CODED FOR MURDER

DIANNE SMITHWICK-BRADEN

DSB
Mysteries

Paperback ISBN: 978-0-9992240-9-0
ebook ISBN: 978-1-7324735-1-5

Published By DSB Mysteries
www.diannesmithwick-braden.com

Cover design by Dave King   kingsize95@gmail.com

Printed in the United States of America
Suggested retail price $14.95

For my Amarillo Friends

CHAPTER ONE

Friday, October 20, 2017

7:30 a.m.

The man, known to only a select few as Ace, stood near his large office window. He sipped his coffee and watched the sunrise slowly illuminate the city thirty stories below.

Towering over downtown Amarillo exhilarated him. It made him feel important. It made him feel powerful. It made him feel like a god.

But his mind wasn't on the view.

His thoughts were interrupted by his secretary clearing her throat. Ace hadn't heard her enter the room.

"Good morning, Nancy," he said turning to greet her.

"Good morning, sir. I'm sorry to disturb you. I knocked before…"

"That's quite all right," he interrupted. "I was enjoying the view. It's going to be a beautiful day."

"Yes, it is," she said before returning to the reason for her intru-

1

sion. "Here are the reports that you asked for, and these letters are ready for your signature." She placed a stack of papers on his desk.

Taking another sip from his mug, he sat down.

"What's on my schedule for the day?" he asked while signing the first letter.

"Mayor Boswell will be here at ten-thirty. You have a lunch meeting at noon with the president of City State Bank. The Panhandle Plains Historical Museum board meeting is at two o'clock."

Ace listened and made mental notes while signing the letters. He returned them to his secretary.

"Call Tony Boswell. Ask him to be here at ten. Then, call Dutch Harvey and push our lunch meeting up to eleven-thirty. I don't want to be late to the museum."

"Yes, sir," Nancy replied and turned to leave.

He watched Nancy Elmore walk away and shook his head. No one would ever accuse him of hiring the middle-aged woman for her looks. Her graying brown hair was trapped in an off-center bun on the back of her head and she wore thick glasses that hid any beauty her eyes may have held. Her hunched shoulders and pigeon-toed walk accentuated her enormous rear end.

He had hired her to avoid any suspicious speculation that might jeopardize the empire he'd built. He'd been surprised to learn that she was the most loyal, efficient, and professional secretary he could have hoped to hire.

Ace leaned back in his leather executive chair and surveyed his office. He'd chosen the most prestigious office space in the tallest building of the city with furnishings and décor of the highest quality. All of it chosen to impress and intimidate those who crossed the threshold. It had taken years to reach this point in his life and career.

His mind drifted to the cryptic text he'd gotten six hours earlier. The sender's phone number was restricted. The message contained three symbols and a letter.

There was no need to reply. He knew who had sent it, and he knew what it meant. It was a reminder of a past he had all but forgotten.

Shaking his head in an effort to clear his mind, Ace focused on the reports that lay in front of him. He read until he heard the chime of the grandfather clock in the corner. It was already eight-thirty.

"The rest of these will have to wait," he said to the empty room.

He stood and picked up his suit coat before walking into the outer office.

"I'm going to run an errand. It won't take more than an hour," he told Nancy. "I should be back in plenty of time for the meeting with the mayor."

"Yes, sir," Nancy replied without looking up from her work.

Ace rode the elevator to the parking garage and pressed the remote start button on his key fob. His black Mercedes sedan roared to life. He got in, and draped his jacket over the back of the passenger seat. He exited the garage, and drove through downtown Amarillo before turning west onto I-40.

His thoughts weren't on the road during the fifteen minute drive. His mind raced through every possibility. What could be so important after all these years?

"Damn it!" he swore aloud when he realized he'd passed his exit. He drove to the next exit and backtracked to his destination.

Cadillac Ranch has been a roadside attraction since 1974, and is located a few miles west of Amarillo. Ten vintage Cadillacs were half buried nose down in a field alongside Interstate 40. All were arranged in a line facing west. All were left to rust in the elements. All were at the mercy of visitors wielding cans of spray paint.

Ace's mindset was practical rather than artistic. He never understood the appeal of the attraction. There was nothing else there, not even a parking lot. He'd have charged admission, put in a concession stand, and a gift shop.

He parked at the edge of the access road and got out of his

car. He surveyed his surroundings before passing through the narrow gate, and walked along the red dirt path toward the old Cadillacs.

A tall man with a shaved head stepped from behind one of the decaying cars. He took a long drag from his cigarette, dropped it, and waited for Ace.

"What's this all about?" Ace demanded when he reached the man.

"Someone is investigating the O'Neal situation," replied Nelson King.

Ace was dumbfounded. He gaped at King for a few seconds before recovering his composure. "That was twenty years ago. Why would someone reopen the case after all this time?"

"The authorities aren't involved. Word is that Erik O'Neal has been investigating for years. It seems that he doesn't believe his brother's death was an accident."

Ace groaned and rubbed the back of his neck with his left hand. King tried not to stare at the stub where Ace's pinkie finger should have been.

"How much does he know?" Ace asked.

"I'm not sure. My source tells me that O'Neal stumbled across some information that rekindled his interest."

"Is your source reliable?"

King nodded. "He was part of our crew."

"What did O'Neal find?"

"He found an old photograph," King paused and took a deep breath. "It was a photo of you standing beside the car used in the hit."

"What?" Ace shouted. "How did…? Where did he…?"

"The details are sketchy, but it's possible that he has that photo or a copy of it in his possession."

Ace began to pace.

King watched his boss quick step around and between the old Cadillacs, rubbing his neck and muttering under his breath. He knew Ace had been blindsided and that it would take some time to process the information.

Ace walked for several minutes before he stopped in front of King, a look of calm resolution on his face. The only indication of his agitation was a clenched jaw.

"How long have you known about this?"

"A couple of weeks. I wanted to check it out before bringing it to you," replied King. "You were a lot younger when the photo was taken. I don't believe he recognized you, but I felt there was enough concern that you should be warned."

"Can he prove anything?"

"It's unclear what he knows or what proof he has."

"What do you know about him?" Ace asked rubbing his neck again.

"O'Neal is ex-military. He returned to civilian life soon after his brother's death. He lives in Canyon and works in the research department at the museum."

"Yes, I've met him, and his work is meticulous. We can expect him to be even more so in this situation." Ace paused a moment before he asked, "Is there anything we can use for leverage?"

"He's squeaky clean as far as I can tell. He has no immediate family. He seems to have a lot of casual friends but no one close. The one person he sees on a regular basis is his niece."

"His niece?"

"She's Jacob O'Neal's daughter."

"How old is she?"

"She's old enough to be a problem. She's a student at the university in Canyon."

"Is she aware of her uncle's activities?"

"I don't believe so. At least, not yet."

"What about the rest of Jacob's family?"

"His parents are dead. His widow lives near Dallas, and his son is a Marine stationed overseas."

"Are the widow and son aware of Erik's activities?"

"I don't know. It's possible that he passed them some information."

"Can we get to them?"

"It would be next to impossible to get to the nephew."

Ace looked at King with determination. "I suggest you find out what they know for all our sakes."

"What do you want me to do about Erik?"

Ace looked down at the dust on his shoes before answering. "I think it would be best to find a way to discourage O'Neal. This whole thing needs to go away without drawing the attention of the police."

"And if he won't be discouraged?"

Ace struggled to keep his fury in check. "Then, he'll have to be eliminated. We can't risk exposure."

"What about the girl?"

"Keep an eye on her. She may know more than you think. Since she's close by, it would be easy and natural for O'Neal to share information with her."

"If she does know?"

"You know what to do."

Nelson King nodded.

"Keep me posted," Ace ordered and walked away.

4:00 p.m.

Jade O'Neal left the Westgate Mall in Amarillo and walked across the parking lot toward her beat up 2001 Chevy Malibu. The red paint was peeling, and the driver's side door was dented as a result of a parking lot hit and run. As a result, she had to get in on the passenger side and crawl over the console or climb through the driver's window NASCAR style.

It had been a busy afternoon at the boutique, and she was looking forward to a quiet evening at her uncle's house. She smiled and thought, *maybe, today will be the day that I get past Teddy.*

She remembered the day that she and Uncle Erik rescued him.

"Jade, I've been thinking about getting a dog," Erik had said. "Why don't we go to the animal shelter and see if there's one there that we want?"

"Are you serious? You want me to help pick out our...I mean your dog?" Jade couldn't contain her excitement. She'd wanted a dog for as long as she could remember.

"Yes, our dog, if you'll come over to play with it and help me take care of it," Erik had said with a wide grin. "You'll also have to dog sit when I'm out of town."

"Can we go now?"

Erik laughed and picked up his car keys. "Let's go!"

They strolled through the aisles between the kennels. Erik had been looking for a medium or small sized dog when a high-pitched yip attracted Jade's attention. Inside the kennel was the cutest puppy she'd ever seen. It was a playful ball of black and brown fur.

"Uncle Erik, what about this one?"

An attendant met Jade and Erik with the puppy in a small fenced area. Jade fell in love with him the moment she looked into those big brown eyes. He licked her face and snuggled into her arms.

"Are you sure he's the one?" Erik teased.

"I'm sure." Jade beamed. "Look at him."

Erik took the pup from her arms and stroked its neck. "He looks like a little stuffed animal."

"Let's name him Teddy!" Jade exclaimed.

"I think Teddy would be a perfect name," Erik replied, "and not just because he looks like a Teddy bear."

It was obvious that Teddy was a mixed breed. They both knew that he would be a bigger dog than Erik had intended to adopt, but they never dreamed that cute little fur ball would grow up to be a cross between a Rottweiler and a Clydesdale.

Jade crawled into her car and started the engine. She drove out of the parking lot and started toward Coulter Street. Radio

Romance's new single "Weekend" began playing on the radio. She cranked up the volume before she stopped at a traffic light. "Because it's the freakin' weekend," she sang along and played imaginary drums on the steering wheel, oblivious to the stares from the neighboring car.

The light turned green, and the song ended before her thoughts returned to Teddy. Almost four years old now, he had long been too big to jump into her arms in greeting. However, Teddy didn't agree. Trying to sneak past him had become a challenge for her and a favorite game for him.

She planned her approach while she drove to her uncle's home. She'd park out front this time instead of in the driveway at the back of the house. She'd leave her backpack in the car.

Maybe, Teddy wouldn't hear her. Maybe, she'd be able to slip past him. Maybe, she'd sprout wings and fly over him.

Her destination was in sight when she put the bucket of bolts in neutral, killed the engine, and rolled to her uncle's front curb. She pocketed her house key and climbed out the driver's side window because quiet was necessary.

Jade tiptoed to the side gate and eased it open. Teddy was asleep on a chaise lounge on the patio. She crept across the lawn, never taking her eyes off the napping dog.

Teddy opened his eyes.

Jade froze.

Teddy lifted his head.

Jade held her breath.

Teddy saw her. He smiled his doggie smile of recognition and charged running full speed to greet his favorite playmate.

Jade backpedaled and turned to run.

It was too late.

Gigantic dog and coed rolled and tumbled across the lawn, stopping inches from a fresh pile of Teddy's poo.

Jade wrinkled her nose and rolled away from the mess. She lay on her back to catch her breath. Teddy woofed and lay across her chest. She covered her face with her arms to ward off the face licks that always followed.

"You win again," she said, her voice heavy with the struggle to breathe. "Let me up, and I'll get your cookie."

Teddy got up and trotted toward the house. He did his "ohboy-ohboyohboy" dance while he waited for her to unlock the back door.

Jade followed Teddy into the kitchen and took a dog biscuit from the Milk Bone box on the counter.

"Just once, I'd like to stay clean when I come to visit you," she said wagging the biscuit at him.

Teddy ignored the exasperation in her voice and gave her a look that said he didn't think that would be any fun at all. She tossed the biscuit and watched him catch it in midair. He gobbled it down and looked at Jade expecting another.

"You just had a cookie; you can't have another one until later," Jade told him with false authority.

Teddy stood on his hind legs and rested his front paws on her shoulders. They stood eye to eye before he licked her face as if to say, "but I love you so much."

"I love you too, but you know the rules," Jade giggled and pushed him down. "You be a good boy while I get my backpack out of the car."

Teddy gave her his "I'm always a good boy look" and followed her to the front door. He waited and watched there until she returned and then settled on the couch with his favorite chew toy.

Jade shoved Teddy over to make room on the couch. "Uncle Erik will be home tomorrow," she told the monstrous dog while she scratched behind his ears. Teddy's tail drummed a cadence on the arm of the sofa.

Half an hour later, Jade went upstairs to change into her workout clothes. There was no need to go to a gym because she got her work out every time she took Teddy for a walk. She put her long brown hair into a ponytail and went downstairs.

"Are you ready to go for a walk?"

Teddy's head popped up over the back of the sofa like a Pop Tart out of a toaster. His body followed a second later. His wagging tail unsettled the lamp on the end table, and Jade managed to catch it before it fell to the floor.

She hooked the leash to his harness, and Teddy drug her toward the back door. "What's your hurry? We have all evening."

Teddy bounded outside. Jade managed to close the back door before he dragged her across the lawn toward the gate.

Jade looked forward to their walks. She saw parts of the campus that she didn't see during her class days, and it gave her a chance to appreciate the history and beauty around her.

West Texas A&M University began as a teacher's college established in 1910, and began as a single building on forty acres of land. The oldest building, called Old Main, stood in the center of a campus that had grown to forty-three buildings on one hundred seventy-six acres, and an additional twenty-five hundred acres provided space for more facilities and future expansion.

More than five hundred trees grew across the main campus, adding beauty and shade while providing a home for birds and squirrels. Students took advantage of the shade for study and socializing when the weather permitted.

Teddy led Jade north on Twenty-Sixth Street to the campus and turned left at the Natural Sciences building. They walked west along Fourth Avenue past the Engineering and Computer Science building and across Captain Donald Blair Drive.

Jade did her best to keep Teddy close to the side walk. Water droplets made by the irrigation system still clung to the grass and dripped from low hanging limbs. She knew there'd be a mud puddle with Teddy's name on it somewhere.

Teddy examined every tree, shrub, and flower bed, marking his territory along the way. He drank from a puddle on the sidewalk and started his examination again.

They were almost to the museum when Jade saw a squirrel on

the ground enjoying the sunshine. The little animal must have missed the memo about staying in the trees when the giant dog was around. She prayed that Teddy wouldn't see it.

Teddy stopped sniffing and raised his head and wagged his massive tail. Jade braced herself holding the leash tight.

"Teddy! Let's go find your prize," she yelled, hoping to distract him.

Teddy charged across the grounds toward the squirrel. Jade pulled on the leash with all her strength. Her feet slipped on the wet grass, and she landed hard on her backside.

Teddy's momentum spun her around and dragged her several yards across the lawn. She was pulled over tree roots, pine cones, sticks, and things that she didn't want to think about before she let go of the leash.

The terrified squirrel dashed up the nearest tree. Teddy kept running full speed and jumped, almost reaching the limb where the frightened animal chattered.

Lying in the grass near the museum entrance, Jade watched Teddy try to reach the squirrel. She closed her eyes and moaned.

"Are you all right, young lady?"

Jade looked toward the voice. A tall slender man in an expensive suit was walking toward her, offering his hand to help her up. She couldn't help but notice that he was trying not to laugh.

His salt and pepper hair was thin enough to see the scalp on top of his head. The sides were thicker and rather bushy.

"I think so," she replied. "I'm just resting."

"Does your dog often drag you across campus?" he said trying to hide his mirth.

"More often than I'd like to admit," she said with a laugh.

The man moved closer to help her off the ground. Teddy was between them in an instant, his growl low and menacing.

The man froze. Jade looked at Teddy in astonishment. She had never known him to growl at anyone that way.

"Teddy! Come!" Jade ordered.

Teddy obeyed and sat down beside her. She grabbed his harness and struggled to her feet.

"I'm sorry, sir. He doesn't usually behave this way," she said pulling grass out of her hair.

"He's being protective. That's what dogs do," the man said. "Are you sure you're not hurt?"

"Just my pride," she replied and rubbed her sore behind."

"That's quite a dog you have there."

"Yes, he's a handful."

"And then some I'd say."

Jade laughed and said, "Sometimes! Thank you again, Mr...?

"Wilson Lee."

"Thank you, Mr. Lee. I'm Jade O'Neal, and this is Teddy."

"O'Neal?" The bright smile on Wilson Lee's face dimmed for an instant. "Are you Erik's daughter?"

"I'm his niece. Teddy belongs to him. I'm dog sitting while my uncle is out of town. He's better behaved when Uncle Erik takes him for a walk."

"Yes, I would imagine so," Lee said staring at Teddy. "Well, if you're sure that you're not hurt, I'll be on my way."

"I'm fine. Thank you," Jade said with a smile. "It was nice to meet you."

"It was nice meeting you, Miss O'Neal."

Jade watched the man walk away before tugging on Teddy's leash. "Come on, Teddy," she pleaded, "Let's finish our walk."

Teddy was slow to obey. Glancing at the man and then the tree where the squirrel had been before, he allowed Jade to lead him away.

They resumed their trek, turning north toward Mary Mood Northern Hall and the Sybil B. Harrington Fine Arts Complex. They followed Russell Long Boulevard until they turned again to walk between Buff Hall and the Caf, also known as the dining hall.

Teddy tugged harder on the leash when they got near the Joseph A. Hill Memorial Chapel. He went to the tree where his jerky treats were always hidden. He dug at the bottom of the Burr Oak until he found his prize, and lay on the ground in quiet contentment.

Jade inspected a scrape on her elbow while Teddy ate. She realized that she was going to feel the impact of this afternoon's adventure for several days.

"Are you ready to go home?" she asked when Teddy stood and wagged his tail.

Jade was thankful that Teddy was much easier to handle on the way home. She supposed that chasing squirrels and protecting masters made even a giant dog tired.

Jade showered before feeding Teddy. She made herself a sandwich, settled on the couch with her meal, and turned on the television. Teddy lay beside her on the floor and chewed on his rawhide bone.

She relaxed in the living room until the ten o'clock news ended. Turning off the TV, she climbed up the stairs and crawled under the covers. Teddy jumped on the bed and lay down beside her. She reviewed her class notes before turning off the light. Gigantic dog and coed were fast asleep in minutes.

CHAPTER TWO

WEDNESDAY, October 25, 2017

11:45 a.m.

Erik O'Neal sat at his desk, leaned back in his chair, and stretched his lean six-foot frame. His research for a new museum exhibit was almost complete. Soon, his work would be in the hands of exhibit, designers, and he'd have a new project.

Looking at his watch, he realized that it was almost time for lunch. He glanced at the picture on his desk. Mollie, Levi, and Jade smiled back at him. He couldn't love them more if they were his own. He felt a sense of pride that his niece and nephew had followed in his footsteps. Levi had joined the Marine Corps, and Jade would soon graduate with a degree in history.

"What are you so happy about?"

Erik jumped, knocked his pen on the floor, and almost tipped his chair over. He laughed when he saw Renee Lanham standing at his office door.

"I was just thinking about Levi and Jade."

Renee laughed and said, "I didn't mean to scare you. Tommy and I are about to go to lunch. Want to come along?"

"Thanks, but I'm meeting Jade for lunch today."

"All right. Maybe tomorrow? You haven't told us about your trip yet."

"Tomorrow for sure."

Renee smiled and waved at him before moving down the hall.

Erik searched the floor until he found his pen. No one else would give it a second thought, but it was his most prized possession. He always carried it with him. It had been a gift from Levi and Jade when they were kids. They had saved their allowances, picked it out together, and had it engraved. The words had become worn over the years, but "We love you, Uncle Erik" could still be distinguished. Putting the pen in his shirt pocket, he left the office.

It was a beautiful day. Fall was Erik's favorite time of year because of the milder temperatures and calmer winds.

He thought of Renee on the drive to the restaurant. He'd been tempted more than once to take things beyond professional friendship with the attractive blonde. She was a good woman and a loyal friend. He enjoyed spending time with her, but he wasn't capable of giving Renee what she most desired.

No one would ever possess his whole heart the way that Mollie did. No one knew how he felt, not even Mollie. He'd never found the courage to tell her. In Erik's mind, being in love with his only brother's widow was the ultimate betrayal.

Erik had been so lost in thought that he almost drove past the restaurant. He parked beside Jade's car and went inside. He looked around the room, searching for his niece.

Jade waved at him from the top of the stairs. Waving back, he walked to the counter to order his meal.

Bear's Burgers and Dawgs was a few blocks from the WTAMU campus. It was popular with college students and local residents alike. Jade loved sitting upstairs so that she could watch the trains roll by while they ate.

"Hello, Erik! What'll you have today?" Bear asked.

"I'll have the loaded Frito Pie." Erik looked around the crowded restaurant. "It looks like business is good."

"Just the way I like it," joked Bear. "Your order will be ready in a couple of minutes."

"Thanks, Bear."

Erik paid for his meal and joined Jade. She was staring out the window at a passing train. He couldn't help noticing that she wouldn't look at him.

"How's school going?" he asked.

"Okay, I guess." Jade stared at a poster on the wall. "Well, it… could be better."

"What's wrong?"

Jade seemed to be fascinated with her fingernails. "I don't know how to tell you this. It's going to ruin all of our plans."

Erik reached across the table and squeezed his niece's hand. "Don't worry. We'll work it out together."

Jade took a deep breath. She was about to explain her problem when Bear brought their food to the table. Jade welcomed the delay while the two men reminisced about their high school days.

After Bear walked away, Erik said, "All right, out with it."

Jade concentrated on her burger. "I went to see my advisor today."

"And?"

Jade looked at Erik, her brown eyes shimmering with tears. "I'm not going to graduate this semester."

Shock waves rippled across Erik's face. Jade was an excellent student and held a near perfect grade point average. "Why not? What happened?"

"You know that I loaded up on my classes so that I could finish this semester."

"Yes, go on."

"There's one class that's much harder than I expected."

"Is that the midterm you didn't feel good about?"

Jade nodded. "The grades were posted this morning. There's no way that I can pass that class now."

"I see." Erik tried to look understanding.

"I'll have to take the class next semester. My advisor suggested that I drop the class now so that the grade won't affect my G.P.A."

Jade stopped and stared at her uncle with apprehension.

Erik smiled at her and wiped a rogue tear drop from her cheek. "I know you're disappointed, but it'll be all right. These things happen."

"But what about the trip you arranged for my graduation? Can you get your money back?"

Erik scratched an imaginary itch above his right ear. "I didn't think about that. I'll have to do some checking."

The look on his niece's face tugged at his heart. "Let me worry about the trip. You need to concentrate on your classes."

Jade smiled with relief. She hadn't expected her uncle to be angry, but she didn't want to disappoint him.

The pair didn't mention school, graduation, or the trip again while they finished their lunch. Waving at Bear, they left the restaurant, and hugged goodbye before getting into their cars.

Erik fought a rising sense of panic during the short drive back to work. What was he going to do? He had already set things in motion, believing his family would be safe. It couldn't be stopped now.

His life had been consumed with finding answers about Jacob's death and caring for his brother's family. He was all but certain that he knew who had been responsible. The proof he needed could be one piece of evidence away.

He believed the murderer was someone well connected, wealthy, and powerful. He didn't know if that person had killed Jacob personally or ordered it done.

Knowing that the killer would stop at nothing, Erik feared that those he loved would be kidnapped or worse in order to get the evidence that he had safely locked away.

He'd thought about warning his family many times, but he knew in his soul that sharing any information would make them targets. How could he warn them without putting them in more danger?

He had to find a solution soon. Twice in the last couple of weeks, he thought there were signs that an uninvited visitor had been in his house. Was he mistaken? Or was he becoming paranoid? He'd have to find out for sure. The safety of his loved ones could depend on it.

When he returned to work, Erik found it hard to concentrate. He'd already taken the precaution of keeping his research and evidence in a secure place away from his home or office. He knew those were the first places anyone would look.

It would be difficult but not impossible for someone to get into his office when he was away or after hours. Looking around the small room, there were things he could do to find out if anyone was snooping.

He spent the afternoon setting up a few indicators that would alert him but wouldn't be noticed by an intruder. He left a neat stack of papers on his desk with one page askew. He closed small pieces of cardboard in the edges of his desk drawers. He left the top edge of a file folder sticking up a bit more than the rest in the file cabinet.

Erik went home that evening and worried about protecting Mollie and Jade. He decided to wait until he was certain they were in danger to warn them.

He took Teddy for a walk before setting up his silent alarms in the house. He hid small pieces of paper in the edges of drawers, rigged items to fall out of cabinets when the doors were opened, and put cellophane tape along the top of his front door and on the edges of his windows at the front of the house. No one would try to get in through the back while Teddy was in the yard.

He collapsed on the couch and ran his fingers through his chestnut brown hair. What was he going to do if someone was breaking in? He knew from his experience as a Marine M.P. that it would be hard to convince the authorities unless something was stolen or there was obvious damage.

A wintry blast of fear rushed through his veins. What if someone broke in while Jade was house sitting?

4:00 p.m.

Jade finished her last class of the day and drove to her apartment. She was thankful that she had the day off from work. She needed some time alone to deal with the disappointment of the day.

She was most upset about missing the trip. It was to have been a three-week driving tour of Ireland with her mom. They were supposed to leave New Year's Day and return the twenty-fifth of January, but the spring semester would be in full swing by that time. She had dreamed of visiting her ancestral home since she had been a little girl. She knew that she might never have another chance.

Jade trudged up the stairs to her second story apartment, her feet as heavy as her heart. She opened the door and blinked. *Did I see what I thought I saw? This couldn't be my place.*

She looked at the number on the door. It was the right apartment. The living room was littered with empty cans, food wrappers, pizza boxes, and chip bags.

She closed the door and stared at the mess.

"Can this day get any worse?" she muttered.

"Hey Roomie!" Heather greeted Jade. "You missed the party. Everyone left a little while ago."

"What happened in here?"

"I had a few friends over. We were celebrating the end of midterms."

Jade bit back the bitter words and shook her head. Picking her way through the garbage to the kitchen, she opened the refrigerator. It was empty.

"I guess it can get worse," she said and slammed the refrigerator door. She stomped back to the living room and stared at her roommate.

Heather Anderton sat on the sofa with her feet on the coffee table, the remote in one hand, a can of beer in the other. She and Jade were about the same height, but Heather was curvy compared to Jade's lean athletic frame.

"Are you…wearing…my clothes?" Jade asked through gritted teeth.

"All my clothes are dirty. I didn't think you'd mind."

Jade had been able to keep herself together until that moment. Rage and resentment merged with the earlier disappointment, and created a storm within her. She wanted to hit something. She wanted to break something. She wanted to scream at the top of her lungs.

She marched to the television and jerked the power cord out of the wall.

"What are you doing? I was watching that!"

"We need to get a few things straight, Heather. I want to make sure you hear what I have to say!"

Heather stood up. "What are you so upset about?"

"Let's start with the fact that you're wearing my clothes! You just took them without asking or considering that I might have wanted to wear them!"

"I'm soooo sorry," Heather scoffed and rolled her blue eyes. "My sister and I traded clothes all the time."

"I'm not your sister! And another thing, we had a system. Half the refrigerator was yours, and the other half was mine. Stop taking things from my half!"

"It was only a few drinks!"

"A few drinks? I went shopping yesterday! Everything I bought is gone! There's a whole lot of nothing in that fridge!"

"It's not a big deal!"

"It is a big deal! It's not just the fact that you take without asking. I'm spending money on food that I don't eat. There's never anything left when I get home. I either have to go out or go shopping again. I don't work enough hours to pay for it all! If this keeps up, I won't be able to pay rent!"

"Why don't you ask your precious uncle for help? Or better yet, why don't you move in with him?"

Jade glared at Heather. She gritted her teeth and took deep breaths in an effort to calm herself.

Heather sensed she had gone too far. "What do you want me to do?" she demanded.

"The first thing I want you to do is return my clothes. Then, I want you to stay out of my room and keep your hands off my things!" Jade shouted. "And clean up after yourself. This place is disgusting!"

Heather opened her mouth to reply and then closed it again. She looked around the room and turned on her heel. She marched to her bedroom and slammed the door. A few minutes later, she opened the door, threw Jade's clothes at her, and slammed the door again.

Jade took her things to her bedroom and then returned to the living room and began to clean up the mess left by Heather and her party friends. Twenty minutes passed before Heather opened her door and said, "You're right, this is a disaster. I'll clean the kitchen."

"I'd appreciate that," answered Jade.

"I'm going to do my laundry after we're finished in here. Do you want me to wash your clothes with mine?" she asked, twirling a strand of her long strawberry blonde hair.

"I plan to do my laundry tomorrow," Jade replied. "I'll wash them."

An uneasy silence hung over the apartment while Jade and Heather worked together to clean up the mess. It wasn't long before everything was back in place, and all of the garbage had been taken to the dumpster.

"It will take me hours to do my laundry downstairs," Heather informed Jade. "I'm going to the laundromat. If I'm lucky, it won't be busy, and I'll be back before midnight."

Heather made three trips to her car with dirty laundry. Jade waved goodbye, went to her room, and flopped onto the bed. Alone at last.

The emotional day and the argument with Heather had exhausted her. She was shrouded in blissful sleep within minutes.

Jade's dream was interrupted by a knock on the apartment door. She groaned and covered her head with a pillow. She hoped whoever was at the door would go away, but the knocking persisted.

Grumbling, Jade went to the door, and looked through the peep-hole. Someone was standing with their back to the door.

"Who is it?"

"It's Logan Rhodes," a voice answered, "from next door."

Jade sighed and opened the door. "Hi, Logan. Heather isn't here right now. You can find her at one of the laundromats in town."

"I wasn't looking for Heather. I want to talk to you."

"Oh!" Jade couldn't hide her surprise. "Um, okay, come in." She stepped aside to allow Logan into the living room. "Would you like some water? We don't have anything else at the moment."

"Sure, I'll take some water."

Logan sat on the couch while Jade went to the kitchen. She filled two glasses with ice and split the last bottled water between them. She joined Logan in the living room and handed him a glass.

"What's wrong with your TV? It won't turn on."

"Um... that's because it's unplugged. Heather and I had a...a... discussion this afternoon."

"I heard." Logan said with a smile. "It was a good one!"

Jade blushed. "I'm sorry you had to hear that. I've had a bad day. I got home and saw," she paused, "let's just say I couldn't take anymore."

"Maybe, it helped."

"I hope so. What did you want to talk to me about?"

It was Logan's turn to blush. He took a deep breath and said in a rush, "I was wondering if you'd be my date to my fraternity's fall formal?"

Jade's surprise was evident on her face. She expected him to ask for help with homework.

"Oh...I...yes," she stammered. "Yes, I'd love to. When is it?"

"It's November eleventh." Logan's brilliant smile lifted Jade's spirits.

"Is it a formal event, or is that just what you call it?"

"It's formal, kind of like a high school prom. My friends and I are talking about renting a limo and going together. I'll let you know what we decide."

"Okay, I'm looking forward to it," she said with a smile.

Awkward silence followed. The pair found themselves with no idea what to say to each other.

"Would you like to go for some pizza?" Logan asked. "I'm starved."

"That sounds good," Jade said nodding her approval. "I'll need to freshen up a bit first."

"I'll grab my wallet and meet you downstairs in fifteen minutes."

"Perfect!"

Half an hour later, Jade and Logan sat in a booth at the local Pizza Hut. They got better acquainted while waiting for their order.

"I have to ask," Jade began. "Why didn't you ask Heather to the formal? I'd have bet you were interested in her.

"I was, at first," Logan admitted. "Then, I met you, and all other women ceased to exist."

Jade raised an eye brow and smirked at him.

Logan laughed and said, "Too corny?"

"Way too corny," she said and rolled her eyes.

"The truth is that I wanted to get to know you better from the start. Making friends with Heather seemed to be the quickest way."

"I see. You were using her," Jade teased.

"We never went out or anything. We've just flirted…a lot."

"Does Heather know it was just flirting?"

"I don't know. Maybe," Logan said unconcerned. "What about you? Is there someone you flirt with on a regular basis?"

Jade didn't answer right away. She looked down at her hands and rolled a straw wrapper into a ball. "I don't flirt."

Logan sensed he had touched a nerve. "Hey, I was only joking. You don't have to talk about anything painful."

"It isn't painful," she said and looked into his eyes, "but it is embarrassing."

"What happened?"

"I was fourteen and had a huge crush on my older brother's best friend."

"How much older?"

"Levi is four years older. Steve is a few months older than Levi," said Jade. She could feel her face reddening as she spoke.

Logan nodded and said, "I'm listening."

"I'd been trying to get his attention for months. I watched people flirt in TV shows and movies. I decided to try some of what I'd seen."

"Did they work?"

"Nope," Jade said shaking her head. "Those words were anything but cool when I said them. Steve got tired of the unwanted attention. Levi tried to tell me that he wasn't interested, but I wouldn't listen. The two of them decided to teach me a lesson."

"Ouch!" Logan grimaced.

Jade nodded. "It was a hard lesson, but I've never forgotten it. I won't go into the details, but they taught me that flirting isn't always harmless and that I'd better be ready for the consequences. I also learned that flirting is a skill that I don't happen to have."

Logan's mouth twitched while he tried not to laugh.

"What about now? Would Steve welcome your attention now that you're a grown woman?"

"I doubt it. He'll always think of me as Levi's little sister. I'm sure his wife appreciates that."

Logan laughed out loud. "How long have they been married?"

"I'm not sure, but they were dating when I was annoying him."

Jade couldn't help but laugh with Logan.

"I'm sorry. I'm not laughing at you," Logan apologized. "I'm laughing at the situation."

Their waitress brought their pizza and refilled their drinks. The couple ate and talked between mouthfuls. They had similar taste when it came to movies and music but disagreed about which sports teams were the best.

Jade had been attracted to Logan from the moment they first met. His baby blue eyes lit up every time he smiled. His curly blonde hair and the freckles on his cheeks accentuated his warm playful personality.

The couple finished their dinner and went back to the apartment building.

"May I see you tomorrow?" Logan asked outside Jade's door.

"I'm sure you'll see me tomorrow. You live next door," Jade teased.

Logan grinned. "Let's go for a drink or have dinner together."

"I'd like that."

They said goodnight and went to their own apartments. Jade went to her room and got ready for bed. *Today turned out better than I expected*, she thought and snuggled under the covers.

CHAPTER THREE

Friday, November 3, 2017

2:15 p.m.

It had been a long week. Erik was ready to relax and enjoy the next two days of downtime. He'd been working too hard, working all day at the museum and half the night trying to solve the puzzle of his brother's murder.

He rubbed his eyes and looked at his watch. Jade would be dropping by in a few minutes, and he wondered if she'd stop by her favorite exhibit before or after she came to see him. She couldn't resist visiting Pioneer Town every time she was in the museum.

Erik focused on his work until a tap on his door broke his concentration.

"Hi, Uncle Erik."

He looked up to see Jade smiling at him from the doorway. "I'm guessing you've already been to Pioneer Town."

"It was a quick tour this time," Jade said with a laugh. "I didn't have time to stay very long today."

"What time do you have to be at work?"

"In forty-five minutes."

"You're cutting it close, aren't you?" Erik teased.

"Maybe a little," Jade replied with a sheepish grin. "It depends on the traffic through the construction zone."

Erik opened his bottom desk drawer and handed her a shopping bag containing a dress shirt. "Thanks for returning this for me."

"You're welcome. I'll take care of it on my break. What reason should I give them for the return?"

"I picked up the wrong size and didn't notice until I tried to put it on this morning. Ask them to refund it to my credit card."

"Do you want me to exchange it for the right size?" Jade offered.

"No, I'll go back when I can take my time. What time will you get off work?"

"I'm supposed to get off at seven. We've been shorthanded, so it might be nine."

"Do you want to have dinner together tonight?"

"I can't," Jade said and blushed. "I have a date."

Erik raised his eyebrows and said, "I see. You'd rather spend time with a handsome young man than your old uncle, would you?" He couldn't resist teasing.

"No, it's not that," Jade protested until she saw the mischievous expression on her uncle's face. "I need to go. I'll tell you all about him later… if you behave."

"I'll hold you to that," Erik said with a smile. "Be careful on your way to work."

Jade waved and scurried down the hall. Erik wondered who the young man might be. He pushed a nagging thought to the back of his mind and returned to his work.

5:00 p.m.

Erik began clearing his desk at the end of the day. He noticed a small piece of cardboard lying on the floor when he opened a cabinet. He picked it up and stared at it. Had it fallen out when he opened the drawer, or had it been there all day? He checked the remaining indicators. All of the alerts were intact.

Could he have imagined that things were out of place? Had he been working so hard that he was becoming paranoid? It had been over a week since he'd put his silent alert plan into action. Nothing had been moved in his office or his home.

He supposed it was possible that someone had been in his home but had no plans to return. *I'll leave everything in place until Monday,* he thought and tossed the piece of cardboard into the nearby trashcan.

Erik was gathering his belongings when Tommy Carlile stopped outside his office door.

"We're going to Burritos Plus for drinks. Would you like to join us?" Tommy invited.

"That sounds good," Erik replied. "I'll meet you there, but I won't be able stay long. I want to take Teddy for his walk and make it an early night."

"See you there."

Erik locked his door and left the museum. He parked near the Science building and walked to a tree near the Chapel. He buried a large jerky treat at the base of the tree before he drove the remaining distance to his home.

Teddy met Erik at the gate. He ran in circles for a few seconds before he stopped, placed his front paws on his master's chest, and licked his chin.

"I'm glad to see you, too," Erik said and rubbed Teddy's neck.

Teddy followed Erik to the back door and waited until it was unlocked. He trotted inside and sat down beside the bar. He looked from Erik to the box of dog biscuits and back at Erik.

"Do you want one of these?" Erik said pointing at the box.

Teddy gave a soft woof.

"Have you been a good boy?"

He woofed a little louder.

"Are you sure?" Erik teased.

Teddy stood and wagged his massive tail. "Woof!"

Erik tossed a biscuit to the begging giant, and it was gone in two seconds.

"I'm going out for a while," Erik told him. "You can eat your dinner outside tonight."

He filled Teddy's bowl and took it to the patio. Teddy followed him and began to eat while Erik filled the water dish.

"You be a good boy," Erik told him. "I won't be long."

Teddy looked up from his dinner and wagged his tail before diving into his bowl for more food.

Erik went back inside, picked up his car keys, and went through the kitchen to the garage. He wondered again if he'd been mistaken about intruders while he drove to meet his coworkers.

He found a parking space and went inside the restaurant. Tommy and Renee waved at him from a table near the bar. He ordered a beer and an appetizer before taking a seat with his friends. Four other coworkers were at a table beside them.

Nelson King was driving down Twenty-Third Street when he received a text and turned into a nearby parking lot. He read the text, then tapped a number, and waited.

"Yeah?" someone answered.

"Our mark is at Burritos Plus. Meet me there." King ended the call and turned his car around.

Erik was relaxed and enjoying himself. The group joked and talked while they enjoyed their meals.

Excusing himself, Tommy went to the bar for another drink.

"I'm glad you came, but I thought you had plans tonight," said Renee.

"I was planning to have dinner with Jade, but she has a date," Erik informed his friend.

"Good for her! Where are they going?'

"I don't know," Erik replied with a frown. "She was running late and didn't share any details with me. I don't know who it is, how long they've been seeing each other, or where they're going."

Renee laughed and squeezed his arm.

"What's so funny?" asked Erik with irritation.

"You have that overprotective parent look on your face."

"What's did I miss?" Tommy asked when he returned.

"Jade has a date." Renee giggled. "Look at Erik's face."

"I wondered who was about to get beat up," Tommy teased.

"All right, all right. Go ahead and laugh," Erik said and glared at his friends.

"Jade's a grown woman, and you've taught her well," Renee assured him. "She'll be fine."

"I know," Erik began. "She usually tells me everything. Today was the first time she's mentioned a date."

"Be happy she told you that much," Tommy chimed in. "I didn't know my daughter was seeing anyone until she showed up with Knucklehead and told me they were engaged."

"I thought you liked him," said Renee with surprise.

"Well, I didn't at first. He's kind of grown on me," Tommy answered.

"When's the wedding?" Erik asked.

"It's the eighth of July. I made her promise to wait until she'd gotten her degree. They'll both graduate in May."

The conversation had turned to wedding plans when Erik suddenly felt that he was being watched. He looked around the room but saw no one who seemed to be interested in what he was doing. His attention returned to the table conversation.

Two men sat at a corner table across the room from Erik and his colleagues. One of the men had the tan muscular appearance of a body builder and the other was a tall man with a shaved head. They appeared to be enjoying the game on the big screen TV while they drank their beer.

Erik looked at his watch. Teddy would be hard to handle if he waited much longer. He finished his beer and paid for his meal.

"Are you leaving already?" Renee asked, the disappointment obvious in her voice. "We're having such a good time."

"I'm sorry," Erik said and squeezed her hand. "Teddy can get destructive if I don't take him to burn off some energy. I've got to take him for his walk."

"Okay, if you must," Renee answered with a sigh. "Promise you'll join us again soon."

Erik smiled at her. "It's a promise. I'll see y'all Monday. Have a good weekend," he said to the group.

He was waving to his coworkers and wasn't paying attention. He turned and ran into a woman, knocking her to the floor.

"Oh my god!" Erik said, his face flushed with embarrassment. "I'm sorry. Are you all right?"

"I'm fine," the woman said and accepted Erik's outstretched hand. "You might want to watch where you're going next time."

Erik helped the woman to her feet. "You're right. I'm so sorry."

"I forgive you," said the woman with a bright smile that lit her entire face. "Mr...?"

Erik stared at her a moment before he realized what she wanted to know. She was an attractive woman.

"Oh, I'm Erik O'Neal."

"It's nice to meet you. I'm Kathy Steen."

"I'd buy you a drink, Kathy, but I need to leave. I'm so sorry."

"Don't worry about it," she assured him. "I'm meeting my date here, and it would be difficult to explain why another man bought me a drink."

"Yes, I imagine it would," he answered. "I'll buy you two drinks the next time I run into you."

Kathy smiled and said, "It's a deal." She turned and walked away.

"That was smooth," Tommy said with a smirk.

The blush on Erik's face deepened. He waved goodbye and left the restaurant without noticing the expression on Renee's face.

The two men at the corner table followed a moment later.

Erik parked his car in the garage and dashed into the house. Grabbing Teddy's leash, he went out the back door. Teddy stood still long enough for his master to attach the leash and then led the way to the gate.

They walked their usual path around the WTAMU campus. They passed the old Education Building and met a large man walking a toy poodle. Erik nodded, giving the stranger the right of way. It wasn't unusual to see other people walking around the campus, but there was something familiar about the man. Erik knew he'd seen the man's royal flush tattoo before. He supposed it was possible for multiple people to have the same tattoo.

Teddy and Erik continued their trek until they reached the area between the Chapel and the Science building. Teddy found the prize that Erik had hidden. He lay on the ground and ate while his master thought about the woman in the bar. It had been a long time since he had made such a fool of himself, and he hoped she wasn't hurt. To his surprise, he also hoped he'd have the opportunity to buy her that drink.

Dog and master were tired when they reached the back gate of their home. They went inside and settled on the couch in front of the TV. Erik flipped through the channels twice before he decided to watch *MacGyver*.

Erik went to the kitchen for a snack when the program ended. He opened the refrigerator and gathered the ingredients for a sandwich. He went to the cabinet for bread and held his hand below to catch the loaf when it fell out.

Nothing happened. He looked inside. The loaf of bread rested in the center of the shelf. He opened another cabinet. Again, nothing fell out.

He opened every drawer and cabinet in the kitchen before

moving to the living room. The tape that he'd placed over the door was still intact. He checked the windows. The tape strip on the window, most difficult to see from the street, had been broken.

Teddy must have sensed that something was wrong because he followed Erik through the house. They checked every room. Nothing was missing, but many of the indicators were no longer in place.

Erik went back to the kitchen and put away the sandwich ingredients. He had lost his appetite. He gave Teddy a dog biscuit and returned to the living room. He again sat down on the couch, but he was no longer interested in watching television.

He hadn't been mistaken, and he wasn't paranoid. Someone had been inside his house. Jade could have opened some of the cabinets and drawers, but she hadn't been there. She'd have no reason to open a window. Someone had been in his home at least twice. How many times had they been here before he noticed?

His mind raced. Was it someone looking for valuables or someone looking for his research? He believed that, if someone had been looking for valuables, the intruder wouldn't have been so careful and would have at least taken a television.

The thought of someone breaking in while he slept was unsettling. The thought of someone breaking in while Jade was housesitting spurred him to immediate action.

He got up and closed all of the blinds and curtains in the house. He then went to his laptop, searched for the best places in the area to purchase an alarm system, and made plans to go first thing in the morning.

Erik was still concerned about his family's safety outside his home. He began to work out a plan to protect both his niece and the woman he loved.

9:00 p.m.

Jade scurried out of the mall and to her car. She was tired after her long shift but excited about having dinner with Logan. She took every short cut she knew to get back to her apartment as fast as possible.

She ran up the stairs to her apartment and into her room to freshen up. She knew that Logan would be there any minute.

She heard a knock on the door and forced herself to take her time answering. Logan stood grinning at her with a bouquet of flowers.

"These are for you," he said.

"They're beautiful. Thank you," Jade said taking the flowers. "Come in while I put these in water."

Logan stood by the door while Jade searched for a vase. She decided to put them in a tall glass to save time.

"Where would you like to go?" Logan asked.

"Anywhere is fine with me. I'm starved," Jade replied.

"I wanted to take you somewhere nice for our first official date, but the nicer places will be closing soon. Do you mind fast food?"

"Fast food would be perfect," Jade assured him.

"Good! I don't think my stomach will tolerate being empty much longer."

Logan took out his phone and searched the local restaurant hours. "It looks like it's going to be a burger place or a Mexican food place."

"A burger sounds pretty good right now."

"A burger, it is," Logan said with a smile. "Are you ready?"

Jade nodded and followed him to his car. The restaurant was all but deserted when they arrived. They placed their orders and found a cozy booth in the corner of the restaurant.

"I'm sorry I was so late getting back," Jade said. "The girl who was supposed to work the last shift didn't show up."

"That's okay. The same thing used to happen to me at my last job," replied Logan. "I had to quit because I didn't have time to do my school work."

"I hope that I won't have to quit. It's an easy job, but it cuts into my study time."

"At least you'll have a nice paycheck," Logan pointed out.

"True!" Jade agreed.

"I've been putting in a lot of applications," Logan told her. "I need the money, but a new job could get in the way of seeing you."

Jade blushed. "We live next door to each other. We'll see each other all the time."

"That's not what I meant," Logan said and took her hand.

Jade was about to reply when their number was called, and Logan went to the counter to collect their meals. They forgot all conversation and concentrated on their food.

The quiet of the restaurant was shattered by celebrating Canyon Eagles fans. Hungry and excited supporters of the local high school football team poured inside. The Eagles had defeated the Caprock Longhorns of Amarillo.

Jade and Logan finished their meal and fought their way through the crowd. They escaped the restaurant and drove back to their apartment building.

"Thank you for dinner and the flowers, Logan," Jade said when they reached her door.

"You're welcome. Do you want to come to my place and watch a movie?"

"I'd love to, but I have to be at work early in the morning, and I need to take an online test before midnight."

Logan's eyes widened, and he gasped. "Oh man! I forgot. I have one, too. I haven't even looked over the notes!"

Jade laughed and said, "School and work strike again."

Logan smirked and leaned in to kiss her. "Goodnight, Jade. We'll try that movie another time."

"Goodnight, Logan. See you around," she teased.

Logan smiled at her and turned toward his own door.

Jade went inside. The smile on her face faded when she saw Heather glaring at her from the living room.

"Hi, Heather," she said and moved toward her bedroom.

"How long have you and Logan been seeing each other?" Heather asked with anger and bitterness.

"He invited me to the fall formal, and we've had dinner together a couple of times," Jade said confused. "Why?"

Heather's face fell. "When did he ask you to the formal?"

"It was the day we cleaned the apartment last week. He came by after you left to do your laundry. Is there a problem?"

"Yes! There's a problem. You talked about leaving your things alone. You need to keep your hands off my things, too!"

"What are you talking about?"

"Don't play dumb. It doesn't suit you," Heather sneered.

"Again, what are you talking about?"

"You knew that Logan and I were getting close. You couldn't stand that could you?"

"I had no idea that you were interested in Logan," Jade answered in surprise. "I know you flirted with him but no more than you flirt with other guys."

"That's not the point. I wanted to go to the fall formal with him. You should have known!"

"How was I supposed to know? We've never talked about Logan. We seldom see each other, and when we do, we argue," Jade pointed out.

Heather stared at Jade for a moment. She took a deep breath and sat down on the sofa. "You're right. There's no way you could have known. I heard voices by the door and looked out the peephole. I was surprised and a little jealous when I saw Logan kiss you."

Jade sat down beside her roommate. "I'm sorry about this. I would have said no if I'd known how you felt."

"That's okay. He wouldn't have asked me anyway. I'm going to bed," Heather said and went toward her room. "Goodnight, Jade."

"Goodnight, Heather."

Jade went to her room still puzzled about the latest argument with Heather. She hoped that Logan hadn't heard.

She took out her notes and studied them once more. She opened her laptop and logged in to the online test. Forty-five minutes later she set her alarm and crawled into bed.

She tossed and turned for half an hour before sleep enveloped her.

CHAPTER FOUR

TUESDAY, November 7, 2017

5:30 p.m.

Erik sat on the sofa and stared at the television. He appeared to be watching the evening news, but he didn't see or hear the broadcast. All he could think about were the events of the past few days.

He had an alarm system installed the day after he'd discovered that someone had indeed been in his home, and he instructed Jade to keep the alarm on at all times.

"Why do you need an alarm system?" she had asked.

"I've been hearing about burglaries around town," he lied. "I thought it would be a good idea to have some added protection. I also want you to keep the blinds and curtains closed so that no one can see inside."

"Do you think someone would try to break in with Teddy around?"

"Teddy won't let anyone near the backyard, but he can't protect the entire house from there," he replied.

Jade seemed to be satisfied with his reasoning and asked no more questions.

Erik had convinced Mollie to take the trip to Ireland as planned. It took several phone calls and all of his powers of persuasion and logic. At last, she agreed during their conversation the previous evening.

"I don't want to go alone," Mollie told him. "Why don't you get your money back? Jade and I will go another time."

"I can't! It's a non-refundable vacation package," he lied. "Take a friend with you if you don't want to go alone."

"Why don't you take the trip with a friend?" Mollie suggested.

"I have to attend a conference the first week in January. I can't be in two places at once. Didn't you tell me you'd already arranged for the time off?"

"Yes, I did," she replied, her resolve weakening.

"I know how much you've always wanted to go to Ireland."

"There will be other opportunities," she said.

"Other opportunities," he answered with irritation, "how many opportunities have you had before now?"

"None," she admitted.

He decided that it was time to play his trump card. "Mollie, I intended for this trip to be a gift for both you and Jade," he told her. "I want you to go and have a good time. There's no reason why you shouldn't go."

"All right, I'll go," Mollie conceded, "But only because you insist."

"I do insist," Erik said, smiling with relief.

They discussed Jade and other family matters before ending the call. He'd had a good night's sleep feeling confident that the people he loved would be safe. Jade was nearby where he could keep an eye on her, and Mollie and Levi would be out of reach.

His confidence was shaken when he got to work. His office door stood open, but he knew that he hadn't left it that way. Renee had mentioned it to him when they were leaving for the day.

"I've noticed that you've started locking your office," she said. "What are you hiding in there?"

"Nothing." His answer was too quick to be convincing.

"I've been wondering about that, too," said Tommy from behind them. "I also heard that you had alarm system installed at your house."

"I did," Erik answered with irritation. "What's wrong with taking extra precautions?"

Tommy and Renee exchanged disconcerted looks. "Not a thing," Renee said. "What's going on?"

Erik scratched the imaginary itch about his right ear. "I'm sorry. There've been some houses burglarized in my neighborhood the past couple of months. I decided to be proactive. I may have gotten a little carried away."

Renee and Tommy seemed to accept his explanation, and the trio left the museum together.

Not only was his door open this morning, but someone had gone through every drawer. All of his indicators had been dislodged. The most disturbing evidence was the fact that the photo of his family had been moved from his desk to the top of the file cabinet.

Erik's one defense he had at work was to keep his office locked. That obviously wouldn't stop someone who had a key such as custodians and security guards. Could it have been one of them? Could it have been someone else? Was someone at the museum working with those responsible for his brother's death?

He could take care of himself, and he believed that Mollie and Levi would be safe. But he worried that Jade was still at risk. He'd like to keep her by his side twenty-four seven. He knew that was impossible, as well as, ridiculous. She had classes to attend, and they both had to work.

Erik heard the jingle of Teddy's tags and looked at this watch. It was time for their walk.

Teddy could be the answer! The monstrous dog was the self-appointed guardian of his family and home. No one would bother Jade with Teddy at her side. His size and muscular build intimidated everyone. His bared teeth and menacing growl would make anyone rethink their nefarious plans.

Teddy stretched into his "let's play" bow before trotting to the back door. Erik attached the leash to the harness before going outside. The huge dog led his master to their destination.

They walked their normal path without seeing anyone else along the way. Teddy found his prize, and the pair made their way home. They were two blocks from the house when Erik noticed an unfamiliar car. It was unusual for anyone to park in that particular place. *The Finchers' daughter must be visiting,* he thought.

Erik looked at the clock on the microwave when they returned home. He'd still have time to go grocery shopping if he hurried. He made a list of the items he needed.

"Why are half of the items on this list for you?" he asked Teddy.

Teddy tilted his head in response but didn't offer an opinion.

"You can eat outside," he said and picked up Teddy's food bowl.

Teddy waited at the door while Erik filled his bowl. He followed his master outside and started to munch when Erik went back inside.

Erik grabbed his car keys, went to the garage, and got in his car. He drove down the alley and onto the street. He turned again and drove down Twenty-Third Street toward one of the local supermarkets. After finding an empty parking space near the entrance, he went inside.

Gaye Fincher was in the checkout line when Erik entered the store.

"Hello, Erik!'

"Hi! How are you doing?"

"I'm doing just fine. How are you?"

"I'm doing well. Is Olen enjoying retirement?"

"Yes, he's loving it."

"Is your daughter visiting this week?" asked Erik.

"No, she's on a Caribbean cruise with some of her friends."

"Oh, I bet that's nice," Erik said. "I noticed a car parked near your house and thought you might have a visitor."

"No, it's just the two of us," replied Gaye.

Erik said goodbye and began his shopping. He went down the pet food aisle first. The thirty-pound bag of dog food took up most of the space in the cart. He managed to make room for the rest of the pet supplies before he moved to the frozen foods section and the meat market.

"Well, hello!"

Erik looked up from a package of pork ribs into a pair of smiling brown eyes. The woman's wavy blonde hair was pulled into a pony tail, and she was wearing navy blue workout clothes that accentuated every curve of her figure.

He ran through his mental card catalog until he remembered where and when they had met.

"Kathy, isn't it?"

"Yes, and you're Erik, right?"

Erik nodded and smiled. "I still owe you a drink."

Kathy laughed. "I believe you said two drinks, but I won't hold you to that."

"I could take you out for drinks tomorrow evening and buy your dinner, too," he suggested.

"I'd love to, but I can't tomorrow night. Why don't you give me a call early next week?"

"I don't have your number."

She pulled a pen from her bag and took his hand. She wrote Kathy and a phone number on his palm.

"Don't lose it," she said and walked away.

Erik watched her hips sway until she turned down another aisle and out of sight. He tossed the package of pork ribs into his cart and went to the checkout counter.

He got in his car and took out his cell phone adding Kathy's name and phone number to his contact list before he started the engine. He drove through the parking lot toward the street, and he noticed a gray Honda Accord parked a few spaces from where he had been. *Is that the same car that was parked near the Finchers'?* he wondered. He knew there were lots of gray cars in the Texas Panhandle. He also knew that he was being silly. It was probably nothing. But why did it bother him so much?

Wednesday, November 8, 2017

12:00 p.m.

Erik parked his car and went inside the restaurant. He ordered his meal and went upstairs to find Jade visiting with Bear.

"Hi, Erik! We were just talking about you," Bear informed him with an evil grin.

"What was he telling you?" Erik asked with mock irritation.

"It had to do with practical jokes and toilet seats," Jade answered, trying not to smile.

"It was just good clean fun," said Bear.

"It was fun, but I don't recall it being clean," laughed Erik.

Bear slapped Erik on the back and walked toward the stairs. He stood aside to allow a tan muscular man to pass before returning to work.

"How has your day been so far?" Jade asked her uncle.

"I'm getting started on a new project," he replied. "Other than that, it's been an ordinary day. How are your classes going?"

"Good! I never would have thought that dropping one class would make the rest seem so much easier. It freed up time for more study and other things."

"Speaking of other things," Erik began, "tell me about your date."

Erik listened while Jade told him about her date with Logan. He was glad that she was getting out more. She spent most of her time studying and working. He wondered if this Logan character could be trusted. He might need to have a talk with the young man.

"Do you like him?" Erik asked when Jade had finished.

"Yes, I do…we've gone out a few times. I'm going with him to a fall formal on Saturday. I don't know if we'll go out again after that."

"Why not?"

"It turns out that Heather likes him, too, and it's causing some tension."

"Is he interested in Heather?" Erik asked.

"I thought so because of the way he flirted with her. Heather flirts with all the guys, so I didn't realize that she was interested in Logan. He said that he was trying to get to me through Heather."

"Did you tell Heather what he said?"

"No, I didn't think that was a good idea."

"Smart girl. Have you talked to Logan about this?"

"No, I haven't." Jade asked, "Should I stop seeing him after the formal to keep peace with Heather?"

"That's up to you," Erik began. "How would you feel if Logan and Heather started dating?"

Jade thought for a moment and said, "I don't think it would help the situation between me and Heather. We'd just be trading sides of the issue."

"My point of view is that Logan would have invited Heather to the formal if he'd wanted to go with her. He didn't. He asked you. He might be interested in Heather too, but he's more interested in you."

"Thanks, Uncle Erik." Jade smiled. "I thought it might be a little weird talking to you about this, but I wanted your opinion."

"You can talk to me about anything anytime," he reassured her, "even if it's a little weird."

"I'm not sure he'll want to go out again after the formal," Jade added.

"Why wouldn't he?"

"We've had a hard time coordinating our school and work schedules. He might want to go out with someone he can see more often."

"If he's smart, he'll make the extra effort," Erik assured her.

They finished their lunch and said goodbye before going about their day.

Erik didn't bother to lock his office door when he left for the day. He said goodbye to Renee and Tommy before driving home.

Dog and master were almost home from their walk when Erik saw it.

The car was back.

It wasn't there when he'd gotten home from work. Was it the same car? It was the same color. He thought it was the same make, but wasn't sure.

He was certain that it didn't belong to one of his neighbors. He supposed that someone could be visiting, but he didn't think so.

Erik took out his phone and snapped a picture of the Accord making sure to include the license plate. He put the phone to his ear and pretended to have a conversation. If he was being watched, he didn't want anyone to know that he was aware.

Thursday, November 9, 2017

6:00 a.m.

It was still dark outside when Erik's alarm clock beeped. Turning it off, he reached for the lamp beside his bed but decided not to turn it on. He got up and walked to his bedroom window instead, and peeked through the blinds toward the houses across the street.

It was still there.

The car, illuminated by the streetlights, was parked a block away from his home. He was startled by the flare of a lighter and the red glow of a cigarette. There was someone inside the car! He waited to see if the car would drive away.

It didn't.

He'd noticed other odd things the past few days. He kept seeing the same two or three men everywhere he went. He saw one at the grocery store last night. He'd seen one of them at the hardware store yesterday and another on his walk with Teddy. He was certain that one of them was at Bear's when he had lunch with Jade.

Were they there before he arrived or after?

These could be normal happenings in a small town like Canyon, but Erik didn't believe any of it was normal. He wondered how long it had been happening before he began to notice.

He knew that he'd become a creature of habit. He needed to change his routine. He'd know for sure that he was being watched if he continued to notice those men.

Erik got ready for work and made a plan. He decided to take a different route to work and stop at a convenience store for some coffee.

Nelson King waited in his car for the man he'd been following. He checked the time on his cell phone. O'Neal was late today.

He was considering having a closer look when he saw O'Neal's car drive down the cross street. He flicked his cigarette butt out the window and started the car. He wondered where his quarry was going and followed him west on Fourth Avenue to the convenience store. He drove several blocks past the store and turned around. Following Erik to the museum, he watched him go inside before driving away. O'Neal would be well watched while at work.

King wanted a shower and a power nap. He looked at the clock on the dash of his car. It was a fifteen to twenty-minute drive from Canyon to Amarillo, depending upon weather and traffic conditions. Construction along Interstate 27 would have traffic backed up by now. He'd have to postpone his personal needs. He didn't want to keep Ace waiting.

8:30 a. m.

King arrived at Cadillac Ranch to find a group of tourists examining the old Cadillacs. He hoped they would be gone by the time Ace arrived.

He parked his car and walked through the gate. Even though he heard another car stop alongside the access road, he didn't turn around. He strolled down the path and lit a cigarette. He smoked at a distance and watched the visitors take selfies in front of the cars.

Ace walked past him and spoke to a woman who appeared to be in charge. "Would you like to have a picture of all of you together? I'd be happy to take one for you."

"Yes, thank you!" the woman said, handing him her cell phone. "We can't get all of us into one selfie. It would be nice to have a group picture."

"Where are you from?" Ace asked.

"Flagstaff, Arizona," she said. "We're on our way to Palo Duro Canyon but couldn't resist stopping here first."

The woman managed to get the rest of her group into position. Ace took the photo and returned the phone to its owner.

"Have a good time and a safe trip," he told them.

King moved toward one of the Cadillacs on the west end while Ace waved goodbye to the travelers. They didn't acknowledge each other until the tourists had driven out of sight.

"Nice touch," King smirked.

Ace scowled at the man. "What have you found out?"

"I've done a casual search of O'Neal's place. If he has anything there, it's well hidden."

"What about his office?"

"My contact inside didn't find anything."

"You don't know anything more than you did before?" Ace asked irritated.

"No, but I think he's spooked. He had an alarm system

installed, and he's keeping his curtains closed. He's also been locking his office door."

"Is he on to you?"

"He may have noticed something after my last visit. I had to leave in a hurry."

"What plans do you have to get the information we need?"

"I've recruited people from McCaslins' team."

Ace rubbed the back of his neck and stared at the ground. "They're good, but we may not have the time to wait for their methods to work." He looked up at King. "A more thorough search is needed."

"It will take a bit more planning to get past O'Neal's alarm system and his dog."

"Do it! And make sure he knows someone has been there. Send him a message."

"Yes, sir." A satisfied smile appeared on King's face.

"What about the sister-in-law and the nephew?"

"Our people did an extensive search of the woman's apartment. There was nothing of interest found there or her office. The nephew is in a remote part of Afghanistan. It's possible that he knows something, but we aren't able to find out."

"It isn't likely that he'll be an issue then. What about the girl?"

"I've arranged for someone to get close to her. My contact found no sign of anything related to her uncle's research in her apartment. She hasn't mentioned anything indicating that she's aware of it."

"Has there been a thorough search of her apartment?"

"I gave orders to be discreet. There have been casual searches when an opportunity was available."

"Search O'Neal's house first. If you find nothing there, search the girl's apartment. That should get his attention."

"I'll contact you when it's done."

"We'll use the secondary rendezvous point next time. We can't risk being seen here again."

"Yes, sir."

CHAPTER FIVE

SATURDAY, November 11, 2017

6:00 p.m.

Jade ran up the stairs to her apartment. She'd been late getting off work and had only an hour to get ready for the fall formal. She showered and dried her hair as fast as she could. She thought about the past few days while she put on her makeup.

She hadn't owned a dress until two days ago. Dresses weren't necessary or practical, given her current way of life. She had a skirt and a pair of slacks for special occasions. Her everyday style leaned more toward tomboy than girly girl.

She preferred jeans and a comfortable shirt most of the time. Her closet held an assortment of colors, but she preferred various shades of pink, yellow, and blue.

She carried a backpack instead of a purse. It gave her hands-free convenience while allowing her to carry her laptop, class supplies, and the few things that she needed on a daily basis.

Owning nothing appropriate for the fall formal, she'd shopped online and at the mall for an entire week. She decided to ask for help when she realized that she was out of her element.

Jade called her friend and former roommate.

"Whitney, it's Jade. I need your help."

"What's wrong?" Whitney asked, alarmed.

"I need a dress for a formal event. Would you have time to go shopping with me?"

Whitney laughed. "I thought you had an emergency. When's the event?"

"This Saturday."

"What? That's only three days away. It is an emergency!"

"I'm sorry I waited so long to call you. I've been shopping when I had the time. I haven't been able to find anything that I like and can afford."

"What's on your schedule tomorrow?" Whitney asked.

"I have classes in the morning, but I'm off tomorrow afternoon."

"I have some comp time that I need to use. I'll take the afternoon off. We'll have a quick lunch, and we'll shop until we find something or the stores close."

Whitney Thomason was an experienced shopper and would know where to find the right dress. She always wore the right outfit for any occasion.

Whitney moved out of their apartment when she graduated and started working full time as a nurse at a local hospital. She was perky, compassionate, and smart.

Jade missed the energetic brunette and her sense of humor. She also missed their late-night talks and study sessions.

They'd still be roommates if Patrick Rugerri hadn't proposed after three years of dating.

Whitney moved in with her fiancé so that they could save money for their wedding, set in June. Jade was to be a bridesmaid.

Jade told Whitney what she had in mind while they ate lunch the following day.

"I'd like to find something that isn't too frilly. No bows or ribbons," Jade said.

"I assume that you don't want lace either."

"It depends on how much lace."

"Something classic and sexy?" asked Whitney.

"I like the idea of classic but nothing too revealing. I've only been out with Logan a few times, and I don't want to give him the wrong idea."

"Classic and modest then," said Whitney, "I think you should find a dress that shows off your figure."

"Do you know where we can find something like that?" asked Jade.

"I do," said Whitney with a twinkle in her eye. "At an old lady's store."

Jade looked at her friend with surprise. She laughed when she realized that Whitney was joking.

"It may come to that before we're through," she replied.

"We'll find something," Whitney assured her. "Don't worry."

They shopped for hours before they found an outfit that they agreed on and was priced within Jade's budget.

It wasn't a dress that she would have considered without Whitney's help. It was light blue tulle and lace with a scoop neck and half sleeves. The asymmetrical, A-line accentuated her figure and showed her legs to their best advantage. Silver high heeled shoes were the perfect finishing touch.

Jade was finishing her makeup when there was a knock on the apartment door. She looked at the clock and thought, *I hope that's Whitney.*

Whitney had volunteered to help Jade get ready for the big event. Jade put on her robe and went to the door. She looked through the peephole and saw Whitney standing on the other side holding a bright pink tote bag.

"Am I glad to see you," said Jade. "I feel like I'm all thumbs, and I don't have much time left."

Whitney put the tote on the kitchen table, followed Jade to her room, and said, "Relax, you've got plenty of time. Take a few deep breaths. I'll wait in the living room while you get dressed."

Jade followed her friend's advice. She put on the dress and stood in front of a full-length mirror assessing her appearance. She would be a lot more comfortable in her jeans, but she had to admit that she was pleased with her reflection.

She peeked out her bedroom door and called, "Whitney? Will you zip me up, please? I can't reach it."

"Let me wash my hands first. Something leaked in my bag. I don't want it to transfer to your dress."

She washed her hands at the kitchen sink and dried them with a paper towel before going to Jade's room. Jade was trying to put her hair up when Whitney knocked on her door.

"You should leave your hair down," Whitney suggested. "I brought my curling iron if you want to use it."

"Thank you," Jade said and turned so that Whitney could reach the zipper. "Will it take long to curl my hair? Logan will be here any minute."

"You could just curl the ends, and it will look gorgeous. I'll do it for you if you like."

"Would you? I'm so nervous. I might drop it and burn a hole in this dress."

"I'll be right back," Whitney said with a grin.

Whitney returned with her curling iron, a small beaded purse, and a wrap.

"There aren't any pockets in that dress. You can use this to carry your keys and your ID," Whitney handed her the purse, "and here's a wrap that I thought might come in handy if it gets chilly."

"Thank you. I hadn't thought about either of those."

Whitney curled Jade's hair while the two women chatted.

"Where's your new roommate?" asked Whitney. "I was hoping to meet her."

"She's either at work or staying away on purpose," Jade replied.

"Aren't the two of you getting along?"

"Let's just say that we've had a hard time getting used to living together."

Whitney stood back to admire her handiwork.

"You look gorgeous."

Jade blushed and was about to reply when there was a knock on the door.

"I'll get it. You wait here," Whitney ordered. "You need to make an entrance, and I want to get a look at this guy."

Whitney winked and went to answer the door.

"Hi, you must be Logan. I'm Whitney."

"It's nice to meet you," he said with a grin. "Is Jade ready? The limo is downstairs."

"I'm not sure," Whitney teased. "Come in, and I'll find out."

Logan stepped inside and checked the time on his cell phone. He didn't notice that Jade had come into the living room.

"It looks like she's ready to me," said Whitney.

Logan glanced up and did a double take. He gaped at Jade trying to find the right words. "Wow!" was all that came to mind.

Whitney giggled. "What's the matter, Logan?"

"It's just...I...wow!" he stammered.

"Do I look all right?" Jade asked unsure of herself.

"You look perfect," Whitney said. "Doesn't she, Logan?"

Logan didn't answer. He couldn't take his eyes off Jade.

"Shouldn't we be going?" Jade asked and walked toward him.

Logan woke from his stupor and said, "Uh, yeah, the limo is waiting."

"You two go on," said Whitney. "I'll lock up when I leave. Have fun!"

Logan offered Jade his arm and a wide grin spread across his face. He escorted her down the stairs to the waiting car. He opened the door for her and kissed her hand.

"You look amazing," he said when he got in beside her.

"Thank you. So, do you," she said. "Where is everyone else?"

"We're going to pick them up on the way."

"Where are we going?"

"We've rented a party room in Amarillo. One of the Mexican food restaurants is catering. There won't be any alcohol served since some of our members and guests are underage. So, no margaritas for you," Logan teased.

"No margaritas!" Jade feigned disappointment.

Jade seldom drank alcohol. It wasn't because she thought it was wrong. It wasn't because she was health conscious. She simply didn't care for the taste or the after effects of drinking too much.

Logan had convinced her to have a margarita while they were having dinner together the previous week. She sipped it at first. She hadn't eaten all day, and their food was slow coming to the table. She drank a little more. She was feeling the buzz by the time they left the restaurant.

Logan opened the car door for her. She opened her mouth to thank him and vomited on his brand-new pair of Jordan's.

She was still embarrassed about ruining his shoes. She'd offered to pay for them at the time. He refused but liked to tease her about it.

Jade hadn't risked having an adult beverage since.

Introductions were made each time a new couple entered the limo. Doug Bentley was a muscular man with sandy brown hair and a winning smile. His date was Nicole Chisholm, slender with high cheek bones and golden blonde hair.

Skeet Bills was tall and thin with an infectious laugh. Jade had met his date Gretchen Law in some of her classes. Gretchen was petite and feisty.

A.J. Vaughan was a burly football player. His date for the evening was Annie Fenhaus, a member of the cheerleading squad.

They arrived at the venue to find an arch covered in fall flowers and twinkle lights had been set up for photos. The couples posed together in turn before having a group photo taken.

They went into a large room that had been prepared for the

festivities. A stage and podium were draped in black and accented with garlands of fall flowers and twinkle lights.

A dance floor separated the stage area from the dining area. Long tables covered with black tablecloths and gold table runners had centerpieces with a white candle surrounded by red, yellow, and orange flowers.

A buffet table was setup at the back of the room and decorated to match the dining tables. Garlands of fall flowers and twinkle lights hung on the walls around the room.

Logan, Jade, and their friends found a table near the buffet and sat down.

A distinguished man in a tuxedo entered the banquet hall. He had a full head of gray hair and a bright smile. He appeared to be accustomed to being the center of attention. He walked around the room shaking hands with all of the fraternity members and talking with their dates.

"Who is that?" Nicole asked Doug.

"That's Jonathan Baxter. He's one of our sponsors and a fraternity brother."

"What does he do?" Annie asked.

"I think he's a lawyer," answered A.J.

The group fell silent when the man approached their table.

"Hello, gentlemen. May I meet these lovely ladies?" the man asked.

Logan stood and shook the man's hand. "Mr. Baxter, I'd like you to meet Jade O'Neal. Jade, this is Jonathan Baxter."

"It's a pleasure to meet you, Mr. Baxter," Jade said and shook his hand.

"The pleasure is all mine, Miss O'Neal," he replied holding her hand in both of his.

Each of the men stood and introduced their dates in turn. Jonathan Baxter seemed to be unable to keep his eyes off Jade. Jade was relieved when he moved to the next table.

"What's up with him?" Gretchen asked. "He's kind of creepy."

"His wife died years ago," answered Skeet. "I heard that he promised her that he'd never marry again."

"Is that true?" asked Annie

"We don't know. He doesn't talk about it," said Doug. "I don't think anyone has ever asked."

"I think he likes getting close to our dates," Skeet offered.

"Why do you say that?" Logan asked.

"Think about it," replied Skeet. "Have you ever known him to bring a date to a fraternity function?"

Doug, A.J., and Logan shook their heads.

"He makes a point to meet all of the ladies," Skeet continued. "He'll dance with most if not all of them before the night is over."

"I'd never thought about it before, but you're right," agreed A.J.

Baxter stood at the lectern and spoke into the microphone. "Welcome everyone to our annual fall formal. There will be awards and announcements later in the evening. The most important thing that I can say at the moment is that dinner is served."

The crowd applauded and made their way to the buffet table.

During dinner, announcements were made and awards were given to deserving fraternity members. The fraternity members and their guests were enjoying dessert when Baxter took the lectern again and introduced the D.J. for the evening.

Logan and Jade danced to several songs before taking a break. Logan escorted her to their table before excusing himself. Jade took advantage of the opportunity to slip her shoes off and rub her aching feet. She slipped her shoes back on when Logan returned a few minutes later with cold drinks.

"I was thirsty and thought you might be too," he said handing her a Dr. Pepper.

"It isn't spiked, is it?" she teased.

"Nope. I learned my lesson. No alcohol for Jade," he joked.

She laughed and said, "Thank you, I am thirsty."

"Are you having a good time?" Logan asked.

"I am. The food was good and the music is great," she paused. "And the company isn't bad either."

"The smile that first attracted Jade to Logan spread across his face. They were interrupted before he could reply.

"Logan, my boy, would you mind if I asked Miss O'Neal for a dance?"

"No, sir. Of course not."

"Miss O'Neal, may I have this dance?"

"I'd be honored," Jade replied with a smile.

Jonathan beamed and led her to the dance floor. Jade noticed that the D.J. was playing a slow song. She tried to make the best of it and smiled when Baxter took her in his arms. She was relieved to find that he was an excellent dancer.

"Are you related to Erik O'Neal?" Baxter asked while guiding her across the floor.

"He's my uncle," Jade replied. "Do you know him?"

"I've been an admirer of his work for years. He's a first-rate historian."

"Are you associated with the museum?" she asked.

"I'm on the board of trustees. I've always loved history. Being involved with the museum is one of the great joys of my life."

"I love history, too. I'm hoping to find a job similar to my uncle's when I graduate."

"Does your uncle involve you in his research?"

"No, I'm afraid not. I've been too busy studying to be of help to him."

The song ended, and Baxter escorted her back to Logan.

"Thank you for the dance, Miss O'Neal."

"Thank you."

Baxter went in search of his next dance partner, and Logan said, "I'm sorry. I didn't see him coming. It wasn't too weird, was it?"

"It wasn't bad. He's a good dancer."

"You didn't mind?"

"I didn't mind," she assured him. "We talked about Uncle Erik and the museum."

Logan and Jade danced several more dances before the party ended. They laughed and joked with their friends during the limo ride home.

The temperature had dropped at least ten degrees by the end of the evening. Jade pulled her wrap over her arms and shoulders when she got out of the limo.

Logan walked her upstairs to her apartment. She unlocked the door and turned to face him.

"I had a wonderful time tonight, Logan. Thank you for inviting me."

"I had a good time, too," he said.

Logan brushed her cheek with his fingertips. He cupped her face in his hand and leaned in for a kiss. It was a long, slow kiss filled with passion. He wrapped his arms around her and pulled her closer.

Jade put her hands on his chest. She was floating in the warmth of his arms and the taste of his lips. It had been a long time since she had felt this way.

A loud noise from inside her apartment brought Jade back to Earth. She broke the kiss and stepped back.

"What's wrong?"

"Nothing. It's just…," Jade hesitated.

"What?"

"I like you a lot. I really do."

"But?"

"Things are moving too fast for me," Jade explained with concern. "We've only gone out a few times. I'm not ready to take the next step."

"I'm sorry. I didn't mean to rush you."

"I know. I'm sorry if I led you to think…"

"No, you didn't. I was just hoping," Logan replied with a grin. "Goodnight, Jade."

"Goodnight, Logan. Thank you for tonight. I had an amazing time."

He kissed her on the cheek and waited until she was inside before he went to his own apartment.

Jade closed the door and took off her shoes.

"I thought you two were going to strip down right there at the top of the stairs," Heather said with a sneer.

Jade looked at her roommate with exasperation.

"You know that wasn't going to happen."

"How am I supposed to know that?" Heather said. "It's like you said. We don't see each other much, and we argue when we do."

"For your information, I'm not in the habit of sleeping with a man after only a few dates."

"Does Logan know that?"

"I hope so."

"What if he doesn't?" Heather continued.

Jade sighed and said, "Goodnight, Heather."

She went to her room and closed the door to avoid any further discussion. She sat on her bed and massaged her feet before getting ready for bed. She hung her dress in her closet and put on her pajamas. She crawled under the covers but was too keyed up to sleep. She took a crossword puzzle book from her nightstand and solved a few pages before turning out the light. She was soon dancing in dreamland.

CHAPTER SIX

SUNDAY, November 12, 2017

9:45 a.m.

Jade lay awake enjoying the comfort of her bed. She was looking forward to seeing Logan again, but it would have to wait until later. She had a full day ahead.

She got up and got dressed, humming a familiar tune. It had been playing in her head since she woke up. It was the song that was playing when she danced with Logan for the first time.

She picked up her backpack and was on her way out of the apartment. She increased her speed when she saw that Heather was waiting for her in the living room.

"Jade, wait! Can we talk?" Heather asked.

"Can't it wait? I'm on my way to brunch with my uncle before I go to work."

"Please. It won't take long."

Jade hesitated before she sat down on the couch. "What do you want to talk about?"

"I'm sorry for the way I've been acting," Heather began. "I had too much to drink last night, and I said things that I know weren't true. It won't happen again, and I hope you can forgive me."

Jade was stunned. She'd been expecting another argument.

"I'll be a better roommate from now on," Heather assured her. "I don't like this tension between us. I'd like for us to be friends."

"I'd like that, too," Jade replied. She stood and extended her hand to Heather. "Let's start fresh and forget that we ever had a disagreement."

Heather smiled and shook hands with Jade.

"I have to go, but we'll talk later," Jade said before she rushed out the door.

Jade got in her car and drove to Erik's house. She parked in the driveway behind the house and hurried across the yard to the back door. Erik motioned for her to come in before she had a chance to knock.

Teddy put his front paws on her shoulders and welcomed her with a sloppy, wet kiss.

"Hi, Teddy," she said and pushed him down. "Hi, Uncle Erik. I'm sorry I'm late," she said wiping her face with her sleeve.

"That's okay," he replied. "It's almost ready. You have time to wash up if you'd like."

"I think I'll do that. Teddy may have missed a spot."

She patted Teddy on the head and went to the bathroom. Erik had a platter of steaming pancakes and sausage on the table when she returned.

"That looks so good," Jade said and sat down.

Erik joined her at the table, and they began filling their plates.

"How was your date last night?" Erik asked.

"It was so much fun," Jade answered.

She told him everything that she could remember about the new friends she'd made. She described the room décor and the food.

"The food was so good," Jade told her uncle. "I'm going to try that restaurant as soon as I find out which one it was. I ate way too much."

Erik had been smirking at her between bites. "I'm glad you had a goodtime. It sounds like things are going pretty well with Logan."

"I think so," she began. "I'm afraid I may have messed things up though."

"Why do you think that?"

Jade blushed and took a big bite of pancake before she continued. "He kissed me goodnight and things were getting... um... interesting. I told him that I wasn't ready for... um..."

"How did he take that?"

Jade was relieved that she wouldn't have to say more. "He seemed okay with it. I won't know for sure until I see him again."

"He won't pressure you if he's a good man," Erik said.

"He didn't last night," Jade told Erik. "I'm afraid that he might have heard an argument I had with Heather. Our walls are thin, and she was kind of loud."

"What did you argue about?"

"Logan."

"So, she's still angry that he asked you out instead of her?"

"She was last night. She said some nasty things. I decided not to argue with her and went to my room. I was late this morning because she wanted to talk."

"How did that go?"

"She apologized and promised she'd be a better roommate," Jade replied. "I accepted her apology."

"I hope that works out for you."

"Me, too! It's gotten to the point that I dread going home."

They ate a bit more before continuing their conversation.

"How are things going with you?" asked Jade.

"The same as always," Erik began, "I'm working on another research project."

"But what about after work?"

"I come home, take Teddy for a walk, and do it all again the next day," Erik answered, avoiding telling her what she wanted to know.

"You're going to make me ask, aren't you?" Jade said.

"I don't know what you're talking about," Erik said. He sipped his coffee and tried to hide behind his cup.

"Okay, have it your way." Jade leaned toward her uncle and put her hand on his arm. "How's your love life, Uncle Erik?"

Erik looked at his niece with mock surprise. She mimicked his expression, and they both laughed out loud.

"Well, are you going to tell me?" Jade asked after the laughter had died away.

"My love life may be looking up," Erik said.

"Renee?"

"No, not Renee," Erik answered.

"What's wrong with Renee?"

"Nothing's wrong with Renee."

"Why don't you ask her out?" Jade persisted.

"Because it could make working together awkward."

"You like her, don't you?"

"Yes, I like her. We've been friends for years. I don't want to ruin that friendship."

"Friends?"

"Yes, friends," Erik replied exasperated. "I met a woman at Burritos Plus last week. I saw her again a few days later, and she gave me her phone number."

"Have you called her yet?" Jade asked with a mischievous grin.

"She asked me to call her at the beginning of this week. I'm planning to call her tonight...or tomorrow."

"What's her name?"

"Her name is Kathy Steen," Erik held up his hand to stop the next question. "Before you ask, no, I don't know where I'm going to take her, and I don't know when we'll go out."

Jade shrugged her shoulders and said, "Okay."

"That's it? No more questions?" Erik asked with disbelief.

"I'll save the rest until you've gone out with her," she said with smile.

Jade helped wash the dishes and clean up the kitchen when they'd finished eating. She hugged her uncle goodbye and gave Teddy a belly rub before she went out the door to work.

7:30 p.m.

Erik had picked up the phone at least a dozen times that afternoon. Twice, he'd gotten to the point of pressing the call button before he changed his mind again.

What is my problem? Erik berated himself. *She gave me her number and told me to call her. All I have to do is dial the number and talk to her. I'll let her pick when and where. The fact that I haven't had a date in years doesn't matter.*

He took a deep breath and picked up his phone. Another deep breath, and he found her number in his contacts. He paced in the living room for several minutes before he pressed the call button. It rang twice. He was about to disconnect the call when he heard someone answer.

"Hi! You've reached Kathy Steen's voice mail. I'm not able to answer your call right now. Leave your name, number, and a brief message. I'll call you back."

Erik waited for the beep. "Hi, Kathy. This is Erik O'Neal. I'm calling to see if you'd be interested in dinner and drinks this week." He left his number and ended the call.

He sat down on the couch and laid his phone on the end table. He picked up the television remote and began flipping through the channels. He was startled when his phone rang. He looked at the caller ID; it was Kathy. He hadn't expected her to return his call so soon.

"Hello," Erik answered.

"Hi, Erik. This is Kathy. I'm sorry that I didn't answer earlier.

I've been screening my calls. Telemarketers have been driving me crazy."

"That's understandable. I do the same thing. "I'd like to keep my promise. I thought we could have dinner and drinks sometime this week if you'd like."

"Yes, I'd like that." Kathy replied. "I'm leaving for a business trip in the morning, but I'll be back late Wednesday night, and available Thursday evening."

"What time should I pick you up?"

"I'd prefer to meet you somewhere. I hope you don't mind."

"No, not at all. Where would you like to meet?"

"We could meet at Burritos Plus at seven Thursday evening," Kathy suggested.

"That sounds great!"

"Then it's a date," she said. "I'm sorry, but I need to finish packing for my trip."

"We'll have time to get acquainted on Thursday. I'll see you then."

The call ended. Erik looked at his phone and smiled. He scratched Teddy's chin and said, "Can you believe it? I have a date."

Wednesday, November 15, 2017

4:30 p.m.

Jade returned to her apartment after a long day. She'd had her toughest two classes and a busy shift at the boutique. She had hours of homework to do before she could sleep. She was relieved to discover Heather had already left for work.

Heather kept her word and was trying to be a better roommate. There had been no more arguments, and it appeared that she had not touched anything belonging to Jade.

Jade still dreaded being at home with her. Heather now seemed to be determined that they should be best friends. She questioned Jade about everything.

The questions were casual at first but soon became intrusive. Jade began to avoid talking with Heather and turned down every invitation to socialize with her.

Jade went to her room and sat at her desk. She needed to get started on the essay that would be due at the end of the week. She opened the desk drawer.

"That's odd," she said aloud. "How did that happen?"

She had arranged everything to accommodate the fact that she was left-handed. The organizer inside the desk drawer was reversed. Had someone been invading her space again?

Looking around her room, her bathroom, and her closet, nothing else seemed to be out of place.

Jade put the contents of the drawer back in order and looked at her cell phone. It was almost five o'clock. She rushed out of the apartment and down the stairs.

Stephanie Hancock was gathering her belongings when Jade entered the apartment manager's office.

"Hello, Jade. What can I do for you?"

"I need to ask you something," Jade replied. "I'd like to put a lock on my bedroom door. Would that be a violation of my lease?"

"Are you having trouble with your roommate?"

"We're getting along better, but she often has visitors that I don't know. I'd rather not have uninvited guests in my room."

"I wouldn't either. Have you talked to your roommate about this?"

"She isn't home at the moment, but I'll talk to her. I wanted to check with you before bringing it up."

"You can put a lock on your door. It will have to be done at your own expense, and you'll have to leave the key when you move out of the apartment."

"All right, thank you," Jade said and turned to leave.

Logan was standing in front of her door when she returned to her apartment.

"Hi, Logan!"

Logan spun around startled by the unexpected greeting.

"Hey! I thought you were inside," he said and stepped away from the door.

"I was, but I had to see Stephanie about something," Jade replied and took her key from her pocket. "Do you want to come in?"

Logan nodded and followed Jade inside.

"Do you want something to drink?" Jade offered.

"No, thanks. I wanted to see if you'd like to go to the mall with me."

"I thought you hated the mall."

"I do, but I have a job interview tomorrow. I don't have the right kind of clothes. I could use your advice, and then we can grab something to eat afterward," he said, with excitement in his voice.

"I'd love to, but I can't tonight. I haven't been home long, and I have a mountain of homework to get through."

"Oh, okay. I guess I'll see you later," he said and started toward the door.

"I'll make it up to you and buy dinner tomorrow night. We'll celebrate your new job."

"That would be great! I'll see you tomorrow."

He kissed her goodbye and went on his way.

Jade closed the door behind him and went to her room. She was finishing a rough draft of her essay when her cell phone rang. She looked at the caller ID before answering.

"Hi, Mom!" Jade said, pleased to hear from her mother.

"Hi, sweetheart. Are you busy?"

"I've been doing homework, but it's time for a break."

"I won't keep you long," Mollie replied. "I wanted to talk with you about Thanksgiving plans. How much time will you have?"

"My last classes before the holiday are on Wednesday morning, but I'm scheduled to work all weekend. The boutique's Black Friday sale starts early Friday morning."

"I was afraid of that," her mother said with a sigh. "I was hoping that you could come and spend your entire holiday with me."

"I'm sorry, Mom. I wish I could." Jade hesitated before asking, "Why don't you come here?"

"Do you have room for me?"

"I'll make room."

"Does your oven work?"

"It did the last time I used it," Jade answered.

"When was that?"

"Six months ago, maybe longer," Jade answered and cringed.

"What have you been eating, young lady?" Mollie asked with her stern tone.

"Stuff that I can heat in the microwave. I've been eating out, too."

"It's a good thing I'm coming. I'll make up some home-cooked meals for your freezer."

"Um, yeah, about that," Jade began. "Anything stored here doesn't last long."

"What do you mean?"

"Let's just say there are often guests who don't care whose food they're eating?"

"Would Erik let you store food in his freezer?"

"I'm sure he would. I'll call him and find out," Jade said. "I need to talk to him about something else anyway."

"All right. Ask him if he'd like to join us for Thanksgiving dinner. Give me a call after you talk with him or when your homework is done."

"It looks like I'll be doing homework most of the night. I'll call you back in a little while."

Jade ended the call with her mother and tapped her uncle's number.

"Hi, Uncle Erik, are you busy?"

"No, I'm just hanging out here with Teddy. What's up?"

"I hate to say it, but I need a favor," Jade said. "I also have a question."

"Okay, what favor?" Erik asked with a yawn.

"I want to install a lock on my bedroom door. Would you show me how to do that?"

"Why do you need a lock on your door?" Erik asked wide awake now.

"Someone has been in my room. I don't know if it was Heather or one of her friends."

Icy tendrils of fear gripped Erik's heart. He did his best to sound unconcerned and said, "I'll do it, but you can help. That way you'll know how if you need to change a lock in the future. I'll go buy a one now and be there in less than an hour."

"Can we wait until tomorrow? I have a lot of homework."

"In that case, I'll take care of it while you do your homework."

"You don't have to do it tonight," Jade protested. "It's late, and I know you're tired."

"I don't want someone walking in on you while you're sleeping. It won't take long."

"I hadn't thought of that. Okay, I'll see you in a little while," Jade conceded.

"What else did you want to ask?"

"We can talk about it when you get here," Jade assured him.

"Okay, see you soon."

Erik ended the call and went to the garage. He collected the tools that he thought he would need. The hardware store had been closed for hours. He'd have to drive a little further and go to the discount department store.

It seemed to Erik that every driver on the road was there to inconvenience him. His nervousness made him impatient. He took chances behind the wheel that he wouldn't have under normal circumstances. He was jolted back to reality when he took a tight curve too fast and bounced off the median.

He had to get a grip on himself. He couldn't let Jade see that he was upset. He took several deep breaths before getting out of his car. It didn't help much.

He walked into the store and continued to take deep breaths. His mind raced. Has the same person who was in my house been in Jade's apartment? There's no reason why anyone would suspect that Jade is part of my investigation. It must have been her roommate snooping around. I'll install the lock, and that will be the end of it.

Erik had almost convinced himself by the time he reached Jade's apartment. Jade explained what she'd found when he arrived. She told him that nothing had been taken, and nothing else was disturbed.

"What else did you want to talk about?" Erik asked, while he installed the lock.

"Mom wants to cook up some meals for me to put in the freezer while she's here. May we store them in your freezer?"

"Of course, you can!"

"She's also planning to be here for Thanksgiving because I have to work most of the weekend," Jade informed him. "We were wondering if you'd join us for Thanksgiving dinner."

Erik felt as though he were having an out of body experience. He heard himself telling Jade that he'd love to have Thanksgiving with them while his mind processed her words. Mollie will be here? She can't! It isn't safe!

"Why don't you both come to my place?" he heard himself say. "My kitchen is bigger and better equipped. You know your mom will cook enough for an army."

"I don't know…"

Erik's face lit up, and he said, "In fact, why don't you both stay at my house for the holiday? I have plenty of room. Your mom can cook to her heart's content. I'll even buy the groceries."

"You'll have to convince Mom," Jade said, her voice filled with doubt. "She won't want to impose."

"Leave your mom to me," Erik said with a wide grin. "This will work out great. I'll call her when I'm finished here."

Erik drove home feeling much better about the situation than he had earlier in the evening. Mollie and Jade had both agreed to stay with him for the Thanksgiving holiday. They'd both be safer at his house than at Jade's apartment.

He pulled into his garage and went into the house. He'd been so preoccupied with Jade's safety that he was unaware that he was being followed. He didn't notice the gray Accord idling at the end of the alley.

Teddy scratched on the back door when his master returned. Erik let him in and patted the large animal's head.

"You've already had your walk today," Erik told him when Teddy looked at his leash hanging on the wall.

Teddy followed his master to the living room. He jumped onto the sofa and rolled onto his back for a belly rub.

"Am I overreacting?" Erik asked while he scratched the dog. "Jade's intruder was just someone being nosy. Mollie and Jade aren't in any more danger than before. Right?"

Teddy responded with a wag of his massive tail.

CHAPTER SEVEN

SUNDAY, November 26, 2017

6:30 p.m.

Jade was exhausted. The boutique had a steady stream of customers all weekend for the Black Friday sales event. She trudged to her car in the mall parking lot and started the engine.

She thought about the past few days during the drive to Canyon. It had been a wonderful Thanksgiving. It would have been like old times if Levi had been there. They managed to visit with him for a few minutes using Skype, but it wasn't the same. She missed her brother.

She had enjoyed the time with her mother and wished it could have been longer. She smiled when she remembered how excited her mother had been during Thanksgiving dinner.

"I have some news," Mollie began with a brilliant smile. "I'm going to New York next month. The company is sending me to be trained for a new job. I'm being promoted!"

"Awesome, Mom!"

"That's great! How long will you be in New York?" asked Erik.

"I'll be there most of the month. I'll get back to Dallas in time to get ready for the trip to Ireland," Mollie replied, unable to contain her excitement.

"Will you be back for Christmas?" Jade asked.

"Yes, for a few days. Will you be working?"

"The schedule isn't set yet, but I'm sure I will."

"Why don't we plan on having Christmas here, too?" suggested Erik.

The O'Neal family discussed Christmas plans while they finished their dinner. Erik made an announcement of his own during dessert.

"The museum is having a holiday event. All employees and their families are invited. The new exhibit that I've been working on will be unveiled, and I'd like you both to be there."

"I'll be there," Jade promised.

"When is it?" asked Mollie.

"It's Saturday, the second of December.

"Oh, I'm so sorry, Erik. I'd love to be there, but my flight to New York is that afternoon."

"That's all right," he assured Mollie. "I guess it's you and me, Jade."

Jade hadn't been able to resist the opportunity to tease her uncle.

"Will Kathy be joining us?" she asked with a grin.

Erik stared at his niece and blushed. "I wasn't planning to ask her."

"Who's Kathy?" Mollie asked.

"She's Uncle Erik's new girlfriend."

Mollie raised one eyebrow and said, "How interesting!"

"She's not my girlfriend. I took her to dinner last week. That's all."

"How did you meet her?" asked Mollie.

"I'd like to hear that story, too," Jade added.

Erik looked at them both. The last thing he wanted was to discuss a recent date with Mollie. He could see that they were both enjoying his discomfort.

"You aren't going to stop until I give you the details, are you?"

"Nope!" the two women replied in unison.

He rolled his eyes and gave them an exasperated sigh. "If you must know, we met at Burritos Plus. I literally ran into her there."

"Ran into her? Do you mean..." Mollie asked.

"Knocked her flat," he admitted his face as red as the cranberry sauce on his plate.

Mollie gasped and covered her mouth with her napkin. She didn't want Erik to see that she was trying not to laugh.

"Oh, no! That must have been embarrassing," Jade replied with sympathy.

"It was. I offered to buy her a drink, but she was there with a date. I left and thought no more about it until I saw her in the grocery store. She gave me her number, and I called her. We had dinner and a few drinks last week. That's all there is to it."

"Where did you have dinner?" asked Jade.

"We met at Burritos Plus had a nice dinner and went our separate ways."

"Are you going to ask her out again?" Mollie asked.

"I don't know. We don't have much in common other than we both travel for our jobs."

Erik had been relieved when the two women dropped the subject and began clearing the table. All too soon, the weekend was over. Jade said goodbye to her mother before going to work that morning because Erik was to drive Mollie to the airport that afternoon.

After work, Jade and Erik planned to finish off the Thanksgiving leftovers and decorate the house for Christmas. She parked in the driveway, went through the gate, and braced herself for Teddy's greeting, but Teddy didn't come. *He must be inside with Uncle Erik,* she thought. She walked across the lawn and noticed that the house was dark. She reached the back door and was surprised to find it standing open. Stepping across the threshold, she turned on the kitchen light, and was dumbstruck.

Every door of the kitchen cabinets stood open. All of the drawers had been pulled out. She crept further inside. Cereal boxes had been emptied. Canisters had been dumped. Both doors of the refrigerator stood open; its contents emptied onto the floor. The kitchen had been ransacked.

"Uncle Erik, are you here?"

There was no response.

"Teddy! Here boy!"

Still, no response.

She tiptoed through the rest of the house turning on lights and stepping over the wreckage. She was terrified that her uncle was hurt and needed help, but she was more terrified that he was beyond help.

Every room had been left in shambles. There was no sign of her uncle or his dog. Where was Teddy? He wouldn't have let anyone in the house or allowed them time to destroy it like this.

Trembling, Jade realized she was functioning on fear and adrenaline. She needed to sit down now that she knew the house was empty. She made her way downstairs and out the front door. She sat on the front step and called the police. She prayed that Teddy and her uncle were together. She tapped Erik's number.

"Hi, Jade," Erik answered.

"Thank God! Is Teddy with you?"

"No, what's wrong?"

"Somebody broke into your house, and I can't find Teddy."

"Call the police! I'm on my way!"

Erik disconnected the call before Jade could tell him anything more. She put her elbows on her knees and covered her face with her hands. This couldn't be happening.

She sat a few minutes before she stood and walked to the next-door neighbors' house. *Maybe, they've seen Teddy,* she thought. She rang the bell and waited.

"Hi, Jade," the elderly man said when he opened the door. "What can I do for you?"

"Hi, Mr. Walters. Have you seen Teddy?"

"No, isn't he in the yard?"

"Someone trashed Uncle Erik's house, and Teddy's gone."

Walters put his arm around her shoulders and said, "I'm sure he's fine. Maybe he's with Erik."

"No, I just talked to him."

"Have you called the police?"

Jade nodded. "They should be here any minute. Do you think someone took Teddy?"

Walters was relieved when the police arrived at that moment. He didn't have an answer that would satisfy either of them.

Jade watched the police officers get out of their car and went to greet them. Mr. Walters followed. She couldn't help noticing that, even in the dark, one of the men was jaw-dropping handsome.

"Miss O'Neal?" the handsome officer asked.

"Yes, I'm Jade O'Neal."

"I'm Hudson Bailey, and this is my partner Ronny Hague. Are you Mr. O'Neal?"

"No, I'm Lewis Walters. I live next door."

"Have you been able to get in touch with Mr. O'Neal?"

"Yes, he's on his way," answered Jade.

"We'd like for you to wait here while we clear the house," Bailey said.

"I've already been inside. There's no one there."

"We'll have a look around anyway."

Jade and Lewis Walters waited on the porch while the police officers went through the house.

"Miss O'Neal, what was your business here today?" Bailey asked.

Jade explained why she had come and what she found when

she arrived. Bailey continued asking questions until he was satisfied that Jade had told him all she knew.

"Did you touch anything while you were inside?"

"I opened the front door, and I turned on all of the lights. I don't think that I touched anything else."

"Does the house have an alarm system?"

"Yes."

"Did you turn the alarm off?"

"No."

"Was is it going off when you arrived?"

"No, it wasn't."

"Does your uncle often leave the house without turning the alarm on?"

"No, it's always on."

Officer Hague searched outside the front of the house with a flashlight while Bailey questioned Jade. He went through the front gate and began his search of the backyard. The grass had been disturbed near the storage shed. It appeared that something large had been dragged across the lawn.

Hague continued his search until he heard a noise coming from the shed.

"Bailey," Hague called. "I may have something."

"Wait here, please," Bailey instructed Jade.

Officer Bailey went through the front gate and joined his partner.

"There's a noise coming from that shed," Hague informed him.

The two men moved into position. Bailey had one hand on the door handle and a flashlight in the other. Hague had his hand on his gun.

Bailey turned the knob. Before he could get clear, he was knocked to the ground. A high-pitched scream echoed through the neighborhood.

"It sounds like they found Teddy," said Walters with a broad smile.

Jade ran to the backyard followed by Walters. Laying across Hague's chest, the massive dog stared at Bailey and growled every time he moved.

"Teddy! Come!" Jade ordered.

Teddy trotted across the yard and stopped beside Jade. She knelt beside him and rubbed his neck while he licked her face.

"I'm glad you're okay," she told him.

"Is this your missing dog?" Bailey asked and got up, keeping his eyes on the huge animal.

"Yes, this is Teddy. He's a sweetheart most of the time."

"If you say so," replied the officer.

"What's that?" Hague asked pointing at something shiny protruding from Teddy's flank.

Bailey picked up his flashlight and turned it toward Teddy. "It looks like a tranquilizer dart," said Bailey.

"Who would do that to Teddy?" Jade asked with anger and fear playing tag through her heart.

"I wouldn't try to get into this yard without one," replied Hague getting up from the ground.

"Do you think he'll let us remove it?" asked Bailey.

"It might be okay if you're quick. I'll see if I can distract him."

Jade scratched Teddy's ears and rubbed his neck. Hudson Bailey took a step toward them, and Teddy growled a warning.

Officer Bailey froze. "I don't think he's going to let me get close enough. You'd better pull it out. I'll leave a bag over there on the patio table."

Bailey kept his eyes on Teddy and moved in slow motion toward the patio. He placed an evidence bag and a rubber glove on the table and then backed away. Jade led Teddy to the patio and put the glove on her hand. She spoke to Teddy in a soft soothing tone and began to stroke his neck.

"Pull it straight out and place it in the bag," said Hague.

Jade pulled the dart out in one quick motion. Teddy winced, and she continued to pet and soothe the animal for a moment.

"Stay!" she told Teddy.

She placed the dart in the evidence bag and carried it to the officers.

"You can pet him now if you want."

"That's okay. I'll take your word for it," said Ronny Hague.

"Jade! Are you okay?" Erik ran toward her.

Teddy ran to greet his master and collided with him knocking Erik to the ground.

"Good ...boy. Teddy! I'm...happy to... see you, too." Erik said between gasps for air. "Now let me up."

Teddy obeyed and stayed close to Erik.

Jade had never been happier to see her uncle. She ran to him and hugged him tight.

"Are you Mr. O'Neal?" Officer Bailey asked.

"Yes, what happened here?"

"We're still trying to determine that, sir. We need to ask you some questions," the officer said and took a step toward Erik.

Teddy growled and barked.

"Jade, will you occupy Teddy while I talk with these officers?"

Jade led Teddy back to the patio and did her best to soothe him. He seemed to dislike the police officers. She wondered if it was because they were strangers or because he thought they had trapped him in the shed.

"I'd like you to go inside with me. We need to make note of the items that have been taken," Bailey said.

Erik toured the house and marveled at the mess. The television and some other electronics were missing. The most significant loss was his laptop computer.

The two men returned to the backyard.

"How many people have keys to this house?" asked Officer Bailey.

"I have keys to both of the outer doors and one to the door from the garage to the kitchen. My niece has a key to the back door. I haven't given anyone else a key."

"What kind of alarm system do you have?"

"It's a stand-alone system. I didn't feel the need for someone to monitor my home."

"Did you turn your alarm on before leaving today?"

"Yes, I did. I keep it on at all times."

"What time did you leave?"

"It was between two and two-thirty. I drove my sister-in-law to the airport. I was running some errands when my niece called."

"This is quite a mess for a simple case of robbery," the officer said and nodded toward the house. "It appears to me that your house has been searched by someone with no regard for your property. Do you have any idea what they could have been looking for?"

"Not a clue," Erik said pokerfaced.

"Do you have any enemies that would do this?" asked Bailey.

"Not to my knowledge."

Officer Hague interrupted the two men. "The scratches on the door lock indicates that lock picks were used to gain access to the house. It looks like the alarm was disabled once the intruder was inside." He pointed at the keypad dangling from the wall.

"Do you have a place to stay tonight?"

"I'll be fine here."

"Mr. O'Neal, whoever broke in here may have found what they wanted. Maybe they didn't. They could come back."

Erik looked at the officer a moment before he answered. "You have a good point, but there aren't many places that would tolerate Teddy."

"Is there someone who could take care of him for the night?" Bailey asked looking at Walters.

"Don't look at me! Erik and Jade are the only people that can handle him," he said, glancing at the dog.

"I think it would be a good idea to have your vet check him," suggested Hague. "We don't know what was in that dart."

"He isn't in his office on Sundays. I'll call and leave a message.

He may not get back to me until morning. I'll take Teddy for a walk and get him out of your way if the vet doesn't return my call soon."

"We'll call you when we've finished," said Officer Bailey, relieved that Teddy would be leaving.

Erik gave the officer his phone number before he called the veterinarian's office. The answering service picked up. Erik explained what happened and was soon speaking with Dr. Leslie Burge.

"Jade, Dr. Burge will meet us at his office. Will you ride along and help me keep Teddy calm?"

Jade nodded and stood. "Come on, Teddy."

Teddy was terrified of the vet. It took both of them to maneuver him through the back door of the veterinary office and into an examination room.

Dr. Burge gave the frightened dog a thorough examination. He found nothing physically wrong with Teddy, but he wasn't himself. He was groggy and short-tempered. Dr. Burge felt that, given the circumstances, Teddy should stay overnight for observation.

Erik and Jade scratched, patted, and rubbed Teddy's belly to reassure him. They coaxed him into a large kennel and told him goodnight. They could hear his anguished howl as they drove away.

"It's going to be a while before we can go back," Erik began. "Are you hungry?"

"A little," Jade replied, "there aren't going to be many places still open at this hour."

"It looks like the Taco Place is open. Do you want to eat there?"

Jade nodded, and Erik turned into the parking lot. They went inside and placed their order. It wasn't until they sat down to eat that Jade felt free to talk to her uncle about the burglary.

"Uncle Erik, who would have done this?"

"I don't know," he answered looking at his food. The truth was that he wasn't sure who it had been, but he knew why.

"They could have just taken what they wanted. Why did they have to destroy the house?"

Erik squeezed her hand. "I know you're scared. I am, too. I'm just thankful that they were gone before you got there."

"Do you think they'll come back?"

"I don't think so. There's nothing left for them to take. I don't keep cash at the house, and they've already taken everything of value."

"Do you think they were looking for money?"

"Money, jewelry, anything that could be pawned."

"Could it have been someone we know?" asked Jade.

Erik took the opportunity to give his niece a vague warning. "I don't know, honey. It might have been. We need to be careful who we trust."

"What do you mean?"

"People aren't always what they seem," he began. "Sometimes people you think you know well will surprise you. It's a good idea to be cautious."

Erik's phone rang before Jade had time to reply. He answered the call and listened for a few minutes. He thanked the caller and hung up.

"The police have finished with the house," Erik told her. "We can go back when we've finished eating."

"Are you really going to stay there tonight?" Jade asked with worry in her voice.

"Why not? The doors still lock. I'll be as safe as I was before I put in the alarm."

"But Teddy won't be there."

"I know it's been a few years, but I was safe before Teddy came along," Erik teased.

"Why don't you stay at my place tonight? Heather won't be home until tomorrow. You can take my bed, and I'll sleep on the couch."

"I'll be fine at home. Don't worry."

Jade wasn't satisfied but didn't argue.

They finished their dinner and drove back to the house. It was almost midnight by the time they'd cleaned up the mess in the kitchen.

"We'd better stop for the night and get some rest," Erik said. "I'll take the day off tomorrow and finish it."

"We'd better clean up your room if you're going to stay here."

They went upstairs to Erik's room and surveyed the damage. The mattress had been slashed and ripped to pieces. The mattresses in Jade's room and the guest room were also destroyed.

"Jade, I think I'll take you up on that offer to sleep at your place, but I'll sleep on the couch."

CHAPTER EIGHT

Monday, November 27, 2017

7:30 a.m.

"Uncle Erik?"

Erik could hear someone calling his name. Who was it? It was a woman. Where was she? It was too foggy to see clearly. He was in an unfamiliar place. Where was he?

"Uncle Erik?"

The building began to shake. He heard the voice again.

"Uncle Erik!"

Erik woke with a start. It took a few seconds to comprehend what was happening. It was Jade. She was standing over him, shaking his shoulder.

"Good morning," she said when he opened his eyes.

"Morning," he replied and looked around the room.

"I made you some coffee," Jade said and handed him a steaming mug.

Erik sat up and took the cup from her. "I was having the weirdest dream. What time is it?"

"Seven-thirty. I'll have to leave for class in a few minutes," she said sitting on the sofa beside him. "You can use my shower if you want."

"Thanks, but I'll go home so that you can lock up. I want to see the damage in the light of day."

"I'm sorry that I don't have anything for breakfast," Jade said. "I wish we'd thought to bring those cinnamon rolls Mom made."

Erik groaned. "We didn't look in the garage last night. All the food your mom made for you will be ruined if the thieves emptied the freezer like they did the fridge."

"Chances are good that it's all gone."

"I'll look in there when I get home."

Erik drank his coffee and looked at Jade. "I'll leave when you do so that I can get started. I've got phone calls to make and a long day of cleanup ahead."

"I'll come and help you when I get off," Jade promised.

The pair left the apartment and hugged goodbye in the parking lot. Erik drove home and used the remote to open his garage door. He got out of the car for a better look. His heart dropped at the sight.

The thieves hadn't just emptied the contents of the freezer. It looked as though they'd thrown the containers out one by one. Thawing food was scattered over the entire floor of the two-car garage.

They hadn't stopped there. The attic ladder was down and items he had stored were spilling out of the opening.

Erik was at a loss. There was so much to do that he didn't know where to start. He closed the garage door and went into the house. He sat down at the bar, took out his phone, and tapped a number.

"Renee? It's Erik. I'm not going to be in today. Someone broke into my house, yesterday."

"That's horrible, Erik," Renee replied. "Are you okay?"

"I'm fine. There's a huge mess to clean up. I need talk to the police and get in touch with my insurance company. It depends on how much I can accomplish today whether I'll be in tomorrow."

"Is there anything I can do?" Renee asked.

"I don't think so. I'm not sure what to do myself."

"I'll let everyone here know what happened. Let us know if we can help with anything."

"I will, thanks, Renee."

Erik tapped in his insurance company's number and arranged for someone to come and assess the damage. He then called the police department and asked for a copy of the police report. Next, he called Dr. Burge's office. The receptionist put him on hold for ten minutes.

"This is Leslie Burge," a voice said at last.

"Dr. Burge, this is Erik O'Neal. How is Teddy doing?"

"The effects of the drug used on him have worn off. He's appears to be back to his old self. You can pick him up when you're ready."

"That's good news! Do you mind if I leave him there a little longer? I have to take care of some things related to the burglary this morning."

"That's no problem. He won't eat the food we have here. He's going to be hungry when you pick him up."

"I'll pick him up when I've finished at the police station," Erik said and ended the call.

Erik made a call to the company who sold him the alarm system. He explained the situation and arranged for repairs and an upgrade.

He wanted to start cleaning the mess in the garage, but he thought it best to wait until the insurance adjustor had come and gone. Instead, he walked through the house and made a list of all the items that would need to be replaced or repaired.

He almost laughed out loud when he thought about the laptop that had been taken. There was nothing useful saved there. All of his work was saved to a flash drive that no one would ever find without his help.

A copy of the police report was ready for Erik when he arrived at the station. Reading through it, he found that most of the report had been discussed with the officers on the scene. There was one item that he didn't understand.

"Excuse me. What does this mean?" Erik pointed out an item on the police report.

The officer looked at the report and said, "That's the analysis of a dart found at the scene. It had traces of Ketamine."

"What's Ketamine?"

"It's a tranquilizer used on large animals. Most people call it 'horse tranquilizer.' It's also a popular street drug," the officer informed him.

Erik left the police station and thought about Teddy. He'd have to discuss this information with Dr. Burge. He hoped that his dog would have no lasting effects from the drug.

He turned onto Fourth Avenue and noticed the time on a bank sign. He decided to pick up lunch at the next fast food establishment he came across because he needed to be home when the insurance adjustor arrived.

The doorbell rang at one o'clock. Erik put what remained of his lunch in the garbage and went to the door.

"Kathy?"

"Surprise!" She said with a smile and handed him her card.

Erik was speechless. He looked at the card and said, "You're the insurance adjustor?"

"I suppose I should have called to let you know that I'd been given your case, but I wanted to see the look on your face," she said still smiling.

"You said you were in the insurance business, but it never occurred to me that... I'm sorry. Please, come in," Erik said stepping out of her way.

Kathy went inside and looked around. "Someone had fun in here."

"You should have seen it before I started cleaning. The barstools in the kitchen are still in one piece. Let's talk in there."

Kathy followed him to the kitchen and sat down at the bar. She took a legal pad and a pen from her brief case.

"Would you like some iced tea or water?"

"No, thank you," Kathy replied. "I think we should get down to business. I have another appointment when I've finished here."

"All right, where do you want to start?"

"Tell me what happened."

Erik told Kathy everything he knew about the burglary while she took notes. He told her what Jade found when she arrived and what had happened to Teddy. He gave her a copy of the police report and copies of the receipts for the repairs he'd already made.

"Who is Teddy?"

"Teddy is my dog. Would you like to see him?"

"Yes, I would," she said taking out her cell phone. "I'll need a few photos of him for your file."

"Let's go outside. I'd rather not let him in just now."

Kathy followed Erik outside.

Teddy was at the corner of the yard lying in the sun. He got up and ran at a full gallop toward Erik when he heard the door open. He stopped and stood on his hind legs with his paws on Erik's chest.

"Oh my God! He's enormous!"

Erik scratched Teddy's ears and neck. "Yes, he is. He's protective of his territory, too."

"I can see why the thieves tranquilized him," Kathy said. "I wouldn't want to be in his path."

Erik pushed Teddy down and told him to sit. Kathy took several photographs before they went back inside.

"All I need now is a tour of the house so that I can photograph the damage," Kathy told Erik.

Erik took her to every part of the house and stood back while she took pictures. He walked her to her car when she finished.

"I'll turn this report in as soon as possible. You should hear back from the company by the end of the week," Kathy told him.

"Do you think there will be any problem with my claim?"

"I don't think so. It's depends on the coverage you have of course."

"Let me ask you one more thing before you go. Are you busy Saturday night?"

4:30 p.m.

Jade returned to her apartment that afternoon and climbed the stairs. She'd had a busy day. She ordered a fast food burger in the drive-thru lane after class and ate in her car on the way to work. She was tired and wanted to relax before going to help her uncle clean up his home.

The apartment door wasn't locked when she arrived. *Heather must be home,* she thought. She stepped inside and turned on the light.

She blinked a few times and looked around. The apartment was wrecked. Worse than Heather had a party wrecked. It looked the same as her uncle's house did the previous day.

Jade looked toward her room. The door was standing open. She knew it had been locked because she double checked it before she left.

She turned around and walked out of the apartment. Standing outside the door, she called the police and her uncle. She decided it would be best to wait outside until help arrived. She was sitting at the top of the stairs when Logan came home.

"Hi, Jade. What are you doing out here?"

"Someone has been in our apartment. I'm waiting for the police," Jade replied, her voice trembling.

"Are you sure?"

"See for yourself," she said pointing at the open door.

Logan looked inside. "What a mess? Are you sure Heather didn't have another party?"

"She went home for Thanksgiving. She hasn't been here since Wednesday afternoon."

Logan sat down beside her and took her hand. Jade liked the warmth of his touch. It helped calm her frazzled nerves.

Erik rushed up the stairs two at a time. Jade let go of Logan's hand and stood.

"Are you okay?" he asked wrapping her in a bear hug.

She nodded and said, "I'm just scared."

"Did you call the police?"

"They're on the way," she said and looked up at her uncle. "What's happening?"

"I don't know, sweetheart."

Jade and Erik looked into each other's eyes. Both knew this wasn't a coincidence. Erik held a finger to his lips. Jade understood that they should talk later. She nodded and noticed Logan was still standing nearby.

"Logan Rhodes, I'd like you to meet my uncle, Erik O'Neal."

"It's nice to meet you, sir."

"It's good to meet you, too. Jade has told me a lot about you."

Logan blushed. Any reply he was about to make was interrupted by two police officers making their way up the stairs.

"Miss O'Neal?"

"Yes."

"I'm Sylvia Morrison," said the woman. "This is my partner, Lance Reeves. Have you been inside?"

"Just long enough to see what happened."

"We'll go inside and have a look around. Please, wait here. "

Jade listened while Erik and Logan seemed to be absorbed in small talk. She soon lost interest in their conversation and peered through the door. She was curious to see what the officers were doing.

Officer Reeves saw her and said, "We'd like for you to take a look around and make a list of anything that's missing."

Jade walked through the apartment. The large television in the living room and a small one that she kept in her room were missing.

"What's going on?" Heather asked when she entered the apartment.

"Someone broke in and did this," Jade replied, indicating the wreckage.

"Who are you?" asked Reeves.

"I'm Heather Anderton. I live here."

"Miss Anderton, please, look around and tell us what's missing."

Heather checked her room and went to talk to the officers. "My iMac is gone."

"Miss O'Neal said the TV that was in the living room belonged to you."

Heather nodded and asked, "Do you think whoever did this will come back?"

"It's possible, but I doubt it," answered Officer Morrison. "Please, step outside while we finish in here. We'll need to ask you both some questions when we're done."

The two women went outside where Erik and Logan waited.

"Can you imagine what might have happened if we'd been home?" asked Heather, fear etched on her face.

"I doubt that anyone would have broken in if you'd been here," Erik said, trying to calm her.

"I hope you're right, Mr. O'Neal."

"Why don't we wait in my apartment where it's more comfortable?" offered Logan.

"You girls go inside," Erik instructed. "I'll tell the officers where to find you."

"I'll leave the door open for you," said Logan.

Jade turned to look at her uncle before following Logan and Heather.

Erik smiled at her and nodded. "I'll join you in a few minutes."

He waited until they were in Logan's apartment before talking to the police officers.

"Officer Morrison, my name is Erik O'Neal. I'm Jade's uncle. I think I should tell you something that I'd rather Miss Anderton didn't hear."

Both officers listened while Erik told them about the burglary of his own home.

"Why don't you want Miss Anderton to know?" Lance Reeves asked.

"She's already afraid. I don't want to frighten her more," he lied.

"Do you think there's a connection between the two burglaries?" asked Reeves.

"It's strange to me that both of our homes have been burglarized in the last two days."

"Any idea what the connection might be?" asked Morrison.

"I'm hoping that you'll be able to tell me," Erik said.

Sylvia Morrison glanced at her partner before saying, "We won't discuss the earlier incident in front of the others."

"Thank you," Erik replied with a weak smile.

He went back outside and looked at the time on his cell phone. He went downstairs to the apartment manager's office. The office was locked. Erik was about to walk away when he noticed a sign with an after-hours phone number. He tapped in the number and waited.

"Ms. Hancock, this is Erik O'Neal."

"Hello, what can I do for you?"

"Someone broke into Jade's apartment today."

"What? Is she all right?"

"Yes, she wasn't home at the time. The police are there now,"

Erik informed her. "I think it would be a good idea for the locks to be changed."

"Yes, I agree. It could be a few days before our maintenance man can get to it. He's taking some time off," said Stephanie. "Was there any damage?"

"They haven't found any yet. They'll have a lot of clean up to do." Erik paused and said, "Would it be possible for the girls to keep my dog with them until the lock is replaced?"

"Pets aren't allowed, but under the circumstances, I might be able to make an exception. What kind of dog?" Stephanie asked.

"He's large, scary, and protective. Most people wouldn't consider entering his domain. He's well trained and won't damage anything."

"How do the girls feel about having the dog?"

"I haven't talked with them about it. It just occurred to me. I know Jade wouldn't mind, but I'm not sure about Heather."

"Is there somewhere else they could stay?"

"I suppose they could stay with me, but my house isn't ideal right now."

"Find out if there are other options before we discuss bringing the dog. I'll have a hard time explaining his presence to other residents and my boss."

"Okay, thank you."

Erik went upstairs and waited with the others in Logan's apartment. The group waited almost an hour before the police officers were ready to talk with Heather and Jade.

"We need to ask you ladies a few questions," Reeves said.

The officers asked similar questions to those that Jade had answered at Erik's house. There was no evidence of forced entry. They believed the door had been left unlocked or someone may have had a key. *Or lock picks,* Jade thought.

Morrison and Reeves suggested that the lock should be changed, and the door kept locked at all times. They told Jade and Heather that it was safe to return to their apartment.

Erik helped Heather and Jade put their home back in order. He told them about the conversation with Ms. Hancock. Heather decided to stay with a friend. Jade packed a bag and followed her uncle to his house.

Teddy welcomed his master and favorite playmate home. He wagged his tail in his "let's play" bow before licking both of their faces.

"Are you hungry?" Erik asked. "I was thinking that pizza sounds good right now."

"That sound good to me," Jade replied.

Erik took out his phone. He ordered their favorite pizza and soft drinks to be delivered.

"It should be here in half an hour," he told Jade.

"Are we any safer here than we were last night?" Jade asked with skepticism.

"The locks still work and the alarm system has been repaired. I've arranged for it to be upgraded by the end of the week. Teddy is here to guard us. We couldn't be safer," Erik replied with more confidence than he felt.

"Where are we going to sleep? The bedrooms are still disaster areas."

Erik looked around the living room and thought for a moment. "We'll have to improvise tonight. There are some cots in the attic. We can camp in here after we've cleared some of the mess."

They ate dinner and made their beds. They watched a movie on Netflix using Jade's laptop before settling down for the night.

"Jade, I know that you're a grown woman and that you like your privacy and independence. But I'd like you to consider moving in here with me," Erik suggested. "I'd feel a lot better if you had more security considering what's happened."

"You're used to privacy and independence, too. I don't want to put you out or be in your way."

"You wouldn't be in my way, and I'd love to have you here," Erik assured her.

"What if you want to bring a date home...for the night...or the weekend?"

"That isn't going to happen any time soon."

"How do you know? You might find out you have more in common with Kathy than you think."

"It's funny you should mention Kathy," Erik said. "She came by this afternoon. She's the insurance adjustor who was assigned to my claim."

"Are you serious?"

"Yep," Erik said with a smile, "I...uh...invited her to join us at the museum Saturday night."

"What did she say?" Jade asked with excitement.

"She'll meet us there."

They talked a while longer before Jade asked, "Why is this happening, Uncle Erik?"

"I wish I could answer that," Erik said truthfully. "I have suspicions but no facts to back them up."

"What kind of suspicions?"

"Nothing specific. Strangers in the neighborhood. Neighbors that I don't know very well. College kids or teenagers looking for trouble or a quick score."

"You think it could have been anyone for any reason or no reason at all."

"That's my point."

"That would explain one break in, but how do you explain them both?"

"My guess is that the thieves found your address here," Erik improvised. "I hope the police will be able to clear it up for us."

Erik lay awake long after Jade and Teddy had fallen asleep. He rolled over on his cot trying to find a more comfortable position. He could hear Jade's heavy breathing and Teddy's soft snores.

He didn't like lying to Jade, but he couldn't risk telling her the truth yet. He hoped those responsible for the burglaries would realize that he was working alone and that his niece was not involved.

His life had become unpredictable, and he found himself second guessing every decision. He was sure of one thing.

These weren't ordinary burglaries. They were a warning.

CHAPTER NINE

6:00 p.m.

Almost a week after the burglaries, Erik's house was being monitored twenty-four hours a day with an upgraded alarm system. The damaged furnishings and stolen items were being replaced little by little. He managed to put up the Christmas tree and add the few ornaments that hadn't been destroyed.

New locks had been installed on the front door of Jade's apartment and her bedroom door. Heather replaced her computer and TV, but Jade hadn't replaced her television. She decided not to spend the money because she seldom had the time to watch.

Their lives were on the road to normal.

Jade had worked most of the day at the boutique. She would have liked nothing better than to hide in her room the rest of the evening, but she couldn't. She'd promised her uncle that she would go to the holiday event at the museum, and she wasn't going to let him down.

She glanced at the time on her cell phone and decided to relax for half an hour before getting ready. She laid on her bed and set an alarm just in case she dozed off. The dress she'd borrowed from Heather hung on her closet door.

The museum event wasn't black tie, but it wasn't a jeans and t-shirt party either. She'd be over dressed in the dress she'd worn to the fall formal. The one skirt she owned wasn't appropriate either. She hadn't been eager to accept Heather's offer to loan her a dress, but lack of time and funds left her no other choice.

Erik knocked on Jade's door at seven-fifteen.

"Are you ready?" he asked when Jade opened the door.

"I am." She smiled at her uncle and added, "Woo hoo! Look at you!"

"What? Do I look too nerdy?"

"You look awesome...except for that tie," she said straightening it. "That's better."

"You look beautiful," Erik told her.

"Thanks. Are you nervous?"

"Does it show?"

"A little," she answered.

"We'd better go and get this over with," he said.

"Are you sure you don't want me to take my car? I don't want to be a third wheel if you decide to take Kathy home."

"I'm sure," Erik replied. "She may not be able to come, and we're nothing more than acquaintances at this point."

They arrived early enough that they had time to visit some of the exhibits before the festivities began. Jade loved the holiday décor.

A Christmas tree stood in each corner of the main entrance. They were decorated identically with white lights and an assortment of colorful ornaments. A golden star topped all four trees. The reception desk was draped with garland and white twinkle lights. Holiday flower arrangements had been strategically placed around the room.

Each exhibit had been decorated with holiday decorations appropriate for the time period. Jade liked the old-fashioned ornaments and lights and wondered where the decorating committee had found them all.

Making their way upstairs, they waited for the official unveiling. Jade couldn't wait to see the results of her uncle's hard work.

"Is my tie still straight?" Erik asked Jade. She could hear the nervousness in his voice.

Jade made a minor adjustment and smiled at her uncle. "It looks like it's time," she said nodding toward the podium.

Erik turned and saw someone stepping up to the podium.

He took a few deep breaths while he waited to be introduced. Jade squeezed his arm when Bryce Ammons the president of the board said, "And I'd like you to meet the man responsible for this magnificent exhibit, Erik O'Neal."

Erik made his way toward the podium amidst applause from the crowd. He shook hands with the board members who stood nearby. Jade noticed that his nervousness was melting away.

He told the audience how the idea for the exhibit had come about. He told them about the interesting people he met while doing his research, and shared a few of the stories that he'd been told. He introduced each member of the team who had built the display. Erik ended his speech by directing the audience's attention to Mr. Ammons who cut the ribbon and opened the exhibit.

Jade marveled at the display. She stood beside her uncle and listened to the comments and compliments of the crowd.

It was the first time in her life that she'd seen Erik as someone other than her uncle. He was in his element. He was an experienced historian whose expertise and attention to detail had earned him the respect of his peers. She had always been proud to be his niece but never more so than tonight.

"Hello, Miss O'Neal. How are you this evening?"

Jade turned to see Jonathan Baxter standing beside her.

"I'm fine, Mr. Baxter. How are you?"

"Doing well, thank you. I was just admiring the new exhibit. Your uncle did an outstanding job."

"Yes, he did," Jade said, beaming with pride.

Erik overheard the conversation and said, "Thank you, Mr. Baxter."

"Well, hello, Erik. I didn't see you standing there," Baxter said with surprise, "excellent work."

A man in a tailored suit joined them. Jade had never seen anyone quite like him. The word flawless came to mind. Not a strand of his dark hair was out of place. Confident and classy, he reminded her of characters from an old James Bond movie.

"Ah, Dino. Have you met Erik O'Neal and his niece Jade?"

"Hello, Mr. Stevens," Erik said and shook the newcomer's hand.

"It's good to see you, Erik, and it's nice to meet such an attractive young lady."

Jade blushed and shook his hand. "Thank you, Mr. Stevens. It's a pleasure to meet you."

"Dino is also a member of the board," explained Baxter.

They exchanged polite small talk before separating to mingle with other guests.

"How do you know Jonathan Baxter?" Erik whispered.

"I met him at the fall formal."

"Good evening, Erik."

Erik turned and greeted a tall slender man. "Good evening, Mr. Lee. I'd like you to meet my niece, Jade."

"I've already had the pleasure." Wilson Lee smiled and shook hands with both of them. "I hope you've recovered from your misadventure."

Jade laughed. "Yes, thank you."

"Misadventure?" Erik asked in confusion.

"Mr. Lee came to my rescue when Teddy decided to chase a squirrel a couple of months ago," Jade explained.

"I'm still amazed that you weren't injured. How is that magnificent dog?"

"He's fine," answered Erik. "He's a good dog until he sees a squirrel."

"It's good to see you both. I should say hello to my fellow board members. Goodnight."

"Goodnight," Erik and Jade said in unison.

"How many of the board members have you met?" Erik asked while they made their way across the room.

"I've met three, counting Mr. Stevens."

Renee Lanham and Tommy Carlile joined the O'Neals at the refreshment table. Jade saw them often when she visited her uncle at work. She talked with them both while Erik schmoozed with the guests and trustees.

Jade saw Erik approach a pretty blonde and give her a hug. She raised an eyebrow and tried to maneuver into position for a better view.

"Who is that with Erik?" Tommy asked. "Wait! Isn't that the woman he ran into at Burritos Plus?"

"He didn't run into that woman," Renee said with disgust. "I saw her when she came into the bar. She ran into him on purpose and let him believe he'd been at fault. She did it just so she could talk to him. He was so embarrassed. I know he felt terrible about it."

Tommy grinned and whispered to Jade, "It looks like it worked."

Erik returned to the refreshment table with Kathy at his side.

"I'd like y'all to meet my friend, Kathy," Erik began. "Kathy, this is my niece, Jade, and these are my friends and coworkers, Renee and Tommy."

"It's nice to meet y'all," Kathy said and shook hands with each of them.

"If you'll excuse us, I'm going to give Kathy a tour of the exhibit," Erik said and led his new friend away.

"Have they been dating?" Tommy asked curiosity shining from his eyes.

"I know they've gone out once," Jade replied. "Other than that, I don't know."

"I hear you've been seeing someone," Renee said, trying to change the subject.

Yes, we've gone out a few times, and I went to his fraternity's fall formal."

"Did you have a good time?" Renee asked but scanned the crowd watching for Erik.

"Yes, it was so much fun."

"You need to bring him by the museum so that we can meet him," Tommy suggested.

"That could be a problem. He started a new job last week, and I've been working until the mall closes almost every night. I'd never see him if we didn't live next door to each other."

"Maybe that will change after the holidays," Renee said and patted Jade's arm.

"I hope so," Jade replied.

Erik and Kathy returned, helped themselves to some refreshments, and moved to a corner where they could be alone.

Renee glared at them for a moment before she said, "I think I'm going home. It's been a long night."

"It's only 9:30," Tommy said surprised. "We've been here an hour and a half."

"Well, I've had a long night," Renee replied. "Goodnight, Jade. Tell Erik I'll see him Monday. Enjoy the rest of your weekend, Tommy."

She stomped out of the room leaving Jade and Tommy bewildered by her behavior.

"What's gotten in to her?" Tommy asked no one in particular.

Jade had an idea what had upset Renee, but she wasn't going to share that information with Tommy. The three of them worked so closely together that he should have been the first to realize that Renee had feelings for Uncle Erik.

Erik and Kathy joined them again.

"Where's Renee?" asked Erik.

"She went home," Tommy informed him.

"I was hoping to get a chance to talk with her before I leave," Kathy said with a glint in her eye.

"Are you leaving so soon?" Tommy asked.

"Yes," Kathy replied. "I have an early flight in the morning, and I still haven't packed. It was nice to meet you both."

"I'm going to walk Kathy to her car," Erik told Jade. "I'll be back in a few minutes."

Jade nodded and waved goodbye to Kathy. She talked with other people she knew who worked at the museum while she waited for her uncle to return. She poured herself another glass of punch and was approached by Wilson Lee.

"Are you having a good time?" Lee asked.

"Yes, I am."

"Jonathan Baxter was telling me that you're hoping to follow in Erik's footsteps."

"Yes, I am. I know it will take some time, but that's my dream job."

"Has your uncle given you any pointers?"

"No, but I hope that he will when I graduate. I've been so busy with school and work that I don't have a lot of free time."

"Will you graduate this semester?" Lee asked.

"That was my goal, but I won't be graduating until May."

"Not much longer then. It'll fly by before you know it."

"I hope so," Jade replied.

"Well, if you'll excuse me, I'll say goodnight."

"Goodnight, Mr. Lee."

Jade was talking with one of her classmates who worked at the museum when Erik returned.

"That was quick," Jade said teasing her uncle.

"I told you'd I'd be back in a few minutes."

"I was expecting twenty minutes not ten," Jade said. "Did you even have time to kiss her goodnight?"

Erik looked at his niece with a mixture of shock and aggravation until he saw her impish grin. He sighed, adjusted his tie, and said, "I'll never tell."

He looked at her through the corner of his eye, and they both laughed out loud.

Erik drove Jade home at the end of evening. He hugged her goodnight and said, "Thanks for coming tonight. It meant a lot."

"I wouldn't have missed it. I'm so proud of you, Uncle Erik."

Erik couldn't hide his surprise or emotion. He beamed at her. "You're proud of me?"

"I don't think I've ever told you, but I've always been proud of you," she said. "I love you."

"I love you too, sweetheart," he replied, hugging her again. "I'll see you tomorrow."

Erik drove home with mixed feelings about the evening. The unveiling of the exhibit had been a success, and finding out that Jade was proud of him made his day...no his year.

The fact that she had already met two board members disturbed him. Why hadn't she told him? The meetings seemed to be coincidental. It worried him that she had now met all three of the men he suspected to be responsible for Jacob's death.

Who else had she met? What if she's met the burglars or the man in the gray Accord? What if she'd met the other men that had been watching him?

There was no doubt in his mind that he was being watched. There was an unfamiliar car parked near his home every night, but it wasn't always the same car. There was also a black Toyota Avalon and a dark blue Dodge Durango. He assumed they were spying on him in shifts.

Three men turned up everywhere he went, a tan muscular man, the man with the royal flush tattoo, and a tall man with a shaved head. They'd never approached him. They were just there. He'd almost spoken to one of them a few days ago, but he thought better of it. He didn't want them to know he had noticed.

It was strange to Erik that he'd never seen one of the cars or the men near the museum. He never saw them when he went to lunch with Renee and Tommy. He didn't see any of them tonight. Was he being watched by someone who worked at the museum? Could it be Renee or Tommy?

Was someone watching Jade? Had she noticed someone showing up everywhere she went? Had she noticed unfamiliar cars parked in unusual places?

Erik knew that he had to make his move soon. Waiting for the final piece of evidence might prove to be disastrous. He might have to force Jacob's murderer into the open without it.

He couldn't sleep that night because he kept running through his plan over and over. The plan was solid. He'd needed to find a way to fool those who were watching him, or it could be the end of him if he were caught.

Frustrated that his mind wouldn't turn off, Erik got up. He took some things from his closet and worked on a special Christmas gift for Jade.

Sunday, December 3, 2017

5:00 a.m.

Erik put the finishing touches on the gift, and hid it in the closet until he had time to buy gift wrap. He imagined the look on Jade's face when she opened it.

He had time for a nap before Jade came for brunch. He showered, set his alarm, and fell into bed. Teddy groaned in protest at being disturbed. They both slept until the alarm went off.

Jade parked in the driveway at ten o'clock and peeked through the fence. Teddy must be inside. Her stomach grumbled when the scent of frying bacon reached her nostrils. She went into the house and said good morning to Teddy and Erik.

"What time do you have to be at work?" Erik asked.

"At noon. I'm opening today, so I shouldn't have to close."

"Will you be able to watch Teddy next week?"

"I've asked to be on earlier shifts. I'll make sure I'm not on the schedule to close."

"It won't interfere with studying for your finals, will it?"

"No, I prefer studying here. There's less noise and fewer interruptions."

They sat down to eat and talked about the previous evening.

"I noticed you were talking with Wilson Lee last night," Erik prodded.

"He said that Mr. Baxter had told him I wanted to follow in your footsteps. He wanted to know if you'd given me any pointers."

"That's interesting. What else did you talk about?"

"He asked when I'm going to graduate and just small talk." Jade took a sip of coffee before she continued. "I thought it was odd. Mr. Baxter asked almost the same thing at the formal."

"What did Baxter ask you?" Erik tried to keep his voice steady.

"He asked if I ever helped you with your research. I told him that I didn't have the time right now."

"Did you and Baxter talk long?"

"Just one dance, he talked about you most of it. He's a fan," Jade said smiling at her uncle.

"Have you had any similar conversations with Dino Stevens?"

"No, the only time we've spoken was when I met him last night."

Erik forced himself to focus on his food rather than questioning Jade further. He wanted to find out more, but he didn't want to alarm her.

"I found out something about your friend, Kathy."

"Oh?"

"Renee told me."

"How would Renee know anything about her? What was wrong with Renee last night?"

Jade rolled her eyes and looked at her uncle. "You don't know?"

"Well...I...know that she'd like to be...more than friends. What does that have to do with Kathy?"

"Renee told me last night that it was no accident that you bumped into Kathy."

"Is that so?" Erik asked with obvious surprise.

"She seemed to think that Kathy saw you when she got inside and walked into you on purpose. I couldn't tell if Renee was more upset that Kathy embarrassed you or that she was your date."

Erik opened his mouth and then shut it again. He had no idea what to say.

"I thought you ought to know," Jade explained. "Things with Renee could be a little chilly at work. A heads up about Kathy won't hurt if Renee is right."

"Kathy approached me the night she gave me her phone number," Erik said. "I might not have seen her otherwise."

"She could be the kind of woman who doesn't wait around for a man to make the first move," Jade suggested.

"That's possible," Erik agreed. "How are things going with Logan?"

"I haven't seen much of him since the formal," she said. "Work and school keep us both busy."

"And how's the situation with Heather?"

"It's getting better. I haven't seen much of her either," Jade said with a smirk.

They finished their meal, and Jade helped with the kitchen cleanup before leaving for work. Erik went upstairs and finished putting the guest room back in order. It was the last room to be completed.

His mind raced while he worked. Two of the three men he suspected had asked Jade about working with him. Were they both just casual questions or was one of them fishing for information?

What about Kathy? Could their meeting have been intentional? It had been a surprise when she turned out to be his insurance adjustor. Was that a coincidence?

Erik finished the repairs in the guest room and took Teddy for his walk. *The Durango is on duty tonight,* he thought, when he turned down the alley toward his house.

A man was throwing garbage in the dumpster across the alley when Erik and Teddy got to the driveway.

"Hi, how are you?" asked the man approaching Erik and offering his hand. "I'm Ed Kinnan."

"Erik O'Neal," said Erik shaking the man's hand.

"It's nice to meet you, Erik. It looks like we're going to be neighbors. I just moved in over here," Kinnan said, indicating the house across the alley from Erik's.

Teddy tugged on his leash.

"I need to feed my dog before he pulls my arm out of socket," Eric apologized. "It's nice to meet you and welcome to the neighborhood."

"It does look likes he's ready to eat. Have a nice evening."

Erik waved goodbye and went into the house. He fed Teddy and made himself a small meal. He sat down at the bar and looked out the kitchen window. He could see his new neighbor on the second-floor balcony. He wondered if the neighbor could see into his kitchen. He thought it strange that he had a new neighbor. He hadn't known the former neighbors had moved or that their home was for sale.

CHAPTER TEN

Tuesday, December 5, 2017

8:00 p.m.

Erik needed to follow a lead that he hoped would be the last piece of the puzzle. He knew that his time would be limited when he returned from his trip, and he needed to have everything at one site. He had to retrieve his flash drive from its hiding place and take it to his secure location before leaving town.

First, he had to ditch the men following him. He'd been planning his escape for several days. He knew it wasn't safe, but he had no choice. He had to risk it.

He'd returned to his old habits, hoping that his life would be so boring to those who watched him that they would drop their guard.

Today had been like any other. He'd gone to work and returned home. Teddy had been walked and fed. He'd had his dinner and was settled in front of the television. Having no idea what was on, his mind was occupied, running through his escape plan.

At ten-thirty, he let Teddy outside and made sure all the doors and windows were locked. He let Teddy back in and pretended to set the alarm. All of the lights inside the house were turned off while the porch lights in both yards were bright as the noon day sun.

Teddy followed his master upstairs and watched him change into black jeans and a black hoodie instead of pajamas. Erik went to the bedroom window and peered out into the street. The black Toyota was on duty out front tonight. He went back to the bed, lay down, and waited.

He'd weighed all of his options. He couldn't be seen if he was going to be successful, which meant that he had to act at night. Driving away from his house and the man watching would mean driving without lights. He couldn't risk his headlights or brake lights being seen.

Walking out the back door and through the alley wouldn't work. It was possible that he was being watched from one of his neighbors' homes. Every light would have to be turned off. Turning off his security lights would alert whoever was watching that something was different, making his escape more difficult.

He couldn't use the doors, but he could get out through a window. The only window that was hidden from the street and the alley was the one used by the intruder.

Teddy groaned in protest when Erik got up an hour later.

"Stay, Teddy!"

Erik made his way downstairs and to the window in the dark. He wanted to avoid alerting anyone outside that all was not as it seemed. He'd already moved everything out of his path so that he wouldn't trip or stub his toe in the darkness.

He heard Teddy panting behind him.

"Teddy! Stay!" he ordered.

Teddy lay down on the floor and looked at Erik as if his master had lost his mind.

"I'll be back soon," Erik whispered and raised the window as high as he could. He squeezed through and took the time to lower it again before he moved toward the front of the house.

He peered through the shrub toward the street. The Toyota was still in position. Erik surveyed his surroundings. He might make it if he stayed in the shadows.

A car turned onto the street, and Erik ducked behind the evergreen bush to avoid being seen. He waited a few minutes before he made his next move.

There was a space between Lewis Walters' house and a shrub that would give him cover until he reached the sidewalk. He crouched and dashed toward his neighbor's house. He slipped behind the shrub and followed it to the sidewalk. He waited on all fours and listened for a moment before he moved again.

Erik stayed crouched in the shadows and maneuvered his way through his neighbors' front yards to the end of the street. He stood up when he was sure he was out of sight. He strolled to the corner of Twenty-Sixth Street and Fourth Avenue. He waited in the shadows to make sure he hadn't been followed.

That was easier than I expected, he thought, feeling proud of himself. All he had to do now was get the flash drive and get back without being seen.

He walked west on Fourth Avenue, crossed Twenty-Third Street, and zig zagged his way to North Fourteenth Street and the Tex Randall statue. He made sure that he was alone before getting on his knees beside a flowering shrub. He dug under the shrub with his hands until he found a sealed plastic container. He took the flash drive from the container and put it in his pocket. He pushed soil back under the shrub and tossed the container in a nearby dumpster.

He meandered his way back to his own neighborhood and repeated the process of crouching low and staying in the shadows. He breathed a sigh of relief when he reached his own property again.

Erik saw no evidence that his absence had been noticed. The

street was quiet, and the man in the Toyota was still parked at the end of the street. He crept to the window and raised it until he heard a low rumble on the other side.

"Teddy, it's me," Erik whispered and squeezed through the window. He managed to close and lock the window in spite of Teddy's excited greeting.

"I'm glad to see you too," Erik said, rubbing Teddy's neck and chin. "Do you need out?"

Erik let his pet in again and this time set the alarm. It was three a.m. when he crawled back into bed and fell asleep in an instant.

Wednesday, December 6, 2017

7:45 a.m.

Erik had arranged to take the day off under the pretext of Christmas shopping. He hadn't shared that information with anyone other than the museum director. He knew that someone inside the museum was passing information to those who dogged his every step.

He waited inside the museum entrance and watched until the Honda Accord passed. He stepped outside, made sure that none of his stalkers were in sight, and returned to his car.

He drove east on Fourth Avenue and turned north onto FM 1541. He reached the Amarillo city limits and made his way to the nearest post office.

Erik parked his car and opened the trunk. He took out two boxes that were ready to be mailed. He hoped that Mollie and Levi would get them in time. Sending packages so close to Christmas was a risk he had to take. Anyone would assume they were gifts.

He knew it wouldn't be long before the men following him were alerted to his absence at the museum. He had to move fast. He had two more stops to make before they found him.

Nelson King followed his mark to the museum. He made sure that O'Neal had gone inside before he turned up the volume on the radio and started toward Amarillo.

"There's been a major accident in the construction zone of I-27 this morning. We've been told that traffic is at a standstill," the radio announcer said. "Emergency vehicles are on the way. You may want to take another route for your commute to work. But if you like sitting still on the highway, listening to the radio, then I-27 is the place to be this morning."

King looked at the clock on his dashboard. He drove out of Canyon as usual but took the Hereford exit. He then turned north onto VFW Road. He was going to be late, but it would still be faster than taking the interstate this time.

He followed VFW Road to Loop 335 and Soncy Road. He turned east onto Amarillo Boulevard and headed toward the medical center.

He parked near the playground at Medi Park and took a canvas chair, fishing pole, and tackle box out of the trunk. He looked around before he walked toward a man feeding ducks near the edge of the lake. A jogger ran toward them on the nearby walking path.

"Good mornin'," King said loud enough for anyone nearby to hear. "Do you mind if I fish here?"

"Not at all," said Ace. "I'll have to leave soon anyway."

King set up his chair and sat down. He opened his tackle box and took out a lure.

"You're late!" said Ace lowering his voice.

"Accident on the interstate. I had to find a different way in," King explained, while tying a lure to his line.

Ace saw another runner coming toward them. "Do you catch many fish here?"

"It's just like anywhere else. Some days are better than others."

The runner passed them by, and they continued talking with lowered voices.

"We didn't find anything in O'Neal's house. No research, no photograph, nothing. There's nothing in his office either."

"He must be keeping it somewhere else."

"I don't know where it could be. He's been watched twenty-four seven for weeks."

"I would have thought he'd make sure it was safe after his home was searched," said Ace.

"He changed his routine for a few days but nothing out of the ordinary," King replied and cast his line into the water.

"O'Neal changed his routine?" Aced asked.

"He started taking different routes to work, shopping at different stores, eating at different restaurants, and walking his dog at different times. He's back to his old routine now. I'm sure he knows he's being watched, but he ignores us and goes about his business."

"What kind of fish do you pull out of this lake?" Ace asked, raising his voice again and tossing a piece of bread to the ducks paddling nearby.

"I catch perch most of the time, but I heard they've stocked it with rainbow trout."

The jogger passed them by.

"And the girl?"

"There was nothing in her apartment either. Her routine hasn't changed at all. She goes to class, to work, and then to her apartment. She goes to O'Neal's place on Sundays before going to work, and they meet for lunch a couple of times a week."

King reeled in his line and made another cast.

"She's gone shopping with a friend and on a couple of dates. My contact says she's never mentioned anything that indicates she knows what O'Neal has been doing."

Ace rubbed the back of his neck with his left hand. He tossed the last of his bread to the ducks and watched them race toward it.

King's line jerked, and he began to reel in a fish. Ace watched until King had removed the perch from the hook and tossed it back into the lake.

"O'Neal is too confident," Ace began. "He thinks he has us where he wants us. I want to know what he has and what he knows."

"What do you want to do?" asked King, although he knew the answer.

"Bring him in!" Ace ordered and walked away.

King fished until Ace had driven out sight. He packed up his gear and walked back to his car. His cell phone rang when he opened the trunk.

"Yeah?"

"He isn't here."

"What?" asked King, shock in his voice.

"He took the day off," said the informant.

"I followed him to the museum and watched him go inside!"

"Well, he isn't here now."

King swore, threw the fishing gear in the trunk, and slammed it shut.

"Contact me if you hear anything else," King ordered and ended the call.

"What are you up to, O'Neal?" King asked aloud and drove out of the parking lot.

2:00 p.m.

Erik enjoyed his freedom while he could. He ran errands and took care of business that he wasn't comfortable doing with his watchdogs in tow. He knew that if he didn't resurface soon that his house could be destroyed again. He drove to the mall where he expected to find at least one of them watching Jade.

He drove through the parking lot until he found Jade's car and parked nearby. A blue Durango was parked at the end of the row. He couldn't see the license plate, but he thought it was one of the cars that he'd seen outside his house. He took a shopping bag from his trunk and walked inside.

He strolled through the mall and window shopped. He stopped to investigate items that caught his eye and made a few purchases. He spotted the large man with the royal flush tattoo outside a store near the boutique where Jade worked.

Stopping to look at a store display, he could see the man's reflection in the store window. The man stared at Erik and took out his cell phone.

Erik went into the boutique and waited while Jade helped a customer.

"Hi, what are you doing here?" Jade asked surprised.

"I'm Christmas shopping. Do you have time to look at something? I bought a sweater for your mom, but I'm not sure she'll like it."

Erik pulled a sweater from the shopping bag he'd brought from the car and waited while Jade inspected it.

"She'll love it," Jade told him. "What else have you got in those bags?"

"Nothing that you need to know about," Erik told her with a smile.

"Mr. O'Neal, why didn't you shop in here?" asked Jade's coworker, Lisa Tarrango.

"I'm sorry," Erik apologized. "But I can't shop for Jade while she's here working. I'm sure that Jade has already purchased everything in the store that her mother would like, and I don't see a single item that would interest my nephew."

The three chatted for a few minutes before Erik said goodbye and continued window shopping. He went into a few more stores and purchased three more gifts before making his way to his car.

He wondered if the tattooed man would follow him or if reinforcements would arrive. He drove out of the parking lot and looked in his review mirror. The man was talking on his phone with one hand and gesturing with the other.

Erik left the mall and drove the short distance to Best Buy. He went inside and browsed. He found a copy of Jade's favorite movie.

He was standing in the checkout line when he saw the Durango enter the parking lot. The tattooed man had caught up with him.

Erik left Best Buy and made one more stop to buy wrapping paper before making the drive back to Canyon.

5:30 p.m.

Jade walked to the Food Court during her dinner break. She wasn't hungry, but it was nice to get out of the boutique for a little while. She ordered a snack and a soft drink and sat down to watch the crowd.

She looked at the time on her cell phone when she'd finished her food. She still had time to window shop. She walked through the mall looking for anything that her brother or uncle might like. She walked into a men's store and met Dino Stevens on his way out.

"Hello, Mr. Stevens," Jade said.

"Miss O'Neal? What a pleasant surprise! Are you Christmas shopping as well?"

"I work at a boutique a few doors down. I'm browsing until my break is over."

"I'm glad I ran into you," said Stevens. "I need a gift for my sister. Would you happen to have any suggestions?"

"We have some nice things in the boutique. I bought all of my mother's gifts there. It's three stores down from here."

"Excellent! Do you mind if I follow you there?"

"Right this way," Jade said with a smile.

The two chatted about what Mr. Stevens' sister might like and what he wanted to buy. Jade had some ideas by the time they'd make the short walk to her store. She chose several items and carried them to the counter for Mr. Stevens to inspect.

Stevens chose three sweaters and coordinating jewelry. Jade took his purchases to the back and gift wrapped them for him.

"Thank you, Miss O'Neal. I appreciate your help. I'm sure that my sister will be delighted."

"You're welcome. I'm happy to help."

"Are you planning to make sales your career?"

"No, sir." Jade assured him. "I'll be graduating in May with a degree in history."

Stevens raised his eyebrows and said, "Is that so? Planning to follow in your uncle's footsteps are you?"

"I'd like to have a job similar to his someday," Jade admitted.

"Have you helped Erik with his research at all?"

"No, I've been too busy with school and work. I'm hoping that I can shadow him next semester."

"You've never worked with him at all?"

"No, sir." Jade hesitated. "At least not on anything for the museum."

"What have you worked on together?" Stevens asked with genuine interest.

"We spent an entire summer when I was in high school researching our family tree. I learned a lot about how to research and about our family. I think that may have been when I fell in love with history."

"How interesting," Stevens replied. "Erik is the best person to learn from in my opinion."

"I think so too," said Jade.

"Thank you again for your help, and I hope you have a very Merry Christmas," Stevens said and left the store.

The store was busy for the rest of the evening. Jade was relieved when it was time to close. She walked toward her car and saw someone standing beside it. She couldn't see the person's face, but there was something familiar.

"Logan?"

Logan beamed at her. "Surprise!" he said and handed her a single long-stemmed rose.

"What are you doing here?" Jade asked with joy.

"I thought we could get something to eat and a couple of drinks before going back to Canyon."

"Awesome! I can't believe this. Thank you!"

"Let's go! We'll take my car."

"Where are we going?"

"It's a place that Skeet told me about. It's on Sixth Street."

"Have you been there?"

"No, this will be a first for us both."

Logan drove east on I-40 and turned onto Georgia Street. It was a few minutes more before they were driving along historic Route 66, also known as Sixth Street. They went inside the Cantina and found a table. They were discussing what to order when the waitress approached the table.

"What can I get for you tonight?"

"Heather?" Jade said in surprise.

"I didn't know you worked here," said Logan.

"Yep, this is where I work," Heather said with an expression on her face that said she'd rather they had gone elsewhere.

"I thought you were working at Willie's," said Jade.

"I'm working both places for now. I wasn't getting enough hours at Willie's. Do you know what you want?"

"I've heard that the green chili cheese burger is awesome," said Logan.

"It's very good," Heather agreed.

"We'll have two of those, an order of fries, and a couple of beers."

"Make that one beer and a Dr. Pepper," said Jade with a grin.

"What kind of beer?" Heather asked.

"Bud Light," Logan replied.

"I'll be right back with your drinks," said Heather and left the table.

"How is your job going?" Jade asked Logan.

"It's good. My boss is willing to work with me, so I have time to get my school work done. The worst part is that I don't have much time to see you."

"I'm not going to have much time off either. Our manager is trying to hire some extra help for the holidays, but so far, there haven't been any applicants. I work most nights until closing and open on weekends."

The food arrived, and they didn't talk again until they'd devoured their burgers.

"Skeet was right. These are good," said Jade.

"We'll have to do this again," Logan suggested. "We might be able to get together after work once or twice a week."

"It will depend on how much homework we have of course."

"That's for sure," Logan agreed. "I was up until three this morning, and I'll be up that late again tonight."

"I have another essay to write when I get home," Jade told him.

"We should go then," Logan said.

He paid the check and gave Heather a generous tip. They drove back to the mall and Jade's car. Logan kissed her and waited until her car started before he returned to his own.

Logan followed her to their apartment building, and they walked upstairs together. He kissed her again. This time it was a long, slow, sweet kiss.

"Goodnight, Jade," he said, his voice husky.

"Goodnight, thank you for dinner. It was such a nice surprise."

"You'd better get inside before we decide to blow off our homework."

They kissed once more before going into their own apartments.

CHAPTER ELEVEN

WEDNESDAY, December 13, 2017

9:40 p.m.

Jade had been staying at Erik's house for almost a week. He had taken a short but well-deserved vacation. She enjoyed having the time to study and being with Teddy. She was going to miss this when she resumed her normal routine.

She was reviewing her class notes when her cell phone rang.

"Hi, Jade," Erik said when she answered the call. "How are things going there?"

"Everything's fine. Are you on your way home?"

"Yes and no. My flight was delayed, and I'll be late getting back."

"Okay, don't worry about anything here. I'm studying, and Teddy is snoring beside me."

Erik chuckled. "I should be back tomorrow morning. I may go to work before I go home, depending on when my flight lands. I'll meet you at Bear's for lunch."

"I'll see you tomorrow then," she said and ended the call.

Thursday, December 14, 2017

8:00 a.m.

Jade had stayed up well past midnight, cramming for her last final exam of the semester. She looked at the clock when Teddy woke her that morning. She got up to let him outside and started a pot of coffee before going back upstairs to shower.

The aroma of fresh brewed coffee beckoned her when she started down the stairs. She opened the back door for Teddy and fed him before pouring herself a cup of wake-up juice. She ate a honey bun and sipped her coffee, enjoying the morning.

She hadn't heard Erik come in and wondered if he had gone straight to the office. She looked in the garage. His car wasn't there.

Having two hours before lunch, Jade decided that Erik should come home to a clean house. She dusted and vacuumed the living room and cleaned the kitchen. It was almost time to leave by the time she finished. She got dressed and drove to Bear's Burgers and Dawgs.

She waited at Bear's for half an hour for her uncle. It wasn't like him to be late. He always called to let her know if he was going to be delayed. She had tried calling his cell and his office but got no answer.

She checked the time on her cell phone again. She walked to the counter and placed her order to go.

"Do you want to order for Erik, too?" Bear asked.

"No, he may be tied up with something at work. I can't wait any longer."

"Okay, I'll put a rush on that for you."

Jade took her meal and drove to the campus. She sat in her car stuffing food in her mouth and reviewing her notes for the last time. She tried to contact Erik again before going inside. This time she left a message on his voicemail.

She finished her exam and checked her answers twice before turning it in. She felt an overwhelming sense of relief and satisfaction when she walked out of the classroom. She thought she had done well, but she wouldn't know for sure until the grades were posted.

Her thoughts turned to Uncle Erik. It had been almost two hours since she last tried to contact him. She turned her cell phone on and checked her messages. He still hadn't responded.

She walked to her car and drove to the museum. The clerk at the reception desk waved at her when she walked in. She went upstairs and started toward her uncle's office. Renee Lanham stopped her in the hallway.

"Is Erik sick today?" asked Renee.

"No, I thought he might be busy here. He was supposed to meet me for lunch. He hasn't answered any of my texts or phone calls."

"He hasn't been here today, and he hasn't called in," Renee said, trying to hide the concern in her voice. "I haven't been able to get in touch with him either."

"He called last night and said his flight was delayed. He thought he'd be home in time to get to work and meet me for lunch." Jade told her. "Maybe the flight was delayed longer than he thought, or it might have been canceled."

"Well, I suppose that's possible," admitted Renee. "His cell phone must be dead, or he's in a place where he can't get reception. He'd have called one of us otherwise."

"Would you like me to call you when I hear from him?" Jade asked.

"I'd appreciate that," Renee replied.

The women exchanged phone numbers, and Jade left the museum.

Jade went back to Erik's house. Teddy greeted her as usual. She gave him his cookie and collapsed on the couch thankful that she didn't have to go to work. She called Erik's cell phone again. It went to voicemail.

"Where are you?" she asked and disconnected the call.

She took her laptop out of her backpack. She intended to search the local airlines for information before she realized that she didn't know Erik's flight number. She didn't even know which airline he had used. The one thing she knew was his destination.

Jade looked for flights from Philadelphia. She knew that she wouldn't find a direct flight to Amarillo. She looked for flights with stops and layovers. She found nothing about delayed or cancelled flights.

She shut down her laptop and put it away. She got up and looked through her uncle's desk hoping to find notes or an itinerary for his trip. There were none to be found. Even his laptop was gone.

She turned on the TV and scrolled through the channels. She found an old movie that she liked and stretched out on the couch. She hoped the movie would help her push the nagging feeling that something was wrong to the back of her mind.

5:30 p.m.

The sound of her cell phone ringing jolted her from sleep. She snatched it up without looking at the caller ID.

"Uncle Erik?"

"I'm sorry, Jade. This is Renee. I take it that you haven't heard from him."

"No, and I'm starting to get worried. Do you happen to know which airline he took or his flight number?" Jade couldn't disguise the hope in her voice.

"I'm sorry, no. Did you check his computer?"

"It isn't here. He must have taken it with him. Could he have made his reservations with the computer in his office?"

"There's no way to find out without his password," Renee told her. "Do you have any idea what it might be?"

"No, I don't," Jade said.

"Maybe you should think about filing a missing person's report."

"It crossed my mind, but I've always heard that you have to wait twenty-four hours. I don't know if I should wait or go ahead and file one."

"How long has it been since he called?" Renee asked.

"It's been about twenty hours."

"You should go ahead and talk to the police. They'll give you the best advice about filing a report," Renee suggested.

"That's a good idea. I'll call you back after I've talked to them," Jade said and ended the call.

She found the phone number and placed the call. She was transferred three times before she was connected with the right person.

"This is Treat," said a voice on the phone.

"I'd like to talk with someone about filing a missing person's report."

"I can help you with that," Officer Damon Treat replied.

Jade explained the situation and gave the officer the necessary information.

"When did you last speak with Mr. O'Neal?"

"He called between nine-thirty and ten last night," Jade informed him and shared the details of the call.

"Have you checked with the airlines?"

"I tried, but I don't have enough of the travel details to get very far."

"All right, you'll need to come down to the station to file the report. Bring all the information about your uncle that you have. We'll also need the most recent photo you have of Mr. O'Neal."

"I'll be there as soon as I can," Jade assured him.

Jade called Renee Lanham and shared the information with her. Renee agreed to meet her at the police station. She wanted the moral support and thought that Renee might know something that she didn't.

The two women met with Officer Treat and told him all that they knew about Erik's vacation plans. He told them to notify him if they heard from Erik or if he came home.

"Thank you for coming with me, Renee," Jade said. "I was nervous about filing a report."

"You're welcome," Renee replied. "Let me know if you hear from Erik and if there's anything else I can do."

They said goodbye, and Jade walked to her car. She stopped when she heard someone call her name.

"Miss O'Neal? Is everything all right?"

Jade turned to face Officer Hudson Bailey. "No, my uncle is missing. I came to file a missing person's report."

"I'm sorry to hear that. Is there anything I can do?"

"I don't think so. Thank you, Officer."

"Please, call me Hudson."

"Thank you, Hudson. You can call me Jade."

"I hope your uncle is home soon."

"Thank you, goodbye."

"Goodbye."

Jade left the police station unsure about what she should do next. She hadn't been to her apartment in days. She had talked to Logan on the phone a few times, but she hadn't seen him.

She went to her apartment under the pretext of picking up a few things in hopes of seeing Logan. Heather was watching TV when she went in.

"Hi, stranger. Are you back for a while?" Heather asked.

"No, I came to get a few things. Uncle Erik hasn't come home yet. I'll have to take care of Teddy a while longer," she explained.

"How much longer?"

"It could be this weekend or early next week," Jade improvised. She didn't want to tell Heather the truth.

Jade went to her room, grabbed some more clothes, and her

puzzle book. She left the apartment and knocked on Logan's door. He didn't answer. She thought about knocking a second time but turned and went to her car.

Jade drove back to Erik's house. She opened the gate and said, "Teddy, are you ready for your walk?"

Teddy stretched, wagging his tail. Jade went into the kitchen for his leash. She hooked it to his harness and hung on while Teddy drug her though the gate.

They were crossing Captain Donald Blair drive when a Siamese cat crossed the lawn near Old Main.

Jade didn't see it in time to brace herself. Teddy woofed and charged after the cat. She tried to hold Teddy back, but the leash snapped.

The leash flew backward, the broken piece hitting her hard on the forehead. She fell flat on her back. Dazed, she sat up and watched the cat run up the nearest tree. It hissed at Teddy from a high limb.

"Teddy! Stay!" Jade shouted and got to her feet.

Teddy seemed to think this was a new game. He bowed into his "let's play" stance until Jade could almost touch him before he galloped away.

"Teddy! Come!"

Teddy ran between Old Main and the Old Education building. Jade almost caught up with him before he darted across the pedestrian mall toward Buffalo Fountain. He drank from the fountain and looked to make sure Jade was coming before he ran again.

He was enjoying his adventure and ran north past the Kilgore Research Center. He found shrubs near the Computer Center that he'd never investigated. Jade caught up to him, panting. She tested the lump on her head for blood while he sniffed every plant and marked his territory.

Jade was inspecting the broken end of the leash when Teddy barked and wagged his entire backend.

"Come on, Teddy. Let's go."

He whined and his tail slowed to a stop.

"Teddy, what's the matter with you? Come on, boy. Let's go get your prize."

He whined again moving further into the evergreen foliage.

"Teddy, come!"

He ignored her.

"No, cookie for you tonight," she said annoyed.

She fought her way through the shrubbery trying to reach Teddy's harness. He was pawing at something under one of the larger bushes. She moved closer. Someone was lying there asleep. She thought it was a man based on the clothing. His arm was draped over his head. She couldn't see his face.

"Hey! Wake up! Are you okay? Do you need help?"

There was no response and no movement.

She gave the man a shake. There was still no response. She couldn't tell if he was breathing. He was cold and his skin was pale. She didn't expect to find a pulse but felt that she should check anyway.

She moved the man's arm away from his head. There was no pulse in his wrist. She crept closer so that she could check for a pulse on his neck and looked at the man's face for the first time.

Jade heard someone shriek, "NO!"

She heard Teddy howl.

She heard screaming.

Teddy licked her face and whined. She wrapped her arms around his neck and wept. It wasn't until the screaming stopped that she realized it had been her.

She had to get help. Maybe they could still save him. She took out her cell phone and called 9-1-1.

"9-1-1, what's your emergency?"

"I...I...just...found...my...uncle," she sobbed. "I...think...he's ...d...," she couldn't say the word. "He's hurt."

Somehow, between sobs, Jade managed to give the operator the necessary information. They waited together beside Erik's body for the ambulance and police. She couldn't stand the thought of leaving her uncle there alone. Teddy whined while she held him close, soaking his coat with her tears.

An incredible emptiness was all that she could feel. She didn't feel her hand holding Teddy's harness or the wetness on her face.

Jade heard the sirens. She heard someone talking to her. She couldn't respond. Her mind wasn't working. All that she could do was to hold on to Teddy.

"Miss O'Neal?" A police officer tried to get her attention. "Jade?"

The officer took a step closer. Teddy stiffened and growled.

Jade looked at Teddy as though she were waking from a deep sleep. She'd forgotten that he was there.

"What's wrong, Teddy?" She looked around her bewildered.

"Jade?"

She looked at the officer and recognized him. "Hello, Officer Bailey."

"I thought we agreed you were going to call me Hudson."

"Did we?"

"Do you mind if I join you?"

She shook her head.

Bailey moved closer and knelt down beside her. Teddy growled again.

"It's okay, Teddy. Hudson is a nice man."

Teddy eyed the officer with suspicion.

"What are you doing here, Hudson?"

"I'm here to help. We need to take care of your uncle. Will you come sit with me?"

"I don't want to leave him. I...can't. He's so cold."

"We won't go far. The emergency crew needs to take care of him, but they're afraid of Teddy. There's a bench close by. Can you lead Teddy to it? You'll still be close to your uncle."

Jade nodded; tears rolled down her face. She kept a tight grip on Teddy's harness and allowed herself to be led out of the shrubbery.

Hudson put his arm around her shoulders both to comfort and warm her. He led her to a bench and sat down beside her. Teddy sat at her feet and laid his head on her lap.

"Jade, can you tell me what happened?"

"I don't know. Teddy and I were out for a walk. His leash broke. He went into the bushes and started acting strange. I tried to pull him out, and I found..." Jade couldn't continue. The words wouldn't come.

Hudson held her while she cried and watched his fellow officers work the scene. They were ready to move the body when an officer approached him.

"Bailey, I think you should take Miss O'Neal home. She doesn't need to see us move him," suggested the officer in charge.

"Yes, sir."

Hudson looked at Teddy and then at Jade. "I'll take you home. Do you think Teddy will ride in my car?"

"You'll have to take me to Uncle Erik's house. Teddy isn't allowed in my apartment building."

"Okay, my car is a block away. Are you ready?"

Jade nodded and stood. "Come, Teddy."

Jade followed Hudson to his car. She coaxed Teddy into the backseat and got in beside him. Hudson chauffeured them to Erik's house.

He watched Jade open the backdoor and put Teddy's broken leash on the hook. She seemed to be on autopilot unaware of what she was doing. He followed them inside and made sure they were comfortable.

He couldn't imagine what she was going through. He knew from their previous meeting that she wasn't the kind of woman to fall apart. He could see that her world had been shattered, and his heart broke for her.

"Is there anyone that I can call to come stay with you?" he offered.

His words seemed to bring Jade back to the present. For an instant, she looked at him as if she were surprised to see him.

"I need to call my mom. I know she can't come tonight, but she'll want to be here."

"I noticed a coffee maker in the kitchen. Would you like for me to make a pot of coffee while you talk to your mom?"

Jade nodded and tapped her mother's number.

Hudson went to the kitchen while Jade sat on the couch talking to her mom.

"Hi, honey. How did your finals go this week?" Mollie asked.

"Mom," she sobbed, "I...I... don't know how to say this."

"What's wrong?"

Jade broke down. "Mom...Uncle...Erik...is...dead."

"Oh my God! What happened?"

"Teddy and I... were taking a walk. Teddy found him in some bushes. I didn't know it was him until I decided to check for a pulse...and...saw...his...face."

"You found him? Are you all right?"

"Mom, can you... come... home?"

"It might take some time to make the arrangements, but I'll be there. Do the police know what happened to Erik yet?"

"I don't think so. They were still there when one of the officers brought me to the house."

"Let me know if you find out any more. I'll call you when I've made my travel arrangements."

"Thanks, Mom. I love you."

"I love you, too, honey."

Hudson waited in the kitchen until Jade's conversation ended. He overheard most of what she'd said and made mental notes. He joined her in the living room and handed her a cup of coffee.

"Thank you, Hudson."

"You're welcome. Is there anything else I can do?"

Jaded started to say no but stopped. "Yes, you can me tell what's happening."

"All I know is what you've told me. The other officers there were still assessing the scene when we left."

"What will happen after that?" Jade noticed the odd look on Hudson's face. "I'm sorry... but I can't stand the... thought ...of Uncle Erik...."

Hudson now understood what she meant. "I'm sure he's been moved by now. There will be an autopsy. You'll be asked to make a formal statement about how you found him."

Jade nodded and stared at the floor. She knew there was something that she needed to do but couldn't remember what it might be.

"Have you eaten?" Hudson asked, breaking the silence.

"No, but I need to feed Teddy." She got up, went to the kitchen, and filled Teddy's food bowl.

Teddy lifted his head but otherwise didn't move.

"Teddy, time to eat."

Teddy's tail wagged twice before he rested his chin on his front paws again.

Jade sat down beside him and scratched his ears.

"I know. I'm not hungry either."

Hudson didn't want to leave Jade alone, but he had no reason to stay. He felt bad for her, but he didn't know what else to do.

"Is your mother coming?" he asked for lack of anything better to say.

"She's in New York right now. She'll be here when she can get a flight."

"What about the rest of your family?"

"My brother is in Afghanistan. He's a Marine."

"Was Mr. O'Neal the only family you had here?"

"Yes, my dad died when we were little. Uncle Erik stepped in. He was always there for us. He taught us how to ride our bikes and never missed a game or school event for either of us." Fresh tears rained down Jade's face.

"I don't mind staying with you, but I think you'd be more comfortable with someone you're more familiar with."

"I appreciate your help, Hudson, but I don't need anyone to stay. I have Teddy. We'll be fine."

Hudson took a business card from his wallet and scribbled on the back. "These are my work and cell numbers. Call me if you need anything?"

Jade took the card. "Thank you, I will."

"I'll be going then. I'll talk with you soon."

Jade followed him to the door and locked it behind him. She reset the alarm and went back to the living room. She was sitting beside Teddy, stroking his head when she remembered what she needed to do.

She picked up her phone and tapped Renee Lanham's number.

CHAPTER TWELVE

FRIDAY, December 15, 2017

7:30 a.m.

Jade hadn't slept more than fifteen minutes all night. She cried herself to sleep only to relive the nightmare of finding her uncle's body in her dreams. She woke up screaming each time she dozed off.

She was relieved when her cell phone rang. Her eyes were so swollen that she had difficulty reading the caller ID.

"Hi, Mom!"

"I'm sorry if I woke you."

"You didn't. I haven't slept much. When will you be here?"

"I'm so sorry, honey. I can't come."

"What? Why not?"

"My boss said that because Erik wasn't legally one of my immediate family members that I'm not entitled to the time off," Mollie said her anger evident in her voice. "I asked him if I could use sick days or vacation time. He said that he'd already approved the use of all of my time in January. He told me that it would be grounds for dismissal if I were to leave before my training has finished."

"I don't want you to lose your job, Mom," Jade replied, trying to hide her disappointment. "You've been so excited about that promotion."

"I want to be there with you, but I can't afford to be out of work. I thought about canceling the trip to Ireland, but it won't change the fact that I can't be there now."

"Mom, I don't want you to lose your job or cancel your trip. I know Uncle Erik wouldn't want you to either. I'll be okay. Have you talked to Levi?"

"Yes, we talked on Skype last night. He's heartbroken about Erik, too."

"I wish he could be here, but I know that's not possible."

"I hate that you're going to have to deal with all of the legal details and funeral arrangements alone."

"Legal details and funeral arrangements? Mom, I don't know how to do that. I don't even know where to begin."

"I can give a few pointers. Do you have a pen and paper handy?" Mollie asked.

Jade picked up a pencil and a notepad from the nightstand and asked, "What should I do first?"

"Call Suzanne Walls. She's the attorney that I used for all of my legal needs while I lived there. I know that Erik used her, too. She should be able to help you with all of the legal issues. The next thing you'll have to do is choose a mortuary. They'll walk you through what needs to be done for the funeral. Keep in mind what you think Erik would've wanted when you talk with them."

"Don't funerals cost a lot of money?"

"They can be very expensive. I'll find a way to pay for it, but try to keep the expenses somewhere in the middle. Erik wouldn't want us to spend a fortune. I don't want to be cheap either. He meant too much to our family."

"I'll do my best," Jade assured her mother. "Are you still planning to be here for Christmas?"

"Yes! My flight lands in Amarillo at eleven-twenty on the morning of the twenty-third. Will you able to pick me up?" asked Mollie.

"I'll be there, but I'll have to drop you off here and go to work for a few hours."

"That's fine. I'll cook while you're working. I shipped your Christmas gifts to Erik's house. They should be there by mid-week. I need to get back to work. I'll talk to you tonight."

"Bye, Mom."

Jade went to the bathroom and washed her face. Her head hurt, and her eyes burned. The bump above her left eye was three shades of purple, but the swelling had gone down a little. She held a cool washcloth over her eyes and forehead for a few minutes before brushing her hair.

She didn't know how she was going to get through this. She had counted on her mother being there, but now, it was all in her hands. Her family needed her to step up and take care of things.

She looked in the mirror and grimaced. First, she had to do something about her appearance. Then, she'd do what needed to be done.

Jade showered, dressed, and covered her bruise and dark circles with makeup before going downstairs. She fed Teddy and remembered that she needed to buy a new leash. She also needed to buy more dog food and a few items for herself.

She made a shopping list and looked at the clock. She decided to wait until later in the morning to make her phone calls.

9:30 a.m.

Jade drove to the store and purchased a heavy-duty leash along with her other items. She went home and unloaded her groceries. She was about to call the boutique when her cell phone rang.

"Jade, this is Hudson Bailey."

"Hi, Hudson. Thank you for your help last night."

"Don't mention it. I'm glad I could help."

"You don't know how much I appreciate it. I was a mess."

"How are you doing today?"

"I'm still a mess, but I'm starting to get it together. Is there any news about Uncle Erik's death?"

"Not yet," he answered. "We need you to come to the station and make your official statement about last night. We'll also need you to identify your uncle's body and give us the name of the funeral home that you want to use when his body is released."

Jade didn't answer right away. Her mind was filled with the image of her uncle lying cold and lifeless under the bushes.

"I...I haven't had time to look into a funeral home yet," she said fighting back tears. "I'll try to take care of that this morning. When do I need to be at the station?"

"There's no specific time, but it would be best to get it taken care of today.

"I'll be there this afternoon," Jade assured him and ended the call.

She placed a call to the boutique manager and explained what had happened. Paula Hicks was understanding and told Jade to take as long as she needed.

Jade then called the office of Suzanne Walls and made an appointment for eleven a.m.

She was looking up funeral homes on the internet when the doorbell rang. Jade went to the door to find Renee and Tommy standing on the front step. They each held something wrapped in foil containers.

"How are you doing?" Renee asked with worry on her face.

"I'm holding up," Jade said. "Come in."

"These are casseroles," Renee said. "I know you won't feel like cooking or going out. Erik told us about all the food your mom made being destroyed."

Jade led the way to the kitchen and opened the refrigerator door. Renee and Tommy placed them inside and stepped back. It seemed that neither of them knew what to say.

"Thank you, I hadn't thought about eating yet," Jade admitted. "Can I get you something to drink?"

"Thank you, no," said Tommy. "We can't stay long. We wanted to see how you're doing."

"Did you get any sleep?" asked Renee.

"Not much," answered Jade. "I dreamed about finding him when I did fall asleep."

"Maybe you should see your doctor," Renee suggested. "You've been through a horrible ordeal."

"I'll be all right," Jade assured them without conviction. "I have a lot to take care of today."

"Are your mother and brother going to be here?" asked Tommy.

"No, Levi is still in Afghanistan, and Mom can't get off work," Jade informed them, trying to hide the tears that threatened.

Renee stared at Jade for a moment and then glanced at Tommy.

"You're dealing with this alone?" Renee asked with disbelief.

"Yes," replied Jade. "Mom told me what I needed to do, and I've made some appointments for today. I'm supposed to go and identify Uncle Erik's body and give my statement to the police this afternoon."

"Would you like for us to go with you?" Tommy offered.

"No, I'll be fine," Jade said bravely.

"You have my number," Renee said. "I want you to call me anytime, day or night if you need anything, anything at all."

"Thank you, I will," Jade said with a weak smile. "Thank you for the casseroles, too."

"You're welcome. Others from the museum will be bringing food, I'm sure," Renee told her. "Most of them didn't know about Erik until they got to work this morning."

Jade thanked Renee and Tommy again and walked them to the

door. She looked at the clock and rushed to her car. She didn't want to be late for her appointment in Amarillo.

10:50 a.m.

Jade was ten minutes early for her appointment with Suzanne Walls. She waited in the reception area and tried to keep her mind off of her uncle. She was flipping through the pages of a worn magazine when her named was called.

"Miss O'Neal," said Zuri, the receptionist. "Ms. Walls will see you now."

Jade followed the young woman to the office. Suzanne Walls was tall and thin with short auburn hair and bright blue eyes.

"Good morning, Miss O'Neal. Please, sit down," the attorney said indicating a chair in front of the desk.

"Good morning," Jade replied and sat down.

"What can I do for you today?"

"My mother, Mollie O'Neal, told me to contact you."

"Yes, I remember Mollie," Suzanne replied.

"I need advice and help," Jade began. "I don't know if you've heard, but my uncle, Erik O'Neal, passed away."

Suzanne sat up a little straighter. "When?"

"He was found last night."

"At home?"

"No," Jade said fighting the tears that she knew would come. "I...I...found him...near the...Computer Center...on campus."

"You'd better tell me everything," Suzanne said.

The attorney sat motionless for a few minutes after Jade had finished. She seemed to be deep in thought.

"What do you need from me?" she asked at last.

"I've never been through anything like this. My mom and brother can't be here to help. I don't know what to do or where to start. I'm supposed to give my statement to the police and identify my uncle's body this afternoon. They also want to know which funeral home I want to use."

The attorney picked up her phone and pressed a number. "Zuri, please bring me Erik O'Neal's file."

She returned her attention to Jade. "I can give you advice about what needs to be done and how to go about it, but I want to show you something first."

They waited in silence until they heard a light tap on the door. Zuri handed the file to her employer.

"Erik brought me these documents last week. He said his house had been burglarized, and he wanted them to be in a safer place," she said, opening the folder and turning it toward Jade.

Inside were prepaid funeral documents and a copy of Erik's will. Both were dated the first of October 2017.

Jade read the documents and looked at the attorney. "I...I had no idea."

"Your family will inherit his estate," said Walls. "There's no mortgage on his home to worry about. There's also a life insurance policy that lists the three of you as beneficiaries."

An unpleasant thought crossed Jade's mind. "Could Uncle Erik have known that he was going to die soon?"

"It's possible, but he didn't share anything with me if he did," replied Suzanne. She pointed at another document in the file. "He made provisions for you. There will be money available for you to pay household expenses and for the care of his dog. He also specified that you're to have the funds you need to finish school."

Tears flowed unchecked down Jade's face. She nodded to acknowledge that she heard what the attorney had said.

"Erik also paid a retainer in the event that you needed my services," the attorney informed Jade.

Jade looked up into the attorney's eyes.

"Police investigations can be intimidating, especially if you're alone," she said and handed Jade her business card. "I want you to call me if you feel threatened by the police or in need of my services."

Jade left the attorney's office with more questions than she had when she went in. The one person with the answers she needed was now lying in the morgue.

She pushed the nagging thoughts from her mind and tapped Renee's number before leaving the parking lot.

"Renee, this is Jade. I know it's almost your lunch time, but could you meet me at Bear's Burgers and Dawgs in half an hour?"

"Of course," Renee replied, "I'll see you there."

"Thanks," Jade said and ended the call.

12:30 p.m.

Jade arrived at the restaurant to find Renee was already there. She waved at Renee and went to the counter.

"Bear? Could I talk with you for a few minutes?"

"Sure, give me a minute to get this order started."

Jade joined Renee at the table and waited for Bear.

"Aren't you going to order anything?" Renee asked.

"I'm not hungry right now," Jade told her. "I'll eat later."

"Now, what did you want to talk about?" Bear asked and pulled up a chair.

Jade introduced Bear to Renee before she began.

"I don't know if you've heard, but Uncle Erik passed away."

"What? No, that can't be," Bear said, clearly shocked by the revelation. "What happened?"

Jade shared the details of the previous evening with Bear before getting to the point of the meeting.

"I was wondering if the two of you would be interested in coming with me to make the funeral arrangements. He thought a lot of you both."

"I'd be happy to," Renee said. "I know Erik wouldn't want you to go through this alone."

"What time are you going?" Bear asked.

"I don't have an appointment yet. I wanted to talk with y'all before I call them. It will have to be this afternoon so that I can tell the police when I see them later today."

"Let me make a phone call and get someone in here to cover for me," said Bear.

"I'll need to let the office know, too," said Renee.

Jade made a call to the funeral home while Bear and Renee made their calls. The appointment was made for two o'clock.

The three of them rode together in Renee's car to the mortuary. They were greeted by Morris Frantz, a pleasant but somber looking man who escorted them to a large room. A table was in the center surrounded by six chairs. They sat at one end of the table while the funeral director located Erik's file.

Mr. Frantz showed them the file that included Erik's wishes. "Mr. O'Neal took care of everything," said Frantz. "It's all been arranged, and the expenses have been paid. All you'll need to do is set the day and time for the services and sign the necessary paperwork."

"Mr. Frantz, my mother and brother won't be able to be here. We don't have any other family. Would it be possible for Uncle Erik's friends here to sit with me?" Jade nodded, indicating Bear and Renee.

"Yes, of course. Anyone you want."

"Will it be possible for my uncle's dog to attend the services?"

"His dog? What kind of dog?"

"He's a big dog, but he's well trained. Uncle Erik and I picked him out and raised him together. It wouldn't be right if Teddy wasn't there to say goodbye."

"Well, I don't think that would be a problem as long as he's on a leash at all times."

"He will be. Thank you."

"When would you like to hold services?"

"I don't know yet," Jade said, wiping her eyes with a tissue. "It will depend upon when the police release his body."

"The police?"

"Yes, sir. I'm going to identify my uncle when I leave here. I don't know how long it will take them to do whatever it is they do."

"We'll have everything ready," he said, indicating where Jade should sign. "I'll contact you when the body has been released. We can set the date for the services then."

"Thank you, Mr. Frantz," Jade said.

The trio got into Renee's car and drove out of the mortuary parking lot.

"Would you like us to come with you to police station?" asked Bear.

"No, I've taken up too much of your time already," Jade said. "I'll be fine."

They drove back to the restaurant. Renee and Bear both returned to work, and Jade drove to the police station.

Jade went inside and told the officer at the desk her name and why she was there.

"Hi, Jade," said Officer Hudson Bailey.

"Hi," Jade answered, trying to keep her nerves under control.

"If you'll follow me, we'll get your statement, and then I'll take you to the morgue."

Jade nodded and followed the officer without saying a word. She was led into a small office where another officer sat behind a desk.

"This is Officer Debbie Cornelius," Hudson told her. "She's going to take your statement and then print it out for you to look over and sign."

"Please, sit down, Miss O'Neal," said Cornelius. "Try to relax and tell me everything that you can remember."

Jade sat down and took a deep breath. "Where do you want me to start?"

"Let's start with why you were in the area where the body was found," suggested the officer.

Jade explained about taking Teddy for a walk.

"Who is Teddy?" interrupted Cornelius.

"He's my uncle's dog. I take care of him when my uncle is out of town."

"Okay, then what happened?"

Jade told the officer about the leash breaking and how she had chased Teddy to the place where Erik was found.

She was unable to stop the flow of tears as she explained how she'd discovered her uncle's body.

"I know that must have been horrible," said the officer with compassion. "Is there anything else that you can remember?"

Jade shook her head and wiped her eyes.

"I'll have this ready for your signature in a few minutes. You can relax while I type it up. Is there anything I can get you? A soft drink or bottle of water?"

"No, thank you," said Jade.

She waited while Officer Cornelius typed and proof read the document. Managing to keep the tears at bay, she read and signed the typed statement.

Hudson was waiting for her when Officer Cornelius escorted her down the hall.

"This isn't going to be easy," Hudson told Jade. "You can take as long as you need."

Jade tried to control the sobs while they made their way to the morgue. She dreaded what she might see when she went inside.

They entered the morgue, and Hudson escorted her to a desk.

"This is Jade O'Neal here to identify the body of last night's victim," Hudson told the clerk.

"She's ready for you," said the clerk.

Hudson led Jade into the morgue and toward a body draped in a white sheet atop a stainless-steel table. She was trembling so much that it was difficult to walk.

Hudson guided her to the table and introduced her to the woman who was standing beside it.

"Jade, this is Dr. Juanita Melendez. She's our medical examiner."

"Hello."

"Hello, Miss O'Neal," said the doctor with a sympathetic smile. "When you're ready, I'll remove the sheet from his face. Take as long as you need."

Jade took a deep breath and said with a trembling voice, "I...I'm ready."

Dr. Melendez removed the sheet, and Jade found herself staring down at her uncle's handsome face. She could no longer stop the tears and sobs. She nodded and turned away.

"Is this your uncle, Erik O'Neal?" asked the doctor.

Jade nodded unable to speak.

"I'm sorry, but I'll need a signed statement verifying that you've identified him."

"I...under...stand," Jade hiccoughed. "What... happened to... his... face?"

"He appears to have been beaten before he was killed. There are bruises and cuts on his body in addition to those on the left side of his head."

"Do...you...know how...he...died?"

"He was killed by a single gunshot wound to the heart," said Doctor Melendez. "He would have died instantly. It isn't likely that he felt any pain."

Jade signed the statement identifying Erik's body. Hudson led her to her car and said goodbye. She sat there a moment trying to collect herself before driving back to her uncle's house.

It had been a long emotional day. Even though she was exhausted, she still had to take Teddy for his walk.

She turned the key in the ignition, but nothing happened. She tried again. It didn't start.

"Not again! Not now!" she said and got out of the car.

She lifted the hood and looked at the engine. She jiggled the battery cables and tried to start the car again. Still nothing.

She went back into the police station and explained that her car wouldn't start. One of the officers gave her car battery a boost, and she was soon on her way.

Teddy was waiting for her when she got home. She took him for his walk right away. She was afraid that if she sat down, she wouldn't get up again until morning. They stayed as far away from the Computer Center as possible. She didn't want to relive finding Uncle Erik in those shrubs.

Her phone rang after she and Teddy returned home. She answered the call and told her mother about her day.

CHAPTER THIRTEEN

THURSDAY, December 21, 2017

8:15 a.m.

Ace was working at his desk signing the letters that had been left by his secretary the previous evening. He looked at the grandfather clock, picked up the phone on his desk, and pushed a button.

"Nancy, would you come in here, please?" he said and ended the call.

"Good morning, sir," Nancy said, when she entered the room.

"Good morning, I've finished these letters," he said and handed them to her. "How many appointments do I have today?"

"You have two this morning, one at ten, and one at eleven. There are three scheduled this afternoon at one, two-thirty, and four."

"I need to attend a funeral in Canyon this afternoon. Reschedule the one o'clock and the two-thirty appointments, please. I should be back in time for the four o'clock."

"Should I send flowers for the funeral?" Nancy asked.

Ace contemplated the idea for a moment. "Yes, I suppose so. It's for a man who worked at the museum. His name was Erik O'Neal."

"Should I send it from you or from the firm?"

"Let's send it from both," he suggested. "Something tasteful but not too expensive."

"I'll take care of that right away."

"Thank you," Ace said. "I'll be leaving in a few minutes to have coffee with an old friend who's passing through town. I'll be back before that ten o'clock meeting."

"Yes, sir," Nancy replied and left the room.

Ace leaned back in his chair with his arms behind his head and chuckled. "Sending flowers to the funeral of a man that I killed. Now, that's funny," he said under his breath.

Nelson King sat at a picnic table at Medi Park. He watched the ducks swimming nearby while he waited. He thought about Erik O'Neal.

O'Neal had made things harder on himself than they had to be. The smirk on his face and his snide responses prompted the beating that he'd endured. The man might have survived if he hadn't been so sure of himself, if he hadn't overplayed his hand, if he hadn't tested Ace's patience.

King shook his head. No, Ace would never have allowed him to leave that warehouse. O'Neal knew too much even if he didn't yet have the proof.

"Do you really think I'm that stupid?" O'Neal had asked, after he'd been searched. "I wouldn't carry the information around in my pocket."

"Who else knows what you've been...researching?"

O'Neal ignored the question. "You know; it's funny. I wasn't sure who'd killed Jacob until a few days ago. I wouldn't have bet that it was you."

"Where is it then?" Ace demanded.

"It's in a safe place."

"That's nice, but I want to know where."

"Every piece of evidence that I've gathered is in a secure place that I'm not at liberty to disclose," O'Neal had said with a satisfied expression on his face.

"It won't matter where it is when you're dead," Ace said and punched him in the face.

O'Neal was dazed, but he laughed as though Ace had told him a good joke. "Are you sure about that? If anything happens to me or any member of my family, everything will be sent to the police."

"I could have that pretty little niece of yours brought to our party."

"Jade doesn't know anything about it. No one in my family knows what I've been doing. I knew, if I told them, they'd be in danger. Bringing Jade here won't make me talk because I know you'll kill her to keep her quiet."

The smile on O'Neal's face and the truth of his words pushed Ace's temper beyond its limit. He walked away from O'Neal and rubbed the back of his neck. Anyone who knew the man would recognize the telltale sign of his rage.

Before anyone realized what was happening, Ace had pulled a pistol from his pocket, turned, and fired. The smile on O'Neal's face faded when he realized he'd been shot; then his body slumped in the chair where he was tied.

King's thoughts were interrupted when Ace joined him at the picnic table.

"Well?" Ace asked.

"The police hadn't received anything as of last night," King told him. "O'Neal could have been bluffing, trying to buy time."

"What if he wasn't? We need to find out what he had, where it's hidden, and who else knows about it."

"Where could it be?" King asked in frustration. "We've searched every logical place."

"Have you found out where he went during those hours that you lost him?" asked Ace, his face flushed with anger.

"No, sir.

"He may have given the evidence to someone or told them where to find it during that time."

"I wonder if someone has the information but doesn't realize it," King speculated, changing the subject.

"He could have mailed the information to someone," Ace agreed. "It would take longer to reach its destination because of the holidays. He might have sent it to his sister-in-law or nephew."

"His sister-in-law hasn't been home in weeks according to my contacts," King said. "I've told them to be on the lookout for mail from O'Neal. His nephew won't be able to do anything with it for some time if it was sent to him."

"He could have passed the information to someone while he was away on his supposed vacation," Ace added. "If that's the case, that person may not have gotten word about his death."

They sat in silence contemplating possibilities.

Ace broke the silence and said, "You could be right about O'Neal trying to buy time, but my gut tells me he wasn't. He acted like a man who was holding all the right cards. We need to be ready whatever the case may be."

"What do you have in mind?"

"What has his niece been doing?"

"She's been dealing with the aftermath of O'Neal's death. Making funeral arrangements and the like. She hasn't been behaving as if she knows anything."

"You said that she discovered the body."

King nodded.

"Can we use that to our advantage?"

King thought for a moment before answering. "Yes, I think we can."

"Keep an eye on her in the meantime," Ace ordered. "O'Neal wouldn't have wanted to put her in danger. Still, she might have the information or know where it could be hidden without realizing what it is."

"Yes, sir."

King lit a cigarette and watched Ace walk to his car.

9:00 a.m.

Jade woke with a start. She rolled over and looked at the clock on her nightstand. She didn't want to get up. She didn't want to face the day. She didn't want to bury her uncle.

She wiped away the tears that had begun to roll across her nose toward her pillow. Teddy barked. Someone was ringing the doorbell.

She got up and put on her robe before going downstairs. She peeked through the peephole on the front door. A UPS truck was pulling away from the curb.

She opened the door to find a large box sitting on the step. She carried it into the house and looked at the label. It was from her mother.

Jade carried the box to the living room and placed it on the coffee table. She went to the kitchen and found a pair scissors. Teddy went to the back door and woofed. She realized that he needed out and opened the door for him before returning to the living room.

She cut the packing tape and opened the box. She took out the wrapped gifts and shook them before she carried them to the tree. She smiled at the memory of past Christmases when she and Levi would shake their gifts, trying to discover the contents before Christmas morning.

Her smile faded when she found Erik's gifts inside. *Mom must have shipped these before Uncle Erik died,* she thought. *What are we going to do with his gifts?* She decided to put them under the tree with the others. They'd decided what to do with them when her mother came for Christmas.

She let Teddy back into the house and went upstairs to get dressed. She was on her way back downstairs when her doorbell rang again. She pasted a smile on her face before opening the door to two people holding another casserole.

"Hi, Mr. and Mrs. Walters."

"We brought you a little something to eat," said Sondra Walters.

"Thank you so much," Jade replied, taking the casserole from her neighbor. "Won't you come in?"

"No, we can't stay," said Mrs. Walters. "I thought you and your mother might enjoy a breakfast casserole."

"Mom can't be here until Christmas, but I'll enjoy it in the meantime."

"Oh?"

"Let's go, Sondra. Jade has a lot on her mind this morning," Lewis said steering his wife away from the door. "We'll see you this afternoon, Jade."

"You can freeze that if you want to save some for later," Mrs. Walters called over her shoulder.

"I will. Thank you!"

Jade took the casserole to the kitchen. It was still warm, and smelled wonderful. She dished some out into a bowl and wrapped up the remainder. She opened the kitchen freezer and realized that it was filled to capacity. She carried the casserole to the freezer in the garage.

She went back to the kitchen and made a note on the clipboard she was using to keep track of everything that her uncle's friends and neighbors had brought. *Mom won't have to cook anything when she gets here*, Jade thought.

Making herself a cup of coffee, she settled down at the bar to eat her breakfast. Teddy sat beside her on the floor with one paw in her lap begging for a bite.

She gave him the last few bits and rubbed his ears. "I need you to be on your best behavior today, Teddy. I think we should take our walk this morning."

The gigantic dog's ears perked up. He stood and wagged his tail before he trotted toward the back door.

"Let me put my shoes on first," she told him and went to upstairs.

She realized on the way downstairs that she hadn't hidden his jerky treat beforehand. She went to the pantry and took a large piece from the package and stuffed it into her pocket. She took his leash from the hook by the kitchen door and attached it to his harness.

"Let's go!"

Teddy drug her as usual toward campus. Jade was thankful there weren't any squirrels or cats in sight. She felt a moment of dread when Teddy looked toward the Computer Center as they took their normal route. She braced herself for a struggle, but he didn't stray.

They reached the trees beside the Chapel, and Teddy ran straight to the Burr Oak tree where his prizes were always buried. Jade let him dig for a minute before tossing the dog jerky into the hole. She watched him enjoy his prize and hoped he would behave this well at the funeral.

Jade was at a loss when they returned home. It was too early for lunch and much too early to get ready for the funeral. She needed something to do to keep her mind off of her uncle's funeral. She had no schoolwork to do. The house was clean. All of the gifts she'd purchased were wrapped and under the tree.

Teddy needed a bath, but there wasn't that much time. She supposed she could brush him for the funeral. She found his brush and ordered him to sit. He liked to be brushed and sat still while she worked. She still had time to kill when she'd finished.

She went upstairs and looked in the closet. She'd already decided what to wear. She bought a black dress at the boutique for the occasion. She closed the closet and looked round the room. Her puzzle book lay on the nightstand.

She picked up the book and found the puzzle she'd been trying to solve before going to sleep. She settled onto the bed and began working on the cryptogram. Teddy jumped on the bed and lay down beside her.

She finished the puzzle and was about to start another when her phone rang.

"Jade? How are you doing this morning?"

"I'm okay, Mom."

"Are you ready for this afternoon?"

"As ready as I'll ever be. I don't have a choice, do I?"

"No, sweetheart, you don't."

"The gifts you sent arrived this morning, and they're all under the tree."

"Good, I was a little worried that they wouldn't get there before Christmas. What else have you done today?"

Jade told her Mom about taking Teddy for his walk and her concern that he might misbehave. She told her about all of the food in the freezer.

"I guess we'll be writing thank you cards while I'm there," said Mollie.

"You won't have to cook unless you want to," Jade joked.

"My break is almost over. I'll be thinking of you this afternoon. I wish I could be there."

"I'll be okay, Mom. I'll talk to you tonight."

The call ended. Jade set her puzzle book aside and began getting dressed for the funeral.

1:00 p.m.

Jade and Teddy were ready when the limousine from the funeral home arrived. The driver held the door open for her while she coaxed Teddy into the back seat.

She couldn't believe it was such a beautiful day. It was sunny and sixty-four degrees with very little wind. She had expected the weather to be as dark and gloomy as she felt.

She was escorted to a comfortable waiting room when she

arrived at the funeral home. It looked like a sitting room or den. Comfortable furniture lined the walls, and the lighting was subdued. The only indication that it wasn't what it appeared to be was the fact that Erik lay in his eternal bed against one wall. It was her time to say a private goodbye.

She led Teddy toward the casket.

Teddy stood on his hind legs and placed his front paws on the edge of the casket. He nuzzled Erik's arm and licked his hand trying to get his master's attention. He whined and looked at Jade when there was no response.

Jade scratched Teddy's ears and looked at her uncle.

He looked so handsome lying there in the same suit he'd worn to the event at the museum. She straightened his tie and smiled at the memory.

She tucked a piece of paper into her uncle's cold lifeless hand. It was a copy of an Irish Blessing that had become their family motto. It read:

> May the blessing of light be upon you, light on the outside, light on the inside. With God's sunlight shining on you, may your heart glow with warmth, like a turf fire that welcomes friends and strangers alike. May the light of the Lord shine from your eyes like a candle welcoming the weary traveler.

"I love you, Uncle Erik," she said and kissed his forehead. "What are we going to do without you?"

She stood there a moment longer before leading Teddy away. Sobbing, she helped herself to a tissue from a box on the end table and sat down in the nearest arm chair. Teddy stood in front of her and leaned against her legs.

"It's okay, Teddy," she whispered while patting him and rubbing his neck. "I don't like this either, but there's nothing we can do about it."

Bear and Renee entered the room, hugged Jade, and fussed over Teddy. Jade watched them as they each said goodbye to Erik.

Tears rolled unchecked down Renee's cheeks while she looked down at the man she had cared for so deeply. Bear stared at the remains of his longtime friend, sniffed, and fought back his own tears.

There was a soft tap on the door, and Mr. Frantz entered the room.

"It's time to go to the chapel," he told them.

They were led into the small chapel and guided to seats on the front row. The room was filled to capacity with Erik's friends, coworkers, and museum board members. Renee and Bear sat on either side of her. Teddy lay at her feet. She was surrounded by people who cared enough about her uncle to pay their respects, but she had never felt more alone.

Jade was led to a limousine after the funeral service ended. Wilson Lee was already outside and held the door open for her. He put his hand on Jade's shoulder, and Teddy growled a warning.

Lee dropped his hand. "That's a good dog." His face smiled at Teddy, but his eyes were wary. "Miss O'Neal, I can't stay for the graveside service, but I didn't want to leave without telling you how sorry I am for your loss."

"Thank you, Mr. Lee."

"Erik was a good man. He'll be sorely missed."

"Yes, he will. Thank you."

"I hope to see you again under happier circumstances," he said and walked away.

Jade coaxed Teddy into the limo and climbed in beside him. Renee got in, and Bear followed, closing the door behind them.

Bear checked to make sure that they were alone and said, "I don't think Teddy likes that guy."

"I was laying on the ground outside the museum the first time we met. Mr. Lee offered to help me up. Teddy may have thought that he had hurt me."

"Why were you on the ground?" Renee asked.

"Teddy chased a squirrel and drug me along with him."

Teddy looked at Jade when he heard his name and soft laughter.

"That could be the reason," Bear said unconvinced.

"Teddy has been growling at people more often since he was drugged and locked in the shed," Jade told them. "He may not trust people in general right now."

"He hasn't growled at us," Bear pointed out. "Dogs have a sense about people. It's a good idea to keep him close."

"Jade, you shouldn't trust too many people either," Renee began. "Both your homes were burglarized within two days. We don't know who killed Erik or why. You need to be careful."

Their conversation ended when the driver got into the car and started the engine. The occupants of the back seats didn't say anything more.

They made their way toward the gravesite and sat in the seats provided. Teddy sat at Jade's feet and leaned on her legs while she stroked his head during the graveside service.

People that Jade knew and others that she'd never met filed past and offered their condolences. Dino Stevens took her hand and Teddy growled. Stevens backed away.

"I'm sorry, Mr. Stevens. Teddy tends to growl at people he doesn't know."

"I'm sure he feels it's his job to protect you now," Stevens said, eyeing the dog.

"Yes, he does." She patted Teddy's back. "Thank you for coming."

Teddy woofed when Hudson Bailey approached. "How are you holding up?" he asked Jade.

"We're hanging on," she replied trying to smile. "Thank you for your help and for coming today."

"You're welcome. Do you still have that card I gave you?" he asked and patted Teddy on the head.

"Yes, and I've put the numbers in my phone."

"Good, don't forget to call me if you need anything," Hudson reminded her and moved away.

"Heather! I didn't expect you to be here!"

"I wanted to let you know that I'm here for you and pay my respects. Your uncle was always nice to me," Heather said and hugged Jade.

Tears ran down Jade's cheeks, and she nodded her thanks.

Erik's neighbors, Lewis and Sondra Walters, and Olen and Gaye Fincher, filed past. They were followed by Tommy Carlile and other people who worked at the museum. Teddy growled when Tommy squeezed her hand.

Jade felt Renee stiffen when Kathy Steen offered her condolences.

Jonathan Baxter was the last person in the line of would be comforters. Teddy growled when he approached them. Baxter didn't get any closer.

"Miss O'Neal, I'm sorry for your loss. Erik was a valuable asset to the museum. We'll all miss him."

"Thank you, Mr. Baxter."

He handed her a business card. "That's my contact information. Please, don't hesitate to call if I can help you in any way."

"Thank you."

Jade watched Bear and Renee walk away before she walked to the grave with Teddy by her side. She stood there with her hand on the casket and whispered "Light on the outside, light on the inside."

Most of the mourners had gone by the time she led Teddy back to the limousine where Renee and Bear waited. They road in silence back to the funeral home.

"Would you like our driver to take you home?" asked Mr. Frantz.

"We'll take her home," said Bear. "If that's okay with you, Jade."

"We'd like to stay and keep you company for a while," added Renee.

"Yes, I'd like that."

Jade and Teddy got into the back of Renee's car and drove to Erik's house with Bear following close behind in his truck.

Renee and Bear stayed with Jade for hours. They ordered pizza and reminisced about Erik. Bear told stories about their high school days, and Renee talked about funny things that had happened with Erik at work and a few stories about conferences they'd gone to together.

"Oh, will you look at the time," Renee said. "I'd better get going. My little dog hasn't been outside for hours. I hope she hasn't had an accident."

"I need to go, too," Bear added. "Fridays are busy at the restaurant. I need my beauty sleep."

Jade walked them to the door and hugged them both. "Thank y'all for being with me today. I don't know how I would have gotten through it without you."

"You're welcome," Renee replied. "Call me anytime. I'll be happy to help."

"Call me if you need anything at all," Bear told her.

"I will. Goodnight"

Jade watched them walk to their vehicles and waved goodbye before she closed the door and set the alarm.

"Come on, Teddy. Let's go upstairs."

Teddy followed her and jumped on the bed. Jade changed into her pajamas and crawled in beside him. She picked up her puzzle book and solved the last puzzle before turning off the lamp for the night.

CHAPTER FOURTEEN

Friday, December 22, 2017

8:00 a.m.

Jade was awake when her alarm went off. She was still having nightmares about finding Erik's body and hadn't slept well.

There were things that she had to get done while she had the day off. She needed to talk to her apartment manager, and she needed to go to the museum to collect Erik's personal items. She wasn't looking forward to either task.

She was excited about her mother being with her for Christmas. Having managed to get through the worst week of her life on her own, she looked forward to having company for the holiday.

She hoped she could get everything done in one day so that she could concentrate on getting the house ready for her mother's visit. Uncle Erik had replaced all of the broken Christmas decorations, and put the lights up on the outside of the house, but all he'd had time to do inside was to set up and decorate the tree.

She showered, dressed, and tended to Teddy before driving to her apartment building. She walked to the manager's office and took a deep breath before she went in.

Stephanie Hancock greeted Jade with a hug. "I'm so sorry to hear about your uncle. He seemed to be such a nice man."

"Thank you," Jade's answer was automatic.

"Do the police know anything?"

"I don't think so."

"I'm sure they'll find out the truth."

"Do you have a few minutes?" Jade asked.

"Of course, sit down. What can I do for you?" Stephanie asked before sitting behind her desk.

"Uncle Erik had a dog. He's a big dog and needs a lot of space and exercise," she hesitated and swallowed hard. "I'm the only one who can handle him now."

"Yes, your uncle mentioned him to me when your apartment was burglarized. I'm sorry, but I can't allow you to bring him here."

"I know, and that's why I wanted to talk to you. I'm going to have to move."

"Your lease isn't up until the end of May."

"I was hoping we could come to an agreement about that."

"What do you have in mind?" Stephanie asked.

"Would it be possible to end my lease early? Heather would be able to find another roommate, and I could move into my uncle's house and take care of Teddy."

"Do you know anyone who might pick up your lease?"

"No, I don't, but Heather might."

"Talk to Heather. If she knows someone, I'll see what I can do."

"Thank you!"

Jade left Stephanie's office and went to her car. She took two boxes out of her trunk and went upstairs to her apartment.

Heather was watching television when Jade opened the door. She eyed the boxes in Jade's hands.

"Are you moving out?"

"Someone has to take care of Teddy, and I can't bring him here. I don't have any other options."

"What about the rent? You're on the lease, too."

"I talked with Stephanie a few minutes ago."

Jade put the boxes on the floor and told Heather about the conversation with the apartment manager.

"I might know of someone. I'll call her and find out if she's interested."

"Thanks, it would help me out a lot," Jade replied.

"I know you're going through a hard time right now, but don't you think it would be better to be around people? Staying cooped up at your uncle's house will be lonely."

"I need time to deal with this, and I don't feel like socializing right now. Besides, I won't be lonely. My mom will be here for Christmas."

"Okay, but remember that I'm here if you need someone to talk to."

"Thanks, but I don't know what there is to say right now."

Jade picked up the boxes and took them to her room. She packed them with her personal belongings and took them to her car. She carried up two more boxes and repeated the process. She was about to start down the stairs with her second load when Logan came out of his apartment.

"Hi, Jade!" His wonderful smile faded when he noticed the boxes. "What are you doing?"

"Hi, Logan. I'm moving."

"Why? Where are you going?"

"I'm moving into my Uncle Erik's house so that I can take care of his dog."

"I'm sorry about your uncle. I wanted to go to the funeral, but I couldn't get off work."

"Thanks," Jade said.

"Let me help you with that."

Logan carried the boxes to her car for her and followed her back upstairs. He watched her take suitcases from her closet and put them on her bed.

"I'll be off work at five today," he told her. "Do you want to have dinner with me?"

"I don't know, Logan. I have a lot to do. I might not get it all done before my mom gets here."

"We haven't gone out in a while. Come on, it'll take your mind off things."

"Okay," Jade conceded. "But just for a little while."

"Great, we'll leave here at seven."

"Logan, I'll be at my uncle's house."

"Oh right, I'll pick you up there at seven."

Jade filled the suitcases with her clothes. Logan helped her carry them downstairs and kissed her goodbye. She waved at him when he drove out of the parking lot.

Heather was waiting for her when she went back upstairs.

"I didn't want to interrupt you while Logan was here," she explained. "I talked to my cousin. She's agreed to take over your part of the lease."

"That's a relief, thanks Heather," Jade said. "I was afraid I'd have to quit school and go to work full time."

"Will you have to make house payments?"

"No, but I'm sure there will be other things that I'll have to do. Mom and I will figure all that out while she's here."

"I can't imagine how hard this must be for you."

"I hope the worst is over," Jade said and went to her room.

Jade was glad that she didn't have to move furniture. The apartment had been furnished when she moved in. She looked around to make sure she hadn't left anything behind and went to the kitchen. There was nothing there that she needed.

"Heather, you can have anything in the kitchen that belongs to me."

"Are you sure?"

"Yeah, Uncle Erik's house is well stocked."

Heather hugged Jade and said, "Will you keep in touch?"

"I'll try," Jade promised. "I have to go unload this and then go to the museum to get Uncle Erik's stuff out of his office."

"Do you want me to go with you?"

"Thanks, but one of his friends at work is going to help. Let me know when your cousin is ready to take over the lease."

"I will, bye, Jade."

"Goodbye."

11:00 a.m.

Jade drove to the house and unloaded her car as fast as she could. She was supposed to meet Renee in ten minutes. She'd have to unpack later. She got back in the car and drove to the museum. Renee was at her desk in an office down the hall from Erik's when Jade arrived.

Jade tapped on her door and said, "Hi, Renee."

"Hi, Jade. How are you doing?"

"I'm okay, I guess. I've never been through anything like this. It never occurred to me it would be so hard."

"It's going to be hard for a long while," Renee said with compassion. "I found some boxes and put them on Erik's desk for you."

"Thank you."

"Did you know the police have been here?"

"No, when?" Jade asked with surprise.

"It was yesterday before the funeral. They went through every drawer and cabinet. They even took his computer."

"Why would they search his office?"

"I don't know."

"Did they take anything else?"

"Not that I noticed." Renee answered. She took a set of keys from her desk drawer and led the way to Erik's office.

Jade took a deep breath and shook her head. "I'm not looking forward to this."

"I know. It's not going to be easy. I'd be happy to keep you company."

Jade nodded and said, "Yes, I'd like that."

The two women went through the office and packed away all of Erik's belongings. Jade found a metal box in the bottom drawer of the desk. There were two photos inside. One was of Erik and Renee.

"Renee, have you seen this?"

Renee looked at the photo and tears filled her eyes.

"I had forgotten all about this. I had no idea he'd kept it."

"When was it taken?"

"It was five or six years ago at a conference in San Diego. There were several of us on that trip. We had such a good time. Erik and I had gotten separated from the group, so we decided to make the best of it and did a little sightseeing. A nice young man took the photo for us."

"Would you like to have it?"

Renee smiled at Jade with gratitude. "Do you mind?"

"I know that you and Uncle Erik were close, and I'm sure he'd want you to have it."

"Thank you," Renee said and hugged Jade. "Who's in that other picture with Erik?"

Jade picked up the picture and stared at it. "That's my dad! I wonder when this was taken."

"Maybe, it's written on the back," Renee suggested.

Jade turned it over. There were numbers written on the back, but there were too many to be a date. She had no idea what it meant. She handed the photo to Renee who didn't know either.

She put the photograph back in the metal box and packed it away with the rest of Erik's things.

"Will you have to sort through all of this alone?"

"I'll talk to Mom about it. We'll have to go through all of Uncle

Erik's belongings at some point. She may want to wait until Levi can be here, too."

Jade looked around the office when they had finished. "I suppose someone else will be using this office soon."

"Yes," Renee couldn't hide her sadness, "Will you keep in touch with me? I'd like to know what's happening in your life from time to time."

"I will. I'll keep you updated about the investigation, too."

"Oh! I almost forgot. Let's go back to my office. I need to give you something."

Jade followed Renee back to her office and watched her struggle to open a file cabinet drawer.

"This darn thing always sticks," she said and gave it a hard yank.

Renee took a gift wrapped in red paper with a large white bow from the drawer and handed it to Jade.

"What's this?"

"It's from Erik. He asked me to keep it here for him until Christmas Eve. You'll have to tell me what's in it after Christmas."

Jade couldn't speak. She was too busy fighting back tears.

Renee turned and picked up the phone on her desk. Two security guards arrived a minute later. They carried the boxes from Erik's office to Jade's car while the two women followed.

Jade waved goodbye and drove away before Renee went back to her office.

1:00 p.m.

Jade could hear Teddy barking when she got back to Erik's house. She called to him, but he didn't stop. She left the boxes in the car and went to see what had him so upset.

"Teddy, what are you barking at?"

"Miss O'Neal?" Someone was standing at the front gate.

"Who's there?"

"It's Hudson Bailey. I need to speak with you, please."

Jade ordered Teddy to stay and went through the gate. Bailey wasn't alone.

"What's going on?"

"Miss O'Neal, we have a warrant to search this house and the property," said Officer Lynn Tredway handing her the warrant.

"Why would you search Uncle Erik's house?"

"We've been trying to trace his movements to find out where he was and who he might have talked to. We hope it will help us solve this case."

Jade couldn't argue with that logic and started toward the back door. Tredway started to follow.

"You don't want to do that," said Bailey.

"I'm in charge here! I'll do what needs to be done!"

"Have it your way."

Tredway followed Jade through the gate. Teddy snarled at him, and Tredway's legs couldn't move him back through the gate fast enough.

Bailey did his best to suppress his laughter.

"Stay, Teddy!" Jade ordered and looked at Tredway. "I'll let you in through the front door. Teddy will stay outside."

"We'll go in through the front," Tredway told his team.

Jade let the police officers into the house.

"Are you moving, Miss O'Neal?" Tredway asked.

"I'm moving in here to take care of Teddy. Those are things from my apartment that I haven't had time to unpack."

"Those boxes and other items will also be searched because they're on the property."

"I understand. There are more boxes from my uncle's office in my car. Should I bring those in?"

"We'll take care of that for you. You're wanted at the station." Tredway informed her.

"Why?" Jade asked in confusion.

"The detective in charge of the case wants to talk to you," Hudson replied.

Jade could see Teddy barking, growling, and jumping on the door, trying to get at the police officers inside.

"Can I try to calm Teddy first? He's not happy, and I'm afraid he might jump through the window."

Bailey and Tredway looked out the window and agreed. They didn't want to have to deal with an angry giant dog.

Jade picked up a chew toy and the blanket that Teddy liked to sleep on. She went to the kitchen and took a handful of dog biscuits from the box.

"It would be a good idea if one of you would close the blinds on this side of the house while I distract him," Jade said before she went outside.

Hudson watched her pet and soothe Teddy. She managed to get him to turn away from the house. Hudson closed all but one set of blinds. He watched from a small window that he didn't think Teddy could see through.

He'd volunteered for this assignment to help ease the blow. He liked Jade and couldn't help being attracted to her, but he had a job to do. He couldn't allow his feelings to distract him.

Teddy had calmed down enough that Jade could walk away. She eased through the back door while he chewed on his toy.

Hudson waited in the kitchen. "I'll drive you to the station."

"Will this take long? I don't know how long Teddy will behave."

"The men inside are going to keep the noise to a minimum, especially on the back-side of the house," he told her. "I don't know how long you'll be at the station, but I'll bring you home when you're done."

2:00 p.m.

Hudson escorted Jade to a room that contained a small table, two chairs, and a large mirror. She'd was pretty sure it wasn't an office. She was introduced to Detective Bob Holloway before Hudson left the room.

"Please, sit down, Miss O'Neal."

Jade sat down in the chair opposite the detective.

"Miss O'Neal, I need to clarify a few things," Holloway began. "We've been tracing your uncle's movements during the time that you said he was on vacation."

"Why would you do that?"

"We're trying to find a clue to the motive for his murder, which should in turn lead us to his killer. Tell me what you know about his trip."

She told Holloway what Erik had told her. He was taking a few days of vacation and going to Philadelphia. He'd always wanted to see Independence Hall and the Liberty Bell. He was supposed to have been back Wednesday evening. She told him about the phone call from Erik and the arrangement to meet for lunch the next day.

"Why did you file a missing person's report?" asked Detective Holloway.

"It wasn't like Uncle Erik to be late without calling. I couldn't get in touch with him. I left voice messages and sent texts, but he didn't reply. He hadn't gone to work or called in, which wasn't normal."

"There are other things about this case that aren't normal," said Holloway. "His car was in the airport parking lot, but he didn't fly to Philadelphia. He got on a plane, but got off in Dallas, and there weren't any other reservations made in his name."

"That's impossible. He told me..." Jade stopped, trying to process what she had been told.

"The coroner placed his time of death between fourteen and sixteen hours before he was found. That would have been between one and three in the morning Thursday the fourteenth. What time did you talk with your uncle?"

"It was between nine-thirty and ten Wednesday evening."

"If that's the case, he couldn't have been stuck in an airport when he called you."

Jade was stunned. None of it made sense to her. Either Erik had lied to her for some unknown reason, or the police were mistaken. She shook her head but said nothing.

"There was very little blood at the scene, which leads us to believe that your uncle was killed somewhere else and the body moved to that location."

"Why would someone do that? Why leave him there?"

Bob Holloway didn't answer. "Do you always walk your dog near the Computer Center?"

"No, that was the first time we'd gone that way."

"Why did you decide to walk in that particular area?"

"Teddy's leash broke. That's where I finally caught up with him," she explained.

Holloway's questions set off warning bells in her mind.

"Are you aware that Mr. O'Neal willed everything to your family?"

"I wasn't until this week," Jade answered, fearing his next words. "We're his only living relatives."

"I've been told that you've moved into your uncle's house."

"Yes, I had to so that I can take care of Teddy. My apartment building doesn't allow pets."

Bob Holloway stared at her for a moment. Jade wasn't sure if he was waiting for her to say more or deciding what to ask next.

"I think it's possible that you and your family are involved in this somehow," he said at last. "I think you knew that you would inherit everything and that you wanted your inheritance now rather than later."

Jade gawked at the man unable to find words.

"You couldn't have done it alone. You had to have had an accomplice. You filed a missing person's report to establish your concern for your uncle. You or your accomplice killed O'Neal and hid his body under those bushes, making sure that you and your dog would find the body," he made quotations marks in the air with his fingers.

"NO! I loved Uncle Erik," she shouted, willing herself not to cry.

"Sure, you did. I'd say that too if I were in your shoes. If you did have anything to do with this, I'll find out. Don't leave the Canyon and Amarillo area."

Holloway stood and left the interrogation room.

Jade was silent during the drive back to the house. She fought back angry tears. She refused to cry. She didn't want to give Hudson Bailey the satisfaction.

4:00 P.M.

The officers searching the house were still there when she walked through the front door. She sat on the living room couch and waited for them to finish. Hudson tried to talk to her, but she refused to acknowledge his presence.

Jade's cell phone rang.

"Are we still on for dinner?" Logan asked when she answered.

"Logan, I'm sorry, but something's come up. I won't be able to go to dinner tonight."

"Oh...I was looking forward to spending time with you."

"I know, I was looking forward to it, too."

"Is someone there?"

"Yes, the police are here searching the house." Logan could hear the anger in her voice.

"Okay, I'll talk to you later."

It was another hour before the officers finished their search and left. Hudson hung back and said, "I know you don't want to talk to me right now, but I swear I didn't know that Holloway was going to accuse you."

"You were behind that mirror, weren't you?"

"Yes, I was. It was my job to listen to what you told the detective and tell him if your story was different from the one you told me."

"I thought you were trying to help, but you've been investigating me all along haven't you?"

"I was trying..."

Jade slammed the door leaving, him on the porch in mid-sentence.

6:30 P.M.

Jade put things in order and rewrapped the gifts before putting them back under the tree. Her stomach grumbled, and she realized that she hadn't eaten since breakfast. Going to the kitchen, she put a frozen pizza in the oven.

After dinner, Jade lay on the couch with Teddy on the floor beside her. The television was on, but she didn't know what was playing. She was lost in anger, grief, and loneliness.

Her musings were interrupted by the ringing of her cell phone.

"Hi, Mom."

"How was your day?"

"Terrible!" Jade said and told her about her day but didn't mention being questioned by the police. She didn't want her mother to worry.

"I'm so sorry that I can't be there with you right now. I know how hard this must be for you. Why don't you come to New York with me after Christmas?"

"I'd love to, but I can't."

"Why not?"

"I've been instructed not to leave the area. The police think I might have had something to do with Uncle Erik's death."

"That's outrageous! Why would they think that?"

"Because the three of us will inherit everything. Since I'm the one living here..."

"That's absurd!"

"Mom, did you know that Uncle Erik left a gift for me at his office?" she asked, trying to change the subject.

"No, I didn't."

"He left it with Renee Lanham. She gave it to me today."

"Did you open it?"

"No, I'm waiting until we can open our gifts together."

"Maybe you should see what's inside. It might take your mind off things."

"I'll think about it."

"I need to go. We're having dinner downstairs. I'll call you tomorrow. I love you."

"I love you too, Mom."

CHAPTER FIFTEEN

SATURDAY, December 23, 2017

6:00 a.m.

Jade was startled awake by the sound of her cell phone ringing. Knocking the phone off the night stand, she searched the floor in the dark. It had stopped ringing by the time she had turned on the light and found it under her bed.

Why would Mom be calling this early? she thought and tapped the number.

"Mom? Did you just call?" she asked with a yawn.

"I'm sorry I woke you, but I had to let you know that my flight was cancelled," Mollie said in a rush. "I'm not going to be able to get there for Christmas."

"Can't you take a later flight?"

"No, I tried. A winter storm has everything grounded. I'm on my way back to my hotel now."

Jade didn't reply. She felt like someone had let all the air out of her birthday bouncy house before she got the chance to jump.

"Jade? Are you there?"

"I'm here. I just don't know what to say."

"I know you're disappointed. I am, too."

"Do you think you could come after the storm blows over?"

"I don't think so. They're predicting more storms through Monday night. I'd have to be back for work on Tuesday morning."

"It's better to be stuck there than in an airport somewhere," Jade said trying to sound positive.

"Do you have to work today?"

"Yes, I go in at two and work until nine."

"Call me when you get home, and we'll talk this evening. Maybe, you can get a little more sleep before you have to go to work."

"I'll try. I'll talk to you tonight. Bye, Mom."

2:05 p.m.

Jade was late. She parked her car at Westgate Mall and hurried across the parking lot.

It had not been a good morning. She had gone back to sleep after talking to her mother and didn't hear her alarm. She rushed to take Teddy for his walk and tripped on a curb, skinning her hands and knees. She showered and dressed but didn't have time to dry her hair.

Her car wouldn't start when she finally made it out the door. She'd had to ask Mr. Walters next door to give her a battery a boost. It was difficult to reach her battery because she was parked close to the garage door and the fence.

"You need to replace the battery on this car," Mr. Walters told her. "Or park on the other side of the driveway, so it's easier to get at."

She thanked him for his help and drove to work with the heater on high, hoping that her hair would dry on the way.

9:05 p.m.

Her workday had been filled with last minute shoppers trying to find gifts for their loved ones. Jade contemplated which casserole she'd have for dinner as she walked across the mall. Her phone rang when she reached the exit.

"Hi, Jade. Are you still at work?"

"Hi, Logan. I'm walking out the door now."

"Do you want to go to the Cantina with me?"

"Yes, I'm starved, and I could use some company."

"Do you want me to pick you up or meet you there?"

"I'll meet you there."

"Okay, I'll see you in about twenty minutes."

She walked across the parking lot and climbed into her car. She prayed it would start and turned the key. The engine puttered to life, and she let it idle while she called her mother.

"Hi, Jade," Mollie answered. "Are you already home?"

"No, I just got off. I'm meeting Logan for dinner."

"Good. I was worried about you being alone. How was your day?"

"It was crazy busy. Tomorrow will be worse. People who wait until Christmas Eve to shop and those who need one more gift will be out in droves."

"I'm sorry you're having to work so hard."

"Honestly, Mom, I'm not. It helps keep my mind occupied. I don't have classes to worry about right now, and I need to stay busy."

"I wish I could be there with you. I won't even have time to see you before I go to Ireland."

"That's okay, Mom. I plan to work a lot between now and the beginning of the semester. I'm going to need the money, and I need to stay busy."

"What's that awful noise?"

"It's my car. I've been having issues with it this week. Uncle

Erik told me that I needed to start looking for another one months ago. I haven't had the time, and I don't have the money right now."

"It would be a good idea to take it in to a mechanic to find the problem," Molly suggested.

"I will when I have the chance. I need to go, but I'll call later."

Jade drove to Sixth Street and parked outside the restaurant. Logan was already inside at a table. He stood and kissed her on the cheek.

"I hope you don't mind, but I ordered for both of us."

"Green Chili Cheeseburgers?"

"Yep."

"That's perfect. I've been eating casseroles for days now. I'm ready for a good burger."

The waitress brought their meal, and they dug in. Jade had expected to see Heather before remembering that she had gone home to be with her family for Christmas.

They had a pleasant meal and talked about their jobs and holiday plans before Logan brought up the topic that he was most anxious to discuss.

"I don't understand why you had to move," Logan told her.

"I talked to Stephanie. Pets aren't allowed, and she can't make an exception for me. Besides, Teddy needs lots of space and exercise."

"But why do you have to take care of him? Can't someone else do it?"

"There is no one else. Levi is overseas; he can't keep him. My mom lives in an apartment that doesn't allow pets, and her job involves a lot of travel. It's up to me."

"Couldn't you take him to a shelter or find him another home?"

Jade stared at Logan. She couldn't believe what she was hearing. "No! Teddy is a member of the family. Uncle Erik and I raised him together. I'd never dream of giving him up. I don't know how I would have gotten through this past week without him."

"I'm sorry. I've never understood people's attachment to their animals."

"Didn't you ever have a pet?"

"I had some goldfish when I was little. I won them at the fair, but they didn't live long."

"Fish are nice, but they're a little hard to interact with."

"Yeah, all they do is look at you and go..." Logan made a face and mimicked the mouth movement of fish.

Jade couldn't help laughing at him. It felt good to laugh. It was almost as if her life was back to normal.

"I have an idea. Why don't you follow me back to the house?" she suggested. "You can meet Teddy, and we can watch a movie together."

"That's a good idea," Logan said with a smile.

Logan paid the check, and they left the restaurant. He followed her back to Canyon and parked in the driveway beside Jade's car. Following her through the gate, he put his arm around her.

Teddy had been asleep on the lounge chair and got up to greet Jade. He saw Logan and ran toward them, barking and growling, his hackles up and his teeth bared.

"Teddy! Stay!" Jade shouted, running toward the dog and grabbing his harness.

"I'm sorry, Logan! You'd better go" she said, struggling to hold the massive dog. "I'll call you later."

Logan didn't argue. He backed through the gate and made certain it was latched. He ran to his car and sped away.

"What's the matter with you?" Jade asked when Logan had gone. "He's my friend, and you'll just have to get used to him."

Teddy stopped barking, but he still stared and growled at the gate.

"Come on. Let's go in."

She unlocked the back door. Teddy followed her inside looking toward the gate once more before she closed the door.

Jade got ready for bed and called her Mom.

"Hi, sweetheart. How was your date?" asked her mother when she answered the phone.

"It was good, but it was cut a little short. I asked Logan to come meet Teddy and watch a movie, but Teddy went crazy when he saw Logan."

"What happened?"

"I don't know. He saw us come into the yard, and then it was like he was a different dog. I didn't think I was going to be able to stop him from attacking."

"What did Logan do?"

"He froze until I told him that he'd better go. Then, he was out of here almost before I got the words out of my mouth."

"I can't say I blame him, but what was he doing when Teddy started misbehaving?"

"Nothing! He put his arm around me, but that's all."

"Well, don't you think that's it?"

"What do you mean?"

"Teddy must have thought that Logan was threatening you. He was trying to protect you."

"I didn't think of that," Jade said and paused. "Teddy growled at people at the funeral, too. I think they were all either trying to shake my hand or hug me. He didn't growl at anyone who kept their distance."

"Next time you bring Logan to the house, make sure he doesn't touch you before he gets acquainted with Teddy."

"That's a good idea. It was so scary. I don't know what I would have done if he'd attacked Logan."

"You should call Logan and explain what we think happened," suggested Mollie.

"I will before I go to bed. What are you going to do tomorrow?"

"I had hoped to be there with you," Mollie began. "I've tried everything to find a way to get home for Christmas. I thought of renting a car and driving, but there isn't a rental car available. Everyone else had the same idea."

"We wouldn't have a lot of time to spend together anyway. I have to work until we close at six tomorrow. We'd only have a few hours together."

"I have an idea. It isn't like being in the same room, but we could use Skype. I could at least see you open your gifts," Mollie said.

"I like that idea. I could open yours, so that you can see them before I ship them to you."

"All we have to decide now is when?"

"I think Christmas morning. It will give me something to look forward to. Do you think Levi would be able to join us?"

"I'll try to get in touch with him and find out. I'll text you later."

"Okay, goodnight, Mom."

Jade ended the call with her mother and tapped Logan's number. It went to voice mail. She left him a message and crawled into bed. Teddy lay down on the bed beside her.

She stroked her guardian's ears and said, "Thank you for trying to protect me, Teddy, but not everyone is a threat."

Teddy looked at her for a moment and laid his head on her lap.

"I'm sorry you didn't get your walk today. We'll go in the morning before I have to go to work."

Teddy tapped his tail and watched Jade turn off the lamp.

"Goodnight, Teddy," she said and snuggled under the covers.

Sunday, December 24, 2017

5:30 a.m.

Jade woke up early and stared at the ceiling. She'd had another nightmare about finding Erik's body. She tried to push it out of her mind by thinking about her plans for the next two days.

She was glad that today would be the last day of the Christmas rush. She'd had some unexpected time off during the past two weeks, but it hadn't been pleasant. All in all, she'd rather have had to work, and the rest of her life remain the same. Uncle Erik would still be alive, and her mom would be there for Christmas.

She shook her head and forced her thoughts back to the present. She'd have Christmas day off, and then she'd have to go back to work for the after Christmas and end of the year clearance sales. She could use the money, and it was nice to have something to do.

Jade dozed thinking about past Christmases. She woke up to the muffled sound of her alarm going off. Tossing the pillow off her head, she turned off the alarm.

She went downstairs and let Teddy outside before making a pot of coffee. She rummaged around the freezer looking for the breakfast casserole that she'd sampled earlier in the week.

She glanced at the oven clock. She'd have to hurry if she was going to take Teddy for his walk and get back in time to get ready for work. She put some of the casserole in the microwave and let Teddy back inside.

Jade ran upstairs to change into her workout gear. She could smell the warm casserole and the coffee on her way back to the kitchen. Sitting at the bar, she ate her breakfast while Teddy begged beside her.

"You can eat when we get back," she told him. "I don't have time to wait on you this morning."

She put the dirty dishes in the sink and went to the back door.

"Let's go," she said, holding Teddy's leash.

Teddy drug her out of the house and through the back gate. They returned an hour later after a brisk and uneventful excursion.

After feeding Teddy, she went upstairs to shower and get ready for work. She tried to call Logan again but got no answer. She hoped Teddy hadn't scared him away forever.

6:30 p.m.

Jade drove into the driveway after a hectic day of work. She got out of the car and trudged to the gate. Teddy greeted her, and they went to the back-door together. Her cell phone rang when she unlocked the door.

"Hi, Jade," Logan said. "Merry Christmas!"

"Merry Christmas!" Jade replied with happiness.

"I got your message. I'm sorry I didn't answer your calls. Something's wrong with my phone. I didn't hear it ring."

"That's okay. I'm sorry about Teddy's behavior the other night."

"I'm not gonna lie. That was scary."

"I know, but I think my mom and I may have figured out why he acted that way," she said and told him their theory.

"That kinda makes sense," Logan said. "I'm not sure meeting him again is a good idea though."

"We'll have to introduce you to him little by little," Jade suggested.

"And from a safe distance," added Logan, "while he's chained up."

"It wasn't that bad, was it?" asked Jade surprised at Logan's attitude.

"All I could see were lots of big teeth headed in my direction. I'd rather not get close enough to see those again."

"I'm sorry. I don't know what else I can do."

"I've got to go. My mom is calling us all to supper. I'll talk to you later," Logan said and ended the call.

Jade stared at the phone. She had a feeling that she'd just been dumped. She couldn't decide if she was hurt or angry. She thought that if Logan couldn't deal with Teddy, there was no point in continuing the relationship. She decided that she wasn't going to call him again. He'd have to make the next move.

She fumed while she made her dinner and fed Teddy. She was still angry when she'd finished cleaning up the kitchen and settled in front of the television. She scrolled through the channels until she found a Christmas movie to watch.

Her anger had subsided by the time her phone rang again. She wasn't ready to talk to Logan yet and looked at the caller ID before she answered.

"Hi, Mom!"

"Hi, sweetheart. How was your day?"

"It could have been better," Jade said and told her about the discussion with Logan.

"I'm sure he was frightened by Teddy's behavior," said Mollie. "You were afraid, too. Don't write Logan off yet. Give him some time to sort things out. He'll call when he realizes you're worth the risk of dealing with Teddy."

"Maybe," said Jade. "I'm sure it's for the best anyway. We aren't able to see each other often, and our relationship hasn't progressed beyond dinner, drinks, and a goodnight kiss."

"So, you two haven't…," Mollie began.

"No and I don't know that we will now," Jade interrupted.

"Jade, honey, if Logan truly cares about you, you'll hear from him again," Mollie assured her.

"I hope you're right," Jade said. "How has your day gone?"

"It was all right, I guess. I've been reading and watching old movies today."

"Is Levi going to join us tomorrow?"

"I haven't been able to get in touch with him," Mollie said. "I'll keep trying. What are you doing tonight?"

"I'm watching *It's a Wonderful Life,* and after that, I think I'll watch *A Christmas Carol,*" Jade replied.

"I'm doing the same thing!" Mollie exclaimed.

The two women compared notes about what was happening in the movie and discussed their plans for the following day.

"I need to get some sleep," Mollie said with a yawn. "I'll talk to you in the morning."

"I think I'll stay up a while longer," Jade said. "I haven't been sleeping anyway."

"You haven't? Aren't you exhausted?"

"I am, but I can't sleep," Jade confided in her mother. "All I can think about is Uncle Erik and how he died. If I do fall asleep, I have nightmares about finding him in those bushes. I'm trying to be strong and keep it together but..."

"I know you are, sweetheart," Mollie said. "This has been a terrible ordeal for you, and the fact that you've managed everything on your own says a lot about your strength. But you don't have to be strong all the time. It's okay to let go and grieve."

Jade began to sob. "I'm...afraid... if I let go...I won't be able to...pull myself together...again. I...don't want... to... let everyone... down."

"You aren't going to let anyone down. You've done everything you can for Erik and the family. It's time to take care of yourself now. You need to rest and recover and then get on with your life."

"I know," Jade said. "You're right, but I don't know how to deal with this. How did you manage when Dad died?"

"Well, I had you and Levi to look after," said Mollie. "I took one day at a time and one crisis at a time until I was able to function again. My life has been different since Jacob died, but it's been a good life. Our lives will be different without Erik, but we'll carry on and keep his memory alive in our hearts."

"Thanks, Mom."

"Try to get some sleep, and we'll have Christmas together tomorrow."

"I'll try. Goodnight"

"Goodnight, sweetheart."

Jade watched another movie before going upstairs to bed. She decided to take her mother's advice and allow herself to grieve for one more night. Tomorrow would be a new day, and the beginning of learning to live life on her own.

CHAPTER SIXTEEN

MONDAY, December 25, 2017

8:30 a. m.

Teddy jumped off the bed and shook himself, making his tags jingle. He went downstairs and waited at the back door for Jade. She didn't follow. He went back upstairs and put his front paws on the side of the bed. He nuzzled her arm.

She still didn't wake up.

He jumped onto the bed and licked her face.

She covered her head with her pillow.

Teddy's playful bark echoed through the house.

Jade screamed, threw the pillow on the floor, and jumped out of bed. "Wha…What's wrong, Teddy?"

Teddy trotted to the bedroom door and looked back at her. Jade was staring at him with her hand over her heart and breathing hard. He went through the hallway to the top of the stairs and looked back.

"Do you need out?"

Teddy wagged his tail and ran downstairs. Jade's heart rate was returning to normal by the time she got to the kitchen and opened the door.

She considered going back to bed until she noticed the kitchen clock. It was almost time to get up anyway. She went upstairs to get ready for the day.

She stood in the shower and let the hot water run over her head while she thought about the holiday. She wasn't in the holiday mood. It wasn't going to be what she'd consider an ideal Christmas. Still, it was better than nothing.

Jade and her mother were trying to make the best of things. They knew that Christmas would never be the same. Nothing would ever be the same.

The house looked festive enough. A six-foot artificial Christmas tree stood in the living room in front of the bay window. Blue and silver ornaments were hung among the multicolored lights, and a twinkling silver star topped the tree.

White rope lights lined the walkway in front of the house, and white icicle lights hung from the eaves. A wreath with white lights adorned the front door.

Jade had always loved this time of year - the colorful lights, the holiday music, the wonder and excitement on children's faces. She'd barely noticed any of it this year. She just went through the motions. The pain was too raw, too fresh.

She wouldn't be spending the day surrounded by her family. Her mother and brother were thousands of miles away, and Uncle Erik was gone.

"Get yourself together, Jade," she said aloud. "You can't let Mom see you like this."

She forced herself to think about the plans with her mother. She finished her shower, toweled dry, and got dressed. She looked forward to talking and spending time with her mother and brother through video chat.

She picked up her comb and looked in the mirror. A stranger

with dark circles below red, puffy eyes stared back at her. She combed her hair and applied some cosmetic enhancement. She forced a smile on her face. The stranger in the mirror sneered.

"Merry Christmas to you, too," she said to the mirror and went downstairs.

Jade let Teddy back inside and prepared for the video chat. They were going to have brunch together before opening their gifts. She moved a comfortable chair in front of the Christmas tree and placed a barstool from the kitchen beside it. The tree would make a nice backdrop and she'd be able to rotate the laptop with the swiveling barstool.

She organized the gifts around the chair with the packages to her mother on one side and those of her own on the other. There were presents from Levi and Uncle Erik in addition to those her mother had sent. She decided to leave the packages for her uncle under the tree for the time being.

Jade took her laptop to the kitchen and set it on the bar. She plugged it in and pressed the power button. She opened the Skype app and began making her breakfast while she waited for her mother's call.

The Santa hat on her head accented the rest of her attire. She wore a green long-sleeved t-shirt with a large Santa on the front and flannel red and green plaid pajama pants. It had been a family tradition for as long as Jade could remember. Every year they ate French toast together while wearing their Christmas pajamas.

She turned when she heard the sound of an incoming call. She was surprised to see Levi's face on the screen.

"Hi, Sis!"

"Hi! I see you have your hat on, but where are your pajamas?" Jade teased.

"They aren't what you'd call regulation," he joked. "I can stuff this hat in my pocket. Is breakfast ready?"

"The bacon is frying, and the bread is soaking," Jade replied.

"Mmmm, sounds good," Levi said.

"It's good to see you. I wish you were here."

"I wish I was there, too. I'm sorry that you're having to deal with everything on your own. How are you holding up?"

"Okay, I guess. I've been trying to stay busy."

"Thanks for the package. The snacks you sent are already gone, and I plan to watch the movie later today."

"I'm glad you liked it. I haven't opened the gift you sent me yet. Do you want me to open it now?"

"I'd love to, but my time is almost up. Can I talk to Mom?"

"She isn't here. Her flight was canceled."

"I'm sorry, Sis. This must be the worst Christmas ever for you."

Jade fought back the tears and nodded.

"I have to go. Tell Mom that I'll talk to her soon. Merry Christmas, Jade."

"Merry Christmas, Levi. Be safe. I love you!"

"I love you, too!"

All too soon, the call ended. Jade wiped away a tear and took a deep breath. Turning back to the stove, she finished making her breakfast. She poured herself a fresh cup of coffee and sat down at the bar to wait for her mother's call. It wasn't long before she heard a familiar sound from her laptop.

"Merry Christmas!" Mollie said, wearing a Santa hat and her Christmas pajamas.

"Hi, Mom. Merry Christmas!"

"How are you doing this morning?"

"I'm okay. Levi called a few minutes ago. He said he'd talk to you later."

"Shoot! I hate that I missed him. I wasn't able to get hold of him to have him join us."

"He was about to go on duty. I don't think he'd have been able to join us anyway. Did you send him the Santa hat?"

"Was he wearing it?" Mollie asked with a grin.

"Yes, he said the pajamas weren't regulation though."

Mother and daughter chatted while they ate a long-distance

breakfast together. Jade moved the laptop to the living room when they'd finished eating.

"Jade, I need to take a little break," Mollie said. "I need to plug in this laptop, but I have no idea where I put the power cord. I'll call you back in a few minutes."

Jade cleaned the kitchen and put the dishes in the dishwasher while she waited for her mother to return. She gave Teddy a cookie and sat down in the chair. She was startled when her cell phone rang.

"Jade? This is Hudson Bailey."

"Hello, Officer," Jade said. He wasn't someone that she wanted to talk to at the moment.

"I wanted to see how you're doing and wish you a Merry Christmas."

"Thank you. Merry Christmas to you."

"Are you doing all right?"

"I'm doing as well as can be expected, considering that I just buried my uncle and that I'm suspected for his murder," she answered with icy bitterness.

"I guess that's true," Hudson said. "Will you be home later this evening? I'd like to deliver your uncle's personal effects."

"His personal effects?"

"His clothing and the items he had in his pockets have been processed for evidence and released. I thought I'd save you another trip to the station and bring them to you when I get off duty."

"I'll be here. I don't have anywhere that I need to be until I go to work in the morning."

"I'll see you later then," he said and ended the call.

Jade was staring at the phone wondering what she'd say when Hudson arrived when the Skype ringtone sounded.

"I'm back," Mollie said with a smile when Jade answered the call.

"Where should we start?" asked Jade.

"Why don't you give me a tour of the house so that I can see the new Christmas décor? The tree is gorgeous."

Jade picked up the laptop and went to the front door. She turned off the alarm and went outside.

"Uncle Erik worked a little bit every day until he got the outside lights up," Jade said and turned the laptop so that her mother could see.

"I'll bet they look beautiful at night," Mollie said.

Jade carried the laptop back inside, closed the door, and reset the alarm.

"Uncle Erik did most of the decorating," Jade told her mom. "I added the final touches a few days ago."

"It looks so nice and so festive," Mollie assured her daughter.

Jade returned the laptop to the barstool and sat down in the chair. She plugged her laptop in again and looked at the screen. "Are you ready to open gifts?" she asked her mother.

"Start with one of yours," Mollie suggested.

Jade opened her gift from Levi first. It was a beautiful red scarf with an intricate gold design. She opened Mollie's present from Levi and found a similar scarf in royal blue.

"He must have found those on his last leave," Mollie said. "I can't get over the color and the detail."

"What should I open next?" Jade asked.

"I think it will be fun to pick one up without looking," Mollie suggested. "You can tell me who it's from after it's opened."

Jade closed her eyes and picked up a package from her mother's side of the chair. She opened it and held the jacket up for her mother to see.

"Oh, that's gorgeous," Mollie said. "It looks so warm. I wish I had that with me right now. Is it from you?"

Jade nodded and said, "I bought it at the boutique. I knew I had to get it for you when I saw it."

"I love it, thank you. Open one of yours now."

Jade closed her eyes and picked up a package from her pile. She didn't bother to look at the name. She knew it had come from her mother. She tore open the paper and found a pair of boots that she'd been wishing for.

"Oh, Mom! How did you know?" she asked and held them up.

"I had a little help," Mollie said. "Erik told me that he'd seen you browsing the web for boots. He snooped a little for me so that I'd get the right ones."

Jade nodded and said, "Thank you, Mom. I can't wait to wear them."

They opened the remaining packages and exclaimed over the ones they'd given to each other and cried over those from Erik.

Teddy had been laying on the floor watching with curiosity. His ears perked up when he heard Mollie say his name.

"Did you give Teddy his gift already?"

"No, I saved it so that you could see him get it," Jade replied. "I should have given it to him before we started."

Jade went to the tree and picked up a long narrow package. She sat down in the chair and tilted the screen so that the mother could see the family pet.

"Here, Teddy," Jade said. "Do you want this?"

Teddy walked to Jade and sniffed the package. He pawed at the paper until it tore. Jade tore away the remaining paper to reveal a massive bone. Teddy wagged his tail and drooled.

"Don't tease him," Mollie said. "Let him have it."

Jade laughed and dropped the bone at Teddy's feet. He picked it up, trotted to his blanket, and gnawed in quiet contentment.

"Are those Erik's packages still under the tree?" Mollie asked.

Jade nodded and said, "I don't know what to do with them. What do you think?"

"I've been thinking a lot about it, and I believe the best thing to do is to donate them in Erik's name to one of the shelters in the area."

"That's a great idea! It's like we're giving them to him another way."

"Have you already opened the package that Erik left with Renee?"

"No, I was saving it for last," Jade said. "Renee told me that he wasn't going to bring it home until Christmas Eve. I don't know why?"

"I'm sure he didn't want you to find it early and figure out what was in there like you and Levi used to do," Mollie said, shaking her finger at her daughter.

Jade laughed and reached for the package. She waited a moment and sighed.

"What's wrong?" asked Mollie.

"It's the last present I'll ever have from Uncle Erik," Jade explained. "I almost don't want to open it."

"Jade, he wanted you to have whatever is inside, and he didn't want it spoiled early. It must be something special."

Jade nodded and opened the package. She found a card inside. She picked up the card and opened it. Tears filled her eyes as she read it aloud.

Merry Christmas, Jade!

I hope that you'll enjoy these as much as you did when you were younger.

I love you,

Uncle Erik

Tears cascaded down her cheeks. She looked at her mother to find her wiping away her own tears. She looked in the box and found something wrapped in tissue paper. She tore the paper away and smiled.

Uncle Erik had given her a large book of word puzzles. She flipped through the pages and remembered how they had worked puzzles like these together when she was growing up. They were some of her fondest memories. She held the book so that her mother could see.

"That takes me back," Mollie said. "I couldn't begin to count the number of hours the two of you spent solving puzzles."

Jade moved the box aside and heard something rattle. There was something else in the box. She reached in and took out a movie. It was her all-time favorite, *National Treasure*. She showed it to her mother and said, "Uncle Erik must have been feeling nostalgic."

"It looks that way," Mollie said.

Mother and daughter looked at each other. There were no more gifts to open. Neither wanted their time together to end.

Jade was the first to speak. "I think I'll take Teddy for his walk. I'm supposed to have a visit from a police officer this afternoon. I'd rather that Teddy was tired when he gets here."

"Police officer?" Mollie asked alarmed. "Why?"

"He said he wanted to deliver Uncle Erik's personal effects and save me a trip to the station."

"I think you should have Suzanne Walls with you before you answer any more questions from the police."

"I don't intend to talk with him more than necessary. I'll call Suzanne if I feel that I'm going to be questioned."

"All right," Mollie said, still not satisfied. "I'll talk to you tonight. Merry Christmas!"

"Merry Christmas, Mom!"

Jade put her laptop, movie, and puzzle book on the bar before putting the house back in order. She picked up the wrapping paper and stuffed it into a garbage bag. She took it to the dumpster before going upstairs to change into her workout clothes. She went downstairs and took Teddy's leash from the hook.

Teddy was by her side in an instant and waited while she attached the leash to his harness. He drug her through the gate and around the campus in record time. He slowed down long enough to dig under the tree for his prize.

Jade had begun carrying the jerky treats in her pocket so that she wouldn't have to make time to bury them. She waited until Teddy had a nice hole and dropped a treat for him. She was pretty sure he knew what she was doing, but he didn't seem to care. He got to dig, and get his prize. She wanted his life to be as normal as she could make it.

They returned to the house, and Jade began moving boxes from the garage into the house while Teddy enjoyed his bone. She packed up Erik's packages and put them in the garage. She'd donate them during her next day off.

She carried her own gifts to her room and put them away. She was in the process of packing her mother's things to be shipped when the doorbell rang.

She went to the door and looked out the peephole. She squared her shoulders and opened the door.

"Come in, Officer Bailey," she said stepping back.

"I thought you were going to call me Hudson."

"That was when I thought we could be friends," Jade replied with her arms crossed over her chest.

"I still think we could be friends if you'd let me explain what happened."

"You said you had something for me," Jade said and closed the door.

"Yes," he said and pointed at the box he carried under his arm.

Jade reached for it, but Bailey moved it away.

"You can have it to under one condition," he said with a smirk.

"What condition?"

"I'll give this to you if you'll hear me out first."

Jade stared at him and fought the overwhelming desire to set Teddy on him.

"I'm listening," she said.

"Why don't we sit at the table?" Hudson suggested. "I wouldn't mind a cup of that coffee I smell."

Jade rolled her eyes and went to the kitchen. She poured two cups of coffee while Hudson made himself comfortable at the dining table.

"Thank you," Hudson said, when she brought his coffee and sat down across from him.

"So, talk," Jade said and sipped her coffee.

"I didn't know that Detective Holloway suspected you of killing your uncle. I was following orders when I went into the next room. My job was to listen to you and inform them if your story was different than what I heard the night your uncle was found. I was doing my job."

"Would you have told me if you'd known?" Jade asked, her anger evident in her tone.

"No, but I wouldn't have done you a favor either."

"You did me a favor?" Jade raised an eyebrow.

"Well, I tried. I thought if I came with the officers who had the search warrant that I might be able to soften the blow. I volunteered to take you to the station because I thought you might need a friend."

Jade stared at him, unable to find words for a reply. She went to the kitchen and brought the coffee pot back to the table. She refilled both their cups before she said anything.

"I get that you were trying to be my friend, but wouldn't a true friend have given me a heads up about the search warrant and the questioning?"

"I thought it would be in your best interest not to tell you beforehand. Your genuine surprise and honest answers were helpful to you. Detective Holloway can spot rehearsed answers and lies in a second. The fact that your story that day matched what you told me is what kept you from being arrested on the spot."

Jade stared into his hazel eyes and searched his handsome face. She could find no sign of deceit. She saw nothing but sincerity.

"All right," she said at last. "I think we can be friends."

"You can have this now," Hudson said, with a smile that made her heart stop.

He handed her the box and watched as she opened it. She cringed when she took the bloody clothing from the box. She opened a manila envelope that had been under the clothing. Erik's wallet, car keys, and pocket change were inside.

"Where's his car?" she asked holding the keys.

"It's still being processed. I'll let you know when they've finished with it."

"I thought his laptop would be in here."

"His laptop?"

"Yes, it isn't in the house. I thought that Uncle Erik must have taken it with him."

"There's a list of the items on the box lid. I don't remember seeing a laptop on the list. Is it important?"

"He did all of his business online. I don't have the information to pay bills or anything else. Could it be in his car?" Jade asked.

"It's possible. I'll find out and let you know."

"Thank you, Hudson. I appreciate everything you've done to help."

"I'm glad to do it, and I'm happy that we can be friends. I'd better get going. I'm supposed to have Christmas supper at my parents' house in ten minutes."

Jade followed Hudson to the door and set the alarm when he'd gone outside. She put Erik's belongings back into the box and carried it to his room. She let Teddy back in and fed him before she finished packing her mother's gifts.

She was about to settle on the couch with a sandwich and watch *National Treasure* when her phone rang.

"Hi, Mom."

"Did the police officer drop by yet?"

"He left a little while ago. He gave me a box with Uncle Erik's things inside. He said the car is still being processed, whatever that means."

"Did he question you?"

"No, he did all the talking," Jade said and told her mother about their conversation.

"Have you worked on your puzzle book yet?" Mollie asked changing the subject.

"Not yet. I'm thinking about making a copy of it. That way I can have a copy to write on, and I'll always have the original to keep."

"Jade, sweetheart, I don't think that's a good idea. Erik intended for you to use and enjoy that book. What would he tell you about making copies?"

"You're right. He wouldn't want me to do that."

"No, he wouldn't," Mollie said. "I talked to Levi a little while ago. I thanked him for our scarves."

"Was he still wearing his Santa hat?"

The two women talked a little longer before saying goodnight. Jade ate her sandwich and took her empty plate to the kitchen. She glanced at the puzzle book on the bar. She wasn't ready to solve the puzzles. She wanted to treasure it for a while.

She called to Teddy, and they went upstairs for the night.

CHAPTER SEVENTEEN

Tuesday, December 26, 2017

1:15 a.m.

It was dark and cold outside. Jade was looking for Teddy. She heard howling and screaming. She couldn't tell where it was coming from. She turned when she heard a noise behind her.

A man was moving toward her with a gun. She ran, but the man kept getting closer. Tripping, she fell hard. She struggled to get up, but something was holding her down.

He was coming closer, but she couldn't see his face. Who was it? He raised the gun. She saw his finger on the trigger.

The man was standing over her, but she couldn't move. She looked to see what lay on top of her. It was a body! Uncle Erik's body!

Jade was jolted awake. Her heart thumped, and she gasped for air.

She tried to sit up, but still couldn't move. Teddy was laying on her chest, whining. He licked her face when she scratched his chin.

"I'm okay, Teddy," she said and turned on the lamp. She lay back on her pillow with relief. "It was just a bad dream."

Teddy jumped off the bed and went to the door.

"Do you need out?"

They went downstairs, and she let Teddy outside. She drank a glass of milk and ate a slice of left-over pizza while she waited for Teddy. When Teddy came back inside, she reset the alarm and made sure all the doors and windows were locked.

She gave Teddy a dog biscuit and saw the puzzle book on the bar. She picked it up and flipped through the pages again. *Mom was right. It might take my mind off of things and I won't be going back to sleep anytime soon*, she thought.

Jade carried the book upstairs, and picked up the pencil that lay on the nightstand. She stacked her pillows for back support and got into bed. Teddy snuggled beside her. The book was filled with her favorite kinds of word puzzles. There were crosswords, cryptograms, hidden word puzzles, and word searches.

She started at the front of the book and worked her way through two pages of short cryptograms. She looked at the clock. It was three in the morning, and she was getting sleepy. She remembered the nightmare, which prompted her to solve another page.

She solved the first four puzzles on the page with relative ease. The fifth puzzle was a bit more difficult than the others had been. Needing a hint, she checked the back of the book and found the solutions section.

She found the answers for the page number she'd been working on, but they were for crossword puzzles rather than cryptograms. She double-checked her page number and the coinciding solutions page.

That was odd. There didn't seem to be a page missing, and the page numbers were in the right sequence. She supposed it was possible that it had been a printing error.

I'll work on it tomorrow, she thought and put the book on the nightstand. She was about to turn off the lamp when she noticed something. Some of the page edges were a little darker that the rest. She picked up the book again.

She opened it to the first odd page. It was the page that she had been working on. She turned to the next odd page and the next and the next. All of the different pages had the wrong type of puzzle solutions in the back of the book.

This wasn't an error. These puzzles had to have been added later. Did Uncle Erik go to all this trouble for her?

Memories came flooding back. Uncle Erik used to bring her puzzles that he'd created when she was a child. He never gave her the answers.

He used to say, "Life doesn't have a solution page at the end. Sometimes you have to figure things out on your own."

All thoughts of sleep were gone. Jade picked up her pencil again and began to solve her special puzzle. The patterns and the words began to form in her mind. The last letter she needed came to her at last. She gasped when she read the entire puzzle.

Jade, you're in danger, and you're being watched. Don't trust anyone. Keep Teddy with you when possible. Stay alert!

Jade felt as if she'd fallen into an icy stream. Her mind was blank. She stared at the page for several minutes. Questions began to bubble to the surface. She wanted to know more.

Why am I in danger? Who could be watching me? He had time to put a message in a book. Why didn't he talk to me instead?

There had to be more information in the book. She solved puzzles and looked for another message until her brain demanded sleep. She put the book on the nightstand and set her alarm. The next message would have to wait until she had some rest.

8:15 a.m.

Two men sat at a corner table in the Big Texan Steak Ranch. They appeared to be sipping coffee and chatting while waiting for their breakfast.

"The girl still doesn't seem to be aware of O'Neal's research," said the tall man with the shaved head. "My contact told me that she hasn't given any opinions about how or why her uncle was killed."

"Was the police search beneficial?" asked the other man.

"There was nothing..." King broke off when the waitress approached to refill their cups. He waited until she walked away to continue, "Nothing in his office, and his office computer was clean. His house was clean, too."

"What about the girl's apartment? Will they be able to get a warrant to search there?" asked Ace.

"There's no need. She moved into O'Neal's house. She hadn't even had time to unpack. All of her belongings were searched, too. They didn't find anything."

"I suppose there's still no indication of where he went or who he talked to when the surveillance team lost him."

"No, sir. We've found nothing to indicate where he was for those few hours or where he went for his vacation."

"Are you telling me that we're no closer to finding out what evidence he had than we were in October?" Ace asked and glared at King.

"Here you are gentlemen," the waitress said. "I have a medium well T-bone with scrambled eggs."

"Right here," said Ace with a smile.

"I guess the medium rare sirloin with two eggs over easy must be yours," she said to King.

"Yes, ma'am," said King. "Thank you."

"If there's anything else y'all need, just give me a holler. My name's Misty," she said and winked at them before she walked away.

The two men cut into their steaks and waited until they were sure no one was close enough to overhear before either of them spoke again.

"There has been an interesting development," King said, before he took a bite of steak.

Ace swallowed the food he had in his mouth and asked, "What kind of development?"

"My contact inside the museum says that Renee Lanham may have been closer to O'Neal than anyone realized."

Ace put his fork down and said, "Go on."

King took a sip of coffee and said, "She has a framed photograph on her desk. She and O'Neal were hugging and smiling in the picture. It turned up a day or two after the funeral."

"That's interesting. I wouldn't have thought she was O'Neal's type," Ace observed.

"He must have been her type. My contact says she was bent out of shape when O'Neal's date turned up at the museum shindig."

"Yes, I saw his date," Ace replied. "But I missed Lanham's reaction."

"There's more. It seems that O'Neal gave Lanham a package to hold for him."

Ace sat up a bit straighter. "Does she still have it?"

"No, it was a gift for his niece. Lanham gave it to the girl the day they cleaned out his office. It happened to be in the girl's car when the police searched O'Neal's property."

They stopped talking when the waitress approached to check on them. King continued after she walked away.

"There was a movie that hadn't been opened, a puzzle book, and a card. There was nothing written in the book and nothing out of the ordinary inside. The card was the standard Merry Christmas, I love you."

"What kind of puzzle book?"

"Word puzzles, the kind you can buy just about anywhere - crosswords, word searches, that kind of thing."

"We need to find out what Lanham knows," Ace said.

"Do you want us to pick her up?"

"No, do a thorough search of her home and office first. Keep an eye on her until we know more. Is there anything that belongs to the girl that you haven't searched?"

"The police searched her car but not as thoroughly as I'd like. There's always someone nearby other than at the house. We have to worry about that damn dog there."

"Yes, I've seen that dog. He is a problem."

"We drugged him to get him out of the way when we trashed the house. I'm not sure it would be a good idea to do that again."

"No, that would alert those members of the police force who don't see things our way."

"I'd like to get a look in that backpack she carries, too, but then again, I'd have to deal with the dog."

"Have your contact that's close to her search it," suggested Ace.

"That angle has proven more difficult since she moved," King said.

"Is there a way to get hold of it while she's at work?" Ace asked.

"There might be if I send in the right person," Nelson replied. "I'll get to work on that and on her car."

Ace nodded. The two men ate the remainder of their breakfast in silence. They asked for separate checks and paid cash. King left the restaurant followed by Ace five minutes later.

10:30 a.m.

Jade overslept. She'd hit the snooze button too many times, and the alarm stopped going off. She'd still be sleeping if Teddy hadn't pawed at her arm. She had little time to take care of Teddy and get to work.

She jumped out of bed and let Teddy outside. She ran back upstairs and changed into her workout clothes. She stuffed a jerky treat in her pocket and grabbed Teddy's leash.

She took Teddy for his walk watching for strangers or someone behind her the entire time. She was relieved when they returned to the house. She fed Teddy and wolfed down the last of the breakfast casserole before she ran upstairs to shower and change.

She pondered what to do with her book. Should she leave it in the house under lock and key or take it with her? She might have some time to work on it during the day if she took it with her. But then again, there was always a chance that her backpack could be stolen.

It would be safer in the house. She didn't want to lose the book, and she didn't want anyone else to read the hidden message. She opened her closet door and took out a large box. She put the puzzle book inside with the boots her mother had given her.

She put the box back in the closet and went downstairs. She thought about leaving Teddy inside. He'd be there to greet anyone who might try to get in, but she could be later than expected. Coming home to a mess didn't appeal to her. She grabbed her keys and headed for the door.

Teddy followed her outside and watched as she filled his water dish before dashing out the gate.

11:54 a.m.

Jade arrived at the mall with only minutes to spare. She hurried inside and went straight to the boutique. There were customers lined up at the counter. Some were spending their Christmas cash while others were making returns.

She tried to behave as if nothing had changed, but she couldn't help staring at the faces of her customers and wondering. She didn't know who might be watching her or where they might be.

She didn't want them to know that she was aware. Not until she had time to figure this out. Not until she had time to deal with her fear. Not until she knew more.

She was soon too busy at work to think about anything other than her job. She took a lunch break midway through her shift and walked to the Food Court. She ordered her food and looked around her.

She wondered if someone was spying on her at that moment. She took her meal to a table and ate while she people watched. She saw nothing out of the ordinary.

She walked to the Hallmark store to buy thank you cards before she went back to the boutique. She was again too busy to worry about anyone watching her. She didn't notice the man who sat on a bench across from the boutique.

6:00 p.m.

Jade breathed a sigh of relief when it was time to go home. She walked to her car and prayed that it would start. She turned the key and was surprised when the motor puttered to life.

She drove out of the parking lot and turned left onto Soncy Road. She stopped at the pet market to get more jerky treats for Teddy. She returned to her car and decided that she'd didn't want another casserole for dinner.

She drove to a fast food restaurant and waited in the drive-through lane. She thought about the warning again. *Could someone be watching me right now?* The thought made her shiver.

She hadn't noticed the car that turned into the parking lot behind her. King had parked his Accord, so that he would be able to see her and follow in any direction she chose to take.

Jade couldn't wait to start work on the puzzles in her book again. She felt both excited and nervous about what she might find.

She ate her food in the car while she drove to Canyon. She looked at the shopping bags on the seat beside her. Teddy had already had his walk for the day. She'd put his jerky treats in the cabinet and save them for the next walk.

The thank you cards were another matter. She needed to take care of those sooner rather than later. She had intended to ship her mother's package before going to work, but that hadn't worked out.

She decided to write the thank you cards right away. It wouldn't take long, and she'd have time to solve more puzzles before going to bed. Then she'd need to make just one trip to the post office.

She parked in the driveway, leaving enough room so that her car could be jumped if needed. She supposed she could park in the garage now, but she thought that parking inside would make it more difficult for anyone to boost her battery. She didn't have the garage door opener anyway.

She hurried through the gate and braced herself for Teddy's greeting. He followed her into the house and begged for his cookie. Jade took one from the box and tossed it in his direction. He snatched it out of the air, and it was gone in seconds.

"I'll bet you're hungry, aren't you?"

Teddy wagged his tail and looked toward his food bowl. She picked up the bowl and carried it to the pantry. She scooped dog food into the bowl and carried it back to its place. She refilled his water dish and patted him on the back.

"There you go," she said.

Teddy looked up from his dinner and wagged his tail twice before burying his face in the bowl.

She gathered everything she needed to write the thank you notes and sat down at the dining table with her clipboard list. The first group of cards were easy to write. She didn't know the people who had sent flowers, and she didn't feel it necessary to include more than a simple thank you.

It was more difficult to write the cards for those people she knew. The neighbors who had been so kind to her and Erik's friends who had stood by her deserved a more personal expression of gratitude.

She was agonizing about what she should write to the Finchers' when her phone rang.

"Hi, Mom."

"Hi, how was your day?"

"I feel like I've been running all day. How was yours?"

"I have mixed feelings about today," Mollie began. "I realized that my time in New York is almost over and that I'll be going back to Dallas."

"Aren't you happy about that?" asked Jade.

"Yes and no. I'm excited about going home, but I'll have to cook and clean for myself there," Mollie replied and laughed.

"I'm glad you'll be closer to home," Jade told her.

"About that," Mollie began. "I found out today that I'm going to be relocated when I get back from Ireland."

"You are? Where will you be going?"

"Well, there are a number of possibilities, but there's only one in the States."

"Wow!" Jade said, for lack of a better word.

"Have you shipped my things yet?"

"No, I was going to do it in the morning."

"Don't ship them until I know where I'll be living," Mollie said. "I'll have to start packing for the trip and the move when I get back to Dallas."

"Will you know where you're moving before you leave New York?"

"I think so, but I'm not sure. I'll let you know as soon as I know. I was hoping," Mollie hesitated. "That you might want to join me when you graduate."

"That would be awesome," Jade said. "It would depend on where you end up though."

"Does it matter?"

"Well, yeah, I don't want to live just any old place," Jade teased. "A college graduate with my credentials needs to live in the right place."

Mollie and Jade laughed long and loud.

"It will depend on the job situation when I graduate," Jade told her mother. "I'll need to go where I can find work."

"I know, and we have a few months before we have to make that decision."

"You won't be able to come visit before you leave for Ireland, will you?" Jade asked.

"No, sweetheart, I won't," Mollie said. "I had planned on it, but I won't have the time now."

"That's okay. We can still talk with Skype and on the phone."

"I'm not sure we'll be able to do either while I'm away. I don't know what kind of internet or phone service I'll have."

"I hadn't thought about that. I know it's hard to talk to Levi at times."

"And he uses the military's service. I'll try to get in touch with you, but I don't want to make a promise that I may not be able to keep."

"Once a week would be great if you can manage it," Jade said.

"I'll do my best," said Mollie. "Have you worked on your puzzle book yet?"

"I worked a couple of pages. I'm planning to work a few more when I've finished the thank you notes."

"Are they helping?"

"You know, I think they are. I have something to look forward to when I get home from work."

Jade chose not to mention the message she'd found. She didn't want her mother to worry.

"I'm sure Erik would be pleased. I'll let you get back to writing those notes. I'll talk to you later. I love you."

"I love you, too, Mom. Goodnight."

Jade labored over the thank you notes for another hour before she finished. She put them away and went upstairs. She got ready for bed and took her puzzle book from the boot box.

She settled into bed with Teddy at her side. She set her alarm and opened the book. She was solving her third short puzzle when she drifted off to sleep.

CHAPTER EIGHTEEN

WEDNESDAY, December 27, 2017

8:00 a.m.

The next thing Jade knew, her alarm was going off. The lamp had been on all night. She'd fallen asleep before she'd found another clue. The puzzle book was on the floor and she had no idea what happened to her pencil.

She picked up the book and put it on the nightstand. She got up and stretched. It was the first good night's sleep she'd had since she'd found Erik's body.

Going downstairs, she let Teddy outside. She started her morning coffee and made herself some toast. She filled Teddy's food bowl and let him back inside before going upstairs to get ready for work.

She had the earlier shift at work today. She'd be home early enough to take Teddy for his walk and still have time to work on the puzzles.

She glanced at the puzzle book. She was tempted to solve one more. She knew that she wouldn't stop at one and would be late for work. Instead, she picked it up and carried it to the closet. She returned it to its hiding place in the boot box and went downstairs.

Jade picked up her keys and her backpack. Teddy followed her outside and waited while she locked the door. She scratched his ears and walked toward the gate. Teddy was making himself comfortable on the patio lounge chair when she closed the gate and climbed into her car.

The car protested when she turned the key. She said a silent prayer and tried again. This time the motor caught. She let it idle for a few minutes before backing out of the driveway. *I've got to get this thing fixed,* she thought, as she drove toward Twenty-Third Street.

She didn't notice the gray Honda Accord that had been parked at the end of the street, or that it was three cars behind her on I-27. She didn't notice that it parked a few rows past where she had parked when she got to work.

Jade arrived at the boutique to find that her manager was already there. Paula Hicks was a tall slender blonde with brown eyes and a toothy smile.

"Good morning, Paula."

"Good morning, Jade," Paula replied and unlocked the door. "How are you doing this morning?"

"I'm okay."

Paula looked at Jade with disbelief. "You look so tired. Are you getting any sleep?"

"Last night was the first good night's sleep I've had in a while," Jade said and tried to hide a yawn.

"I hope that continues."

"Me, too!"

They worked together to open the store for the day before Paula went to her office.

Jade kept herself busy straightening the merchandise and dusting shelves until her coworker Lisa arrived for her shift.

"Jade would you come to my office for a minute, please?" Paula asked from the back of the store.

Jade went to Paula's office and sat down in the chair across from her boss.

"Jade, I can't begin to tell you how much I've appreciated the way you've stepped up during the holidays. You've worked double shifts and covered shifts when some of your coworkers didn't bother to show up. Thank you."

"You're welcome," Jade replied but sensed that Paula had more to say.

"Corporate appreciates your hard work, too. However, my supervisor has informed me that I've been violating company policy by allowing you to work so many hours.

You were hired as a part-time employee with a maximum of thirty-five hours a week. You've surpassed that limit every week since Thanksgiving and have approached forty hours at least twice."

Jade's stomach began to do flip flops.

"What are your plans for the future?" Paula asked.

"I'll graduate with a bachelor's degree in May. I plan to work for a while before I start on a master's degree. I'd like to be a museum curator someday."

"I see," Paula said and paused. "You're my best employee, but I risk being fired if I continue to violate company policy by letting you work more than thirty-five hours a week."

Paula took a sip from her coffee mug.

Jade swallowed hard trying to get rid of the lump that had formed in her throat. She clasped her hands and hoped that Paula couldn't see them shaking. *Am I about to be fired?* she wondered.

Paula looked at Jade and folded her arms on the desk. I have two options. One, is to cut your hours back.

Jade nodded. Fewer hours was much better than being fired.

"The second option is to offer you the position of assistant manager."

Jade gaped at her boss.

Paula smiled. "Are you interested?"

"I don't know what to say. I never expected..." Jade couldn't find the words to continue.

"We can work around your school schedule, and as a full-time employee, you'd qualify for the benefits package. You'd have health insurance, a retirement fund, and paid time off."

"That sounds great!" Jade replied. "What would I be responsible for?"

"You and I would alternate shifts. You'll cover for me when I have to be away. You'd be responsible for creating the work schedule and doing a lot of what I do on a daily basis."

"Will I need to sign a contract?" asked Jade.

"Yes. The contract is for two years. That's why I wanted to know about your plans."

"When would I start?"

"The position won't be available until the first of February. In the meantime, I'll have to cut your hours, but I'll make sure you get at least thirty a week. That will give you an additional five hours to work if needed."

"I'd like to think about it," Jade said. "When do you need an answer?"

"There's no rush. I'd like you to keep this conversation between the two of us. You can talk to family members of course, but don't tell the other girls. Corporate didn't want word getting out about the position, but I don't want to lose you. I'll let you know when the job is posted, and we'll take it from there."

"Thank you. I can't tell you how much this means to me," Jade said with a smile.

"Let's take a look at the schedule and see what hours you want to work for the next couple of weeks," Paula suggested.

"Would it be possible for me to have tomorrow off? I need to take my car to a mechanic, or I might not be able to get here at all."

Paula and Jade planned her work schedule for the following

two weeks. She would be opening the store five times a week and working six-hour shifts. That would give her time to take better care of Teddy and to work on solving the puzzles.

Jade left Paula's office and went to the front of the store. Lisa was helping a customer at the checkout counter. Jade approached a woman who was standing by the shoe section.

"Is there something that I can help you find?" Jade asked.

The woman didn't look at Jade. "Yes, do you happen to have these in size seven?"

"Hi, Ms. Steen," Jade answered with a smile.

"Oh! Hello, Jade. Please, call me Kathy."

"I'll see if we have your size in the back," Jade said, taking the red kitten heel shoe from Kathy's hand.

Jade returned a few minutes later with the right size shoe and waited while Kathy Steen tried them on.

"May I return these if they don't match my dress?"

"We accept returns with a receipt for up to thirty days," Jade informed her.

"I think I'll give these a try then."

"Is there anything else that I can help you with?"

"I'd like to try a pair of jeans that I found earlier. Where are the dressing rooms?"

"They're right over here," Jade said, leading the way.

Jade gave Kathy her privacy and returned to straightening the merchandise. She was startled by someone tapping her on the shoulder.

"Hi, Roomie!"

"Heather? What are you doing here?"

"I came to the mall to return an ugly sweater that I got for Christmas. I decided to stop by and see you."

"Did you have a good Christmas?" Jade asked.

"It was all right. How are you doing?" asked Heather.

"I'm doing okay."

"Liar," said Heather and changed the subject. "My cousin is

moving in next week. Stephanie needs you to sign some paperwork as soon as you can."

"I'll try to get by there tomorrow."

Kathy Steen exited the dressing room and said, "Jade, I'll take the shoes and the jeans."

Jade took the items to the cash register. Heather took a skirt and a sweater into the dressing room while Jade completed Kathy's transaction.

"It was nice to see you again, Jade." Kathy said with a warm smile.

"It was good to see you, too. Have a Happy New Year."

"Who was that?" Lisa asked.

"She went out with my uncle a few times before he died," Jade answered. "I don't know anything else about her."

"Jade, I want this sweater, but the skirt isn't for me," Heather said when she left the dressing room.

"I'll put the skirt away," Lisa offered.

"Thanks," said Heather. "This sweater is a lot nicer than the one I returned at the other store. I don't know what my aunt was thinking when she picked that one."

Jade rang up the sweater and waved Heather out of the store. The rest of her shift was uneventful, and she drove right home when she got off work.

4:30 p.m.

Teddy had been sleeping on the patio lounge chair when Jade opened the gate. He bounded toward her but obeyed her command to stay rather than running over her.

"Good boy, Teddy! I think you deserve two cookies."

Teddy looked at her as if he agreed and followed her into the house. Jade tossed a dog biscuit to him and waited until he'd finished before she tossed the second.

Jade wanted to relax on the couch with her puzzle book. She

knew that if she did, she wouldn't want to stop and take Teddy for his walk. She decided to take him right away and went upstairs to change.

She was dressed in ten minutes and went downstairs. She put a jerky treat in her pocket and took the leash from the hook. Teddy was ready and waiting. She hooked the leash onto his harness, and they were on their way.

They followed their normal track around the campus. She gave Teddy his prize when they reached the tree near the Chapel. A tall man with a shaved head walked a toy poodle on the sidewalk nearby. Something about the man seemed familiar. Jade wracked her brain but couldn't place where or when she'd seen him before.

Teddy finished eating the jerky and rolled around on the grass for a few minutes before Jade tugged on the leash. She was ready to go home and relax.

Nelson King followed a block behind. He put the little dog back in the yard where he had found it and made his way to his car.

Jade went upstairs to the closet. She took the puzzle book from its hiding place in the boot box. She propped the pillows up on her bed and sat down to finish the puzzle page she'd already begun.

The third short puzzle on the page wasn't an easy one to solve. At last, the patterns began to take shape, and she found the solution. Her pulse quickened as she read.

Don't share this book or its contents with anyone. Not even your mother and brother. It's possible that someone could be listening to your conversations. Keep the book safe. Keep Teddy close. Be careful and alert.

Jade was frustrated. She didn't need another warning. She needed answers. Who could be listening and how? Was her phone bugged? Were there listening devices in the house? What's going on?

She got up, tucked the book under her arm and her pencil behind her ear. She went downstairs to the refrigerator and rummaged for a snack. It occurred to her while she opened a container of ranch dip that she hadn't been alert today. She'd been so busy at work that she hadn't paid attention to her surroundings. Her thoughts were on the book rather than what was going on around her while she and Teddy walked.

She thought about the man she'd seen walking the poodle. She still didn't know where she'd seen him before.

She took a bag of chips and the dip to the living room and settled on the couch. She snacked and solved another page. The next section of puzzles were crosswords. She'd been working on the puzzle for more than an hour when the doorbell rang.

She closed her book and tucked it under the couch cushion before answering the door. Teddy's ears were at attention, and he followed her to the door. She peeked through the peep hole to see Hudson Bailey.

She opened the door and said, "Hi, Hudson. What's up?"

Teddy woofed hello.

Hudson smiled and held up a small device. "I thought you might like to have the garage door opener from your uncle's car."

"Thank you! Come in."

"I can't stay. We're on our way back to the station," he said pointing toward his police cruiser and his partner Ronny Hague. "We were on a call a few blocks from here and thought we'd bring this by."

"Is Uncle Erik's laptop in his car?" Jade asked.

"No. I checked the contents list and asked the man in charge."

"I wonder where it could be."

"We may never know," Hudson told her.

Hague honked the horn, and Hudson waved at him. "I'll talk to you later. We have to do reports before we can call it a day."

"Thanks again, Hudson."

She closed the door and watched him walk away through the peep hole. There was no denying that Hudson Bailey looked even more handsome in uniform.

Teddy nuzzled her hand while she watched the officers drive away.

"Are you hungry, Teddy?"

Teddy wagged his tail and woofed. He went to the kitchen and waited beside his empty food bowl. Jade filled the bowl before returning to the couch and her puzzle.

She took the book from under the cushion and opened it to the crossword she'd been working. She gasped when she realized it was another message. She needed to find five more words, two words across and three words down.

She worked half an hour before she finished and was able to read the message.

Jade watch National Treasure movie.

Jade took the stairs two at a time to her room. She searched for several minutes before she remembered that it was downstairs but never got around to watching it.

She ran downstairs and found the movie on the bar. She tore the shrink wrap away and put it into the Blu-ray player.

She went to the kitchen and popped a bag of microwave popcorn and grabbed a Dr. Pepper from the fridge. She settled on the couch with Teddy and pushed play.

She watched and enjoyed her popcorn until the characters in the movie were examining the Declaration of Independence. She watched until the end of the scene and then backed it up and watched again.

Jade gaped at the screen and dropped a handful of popcorn. Teddy gobbled up the kernels that had fallen to the floor. She stopped the movie and went upstairs to her uncle's bedroom. She searched through the boxes she'd stored there until she found the metal box that had been in Erik's office desk.

She took out the photograph and turned it over. The numbers were arranged in groups of three. It had to be a cipher like the one in the movie.

"How am I going to break this code?" she asked the ceiling. "Which book or text am I supposed to use?"

She turned the photo over and stared at the young smiling faces of her dad and her uncle. She left her uncle's room and returned to the living room. She sat on the couch with the picture against her chest and started the movie again.

"There might be more clues for me in the movie," she told Teddy.

Jade watched the movie three times. She was no closer to breaking the cipher than she'd been when she found the photo. She wandered around the house looking for anything that would point her in the right direction.

It was getting late, and she needed to be up early. She let Teddy out and stared at her puzzle book. *There could be another message in the book,* she thought.

She cleaned up her mess and made sure the house was secure. She picked up the book and the photo before letting Teddy inside. The two of them went upstairs for the night.

Teddy made himself comfortable on Jade's bed while she changed into her pajamas. She crawled into bed and solved two more crossword puzzles. Neither of them held messages or answers for her.

She looked at the time on her cell phone. *Mom hasn't called tonight,* she thought. She tapped her mother's number into the phone and waited. It went to voice mail.

Jade left a message. "Hi, Mom. I thought I'd check in and see how your day has been. I'll call you tomorrow. I love you."

She tried to focus on the next puzzle. Brain fog was rolling in, and she couldn't concentrate.

"Do you think the answers will come to me in my sleep, Teddy?" she yawned.

Teddy tapped his tail twice and looked at her as if he thought sleep was a great idea.

"Good night, Teddy," she said and turned off the lamp.

CHAPTER NINETEEN

Thursday, December 28, 2019

8:30 a.m.

Jade got up and dressed in jeans and a sweatshirt. She brushed the tangles out of her long brown hair and went downstairs. She hoped to have all of her errands run early, so that she could spend the rest of the day looking for the next message from her uncle.

She let Teddy outside and made a list of all the things she needed to do. She picked up the garage door opener, her backpack, and her keys and headed out the door.

The first stop was the post office to mail the thank you cards she'd written. Next, she took her uncle's gifts and donated them to one of the churches. She knew that the various clothing items would be given to those who needed them.

She then went to the City of Canyon offices to find out about paying the water bill. She explained her situation to the clerk and was directed to a desk in the far corner of the room.

Jade made her way to the desk of a large round woman with a bright smile and dancing brown eyes.

"Sit down, relax," said Chela Maldonado. "I was about to refill my coffee cup. Would you like some coffee or a donut?"

"No, thank you."

"I'm not myself until I've had four or five cups in the morning. This will be my third. I'll be right back."

Jade watched the woman waddle to the break room. Chela returned with a fresh cup of coffee and a chocolate donut.

"Now, what can I do for you?"

"My name is Jade O'Neal. My uncle, Erik O'Neal, recently passed away. He paid all of his bills online, but the laptop he used is missing. I don't know how much is owed, or when the payments are due."

"I'm sorry for your loss," Chela said with empathy. "When did he pass?"

"Two weeks ago."

She reached across the desk and squeezed Jade's hand. "I'll keep you in my thoughts and prayers."

"Thank you," Jade said fighting back tears.

"Let's see what I can do here," Chela said changing the subject. "What's the address?"

Jade gave the woman the address and waited while she tapped the computer keys and pulled up the file.

"The account is current. The payments are due on the first of the month," Chela informed her. "Is anyone living in the home now?"

"Yes, my family inherited his house. I'm living there for the time being, so that I can take care of his dog," Jade replied.

"The account is enrolled in paperless statements. Do you have access to that email?"

"No, I don't."

"All right, let's add your email address so that you'll get the statements, too. The account is set up for automatic draft from the bank. Would you like to change that?"

"I'd rather wait until everything is settled," Jade replied. "My family and I haven't discussed our options yet."

"That's fine. What's your email address?" asked Chela.

Jade gave her the information and watched the woman tap the keys on the keyboard.

"You're all set," Chela said. "Let us know if there's anything else we can do for you."

"I will, thank you," Jade said and waved goodbye.

She visited the electric company and the gas company. She learned that their statements were also emailed and setup for automatic draft. She arranged to have those sent to her email address as well.

Her next stop was the bank. She needed to know if there was enough money available in Erik's account to pay the bills. She'd have to figure out another way to make the payments if not.

Jade went inside the bank and explained why she was there to the first person she saw. She was directed to a small office across the lobby. She tapped on the door with the nameplate Marcie Johnson, Vice President.

"Come in," said Ms. Johnson. "Please, have a seat. What can I do for you today?"

"I'm Jade O'Neal. Erik O'Neal was my uncle, and he had an account here. He passed away two weeks ago."

"I'm sorry to hear that. Erik was a nice man."

"Yes, he was," Jade replied. "I've been to all the utility companies today to find out about paying his bills. I've been told that he had them set up for automatic draft from his account each month. I need to know if there's enough money in his account to pay those bills."

"Let's find out," said Marcie. "Do you happen to know his account number?"

"No, I'm sorry."

"What about his social security number?"

"Yes, I have it saved in my phone," Jade replied and took her phone from her backpack.

She tapped the phone a few times and read the number. Ms. Johnson entered the information into the computer.

"Your uncle's check from the Panhandle Plains Historical Museum is deposited into this account every month. I'd say, based on his past expenses, there's enough to pay drafted bills for another month. It could be more depending on when his last check is received."

"Can you tell me how much is in there?"

"I'm sorry, no. Your name isn't on the account. I can tell you that you are listed as payee in the event of death. I'll need a copy of the death certificate before I can release the money to you."

"I see. Can I make deposits into the account?"

"Yes, but you wouldn't be able to get a balance or make withdrawals."

Jade sat in thought for a moment. "Will I be able to keep this account open once I have the death certificate?"

"No, we'd have to set up a new account in your name and then transfer the money."

"I'll take care of that when the copies of the death certificate arrive. Thank you for your time."

"You're welcome."

Jade left the bank feeling that she'd accomplished nothing. She knew there would be enough money to pay the bills at least once more. She'd have to transfer everything into her name and set up payments at some point. Her hands were tied for now.

She got into her car and turned the key. Clickclickclick.

"No, not again," Jade said and smacked the dash with her fist. "I just have one more stop, and then I'll take you to the mechanic. I promise."

She turned the key again. Nothing. She got out of the car and raised the hood. She jiggled the battery cables and noticed they were corroded. She grabbed her backpack and her keys and walked to a convenience store across the street. She bought a bottle of Coke and walked back to the car.

She opened the bottle and poured the soda a little at a time over the battery cables. The corrosion dissolved and Jade tried the start the car again. The motor caught. She pumped her fist in the air, got out of the car, and slammed the hood down. She let the car idle and debated about going to the mechanic next.

She wouldn't be able to finish her errands if she had to leave her Malibu for repairs. She had one more stop to make, and she didn't relish the idea of walking that far. There was no one that she could call for a ride. She supposed she could call an Uber, but she had no idea how much the car repairs were going to be. She needed to save as much money as she could.

Jade put the car in gear and drove to her old apartment building. She parked the car and walked to Stephanie Hancock's office.

"Hi, Stephanie."

"Hi, Jade. How are you?"

"I'm doing okay. Heather said that I need to sign some papers."

"Yes, give me a minute to find them. Have a seat."

Jade obeyed and watched Stephanie search through file cabinets and her desk drawers.

"Someone was in here asking about you the other day," Stephanie said while she searched.

"Do you know who it was?" Jade asked surprised.

"No, I can't remember his name. I'd never seen him before. He said he was an old friend of your uncle's."

"What did he look like?"

"He was tall and muscular. He was good looking even with his head shaved."

Jade felt every nerve in her body tingle on high alert.

"Here it is," Stephanie said and handed Jade the paperwork. "If you'll sign beside the sticky notes, you'll no longer be a tenant here."

Jade signed the papers and handed the apartment keys to Stephanie. "What did the man want to know about me?"

"I don't remember exactly. It was just small talk. He was asking about renting an apartment and mentioned that he knew your uncle."

Jade was curious but knew she'd get no more information. "Thanks, Stephanie. I appreciate your help." Jade said.

"You're welcome," Stephanie said. "Just don't spread it around. I don't want the other tenants to get the idea that I'm an easy touch." She smiled and said, "Take care of yourself, Jade."

"I will."

Jade walked to her car and took in her surroundings. She tried to stay alert, but she often forgot during her day to day activities. She wondered if the man who had questioned Stephanie about her was the man she'd seen on her walk with Teddy.

She got into her car and prayed it would start when she turned the key. It started without a problem, and she pointed it in the direction of the mechanic.

She arrived at Tyree Automotive to find the owner standing outside the shop. Chris Tyree was a tall, thin man with long salt and pepper hair tied back in a ponytail. A handle bar mustache and a goatee adorned his face. He raised his bushy eyebrows when he saw Jade climb out of her car.

"What can I do for you, young lady?"

"My car needs help," Jade told him. "My uncle told me you're the best mechanic in town, so I brought it to you."

"Who's your uncle?" asked Tyree pleased with the compliment.

"Erik O'Neal."

Tyree's face dropped. "I was sorry to hear about Erik. He was a good guy."

"Yes, he was," Jade replied. "Can you help me?"

"What's the problem?"

"The most immediate problem is that sometimes it starts; sometimes it doesn't. I've had to be boosted a few times."

"The motor doesn't sound too good either," Chris said. "Let's pull it into the bay here, and I'll take a look at it."

Jade climbed in and drove into the garage guided by Chris. She left the keys inside and climbed out.

"What's wrong with your door?"

"It was hit in the parking lot at work one day, and I haven't been able to open it since. Can you fix that?"

"I don't do body work, but I'll send you to someone who does."

"Do you have any idea how much this is going to cost? I'm a little strapped for cash right now."

"I'll run diagnostics on it and see what it needs. We'll talk about what has to be done right away and what can wait. You can wait in the office there until I'm done."

Jade walked to the office and sat down in an upholstered chair. The arms and the seat were worn and dingy. The room had the smell of oil, grease, and tires.

She'd been waiting for half an hour when her cell phone rang.

"Jade, this is Logan."

"Hi, Logan," she answered with surprise.

"Are you working today?"

"Not today. I'm running errands."

"Cool! Would you like to have dinner with me tonight?"

"Yes, I'd love to."

"I thought we'd have a nice dinner and maybe see a movie."

"That sounds good."

"I'll pick you up at six."

"Okay, I'll see you then."

Jade ended the call and smiled. *Teddy didn't scare him away after all,* she thought.

Chris Tyree walked into the office and sat at the counter. He typed some information into his computer, and his printer began to spit out sheets of paper. He collected the papers and called Jade to the counter.

"There's a lot of work that needs to be done to get your car running the way it should," he told her and handed her the printout.

Jade's mouth dropped open. "Holy Cow! That's a lot of money! I can't afford all of this right now!"

"I know," he told her. "Most of this can wait for a little while. The battery needs to be replaced now. It also needs an oil change. The rest of the repairs can be done later, but you can't wait too long."

"How much for the battery and the oil change?" Jade asked concerned.

"It'll be about seventy-five dollars."

"Will that solve the starting problem?"

"Yeah, your battery is bad. I didn't find an issue with your starter or your alternator."

"Okay, let's do it," Jade said. "I'll take care of the rest when I have the money."

"I'll get started on it."

"Will I have time to grab some lunch while you're working?"

"Sure, if you'll leave me your number, I'll call you when it's done."

Jade walked down the street and got a hamburger. She was excited about having dinner with Logan. She sat in the restaurant and planned the rest of her day. She'd take Teddy for his walk when she got home, giving her time to solve more puzzles before she had to get ready for her date.

She looked at her cell phone. Her mother hadn't returned her call. She thought about calling her again but didn't want to disturb her at work. She made a mental note to call before going out with Logan.

She finished her lunch and was refilling her soda when her cell phone rang.

"Your car is ready," Tyree said.

"I'm on my way," Jade said and walked back to the garage.

She was a block away when she saw a tall man with a shaved

head leave the garage. She slowed down and watched him get into a gray Honda Accord and drive away. Was he the man who'd asked Stephanie about her?

Jade went into the office and paid for her car repairs.

"Who was that man?" she asked Tyree. "He looked familiar."

"I don't know. He asked for directions and left. He didn't give his name." Chris handed her a receipt and said, "Don't wait too long for those other repairs. You might find yourself on foot."

"I won't. Thank you."

Jade made her way home and took Teddy for his walk. She kept an eye out for the man she'd seen at the garage. She saw no one else during their walk and hurried home.

She dressed in her favorite jeans and a blue sweater she'd gotten for Christmas. She pulled on her new boots and freshened her makeup. She was ready when Logan rang the doorbell.

"Hi, Logan," she said when she opened the door. "Let me put Teddy outside, and I'll be ready to go. You can come in if you'd like."

"Thanks, but I'll wait here."

She let Teddy outside and joined Logan on the porch.

"Is it safe to kiss you now?" Logan asked with a grin.

"I think so."

He put his arm around her and pulled her close. He caressed her cheek with his free hand and leaned in to kiss her. It was a soft, gentle kiss that left Jade wanting more.

Logan stepped back and said, "We'd better get going."

He escorted her to the car and opened the door for her. He made sure that she was inside before he closed the door and walked to the driver's side.

"I thought we'd go to a steakhouse," he said as he started the engine. "We may not make it to a movie if we have to wait a long time."

"That's okay with me," Jade said.

They arrived at the steakhouse to find that their wait would be only twenty minutes. They sat down to wait their turn when Jade heard someone calling her name.

"How are you this evening, Miss O'Neal?"

"Hello, Mr. Lee," Jade said. "I'm doing well. How are you?"

"Very well, thank you."

"I'd like you to meet my friend, Logan Rhodes," Jade began the introduction. "Logan this is Wilson Lee."

The two men shook hands and exchanged pleasantries.

"Are you here alone?" Jade asked.

"No, my dinner partner has gone to the ladies' room," Lee said. "Ah, here she comes."

He held his arm out in welcome to a pretty blonde. "I'd like you both to meet Kathy."

"Jade and I have met," said Kathy Steen. "But I haven't met this handsome young man."

Logan blushed with pleasure and said, "It's nice to meet you. I'm Logan Rhodes."

"It's nice to meet you, too."

"How are you doing since Erik passed away?" Lee asked.

"I'm getting by," Jade replied. "Some days are harder than others"

"I'm sure that's true," said Lee. "Do the police have any ideas who might have killed him?"

"I hope they do," said Jade. "But they haven't been sharing information with me."

She was relieved when the hostess called, "Lee, party of two."

"Enjoy your evening," said Lee and turned to follow the hostess.

Jade and Logan were soon shown to their table as well. They ordered their drinks and perused the menus.

"That was kind of awkward, wasn't it?" said Logan.

"Yes, it was, but I'm getting used to it," Jade replied.

The waiter returned with the drinks and took their orders. Logan reached across the table and took Jade's hand.

"I'm sorry that I haven't been around much. I went home for Christmas, and I've been working a lot of hours since I got back."

"That's okay. I've been working a lot, too," Jade told him. "That's going to change now that the holidays are over."

They talked about the holidays and their busy schedules until their food arrived. Both were hungry and their conversation stalled while they ate. They ordered dessert and continued their conversation.

"I'm sorry about Teddy's behavior the last time we went out. I think if we try introducing you to him a little at a time, he'll come around."

"I don't know, Jade. It was obvious that he didn't like me."

"We'll have to make sure you aren't touching me when you meet him again."

"Do you think that's why he acted that way?"

"It's possible. There's one way to find out." Jade said.

Their dessert arrived, and Logan ate without looking at Jade.

"Are you okay?" she asked.

"Yeah," Logan replied. "But I don't think I'm ready to meet Teddy again just yet."

"Oh, okay," Jade replied with surprise. "You don't have to meet him tonight. We can try it another time."

"I think another time would be great."

Logan paid for their meal, and they walked to his car.

"Are you a Star Wars fan?" Logan asked. *The Last Jedi* is playing."

"I love Star Wars. What time does it start?"

"If we hurry, we can get there by the time all the previews are over."

"Let's go."

They drove to the movie theater and skipped the concessions. They bought their tickets and found two seats near the screen. It was so close that Jade felt as if she were part of the action.

Logan drove her home and walked her to the door. He held her face in both hands and gave her a slow, sweet kiss. She was disappointed when the kiss ended, and he backed away.

"Would you like to come in?" she asked.

"Not until I'm ready to make nice with Teddy," Logan replied. "I don't want him to take a bite out of me while we're...uh...close."

"He wouldn't do that! He's a sweetheart."

"I'm sure you see him that way, but he scares the shit out of me," Logan said with a smirk.

Jade laughed and said, "I hear that he takes some getting used to."

"Goodnight, Jade," Logan said and kissed her again.

Jade waved at him and closed the door. She let Teddy inside and set the alarm. She went upstairs with Teddy at her heels.

"Teddy, you're wrecking my love life," she told him as she got ready for bed.

Teddy ignored her and settled himself on the bed.

She was about to crawl under the covers when her phone rang.

"Hi, Mom!" Jade answered. "How are things going?"

"Good! How are things there?" Mollie replied.

"I'd say things are improving."

Jade told her mother about what she'd learned while running errands. She told her about her car repairs and about her date with Logan.

"Paula offered me a full-time job today," Jade said. "I'd have benefits, and we can work around my school schedule."

"That's wonderful news, sweetheart. Are you going to take it?"

"I think so. It won't start until February. I'll be getting fewer hours until then, but I could start working toward my master's sooner."

"I have some news, too," Mollie began. "I'm moving to New York."

"That's great, Mom!"

"I've been looking at apartments. That's why I didn't call last night."

"Have you found one?"

"There's one a few blocks from the office. I could walk to work. Apartments here are much more expensive than in Dallas. They're smaller too. I'll have to sell some of my furniture and maybe my car."

"I might be interested in your car if mine keeps giving me problems," Jade joked. "When are you going to have time to pack?"

"I fly back to Dallas tomorrow afternoon. I'll pack until I have to leave for the trip to Ireland, and I'll finish what's left when I get home."

"Don't worry about calling me when you get home," Jade told her mother. "I know you're going to be busy."

"I'll try to call you while I'm away. I need to start packing for the trip back to Dallas."

"Okay, have a good trip and take lots of pictures. I love you."

"I love you, too.

The call ended, and Jade stared at the phone, wishing that she could see her mother. She pushed that thought from her mind and turned off the lamp.

CHAPTER TWENTY

3:25 a.m.

Jade and Teddy were walking around campus. The sunny afternoon turned dark and ominous. Quickening their pace, they turned the corner toward the house. Someone was shouting at them.

"Jade! Run!" yelled Uncle Erik. "Get out of here!"

She looked around her. She wasn't on the street anymore. She was in a strange building. It was dark. Someone stood in the corner. Teddy was gone.

"Don't trust anyone!" her mother said.

"You're in danger!" Levi shouted. "Stay alert!"

"You can trust us," said several voices in unison.

Faces of people she knew and of those she'd seen floated in front of her. "We'd never hurt you," they said. "We're your friends."

She ran out of the building. The faces of Logan, Tommy,

Heather, Renee, Bear and half a dozen nameless people followed as if they were balloons on a string.

Terrified, she ran down the street and into a convenience store.

"You're coming with me," said the tall man with a shaved head.

She had nowhere to run. She was surrounded by the faces. The man reached for her with a sinister smile.

Jade woke up screaming. Teddy whined and licked her face. She turned on the lamp and sat on the edge of the bed. She sat there until her heart rate slowed, and she could breathe again.

"It's okay, Teddy," she said rubbing the giant dog's neck. "It was another bad dream."

She went to the bathroom and splashed water on her face. Her reflection in the mirror looked pale and frightened.

"You need to get a grip," she said to the mirror and went back to the bedroom.

She crawled back under the covers and wrapped her arms around Teddy. He was warm and comforting, and she drifted off to sleep again.

8:30 a.m.

Nelson King waited at a diner and sipped his coffee. He was worried. Two meetings within a week meant that Ace was getting impatient. He was already dangerous, and impatience made him reckless and unpredictable.

Ace was rubbing the back of his neck with his left hand when he entered the restaurant. He didn't like meeting with King in front of witnesses, but the chill of the late December mornings would make outdoor meetings noticeable.

He sat down in the booth across the table from King. The two men gave their waitress their orders and waited for her to move away.

Ace stared at King and waited.

"We've got nothing," King began. "Lanham's house, office, and car are clean. The girl uses that backpack as a purse, and there was nothing out of the ordinary inside. She's started parking her car in the garage, so I haven't been able to search it."

The waitress brought their drinks and walked away before Ace spoke.

"I think it's time to talk to the Lanham woman in person."

"She trusts the contact in the museum. He could talk to her."

Ace thought for a moment while he sipped his coffee.

"All right. I'd rather not risk exposing my part in this."

"And if she won't talk?" King asked.

"Dispose of her. We can't risk her talking to the authorities."

"What about the girl?"

"We need to discredit her, or better yet, make sure she's in jail and can't hurt us," Ace said. "Our police contacts haven't been successful so far. Make sure she's their number one suspect, and that they find the evidence they need."

Their food arrived, and they busied themselves with eating their breakfast.

King swallowed a bite of eggs and asked, "Is there a plan B?"

Ace took a bite of his toast and sipped his coffee before answering.

"Bring her in if all else fails. We'll make it look like a suicide or a tragic accident when I've finished with her."

"Yes, sir."

With their business was concluded, they appeared to be old friends having a meal together. They talked about sports and the weather. They discussed their plans for the New Year. No one in the restaurant would have guessed their true purpose.

They finished their meals and shook hands. King paid his check and left the restaurant. Ace waited until he saw King drive away before paying for his meal and going to his office.

9:45 a.m.

Jade was stopped at a traffic light on the way to work when she noticed a black Toyota Avalon much too close to her rear bumper. *Is that car following me?*

The warnings from her uncle and the dream she'd had made her tense and nervous. She knew she hadn't been on guard enough during the past week. That had to change. She'd seen the man with the shaved head too many times to think it was just coincidence. She was sure he'd been watching her. She had no idea how many others might be watching her as well.

The light turned green, and she sped away. She turned right onto a side street without using her turn signal and held her breath. The car didn't follow.

She exhaled with relief and drove to the mall. She parked near the entrance and walked inside. She was a few minutes early and had to wait for Paula to arrive and open the store.

"Good morning, Jade," Paula said, pulling her keys from her pocket. "You didn't sleep well last night, did you?"

"No, I had another nightmare. It was creepy."

"I have insomnia from time to time. It gets to the point that I sleep when I can. Maybe you should take a nap when you get home," Paula suggested.

"I might do that," Jade replied. "Do you have a minute to talk?"

"Let's get the day started. I'll get us something from the Food Court, and we can talk until we get busy."

Jade and Paula opened the store. The mall was seldom busy this early in the day. Paula made her way through the mall while Jade waited for customers.

Paula returned with coffee and cinnamon rolls. They sat at the checkout counter and enjoyed their snacks for a few minutes.

"What did you want to talk about?" asked Paula. "I hope you're going to tell me you want the job."

"Actually," Jade replied with a grin. "I do. I'm excited about it."

"Wonderful! That's a load off my mind."

"There is something you should know first," Jade began. "I

haven't told anyone except my mother about it. You may not want me to take the job."

"It sounds serious," Paula said.

"It is." Jade hesitated before continuing. "The police seem to think that I had something to do with Uncle Erik's death."

"Are you kidding?" Paula asked flabbergasted.

"They've searched the house, my car, and all my belongings. I had to go in for questioning the day after the funeral. I don't know if they'll question me again or if they'll arrest me at some point. I don't know what's going to happen."

"No wonder you're not sleeping and having nightmares! Finding your uncle was bad enough, but to be suspected of killing him...I just can't believe it."

"I've been told not to leave the area. I haven't heard anything from the police since then, and I don't know what's happening with the investigation. I don't know if there are any other suspects. I don't know what to do."

"Do you have a good attorney?" Paula asked.

"Yes, I do. I haven't told her about being questioned. Should I call her?"

"Yes! Call her and tell her everything the police said. She might be able to find out how their investigation is taking shape. You'll need her if they question you again or arrest you."

"I'll call this afternoon."

"I think you should call her now," Paula suggested. "We aren't busy, and this is important."

"Will this affect the job offer?" Jade asked.

"Not as far as I'm concerned. You haven't been arrested or charged with anything, and I know how much your uncle meant to you," Paula assured her. "We'll worry about the rest if it happens."

"Thank you, Paula."

Paula hugged Jade and went to her office. Jade found her attorney's number and informed Suzanne Walls about being questioned and the search.

"You haven't heard anything else from the police?" Walls asked.

"No," Jade replied. "There is one officer who seems to want to be my friend. I don't know if I should trust him or not."

"Tell me about him."

"He was one of the officers who responded to the burglary of Uncle Erik's house. He took me home and stayed with me the night Uncle Erik was found."

"That sounds harmless enough," Walls replied.

"Yes, but he's also the officer who took me to the station for questioning and was in the next room listening at the time. He's been helpful since then, but I don't know."

"Has he asked you about the case or questioned you in anyway?"

"Not really. I've been asking most of the questions."

"I don't think you should discuss the case with him at all. He has a job to do, and anything you say to him about your uncle's death could be used against you even if he isn't on the job at the time."

"What about otherwise? He comes by or calls to check on me from time to time."

"That's up to you. Trust your instincts. Call me right away if anything else happens."

"I will. Thank you."

Jade wondered about Hudson. Was he trying to get close to her, hoping she'd tell him something incriminating? Or, did he truly want to be her friend and get to know her better?

She thought about his handsome face and his hazel eyes that lit up when he smiled. She liked the way a lock of his hair fell across his right eyebrow. She liked that he made her feel safe. Was it all an act?

A customer entered the store and woke Jade from her daydream. She pulled out several pairs of shoes for the woman to try on, and carried countless clothing items to the dressing room for her. In the end, the woman left without buying a thing.

Jade kept busy putting the items away until her break. She left the boutique and took stock of her surroundings.

There were half a dozen women walking the mall for their daily exercise. A young woman drug two small children past center court. There were a few window-shoppers and some folks who seemed to be in a hurry.

She made her way to the Food Court and ordered a soft drink. She sat down at a table to relax and enjoy her drink. There were all sorts of people there.

People who worked in or near the mall came for lunch. Shoppers took a break with a snack or a drink. People passed through on their way in an out of the mall.

Jade noticed a tan muscular man enter the Food Court and sit down a few tables away from her. He hadn't ordered anything to eat or drink, and he carried no shopping bags.

She scanned the room and wondered if he was waiting for someone who was in line at one of the restaurants. She looked at him again and discovered that he was looking at her. He turned away and didn't look her direction again.

She finished her soda and walked to the nearby trash can. She dropped her cup inside without stopping and went back to the boutique. She didn't turn to see if he followed. She watched through the store window while she kept herself busy for the rest of her shift.

4:00 p.m.

Jade clocked out and rushed out of the mall to her car. She hadn't seen the man again, but she felt as though someone was watching. She climbed into her car and drove home. She didn't relax until she'd closed the garage door behind her.

The adrenaline rush that had kept her on high alert was ebbing away. Feeling drained, she struggled to keep her eyes open. She decided to take Paula's advice and have a nap before taking Teddy for his walk.

She let Teddy in the house and went upstairs. She set the alarm on her phone and was asleep before Teddy could get comfortable beside her.

Her alarm sounded half an hour later. She groaned and looked at the clock. She wanted to sleep longer, but instead, she got up and changed into her workout clothes.

She went downstairs with Teddy at her heels, hooked the leash to his harness, and they started their walk.

A black Toyota Avalon was parked at the corner. Jade wondered if it was the same one that had followed her to work. The windows were tinted, and she was unable to see if anyone was inside.

She kept a look out for the man with the shaved head and the tan muscular man she'd seen in the mall. She met no one on the path but was relieved when Teddy had found his prize, and they headed home.

The car was still there when she turned the corner and walked down the alley. She was preoccupied and was startled when Teddy began to growl. A man she'd never seen before was standing beside the dumpster near the house.

"Howdy! I don't believe we've met," the stranger said. "I'm Ed Kinnan. I moved into the house behind you a few weeks ago."

"It's nice to meet you. I'm Jade O'Neal."

"That's some dog you have there."

"Thank you," Jade replied over Teddy's growl.

"I was sure sorry to hear about your dad. I only met him one time, but he seemed like a real nice fella."

"He was my uncle, and yes, he was. I'm sorry, Mr. Kinnan, but I need to feed Teddy. He gets cranky when he's hungry," she lied.

"I don't blame him for that. I get cranky when I'm hungry, too. I'll see ya around."

"Goodnight."

Jade and Teddy scurried through the gate and into the yard. They wasted no time getting into the house. She locked the door and set the alarm before unhooking Teddy's leash and putting it away.

After filling Teddy's food bowl and water dish, she began finding her own dinner. She wanted to spend the rest of the evening solving the puzzles in her book. She hoped there would be another clue that would explain what was happening.

She cleared away her dishes and went upstairs to retrieve her book. She was about to go downstairs again when her phone rang.

"Hi, Logan."

"I know it's a little late to be asking, but do you have plans for New Year's Eve?" Logan asked.

"No, I hadn't thought about it to tell you the truth."

"Will you have to work?"

"Yes, but I'll be off by six."

"How about I pick you up at eight?"

"I'd like that."

"Great! I'll see you Sunday," Logan said and ended the call.

Jade settled on the couch and turned on the television. She found an all music channel and opened her book. Teddy lay on the floor beside her and chewed on his new bone.

She solved the remaining crossword puzzles but found no more clues. She began solving the Acrostic puzzles. She solved four before she got up to stretch and let Teddy outside.

It was getting late, but she didn't have to go to work tomorrow. She could work as late as she wanted. Her mind wandered to the black Toyota, and she wondered if it was still parked outside.

She let Teddy back inside and gave him a cookie. She took a chocolate chip cookie for herself from the cabinet. She made sure the house was secure and turned off the television before she started upstairs. Teddy followed at her heels, hoping she'd drop one of her cookies for him.

Jade put the puzzle book on the nightstand and got ready for bed. Curiosity got the better of her

"Stay, Teddy!" she ordered and went across the hall to her uncle's room.

She wove through the maze of boxes in the dark and peeked through the blinds at the street below. The Toyota hadn't moved, and there was a man standing beside the driver's door. It was hard to tell for certain, but she didn't think it was the man with the shaved head.

She watched until the man got inside the car, expecting him to drive away. The car and its occupant remained in place. She went back to her room and crawled under the covers.

There was no doubt in her mind that she was being watched by more than one person. The man with the shaved head, the man in the Toyota, and she suspected the new neighbor she'd met in the alley. No wonder Uncle Erik wanted her to keep Teddy close.

She focused on her puzzle to dispel her growing fear. She needed to find out why she was being followed, and why her uncle had been killed.

Jade began working another acrostic puzzle. It was shorter than the previous puzzles but the clues were more difficult. She worked for two hours before the words began to make sense.

She stared at the message for a moment.

"The President holds the key," she read aloud. "What's that supposed to mean? Which president and the key to what?" she asked Teddy.

Teddy continued to snore.

"I wonder if it's the key to the cipher or an actual key."

Jade thought about searching the house for the president. She looked at the time and decided against it. She didn't want to alert those who were watching that something was different inside the house. She decided to wait until morning so that she could search without light being noticed from outside.

She turned off the lamp and tried to sleep. She tossed and turned wondering if the president and the key were in the house. She thought about the portraits and statues that Uncle Erik had.

She hadn't paid attention to them in so long she wasn't sure what they were.

She made a mental plan for the following day. She'd search room by room looking for a president. She'd start upstairs and work her way down. She was sure to find it if she was methodical.

Having made her plan of attack, she set her alarm, and fell asleep.

CHAPTER TWENTY-ONE

Saturday, December 30, 2017

8:30 a.m.

Jade slept later than she'd intended. She'd wanted to get an early start searching for the president and the key. It had taken her hours to fall asleep because she couldn't stop going over all of the messages she'd found and wondering what they all meant.

Getting up and going downstairs, she let Teddy outside and started a pot of coffee. She was going to need it to get moving this morning.

She let Teddy inside and stood in the kitchen looking around the room. She saw nothing that looked like a president or a key. She searched every cabinet and drawer. She searched the pantry, refrigerator, and freezer. She found nothing.

She fed Teddy and sat down with her second cup of coffee. *Were the burglars looking for the key?* she wondered. *It would have to be a physical key if they were. What did the key unlock?*

She finished her coffee and went upstairs to get dressed. She put on her workout clothes and pulled her hair into a ponytail. There was still a lot of house to search.

Jade searched each room. She looked behind paintings, under furniture, inside drawers, closets, and cushions. She went through all of the boxes in her uncle's room. She still found nothing.

She went through the garage and the attic. She found some old books and pictures there that she thought might point her in the right direction. That idea also ended in disappointment.

The entire inside of the house had been searched by two o'clock. Jade made herself a sandwich and sat at the bar wondering if the president was outside the house. She couldn't think of anything having to do with a president out there.

She finished her lunch and started her search outdoors and the shed. Then, she searched shrubs and trees. She looked for loose stones and concrete but found none.

She had almost finished with the backyard when she felt someone watching her. She made a show of searching through the patio cushions and threw up her hands.

She looked at Teddy and said, "Did you eat your toy? I can't find it anywhere?"

Teddy tilted his head in confusion.

"Are you ready for your walk?"

Teddy wagged his tail and started toward the gate.

"Wait until I get your leash," Jade told him.

She went inside and grabbed the leash. She pocketed her house key and a jerky treat and went back outside. She hooked the leash to Teddy's harness, and they were on their way.

A dark blue Dodge Durango was parked at the end of the street. Jade could see someone sitting in the passenger seat but couldn't see details. She forced herself not to stare as they passed.

Teddy knew where he was going. All she had to do was keep him under control and think. She wondered if the president was somewhere on campus. She couldn't imagine Uncle Erik risking the key being found by the wrong person, but it wasn't in the house.

She paid particular attention to the buildings and objects they passed on their walk. She saw nothing that she felt was the president or a key.

She looked toward Old Main and an idea immerged. *Maybe, it's a university president,* she thought. She couldn't take Teddy inside, and she couldn't tie him up. She'd have to come back to see what she could find.

Jade let her attention to Teddy lapse a moment too long. The giant dog felt the lack of tension on his leash and began to run. The leash was jerked out of Jade's hand before she realized what was happening.

She ran after Teddy but never got close enough to grab him or his leash. He sniffed the air and ran across Fourth Street. He moved so fast that Jade saw a black blur when he turned toward a nearby fast food restaurant.

Teddy stopped beside the restaurant's dumpster. Its contents overflowed onto the parking lot. The pungent smell of rotting food and the putrid odor of old cooking grease was overwhelming.

Jade called to Teddy, but he was too busy rolling in the stench and eating the scraps to obey. She waded into the mess almost reaching him when she slipped and landed in something green, slimy, and disgusting.

She held her breath and pushed herself to her knees. Her eyes watered, and she could taste the foul odor. She managed to find her footing and stood up. She inched her way toward Teddy and grabbed his leash.

She led him away from the dumpster overflow and surveyed the damage. There was no way either of them was going into the house like this. Jade wondered if she'd ever get rid of that horrible smell.

Teddy looked at Jade. She knew what was coming.

"No, Teddy! Don't shake!"

Jade hadn't been able to get the words out before the grunge that had been clinging to Teddy's coat flew through the air toward Jade and into her open mouth.

She gagged and choked before she bent over and retched. The taste, the smell, the slime running down her legs, and dripping from her chin was more than Jade's stomach could take.

A teenager who worked in the restaurant opened the back door.

"Hey lady, are you okay?" he asked and walked toward her. "Whoa," he said, stopped in his tracks, and covered his nose with his hand.

"We're fine," Jade replied. "Be careful by the dumpster over there. It's slippery."

"What's that stuff all over you?"

"Trust me. You don't want to know."

The teenager went back inside, and Jade could hear him telling his coworkers about what he'd seen. Not wanting to be their entertainment for the evening, she tugged on Teddy's leash.

"Let's go home, Teddy. I don't think you need a prize today."

Teddy answered with a low growl. She turned to see a large man walking a toy poodle. The man raised his hand in a wave and walked past. He had a royal flush tattoo on his forearm.

Jade nodded at the man and tugged on Teddy's leash. They started to walk away, but she turned and looked at the dog. She was almost sure it was the same poodle she'd seen with the other man.

They rushed home and went through the gate. She found a garden hose in the shed and connected it to a spigot in the backyard.

"This is going to be cold," she told Teddy. "But it's your own fault for playing in that stuff."

She unhooked the leash and carried it toward a tree. She wrapped it around the trunk and slipped the clasp through the hand loop. She called Teddy to her and hooked the leash to his harness again.

"I'm sorry I have to tie you up," she apologized. "I want to get this done without a chase."

She turned on the faucet and approached Teddy with the hose. He didn't like what he saw and tried to escape his tether.

Jade started at his head and rinsed the gunk from Teddy's coat. He shivered and whined. She would have felt sorry for him if he hadn't brought it on himself.

She stood back and let him shake off the water before she rinsed him again. She left him tied to the tree while she rinsed herself off. The slime was gone, but the smell lingered.

She turned the water off and ran inside for towels. She returned to the backyard and dried Teddy as best she could. He was damp but no longer dripping when she unhooked the leash. They went into the house and finished toweling off in the kitchen.

Teddy shivered and glared at Jade. He seemed to think she had ruined his fun.

"I know you're cold," she told him.

She picked up his favorite blanket and wrapped it around him. She waited until he'd stopped shivering before going upstairs to shower.

She stood in the hot shower and scrubbed until the water began to get cold. She still didn't feel clean, and she could still smell that awful odor.

She toweled dry and put on clean clothes. She held her breath, picked up her workout clothes with two fingers, and carried them at arm's length to the laundry room. She dropped them in the washing machine with an extra dose of detergent and slammed the lid. She set the machine to the longest wash cycle.

The smell still lingered when she returned to the kitchen. She looked at Teddy. She knew there was no way she was going to get him into the bathtub tonight.

She went to the pantry and found a bottle of pine scented air freshener. She sprayed it in every room of the house with a double shot in the kitchen and bathroom. It helped a little, but she knew she needed to spray the source of the stench.

She lifted Teddy's blanket and sprayed his back. He woofed at her and stood up to shake. She waited until he'd finished and gave him another blast.

"That'll have to do for now," she told him.

He ignored her and settle onto his blanket again.

Jade looked at the time on her cell phone. The campus buildings might still be open if she hurried. She wondered if she could get there without drawing the attention of the man in blue Durango.

She went upstairs to her uncle's room and peeked through the blinds. The Durango was still parked at the end of the street. The man with the royal flush tattoo walked to the vehicle, unlocked it, and got inside. There was no poodle in sight.

She went downstairs, picked up her keys and her back pack, and went to the garage. She drove to the WTAMU campus and found a parking space near Old Main. She saw the dark blue Dodge Durango park in the lot when she reached the top of the steps.

She went inside and took the stairs to the top floor. She hurried down the hall and found the portraits of the current and former university presidents. She didn't want the man in the Durango to see what she was doing.

She looked at each one, inspecting the frames and lifting each away from the wall. There was nothing hidden in or behind any of them. She ran downstairs and across the pedestrian mall to the Jack B. Kelley Student Center and the Classroom Center.

She roamed the halls of each floor looking at portraits and photographs. It occurred to her on the way back to her car that the president could be at the museum. She checked the time on her cell phone.

It was already four forty-five. The museum would close in fifteen minutes. There wasn't enough time to search one floor let alone the entire museum.

Jade got back in her car and drove home. She was tired and disappointed. She wouldn't be able to look through the museum until Tuesday. If the answer wasn't there, she had no idea where else to look.

She parked in the garage and went inside the house. Something nagged at the back of her mind.

She sat at the bar and looked up the number for Teddy's groomer. He needed a bath, and she knew they had everything they needed to handle him.

"Hi," Jade said when a woman answered. "My name is Jade O'Neal. I was wondering if I could bring my dog in for a bath tomorrow. He got into some nasty stuff and smells terrible."

"Has your dog been here before?"

"Yes, his name is Teddy. The account is under my uncle's name, Erik O'Neal."

She heard the tapping of computer keys and then, "Oh! Teddy!

"Yes, will that be a problem?"

"Ummm, I don't know. Let me check. I'll have to put you on hold."

"Okay, I'll hold."

Jade waited on hold for ten minutes before the voice returned.

"Yes, we can take Teddy tomorrow at eleven-thirty. Does he need a trim or just a bath?"

"Just a bath. His nails could use a trim if he'll let you. It's okay if he won't."

"All right, we'll see you tomorrow morning."

"Thanks, I'll see you then."

She looked at Teddy and said, "You can go with me to Amarillo in the morning. I'll drop you off on my way to work and pick you up when I get off."

Teddy still felt mistreated. He looked at her and resumed pouting on his blanket.

"Okay, then be that way. No cookies for you tonight."

She stared at the phone for a minute before she tapped the screen on her phone again.

"Hello," said a woman's voice

"Renee, this is Jade."

"I was wondering about you a little while ago," Renee replied. "How are you doing?"

"I'm okay, I guess. Do you have a few minutes to talk?"

"Of course, I do. What can I help you with?"

"Its...I was wondering...." Jade began. "Is there anything else that you were keeping for Uncle Erik?"

"No, just your package. I've been curious about that since he gave it to me," Renee said. "What was inside?"

"It was a puzzle book like we did together when I was young. There was also a copy of my favorite movie."

"Oh, I bet that was a nice surprise."

"Yes, it was. It brought back a lot of good memories," Jade said and paused. "Do you think Uncle Erik might have left something for safe-keeping with someone else at the museum?"

"I don't know. I suppose he could have. What are you looking for?"

"His laptop is missing," Jade said, opting not to divulge her true purpose. "It isn't here, and it wasn't in his office. The police didn't find it in his car. I thought maybe he'd left it with you or another friend."

"I can ask around. Is it important?"

"He did all of his business online with that laptop. I don't have account numbers or any other information that I need to pay his bills."

"That could be a big problem," Renee replied. "I'll see what I can find out and let you know."

"Thanks, Renee. I'd appreciate it," Jade said. "I was thinking about visiting the museum before I go to work Tuesday."

"Stop by my office if you do. We can have a cup of coffee and talk."

"I'd like that. I'll see you Tuesday then."

Tired and frustrated, she sat on the couch and turned on the TV. She flipped through the channels but found nothing that she wanted to watch. She decided to watch *National Treasure* again. She wanted to relax and enjoy it this time without looking for clues. She fed Teddy and made herself a snack before starting the movie.

Jade lay on the couch, and Teddy snored on the floor beside her. She was considering going upstairs for the night when one scene made her sit up and reach for the remote. There was a clue on the hundred-dollar bill in the movie.

Was it possible that the answer she was looking for was on her money?

She got up and found her backpack. She knew she didn't have a hundred in her wallet, but she'd inspect what she did have. She found a handful of ones and a five.

She took a one and the five to the living room and held them under the lamp. She still couldn't see enough detail. She went to her uncle's desk and found a magnifying glass she had seen during her search.

She looked at the bills with the magnifying glass. There was more detail but nothing that looked like a key or a clue. She needed to look at different denominations of bills.

"Where am I going to find bigger bills at this time of night?" she asked Teddy.

Teddy laid his head on his front paws in response.

"I don't have that kind of money in my bank account. Uncle Erik didn't keep cash in the..." Jade paused.

She ran upstairs to Erik's room and found the box that Hudson had delivered with her uncle's belongings. She thought she remembered seeing some cash in his wallet.

She found the box at the foot of Erik's bed. She ignored the queasy feeling in her stomach when she opened it and found the envelope. She dumped the contents of the envelope onto the bed and picked up the wallet.

Inside, she found two twenties, a ten, and some ones. She took the bills downstairs and examined them with the magnifying class. She was disappointed again.

She decided to see if she could find images of larger bills on the internet. Her laptop was tucked away upstairs.

She let Teddy outside and put her dishes away. She turned off the lights and made sure the house was secure before letting Teddy back inside.

She changed into her pajamas, and plugged in her laptop. She sat on her bed and searched the internet for an hour but still found no hint as to which president had the key.

The nagging feeling she'd had at the back of her mind became a clear and conscious thought.

"What if the information I'm looking for is on Uncle Erik's missing laptop?" she asked aloud. "How am I supposed to find it? What am I going to do, Teddy?"

Teddy sighed and rolled over without giving her an answer.

She put the laptop away and went to her closet. She took her puzzle book from the boot box and settled on the bed again. She needed to clear her mind and think about something else for a while. She also hoped she'd find another clue.

Jade solved all of the puzzles. The last one held a personal message for her.

Jade, stay strong and be brave. I know that you can finish what I couldn't. Be careful and alert. I love you, Uncle Erik.

She wiped tears from her eyes and got out of bed. She put the book back in the boot box and hid it in the back of the closet. She went back to bed and turned off the lamp. Tomorrow was going to be a long day.

CHAPTER TWENTY-TWO

Sunday, December 31, 2017

7:30 a.m.

Jade got up before her alarm went off. She had a lot to do before she went to work. She got dressed in workout clothes and went downstairs. She let Teddy outside and made toast and coffee.

Wrinkling her nose, she got out the can of air freshener again. She sprayed every room in the house, but the odor lingered. She looked at Teddy's blanket. *It must be on the blanket and the towels,* she thought with a sigh.

She went to the laundry room and moved her clothes to the dryer. She held her breath and carried the towels and the blanket to the washer. She knew that the smell wouldn't go away until Teddy had a bath, and she had laundered everything he'd lain on.

She let Teddy back inside and filled his food bowl. They both enjoyed their breakfast while Jade made her plan of attack.

Teddy hated baths.

She intended to take him on an extra-long walk this morning in an effort to tire him out. If she got ready for work fast enough, he wouldn't have a lot of time to nap. He wouldn't sleep in the car because he liked to bark at all the cars they passed.

Avoiding a repeat of yesterday's disaster was a must. She'd take him around campus as usual but extend the walk north to the Randall County District Court building and east past the Virgil Henson Activities Center before turning back to their normal path.

They finished their breakfast, and Jade cleaned up the kitchen. She took Teddy's leash from the hook and gagged. She hadn't thought to wash his leash.

She filled the kitchen sink with hot soapy water and dunked the leash to the bottom. She washed and dried her hands before putting on rubber gloves. She didn't want to get anything else on her.

She found a scrub brush under the sink and scoured the leash from clasp to hand loop three times. She pulled the plug and let the dirty water run down the drain before she filled the sink with clean hot water. She rinsed the leash several times before she laid it on a dish towel and patted it dry.

She considered throwing it in the dryer, but she knew it wasn't a good idea. She went upstairs instead, unplugged her hair dryer, and carried it to the kitchen. She turned it on high and dried the leash until it was almost as good as new.

It was already eight forty-five. She needed to leave by eleven to get Teddy to the groomer and to work on time. She needed to shower after their walk. There may not be time to extend the walk as much as she'd planned.

She put on her jacket and stuffed a jerky treat into one pocket and her house keys in the other. She picked up the sparkling clean leash and held it up.

"Let's go for our walk, Teddy."

Teddy trotted to the back door and waited while she attached the leash to his harness. He did his "ohboyohboyohboy" dance while she set the alarm and locked the door.

He was more excited than usual, and she wondered if memories of the garbage pile danced in his head. He led her through the gate and toward campus.

Jade felt a moment of alarm when Teddy sniffed the air and looked in the direction of the fast food restaurant. She gripped the leash tight and tugged him in the opposite direction. He obeyed, and the rest of the walk was uneventful.

There were no squirrels or cats to be chased. There were no men walking the toy poodle, few cars on the streets, and no one out for their morning exercise. It was a peaceful Sunday morning.

She extended their walk as planned and walked across Russell Long Boulevard and did a couple of laps around the parking lot of the District Court building. She looked at the time on her cell phone and decided to return to their normal routine.

They stopped at Teddy's tree. She allowed him to dig and tossed his prize into the hole. She kicked the dirt back under the tree while Teddy enjoyed the jerky treat. They walked through the gate five minutes ahead of schedule.

They went inside, and Jade ran upstairs to get ready for work. Teddy was chewing his bone on the couch when she returned. She moved the blanket and towels to the dryer and put her stench free clothes away.

She thought about spraying Teddy with air freshener again but decided against it. She had a feeling that it wasn't good for him.

11:00 a.m.

She looked at the kitchen clock and took a deep breath. She couldn't put it off any longer. She needed to leave now.

She picked up her keys and her back pack. She stuffed the can of air freshener in her jacket pocket just in case. She looked at Teddy and took his leash from the hook. Teddy's stopped chewing and looked at her with his ears at attention.

"Do you want to go?"

Teddy jumped off the couch and trotted toward her. She hooked the leash to his harness and led the way to the garage. She opened the passenger side door, and Teddy jumped in. He made himself comfortable on the back seat while Jade got in and opened the garage. They were on their way.

Teddy barked and woofed at the cars they encountered on the drive to Amarillo. Jade hoped he was tired enough that he wouldn't give them a bad time at the groomer.

She turned into the parking lot and parked close to the entrance.

"Stay, Teddy!" she ordered and got out of the car and went inside.

A young girl stood at the counter, picking at her nails. She had short hot pink hair and sparkly, blue eyeshadow caked on her eyes. Her name tag proclaimed that she was known as Lori.

"Hi, Lori. My name is Jade O'Neal, and I've brought Teddy for his bath. Are you ready for him?"

The girl sighed, popped her gum, and asked, "Did you have an appointment?"

"Yes, his appointment is at eleven-thirty."

"Okay, let me check," Lori said and drug herself to the back room.

Jade waited for five minutes before the owner came to talk with her.

"Have you been helped?" Hippy asked.

"Lori is supposed to be finding out if you're ready for Teddy."

"Teddy?"

"I'm Jade O'Neal. I made an appointment for eleven-thirty today for my Uncle Erik's dog, Teddy."

Hippy blanched and tapped the computer keys. "Yes, here it is, but no one told me about it. Are you in a hurry?"

"I have to be at work by noon," Jade replied unable to keep the irritation out of her voice.

"We'll have to make the best of things then," Hippy replied. "Bring him in, and I'll get my crew to work."

"I told the person that I made the appointment with that I won't be able to pick him up until I get off work at six," Jade informed him. "Will that be a problem?"

"No, that will be fine," he replied and turned toward the back room. "Lori! Spiker! Everyone! Red alert! We have a big boy coming in who detests being bathed. Start the water in the biggest tub. Make sure it's warm!"

Jade went to the car and opened the back door. She picked up the leash, and Teddy jumped out beside her. He trotted to the door of the building excited for another adventure. Everything was fine until he saw Hippy.

Teddy did his best to get out the door before it closed, but Jade stood in his way. He whined and scratched at the door begging to go back to the car.

"I'm sorry, but you had a lot of fun yesterday," Jade told him. "It's time to wash all that fun off now. You stink. You played; now, it's time to pay."

Jade scratched his ears and patted his head. Hippy opened the gate and Jade handed him the leash. Teddy put on the brakes and refused to move. Jade pushed Teddy from behind while Hippy tugged on the leash.

"Whew, what is that smell?" Hippy asked. "It smells like fermenting garbage with a hint of pine."

"It's Teddy," Jade replied and pushed.

Teddy was moved a little at a time toward the back room. It took Hippy and all of his workers to pick him up and get him into the tub. Jade left as soon as they had him under control. She could hear him whining when she went through the door.

She went to her car and got inside. She took the can of air freshener from her pocket and sprayed the back seat before driving out of the parking lot toward the mall.

She arrived for work with five minutes to spare. It was a long dull afternoon. There were few shoppers other than those looking for last minute accessories for their New Year's Eve celebration.

Six o'clock arrived at last, and she rushed out of the mall. She drove to the groomers and picked up a sparkling clean, although out of sorts, giant dog.

She had no trouble getting Teddy out of the building and into the car. He was more than ready to go.

"You smell so much better, Teddy," she told him. "I'll bet you feel better, too."

Teddy was in pout mode again and refused to look at her or acknowledge that she was speaking to him.

They were halfway home when Radio Romance's song "Weekend" began to play on the radio. Jade sang along, and to her surprise, Teddy joined in.

"Because it's the freakin' weekend," she sang, and Teddy woofed and howled.

She drove into the garage and opened the door for Teddy. He jumped out and followed her into the house. She unhooked his leash and put it on the hook.

"Do you want a cookie?"

Teddy sat down and woofed his approval. Jade took a dog biscuit from the box and tossed it to him. He snatched it out of the air and swallowed it whole.

"Am I forgiven now?" Jade joked.

Teddy stood on his hind legs, put his paws on her shoulders, and licked her face.

Jade scratched his neck before she pushed him down. She let him outside before she filled his food bowl and water dish and retrieved his blanket from the dryer.

She went upstairs to freshen up and change clothes for her date with Logan. She hoped he would agree to meet Teddy tonight, but she wouldn't push it.

She stripped the sheets and comforter from her bed and took them to the laundry room. She let Teddy back inside and sprayed the house once more with the air freshener.

She had just finished putting fresh sheets and a quilt on her bed when her phone rang.

"Hi, Mom! Are you back in Dallas?"

"Yes, and I've been packing all day. What have you been doing since we last talked?"

Jade told her mother everything she could remember. Mollie laughed long and loud when she heard about Teddy's recent adventure.

"I'll let you get ready for your date," Mollie said. "I wanted to talk to you before I leave tomorrow."

"I'm glad you called," Jade replied. "Have a great time and be safe."

"I will. I'll call when I can. I love you."

"I love you, too."

The call ended, and Jade fought the urge to cry. She didn't want Logan to find her with puffy eyes and a blotchy face.

She went downstairs and rubbed Teddy's belly while she waited for Logan to arrive.

"I'm going out, and it will be late when I get back," she told him. "I'll put your blanket outside for you so you can curl up on it until I come home."

8:00 p.m.

The doorbell rang, and Jade went to the door. Teddy followed at her heels. She looked through the peephole and saw Logan waving at her.

"I'm going to put Teddy out, and I'll be right back," she shouted through the closed door.

Logan nodded his approval.

Jade picked up Teddy's blanket on the way through the living room and led the way to the backyard. Teddy was making his bed when she locked the back door. She opened the front door for Logan and smiled.

"Are you ready?" he asked.

"I just need to get my jacket and keys. Come in."

Logan stepped inside and waited by the door. "This is a nice house."

"Thanks, Uncle Erik worked hard to remodel it," Jade said, while she put on her jacket and stuffed her wallet and keys into the pockets. "I'm ready."

Logan waited on the porch while she set the alarm and locked the door. He escorted her to the car and held the door open for her.

"Where are we going?" Jade asked, when Logan drove away from the house.

"I thought we'd start at the Cantina and have a green chili cheese-burger before we go to any parties," he told her.

"That's a great idea. You know how well liquor and I get along."

They talked and laughed until they reached the restaurant. Logan found a parking space two blocks away. They walked arm in arm down the street.

Heather greeted them at the door and showed them to a table in the back corner of the room.

"It's been crazy busy tonight," she told them. "What can I get for you?'

They gave her their order and resumed their conversation when Heather walked away.

"Are you okay?" Logan asked. "You seem to be tired."

"I am," Jade replied. "The last few days have been hard."

She told him about work and her ordeal with Teddy. She was surprised when he didn't laugh at the story.

"I don't get why you want to keep that dog," Logan began. "He drags you into trouble all the time. Why don't you get rid of him?"

Jade couldn't believe her ears. It took her a minute to process what he said and to respond.

"We've had this discussion before. Teddy is a member of the family. Uncle Erik and I raised him. You don't get rid of a child when he misbehaves. I know you're afraid of him, but I'm not giving Teddy up!"

Heather arrived with their drinks, and Logan said nothing more about Teddy. They talked about work and the upcoming semester until their food arrived.

They ate in silence, and Jade pondered what Logan had said. She was upset with him but tried to make the best of things. She believed that his remarks came from his fear of Teddy. She didn't know if he'd ever get past it. She knew that they had no future if he didn't.

Heather took a short break and stopped by their table to chat.

"How are you doing?" she asked Jade.

"I have good days and bad days," Jade replied. "Some days are both good and bad."

"I don't know how you've managed to get through it all by yourself," Heather said. "I'd spend most of my time in bed, crying myself to sleep."

"I do that more than I'd like to admit."

"I wish I had your strength," Heather said. "I'll bring you some drink refills. Do you want dessert?"

"I'm stuffed," Jade said.

"No, thanks," Logan replied.

"I'll be right back with those refills," Heather said and left the table.

"Do you really cry yourself to sleep?" Logan asked.

"Not every night but yes," Jade answered. "I have nightmares pretty often, too."

"Why? It's been two weeks since that happened," Logan said. "I could understand if he'd been your dad, but he was just your uncle."

Jade was stunned. She couldn't believe what she was hearing. She searched her mind for the perfect words to express her anger and contempt for Logan at that moment. How could he say such a thing?

Heather brought their drinks and looked at Jade. "Is everything all right?"

"Excuse me, I need to go to the ladies' room," Jade said and left the table.

Heather watched her walk away and glanced at Logan. She frowned at him and asked, "What did you do?"

"Nothing," he said and put something in his shirt pocket.

Heather didn't say anything else, but she watched for Jade to return.

Jade left the ladies' room and went back to the table. Heather tried to get her attention, but Jade didn't notice. She took a sip of her soda and looked at Logan.

"I'm going home," she said, looking him in the eye.

"Why? It's New Year's Eve, and we haven't even begun to party."

"I don't think there's any point in continuing to see each other," she said bluntly. "It's obvious that we aren't going to have a good evening, and I want to go home."

Logan stared at her. "I'll take you home if you want to go home," he said irritated.

"No, I'll call a cab or an Uber. I don't want you to have to worry about running into Teddy."

"I said I'd take you home, and I'm going to take you home!" Logan shouted.

"No, you're not," Heather said with authority.

"Is there a problem here?" said the restaurant manager.

Jade's head began to spin. The conversation between Logan, Heather, and the manager seemed to be far away. She drank some more of her Dr. Pepper and shook her head trying to clear away the cobwebs. She tried to stand but fell back onto the table.

"Jade!" Heather shouted. "What's wrong?"

"I don't feel well," Jade muttered.

"What did you do to her?" Heather shouted at Logan.

"Nothing! She's probably got food poisoning or something."

"I think it's best that you leave right now," said the manager.

Logan started to argue but thought better of it when he saw the manager's angry expression and clenched fists at his side. He stormed out of the restaurant and slammed the door.

"You'd better get her home," the manager said to Heather. "Your shift is almost over anyway."

Heather led Jade to her car with the manager's help. Jade was unconscious by the time they left the parking lot.

Heather was scared and drove much too fast. She managed to get into the Canyon city limits without having an accident, but her luck ran out when she passed a patrol car.

Red lights flashed in her rearview mirror. She wiped tears from her face and pulled into a parking lot. She dug for her driver's license while the police officer approached her vehicle. She rolled down her window and waited for the officer.

"Good evening, ma'am," said the officer. "Is there an emergency?"

"Yes, there is," Heather began. "My friend's date put something in her drink. I'm trying to get her home. She passed out, and I don't know what to do."

"What's your friend's name?"

"Jade O'Neal."

"Jade?" said Officer Hudson Bailey. "I know Jade. What happened to her?"

"She was at the restaurant where I work with her date. She went to the restroom, and I thought I saw him put something in her drink. They'd been arguing, and she told him she was going home. A few minutes later she said she wasn't feeling well. She passed out right after we left the restaurant."

Hudson signaled to Officer Ronny Hague to join him. He explained the situation to his partner while he opened the passenger side door to assess Jade's condition.

"We'd better call the paramedics," suggested Hague. "We don't know what that guy drugged her with or how much he gave her."

Hague called for an ambulance while Hudson and Heather talked.

"What is your name?"

"Heather Anderton."

"Where do you work?"

"At the Cantina on Sixth Street in Amarillo."

"How do you know Jade?" asked Hudson.

"We were roommates until her uncle was killed. She had to move out to take care of the dog."

"Did you know the man she was with tonight?"

"Yes, he lives next door to me. His name is Logan Rhodes."

"How long have he and Jade been seeing each other?"

"Since October, I think. They haven't gone out a lot because of their schedules."

"Did you see him put something in her drink?"

"I thought so, but I wasn't sure until she started feeling sick." Heather replied. "I tried to get her attention to warn her, but she drank it before I could say anything."

"When did she start feeling ill?" Hudson asked.

"Half an hour ago maybe. I know it's been less than an hour."

The ambulance and the paramedics arrived. They examined Jade and decided it would be best to take her to the emergency room.

"Go with her," Ronny said to Hudson. "Our shift is over. I'll do the paperwork. She needs her friends with her in case that guy tries to get at her again."

"Thanks, Ronny. I'll see you tomorrow."

Hudson turned and walked toward Heather. "Are you planning to go to the hospital with her?"

"Yes, I am." Heather replied. "I don't want her to be alone."

"Do you mind if I ride along with you? I want to be around just in case Rhodes turns up."

"I think that's a great idea," Heather replied. "I might get arrested for assault if he shows up."

They got into Heather's car and followed the ambulance to the emergency room.

CHAPTER TWENTY-THREE

Monday, January 1, 2018

1:25 a.m.

Jade felt like she was rising out a deep dark pit. A light above her grew brighter as she ascended, and voices above her became louder and clearer.

She opened her eyes and blinked a few times. The light was so bright. She shaded her eyes with her hand.

"She's coming around," an unfamiliar voice said.

"Thank God!" said a woman.

Her voice sounded familiar.

"Jade, it's Heather. Can you hear me?"

"Heather? Where am I? What happened?"

"You're at the emergency room. You were drugged," said the unfamiliar voice. "You've been sleeping for several hours."

"Drugged?"

"Yes, but nothing else happened to you," Heather assured her. "I've been with you the whole time."

"She's been taking good care of you," said another familiar voice.

Jade turned toward the voice and saw Hudson Bailey.

"Thank you, Heather," mumbled Jade before she fell asleep again.

"She'll sleep a lot for the next several hours," said Dr. Ransom. "She may feel like she has a hangover for the rest of the day. Her vital signs are good, and she should be back to normal once the drug is out of her system."

"Does she need to stay here, or can we take her home?" Hudson asked.

"You can take her home when she wakes up again. I'll sign the paperwork, so you can be on your way," Dr. Ransom said and left them alone with Jade.

"Officer Bailey, I don't think we can take her home," Heather said. "I don't know the alarm code, and I'm scared to death of her dog."

"Maybe, we should take her to your place," suggested Hudson.

"That's not a good idea either. I live on the second floor. We'd have to get her up the stairs, and we might run into Logan."

"I can't take her to my place," said Hudson. "It's an ethical issue."

"What are we going to do?" asked Heather.

"She might be able to tell us the code when she wakes up again," Hudson said. "Teddy and I have gotten along so far. Maybe, he'll let us in the house."

"What if she can't tell us the code?" Heather asked with skepticism.

"I'll make an official phone call to the alarm company."

4:00 a.m.

Jade was in the backseat of Heather's car. She didn't know how she'd gotten there or where they were going. Heather was driving and Hudson Bailey was in the passenger seat.

"Jade, we're almost to your house," Hudson was saying. "Can you stay awake long enough to get us inside?"

"I'll try," she said. "Where have we been?"

"We've been at the emergency room," Hudson said. "We need you to convince Teddy that it's okay for us to be with you. Can you do that?"

"Teddy? He wouldn't hurt a fly," Jade said feeling the urge to sleep.

"Jade! You have to stay awake a little longer."

"I'm awake."

"We're at your house now, and we need to get you inside," Hudson coaxed. "Can you tell Teddy to stay?"

"I will but don't touch me or stand too close," Jade replied in a moment of clarity. "He doesn't like that."

Heather stayed in the car while Hudson helped Jade out of the backseat and to the gate. He pushed the gate open and saw Teddy at full alert on the patio.

"Stay, Teddy!" Jade ordered and fumbled for her key.

She unlocked the door and turned off the alarm.

"See, nothing to it," she said and went inside with Teddy at her heels.

Hudson signaled to Heather that everything was all right. She got out and went inside. They helped Jade upstairs. Heather helped her change into her pajamas while Hudson waited in the hall.

Jade was safely tucked in bed when they reset the alarm and locked the door behind them.

10:00 a.m.

Jade woke up with a terrible headache. Her mouth felt as dry as fresh surgical gauze. She got up and went to the kitchen for a drink of water. She let Teddy outside and noticed a hospital ID bracelet on her wrist.

"How did I get this?" she asked aloud. "When was I at the hospital and why?"

She sat down at the bar and tried to remember the night before. She remembered going out with Logan and remembered eating dinner. Logan said something that hurt and made her angry.

She had no idea what he had said, but she knew it was over between them. The rest of the night came to her in bits and pieces. Heather... Heather was there and...Hudson.

Teddy scratched at the door, and Jade let him inside. She went upstairs to take some aspirin and shower. She was happy that she didn't have to work today. All she wanted to do was sleep.

She got back into bed, and Teddy lay down beside her.

"I don't think we're going to walk today, Teddy," she told him. "I'm sorry, but I'll make it up to you tomorrow."

Teddy looked at her as though he understood, and they both went back to sleep.

2:00 p.m.

Jade woke up feeling much better. Her headache and dry mouth were just a memory. The ID bracelet on her arm worried her. She picked up her phone and tapped Heather's number.

"Hi, Jade. How are feeling?"

"I'm okay, but I'd feel a lot better if I knew what happened last night."

Jade listened while Heather told her the details about the previous evening. She was frightened by what might have happened, embarrassed by her own actions while under the influence, and thankful that she had such good friends after all.

"Heather, thank you. I can't imagine what might have happened if you hadn't stepped in."

"I still don't understand why he drugged you. Haven't you been sleeping together?"

"No, we haven't," Jade admitted. "Every time we got close, something happened."

"He must have wanted to make sure nothing got in his way this time, but it was still a lousy thing to do."

"Yes, it was," Jade said with anger. "What were we arguing about?"

Heather explained what she'd overheard.

"Oh yeah, it's never going to happen," Jade said.

"You let him know that the two of you were finished before you started to feel bad."

"That's good to know. One more thing, how did I get home?"

Heather filled her in and told her how nice Officer Bailey had been.

"Thanks again, Heather," Jade said. "I'll talk to you later."

They ended the call, and Jade looked up the number for the emergency room. She tapped the number into her phone and asked for someone who could answer her questions.

She waited on hold for a few minutes before Dr. Ransom answered the call.

"Miss O'Neal, this is Brad Ransom. I was on call when you came in last night. How are you feeling?"

"I feel like I've got a hangover after a two-day drinking binge," Jade told him.

"Yes, I thought you might."

"I don't remember anything about last night. My friend, Heather, told me everything she knew, but I'd like to hear the medical information from you," Jade explained.

"Of course," said Dr. Ransom. "Your blood work showed Ketamine in your system. Once the effects wear off, you should be fine. You were given enough to make you sleep, but not enough to cause any serious harm. Your records will be available if you're planning to file charges against your date."

"I hadn't thought about that," she admitted. "Thank you, Dr. Ransom. Do you have any idea who I need to talk with about paying for my visit?"

The doctor gave her the number, and they ended the call. She was about to dial the business office when she realized it was a holiday.

"Happy New Year to me," she said with sarcasm.

Her stomach growled, and she realized she hadn't eaten since dinner with Logan. She looked at Teddy who was sitting beside his food bowl.

"You're hungry too, aren't you?" she said.

She filled his food bowl with dog food and put fresh water in his water dish. She rummaged in the refrigerator for something to eat, but there were no leftovers, and she didn't feel like cooking.

She found her backpack and opened it, searching for her wallet. It wasn't there. She tried to remember when she last saw it. She went upstairs and picked up the jacket she had worn. Her wallet was still in the pocket. She had a grand total of twenty-seven dollars to last her until payday.

She was weighing her options when her cell phone rang.

"Hi, Jade. This is Hudson Bailey. How are you feeling?"

"Hi, Hudson. I'm better. Thank you for your help last night."

"You're welcome. I thought I'd stop by to see you if you're feeling up to it."

"I'd like that," Jade said. "I have a lot of questions."

"Would it be all right if I dropped by in half an hour?"

"I'll be here."

"I haven't had lunch yet. Are you hungry?" Hudson asked.

"I am. I was trying to decide what I wanted when you called."

"How does pizza and beer sound?"

"The pizza sounds great, but my head and stomach can't handle the beer," Jade replied.

Hudson laughed. "All right pizza and Pepsi, I'll see you soon."

Jade ran upstairs to change. She put on a pair of jeans and her favorite sweatshirt. She put two drops of Visine in each eye and put on some makeup. She didn't want to frighten Hudson with her bloodshot eyes and crazy hair.

The doorbell rang when she reached the bottom of the stairs. She looked through the peephole and saw Hudson standing on the porch.

She opened the door, and her mouth watered when the savory scent of pepperoni reached her nostrils.

"Hi! Come in," she said.

Teddy woofed his welcome to Hudson and wagged his tail. He sniffed the air and began to drool.

"Does Teddy like pizza, too?" Hudson asked.

"Teddy likes everything, but pizza is one of his favorites," Jade replied.

They went to the kitchen and sat at the bar. Jade found paper plates and handed them to Hudson. He dished out the pizza while Jade filled glasses with ice and poured them each a soft drink.

Jade and Hudson talked about the events of the previous evening. She told him what she'd learned from Dr. Ransom.

"The doctor told me that I'd been drugged with Ketamine," Jade told him. "I'm almost certain that was the drug that Uncle Erik said the burglars used on Teddy."

Hudson stopped in mid bite. "What's on your mind?"

"I'm thinking that Logan might have been the one who drugged Teddy," Jade said. "Teddy doesn't like Logan. It's possible he remembered Logan or something about him. And Logan is terrified of Teddy."

"Go on." Hudson said taking in every word.

"I noticed things missing or moved when I lived in my apartment. I always thought it was Heather or her friends," Jade continued. "It could have been Logan. My apartment was burglarized the day after this house was broken into. It was trashed in the same way."

"You may be right," Hudson said, "but do you have any

evidence?"

"No, I don't," Jade admitted.

"And it doesn't explain why he drugged you," Hudson pointed out.

"I know," Jade replied. "I can't figure out why he did that."

"Are you going to press charges?" asked Hudson.

Jade sighed. "Part of me wants to just forget it ever happened, and part of me wants to make him pay."

Hudson laughed at the look of determination on her face. "I wouldn't want to be in his shoes right now."

"What do you think I should do?" she asked and helped herself to another slice of pizza.

"You have evidence and enough witnesses if you decide to press charges. He didn't do anything other than drug you, regardless of what he had planned. A good lawyer could get him off," Hudson told her.

"Either way, he'd get away with it."

Hudson nodded and took another bite of pizza.

"You should file for a protective order whether you decide to file charges or not," Hudson suggested.

"Will that help?"

"It can't hurt."

Hudson tossed a pizza crust toward Teddy who caught it in midair.

"Nice catch!" Hudson said.

"He doesn't miss very often," Jade told Hudson.

"A lot of people are afraid of big dogs," Hudson began. "That's one of the reasons I like them. That fear keeps the bad guys away most of the time."

"You were afraid of Teddy too, at first," Jade teased.

"Well, yeah," Hudson said with a smirk. "He was angry and seemed to think that Ronny and I had locked him in that shed. Anybody would have been scared."

"He hasn't growled at you since the night that we found Uncle

Erik."

"Does he growl at other people?"

"Not everyone. I noticed that he growled at anyone who touched me or got too close to me. Logan had his arm around me when he brought me home one night. Teddy went berserk."

"He could be protecting you," Hudson said, "but he could also have sensed something about those people."

"How can I tell the difference?

"I don't know," Hudson admitted.

They finished their pizza and saved the crusts for Teddy. Jade cleaned the bar while Hudson played with Teddy, tossing the crusts in different directions to see if he could catch them. He never missed.

"Teddy's enjoying your attention," Jade told Hudson.

"I'm having fun, too."

She felt a surge of affection for Hudson. He was attractive, and he liked her dog. Hudson Bailey was a good man. Single men like Hudson were hard to find.

"I'm sorry I ruined your New Year's Eve, Hudson"

"You didn't ruin anything. I was on duty and had no plans to do anything when I got off."

"I was afraid I'd spoiled your date plans. Thank you for helping last night."

"Hey, what are friends for?" he asked. "And I didn't have a date."

"Oh...I'm sorry. I didn't mean to pry. I assumed..."

Hudson crossed his arms and leaned back in his chair with a wide grin on his face.

"What did you assume?" he asked.

Jade blushed and could feel the heat spreading to the roots of her hair.

"I assumed you had someone in your life," she began. "I thought you might be in a serious relationship or engaged. Maybe even married."

"Nope," he said and leaned toward her, resting his elbows on the bar. "I've never been married or engaged. I'm recovering from the last serious relationship I had. What about you?"

"What about me?" Jade said, recovering her composure.

"Are you married, engaged, or in a serious relationship?" Hudson asked with mock irritation.

"I've never been married or engaged. I was dating Logan until last night. It was never serious or physical."

"What about a serious relationship?"

Jade thought about his question before she answered. "I had one a long time ago. At least, I thought it was at the time. Since then, I've dated but never more than a few months."

"What happened?" Hudson asked. "If you don't mind telling me about it."

"We met when I was a junior in high school. He was a senior. We dated for two years and talked about getting married someday. He was driving home after work one night and was hit head on by a drunk driver. He died on the way to the hospital. Since then, I've been focusing on school and making a future for myself."

"I'm so sorry, Jade. I shouldn't have asked."

"That's okay. It felt good to talk about it. I haven't for a long time."

"It sounds like it was a serious relationship. Why do you think it wasn't?"

"I suppose it was, but we were both just kids. The truth is that we had begun to drift apart. He'd gone off to college and came home for the weekends. It wasn't long until he came home every other weekend and then once a month. I made excuses for him, and I was devastated when he died. When I think about those days, it seems that we were playing house rather being in a real relationship."

Jade looked at Hudson and said, "That's my sad tale. Tell me about that serious relationship you mentioned."

"Oh well, I'm sure you've heard stories like this before,"

Hudson began. "I'd been dating a woman for almost a year. One thing led to another, and we got an apartment together. There was no discussion of marriage or our future. We were taking things one day a time. We'd been living together for three months, so I decided to surprise her with flowers at work to celebrate. I found her with one of the interns in the break room. It turned out that she moved in with me to save money, and she had a reputation for being too friendly with the male members of the medical staff."

"That must have hurt," Jade said with sympathy.

"It did at the time," Hudson replied. "But now I'm thankful that it didn't last. She was arrested for stealing drugs from the hospital where she worked and selling what she didn't use. She'll be in prison for a long time."

"How long ago did you break up?"

"It was two years ago. I haven't gone out with anyone more than half a dozen times since then," Hudson said. "I'm out anytime a woman says or does something that reminds me of her."

They talked a while longer until Jade yawned.

"I'm sorry," Hudson said. "I didn't mean to stay this long. I'll go and let you get some rest."

"You don't have to go," Jade replied. "I've been enjoying your company."

"You need to rest. Dr. Ransom told us you'd sleep a lot today. I don't want to keep you up."

"I'm fine. I just need some aspirin, and I'll be as good as new," Jade said.

"All right, take some aspirin and go to bed," Hudson said and started to the door. "I'll see you again soon."

"Wait, let me pay you for the pizza."

"No, it was my treat," he said. "I'll call you tomorrow to see how you're feeling."

Jade followed him to the door and waved goodbye. She reset the alarm and went upstairs. She took another dose of aspirin and collapsed on her bed.

CHAPTER TWENTY-FOUR

TUESDAY, January 2, 2018

7:30 a.m.

Jade's alarm went off and startled her out a deep sleep. She would have loved to stay in bed longer, but Teddy needed his exercise. She also wanted to look through the museum and visit with Renee before going to work. If she timed everything right, she'd be there when the museum opened at nine.

She let Teddy outside and started her coffee. The effects of the drug she'd been given had worn off, and she felt energized after having so much sleep.

She ran upstairs, changed into her workout clothes, and a hoodie. She went back to the kitchen and decided to have her coffee when they returned. She took Teddy's leash from the hook and went outside.

Teddy ran toward her and stood still while she attached the leash to his harness. He was ready to stretch his legs and dragged her through the gate and toward campus. The gray Honda was parked at the corner. She wondered if the man with the shaved head would be walking his poodle today.

Their walk around campus was uneventful, and they met no one else on their trek. The Honda was still parked at the corner, but Jade couldn't see if anyone was inside.

Jade fed Teddy when they got back to the house. She made herself some toast and drank her coffee before going upstairs to get ready for work. She bounded down the stairs and let Teddy outside. She patted him and told him goodbye before going back inside and gathering her things.

She drove out of the garage and to the convenience store. She saw the Honda drive past while she stood at the gas pump. She saw it cruise by again after she'd paid the clerk. She got in the car and drove to the museum.

9:15 a.m.

She found a place to park near the entrance and hurried inside. She took out her wallet to pay for admission, but the receptionist waved her through.

"I'll take care of it," Pam said. "Your uncle was always good to me. It's the least I can do."

"Thank you," Jade replied. "Is Renee Lanham here?"

"Yes, I saw her come in. I'm sure she's in her office."

"I'll go up and say hello before I tour the museum."

Jade waved goodbye to Pam and took the elevator to the second floor. She almost expected to see her uncle walking down the hall when the elevator doors opened.

She walked toward Renee's office and tapped on the door.

"Jade! It's so good to see you," said Renee. "Come in."

"Hi, Renee. I thought I'd stop by and see how you're doing."

"I'm doing okay. How are you doing?"

"I'm okay," Jade replied. "I'm settling into the house and my new routine."

"You look like you're getting more rest than you did the last time I saw you."

"The nightmares have almost stopped, and I'm not working as many hours since the holidays are over."

"Well, look who's here," said a familiar voice from the hallway.

"Hi, Mr. Carlile," Jade said with a smile. "How are you?"

"I'm doing all right," Tommy said. "Are you doing okay?"

"I'm making the best of things."

"That's good. Give us a call if you need anything," Tommy said.

"I will, thanks."

"Renee, I'm sorry to interrupt," said Tommy. "But Jacqui wants to have a staff meeting in ten minutes."

"We had a staff meeting on Friday," said Renee confused. "What do we have to meet about today?"

"I guess we'll find out in a few minutes," Tommy said with a grin.

"But Jade just got here," Renee complained.

"That's okay. I was planning to tour the museum. I can do that now and come back to visit you before I leave for work," Jade said.

"The meeting shouldn't last long," Tommy added.

Jade waved goodbye and went back to the first floor. She'd been in the museum so many times that she knew exactly what route she wanted to take. She sped through the exhibits looking for anything having to do with a president. The few items she found were roped off or behind glass. She knew her uncle wouldn't have made his hiding place impossible for her to reach.

She fought back tears when she came upon the exhibit that had earned Uncle Erik such praise. It occurred to her that he might have hidden something there, but she found no president and no key.

She checked the time on her cell phone. It was already ten-thirty. She decided to make a quick tour of Pioneer Town before visiting with Renee again.

Renee and Tommy were talking in the hallway when Jade got off the elevator. Tommy looked at her and walked away.

"How was your meeting?" Jade asked in an effort to dispel the awkwardness she felt.

"Uncomfortable," Renee replied. "They've hired a new researcher to fill Erik's position."

"That's good isn't it?"

"It is, but Tommy was expecting to get that job. He has seniority. The new person will be given Erik's position and all that goes with it."

"Ouch!" said Jade.

"Yeah, Tommy isn't happy to say the least."

"I'm going to have to leave for work in a few minutes," Jade began. "Did you happen to ask around to see if anyone had Uncle Erik's laptop?"

"Yes, I asked during the meeting," Renee replied. "No one knows anything about it."

"I don't suppose he left anything else for safe keeping," Jade asked trying to sound casual.

"No one mentioned it if he did."

"Thanks for checking for me," Jade told Renee. "I'm beginning to think that whoever killed him must have it. Why, I don't know."

"Do the police have any leads?" asked Renee.

"I don't know," Jade said. "I need to get going, or I'll be late to work. Thanks again for your help."

"Come by anytime," Renee said.

They walked to the elevator together and waved goodbye before the elevator doors closed.

Jade drove to work and thought about her uncle. *Why would he leave me such a vague clue? What president? What kind of key? Where else could I look?*

She wasn't paying attention and didn't see that the traffic light had turned red. It wasn't until she saw the flash of the camera that she realized what she'd done. She wondered how long it would take for the citation to arrive in the mail.

She found a parking space near the mall entrance and went inside. She expected the day's shift to be long and boring. She squared her shoulders and pasted a smile on her face, intending to make the best of it.

12:00 p.m.

Renee Lanham sat at her desk and looked at the photograph on her desk. She remembered the day it was taken as though it were yesterday. Erik had wrapped his arm around her and held her close while the picture was taken. She was unable to express how much Jade's gift meant to her.

Memories of Erik followed her like a ghost. She missed him. They'd been colleagues and friends for years. She had hoped that friendship would one day turn into something more.

There were times when she thought Erik was close to crossing that fine line between friendship and romance. But then, he'd pull back.

He'd been distant in the weeks before his death. It was obvious that something weighed on his mind, but he never talked about it.

Her romantic hopes were gone now and so was her friend. She'd have to get used to seeing someone new sitting at Erik's desk. She'd have to work with someone she knew nothing about. Someone that she might not even like.

Renee didn't want to eat at her desk again today. She needed to get out of the office for a while and hoped a change of scenery and fresh air would revive her spirits.

She stood and went to the file cabinet where she kept her purse. Her cell phone buzzed before she unlocked the drawer. It was a text asking her to report to the Goodnight Cabin in the Pioneer Town.

She didn't recognize the number but assumed that it was from the new hire who'd been assigned to the exhibit. She hoped this would be quick and went downstairs.

5:00 p.m.

280

It was closing time, and Jennifer Havins was relieved that the last group of guests in Pioneer Town were making their way toward the exit. She overheard part of their conversation when they passed her booth.

"I'd swear that was a real person if I didn't know better," said one of the guests.

"I expected to hear snoring," said his companion.

Jennifer wondered what the visitors had been talking about. There were no mannequins in the exhibit. She hoped that no one had tampered with the scenes.

When the guests had gone, she walked through the replica to make sure that everything was in order. She found nothing unusual until she went into the Goodnight Cabin.

She could see something on the old bed. It was too dark to see detail. She used the flashlight on her cell and moved closer. Someone was lying there asleep.

"Excuse me," she said. "The museum is closed."

Jennifer waited for a response, but there was none.

"Hey, wake up! It's time to leave!" she shouted and touched the person's shoulder.

Jennifer's scream echoed through the museum.

6:00 p.m.

Jade was relieved when her shift came to an end. She was hungry and tired and couldn't wait to get home.

She thought about taking Teddy for another walk but decided against it. She needed to keep searching for the president.

She was tempted to stop for a burger and fries on her way out of Amarillo, but she knew that she'd regret it. She had food at home and little money in her wallet. It had to last her until she got paid on Friday.

She turned into the drive and pulled the car into the garage. She went into the house and opened the door for Teddy. He was so happy to see her that he almost knocked her to the floor.

"I'm glad to see you, too," she said and scratched his chin. "I'll bet you're hungry aren't you?"

Teddy followed her to the pantry and watched her fill his bowl. He dove in as soon as she put it on the floor. She refilled his water bowl and went to the refrigerator.

She found a microwaveable dinner in the freezer and read the directions. She took the dinner out of the carton and set the timer on the microwave. Ten minutes later, she was on the couch watching a *Friends* rerun and enjoying her meal.

Her cell phone rang, and she smiled when she saw Hudson's name on the caller ID.

"Hi, Hudson."

"I can't talk long, and don't tell anyone we talked," Hudson said.

"What's wrong?"

"All I can say is that you need to have your lawyer's number handy," Hudson said and ended the call.

Jade was alarmed. What was happening and why wasn't she supposed to be talking to Hudson? She looked at her cell phone and deleted the record of Hudson's call. She found the card that Suzanne Walls had given her and added the attorney's contact information to her phone.

She wondered if she should call Suzanne right away, but she didn't know what to tell her. She didn't want to have to explain why Suzanne had already been contacted.

She was restless with anxiety and fear. She cleared away her dinner tray and refilled Teddy's water dish. She went upstairs to change into more comfortable clothes and carried her laundry to the washing machine. She tried to stay busy and not worry about Hudson's phone call.

The doorbell rang at eight-fifteen. She looked out the peephole and saw two police officers waiting for her to answer. She didn't know either of them.

She opened the door and asked, "Is something wrong?"

"Are you Jade O'Neal?" asked Officer Cummings.

"Yes," Jade replied, "what can I do for you?"

"We'd like you to come to the station with us," answered Officer Patchin.

"Why? What's happened?"

"There are some questions that you need to answer," said Patchin.

"Can't I answer them here?" Jade asked.

"No, ma'am," replied Cummings. "We won't be the ones asking the questions."

"I...I need to put my dog outside and get my things. Do you want to come in?"

Officer Patchin moved toward Jade. Teddy appeared in the entry hall and growled at the intruders.

Patchin stepped back and said, "We'll wait right here."

"Come, Teddy," Jade said and took hold of Teddy's harness.

Teddy was slow to obey but gave in and followed Jade through the kitchen. She locked the back door behind him and picked up her jacket and backpack. She reset the alarm and joined the officers on the front porch.

Officer Cummings took Jade's arm and escorted her to the police car. He opened the back door, and she got inside.

The officers didn't speak during the ride to the police station. Jade said a silent prayer and tried to calm her nerves.

Her belongings were taken from her when she entered the station, and she was escorted to the room with the large mirror where she was questioned about her uncle's death. She wasn't surprised when Detective Bob Holloway entered the room.

"We meet again, Miss O'Neal?" said Holloway.

"Am I being arrested?" Jade asked.

"I'll be asking the questions," he said with a nasty smirk. "Where were you between noon and five this afternoon?"

"I was at work." Jade answered confused. She had a feeling this wasn't about her uncle.

"Where do you work?"

"I work in a boutique at the mall in Amarillo."

"What time did you go to work today?"

"My shift started at noon, and I worked until six?" Jade answered.

"Is there anyone who can verify that statement?" Holloway asked and stared into Jade's eyes trying to intimidate her.

"Yes, my manager and my coworker," Jade replied. "What's going on? Do I need to call my attorney?"

Holloway glared at her for a moment before answering. "You may have your attorney present during questioning if you wish."

"I think I'd better call her. I'm not saying anything else until I talk to her," Jade said with determination.

Holloway left the room. Jade heard him speak to someone in the hall.

"She wants to call her lawyer. I'll be in my office."

Officer Debbie Cornelius appeared in the doorway. "If you'll follow me, I'll take you to make your phone call."

Jade stood and said, "The number is in my cell phone. May I call her from it?"

Officer Cornelius nodded and led Jade to small vacant office. She took Jade's belongings from a file cabinet and handed her the cell phone.

Jade called the number and told her attorney what she knew. She handed the phone back to the officer when the call ended.

Cornelius returned Jade's things to the file cabinet and escorted her back to the interrogation room. She waited there for half an hour before Suzanne Walls joined her.

"Do you know anything more than you told me?" Suzanne asked.

"No, but I don't think this is about Uncle Erik."

"What were you asked?"

Jade relayed the conversation she'd had with the detective. Suzanne frowned while she listened.

"I don't think this is about Erik either," she said. "Sit tight, and I'll try to find out what's going on. Don't say anything to anyone unless I give you a nod."

Suzanne went into the hallway and disappeared. She returned a few minutes later with a grim expression on her face.

"Tell me everything you did today, every detail."

Jade told Walls everything she could remember about her day.

"Why did you go to the museum?"

"I had arranged to visit with Renee Lanham, and I wanted to go through the museum. I hadn't talked to her or been to the museum in a while."

"Did you have an argument or any issues with Renee?"

Jade couldn't hide her surprise. "No, Renee is my friend. She was there for me when Uncle Erik died. She sat with me at the funeral. I promised I'd keep in touch with her. What's happened?"

Suzanne's reply was interrupted when Detective Holloway entered the room.

"Are we ready to talk now?" he asked with sarcasm.

"My client should be informed as to the reason for her presence here tonight," said Walls.

"I would have thought you'd already done that."

"I was about to when you came in."

"By all means, continue your conversation. I can wait," he said and leaned back, balancing on the back legs of his chair.

Suzanne Walls glared at the officer. "That information should have been given to my client when she was brought in. If you refuse to do so, there's no reason for her to remain here."

Anger flashed across the officer's face, and his chair landed with a thump.

"Renee Lanham was found dead at the museum this afternoon," he informed her.

Jade gaped at the officer. "Renee is dead?"

"We know you were there, and we know the two of you had a disagreement," he added. "What was the argument about?"

Jade looked at Suzanne. The attorney nodded.

"I was there, but we didn't argue. We've never had a disagreement of any kind."

"I have a witness who says otherwise."

"We talked about Uncle Erik and the fact that someone was going to be taking over his job, but we didn't argue."

"Why were you at the museum this morning?" Holloway asked.

Jade told him what she had told Suzanne.

"She was your friend and you…"

Holloway was interrupted by a tap on the door. He went into the hallway and returned a few minutes later with a look of disappointment on his face.

"You're free to go," he told Jade. "Your manager verified that you were at work at the time of Ms. Lanham's death. You can collect your belongings from Officer Cornelius."

The detective turned and left the room without another word. Jade and Suzanne exited the building before they spoke to each other again.

"We need to talk," Suzanne said. "Did you drive here?"

"No, two police officers picked me up at my house."

Suzanne swore under her breath before she said, "I'll take you home. Do you have coffee?"

"Yes, I do," Jade replied. "I'll keep your cup full as long as you promise to tell me what happened."

They got into Suzanne's car and drove away from the police station. Jade directed her to park in the driveway so that they could go in through the back door. She introduced Suzanne to Teddy and made a pot of coffee. They sat down at the dining room table, and Jade waited for Suzanne to begin.

"You know now that Renee was found dead at the museum," Suzanne began. "What Holloway didn't tell you was that her body was found in the Pioneer Town exhibit. You were seen there only a few minutes before Renee went in."

"Renee was standing by the elevator when I last saw her," Jade began.

Suzanne held up her hand indicating that Jade should listen. "One of her coworkers told police that the two of you appeared to be having a serious discussion. The witness said that you appeared to be arguing but couldn't be sure because he couldn't hear what was being said. Those two circumstances were what led the police to suspect you. Knowing how she was killed should have put that suspicion to rest."

"How was she killed?" Jade asked with wide fearful eyes.

"Her neck was broken," Suzanne began, "by someone who knew how to do it."

"Why would the police suspect me then?"

"I got the impression that Detective Holloway has some grudge against you."

"I'd never met him before the night he questioned me about Uncle Erik's death," Jade said. "Why would he have a grudge against me?"

"I don't know, but if he had any evidence against you at all, you'd have been arrested by now."

The women talked a bit longer before Suzanne said goodnight and went home. Jade locked the door and set the alarm before going upstairs.

She got ready for bed with an aching heart and a troubled mind. She was sure that Renee had somehow gotten caught in the middle of things, and she knew she had to find the answer soon.

CHAPTER TWENTY-FIVE

F<small>RIDAY</small>, January 4, 2018

8:00 a.m.

Jade got up when her alarm sounded. She had traded shifts with Lisa so that she'd be able to attend Renee's funeral on Monday afternoon. She'd work today and be off until Wednesday.

She knew that Renee had two grown sons but didn't know if she had any other family. She'd used her emergency credit card to buy food and soft drinks. She delivered them to Renee's house and met some of her family.

She ate breakfast and fed Teddy before getting ready for work. She had an early shift today and wouldn't have time to take Teddy for some exercise until she got home.

She backed out of the driveway and drove toward Amarillo. She saw the man in the black Toyota following two cars behind her. She didn't know if it was the police or the people responsible for her uncle's death.

The three men had never approached her or tried to get into the house, not while she was there at least. She worried about what would happen if they decided to do more than follow.

She pushed those thoughts out of her mind and began her shift at the boutique. It promised to be another long uneventful day. She kept herself busy until time for her break.

With her paycheck in her wallet, she hurried to her car. She needed to deposit it in the bank and grab some lunch before her break was over. She knew Paula wouldn't mind if she was a little late getting back, but she didn't want to take advantage.

The drive-up windows at the bank were lined up three cars deep. She decided it would be faster to go inside. She parked in the only available space and ran to the door.

She groaned when she realized all of the tellers inside were busy as well. She consoled herself with the thought that the lines seemed to be moving faster than those in the drive-up lanes.

Her check was deposited, and she had some cash in her wallet when she left the bank and headed back to the mall. She parked near the Food Court so that she could at least buy a soft drink before going back to the boutique.

The rest of her shift was more of the same. There were few customers and a lot of looking for things to do.

4:30 p.m.

Her cell phone rang when Jade drove into her garage. She answered the phone and closed the garage door with the press of a button.

"Hi, Jade. Are you home?" Hudson asked.

"I just got here."

"I'd like to drop by and see you if that's okay. I need to talk to you."

"What time?"

"I'm getting ready to go on duty," Hudson told her. "I'll be there in twenty minutes."

"We'll be here," Jade said and ended the call.

She thought she knew what he wanted to talk about. She hadn't heard from him since Tuesday evening.

She went inside and opened the door for Teddy. He greeted her with wet, sloppy face licks, and she gave him his cookie.

Jade went into the living room and settled on the couch. She scrolled through the TV channels trying to decide what to watch while she waited for Hudson.

Teddy found his chew bone and was about to jump on the couch with her when he froze. His hackles up, ears perked, eyes fixed, a low grumble in his throat. He dropped his bone and bolted toward the living room window barking and snarling.

Jade stood up in surprise. "What's wrong, Te...?"

She didn't get the words out before there was a loud bang and the blinds on the window rattled.

The world seemed to be in a state of suspended animation. She couldn't think, couldn't breathe, couldn't move.

And then Teddy whined.

Jade ran toward him. He was lying on the floor. Blood covered his chest. She heard herself crying for help. She found the wound and pressed her hand firmly against it.

Hudson pounded on the front door. "Jade! Are you okay? Jade!"

She ran to the front door and opened it to find Hudson breathing hard with his weapon drawn.

"Help me, Hudson! Teddy's hurt!"

Hudson walked in the room, holstered his weapon, and bent over Teddy. "We need to get him to the vet, now! We need a blanket or a sheet and a thick towel. It'll be faster if you get them. I'll keep pressure on his wound."

Jade didn't argue. She left Teddy in Hudson's hands and ran to the linen closet. She ran back to Teddy and waited for instructions.

"I'll take the towel. You spread that blanket on the floor. It will make carrying him easier if we can move him onto it."

Jade laid the blanket on the floor beside Teddy and watched Hudson stuff the end of the towel into Teddy's wound.

"Do you have an ace bandage or something similar?" Hudson asked.

"I think there's a roll of gauze in the bathroom," she said wiping away tears.

"That'll do."

Jade ran to the bathroom and back to Hudson and Teddy. She opened the roll of gauze and handed it to Hudson.

Hudson wrapped the gauze around Teddy's chest, over the wound, and around his back. He tore the end in half and tied the gauze in place.

"I've got his head and shoulders. I'll need you to get under his hips. We'll lift him just enough to get him to the center of the blanket."

Jade nodded and followed Hudson's instructions. They lifted Teddy together and moved him, being careful of his wound.

"I'm going to bring my car as close as I can to the door. I'll need you to call your vet and tell him that we're on our way."

Nodding, she took her cell phone out of her pocket. Her hands shook so much that she had difficulty making the call.

"They want us to take him in the back way," she said when Hudson returned. "It's closer to the examination room."

"That's good," Hudson replied. "This is going to be the hardest part because of his weight. I'll take this end of the blanket while you take that end. We need to maneuver him into the back seat without hurting him."

"I'll do whatever you say," Jade said.

"We'll lift him together on the count of three. Wrap the corners of the blanket around your hands if you need a better grip. I'll back into the car and pull him across once his shoulders are on the seat."

Jade nodded and made sure she had a tight grip. Hudson counted to three, and they lifted Teddy together. They got him into the car, and Hudson closed the doors.

"Get what you need from the house and lock up," Hudson told her. "I'll get the car back on the street."

She turned and ran inside grabbing her backpack and her keys. She locked the door and set the alarm. They were on their way in seconds.

They arrived at Dr. Burge's office to find two members of his staff waiting for them. The staff members moved Teddy from the car to a nearby gurney and wheeled him into the exam room.

Jade stood by Teddy's head and stroked his ears while the veterinarian assessed the damage. Teddy looked at her with his big brown eyes and whined.

"I need to get an x-ray to see what I'm dealing with," said Dr. Burge. "I'll have to sedate him first."

Jade sniffed and nodded.

"You can stay with him until he goes to sleep, and then I'll have to ask you to wait in the lobby."

Jade stroked Teddy's ears until he fell asleep. Hudson led her to the lobby and the most comfortable seat he could find. He sat down beside her and held her while she cried.

His presence made her feel a little better. She was thankful that she didn't have to deal with another bad situation alone. She liked the feel of his arms around her and allowed herself a good cry while she melted into him.

Hudson went in search of tissues when she stopped crying. He found a box behind the counter and returned to Jade's side.

"Can you tell me what happened?" Hudson asked.

Jade blew her nose before she told him how Teddy had acted right before she heard the shot.

"I saw someone standing in front of your window when I turned onto your street. I heard the shot and saw him run. I was going after him until I heard you scream."

"Did you see who it was?"

"I didn't see his face."

Dr. Burge's assistant entered the lobby. "We're taking Teddy into surgery to remove the bullet," said Janie Strickland. "You can wait here, or leave us your number, and we'll call you with updates."

"No, I'll wait here," Jade replied.

"Would you like to keep his harness with you?" Janie asked, handing it to Jade.

"Yes, thank you."

"Make yourselves comfortable. I'll be back when I have news."

Jade held the harness and struggled to control her emotions. The identification tag reflected the overhead light and drew her attention.

"I need to report what happened. Will you be okay while I call it in?"

"I'll be fine," Jade said and tried to smile at Hudson.

She watched Hudson leave the room and returned her attention to the harness. She stared at it for a moment, waiting for her brain to process what she saw.

The name etched on the tag read Theodore Roosevelt O'Neal aka Teddy.

Jade felt as though someone had opened the drapes of her mind and allowed the light of realization inside. *Why hadn't I thought of it sooner? Teddy Roosevelt was Uncle Erik's favorite president. The president holds the key! There was no better hiding place. No one else would be able to get that close to Teddy.*

She ran the harness through her fingers and felt something inside the chest strap. It didn't feel like it was part of the material. She lifted it toward her face for a better look. There was a small part of the stitching that was different than the rest.

Hudson startled her when he returned, and she stuffed the harness into her pocket.

"I've filed my report, but you'll need to make a statement about what happened," he told her. "A patrol car will be in your neighborhood looking for anyone matching the description of the man I saw."

"What did he look like?" asked Jade.

"He was about five ten and about a hundred seventy pounds. He was wearing jeans and a dark hoodie. His head was covered, so I couldn't see anything else."

She knew from Hudson's description that it wasn't one of the three men who'd been following her. One was taller and the other two were heavier.

"Do you have any idea why he was there or what he was after?"

"Not unless it has something to do with Uncle Erik's death," she said. "Or Renee's."

"I can't help but believe that you were his target, but he had to get Teddy out of the way first."

"What do you mean?" Jade asked although she knew he was right.

"I have a feeling this is all connected somehow," he said and looked into her eyes.

Jade returned his gaze and felt an overwhelming urge to tell Hudson everything, but the memory of her uncle's warning changed her mind. Don't trust anyone!

"What did you want to talk to me about?" she asked, trying to break the spell.

"I wanted to tell you to watch your back. I couldn't risk being overheard at the station," he began. "Detective Holloway seems determined to arrest you. There was no evidence at either crime scene that indicated you were involved, yet you were the only person questioned."

"My lawyer seems to think that Detective Holloway has something against me."

"It sounds like you have a good lawyer, and I think she's right."

"I don't know why. I'd never met him before."

"I don't know either, but he wanted to bully you like he did before. He wasn't happy that you called her, or that she got the better of him."

"Do you think the man today is connected to Detective Holloway?"

"I don't want to tell you what I think until I have some evidence to back it up," Hudson said.

Their conversation was interrupted by Janie Strickland. "The doctor was able to remove the bullet," she said and handed Hudson a plastic bag. "He thought you might need this for your investigation."

"How is Teddy doing?" Jade asked.

"Dr. Burge is still working on his wound, but he seems to be doing fine. It should be over soon."

Janie disappeared into the back room, and Hudson stuffed the bag into his pocket.

Hudson's radio beeped, and he excused himself to take the call. He returned ten minutes later.

"I've got to go into work, but I'll take you home first. I'd rather you were in protective custody but under the circumstances...," he broke off.

Dr. Burge entered the room. "Teddy's going to be fine. The bullet missed his vital organs and was lodged against a bone in his shoulder. He's in recovery now. I want to keep him here for a few days under observation."

"Can I see him?" Jade asked, willing herself not to cry.

Dr. Burge smiled at her with compassion. "Follow me. You can wait with him until we move him to a kennel."

Hudson and Jade followed the vet into a back room. Teddy was on a table covered in a blanket. Jade sat on a stool near his head and stroked his ears.

Teddy moved his head and opened his eyes.

"We're keeping him on a mild sedative so that he doesn't thrash around," Janie told her. "He's going to be sleeping a lot for the rest of the night and tomorrow. You should go home and get some rest."

Jade nodded and followed Hudson to the lobby.

"I moved my car around front," he said and escorted her

outside. "I don't think you should be alone tonight. Is there somewhere else you can stay?"

"I have a friend I can call," she said but had no intention of doing so.

"Good, go to her place and call me when you get there."

Jade nodded but said nothing more.

7:15 p.m.

Hudson stopped in her driveway and escorted her to the door. He went inside to make sure the house was safe before leaving her there alone.

"Make sure the house is locked down, and the security system is on," he told her. "Don't stay here too long. That guy might come back."

"I'll be fine," Jade assured him. "Don't worry."

Hudson looked at her as though he wanted to say more, but his radio beeped, and he went to his car and drove away.

Jade did as Hudson had suggested and made sure the house was secure. She went upstairs to her closet where she found a small pair of scissors. She took the harness from her pocket and turned on the lamp beside her bed.

The light wasn't bright enough, so she went into the bathroom and turned on her makeup mirror. She put it on the highest setting and went to work on the seam.

She made the opening larger than she had to so that she could get it out quickly. She set the scissors aside and pulled the seam apart. She turned the harness upside down and a key fell onto the bathroom counter.

She tossed the bloody harness into the bathtub and washed the blood off her hands before she picked up the key. It was on a small keyring and had a tag attached. The tag had a number on it and the words "Fun 2 Bowl."

It was a key to her uncle's bowling locker. He'd always enjoyed bowling and was part of a league team. He must have hidden something in his locker for her to find.

Jade's heart knocked in her chest like the engine of her old Chevy Malibu.

It wasn't fear that made her heart pound, but anger and determination. She knew that Teddy would be safe at the veterinary office. She wanted to catch whoever was responsible for tearing her family apart and killing her friend. She had to find out what was going on.

She went to her closet and changed clothes. She dressed in layers to ward off the chill of the winter night. She tossed her bloody clothes into the bathtub with Teddy's harness.

In her dresser, she found the photo of her dad and uncle. She carried it to the closet and took her puzzle book from its hiding place. She tucked the photo into the book and looked around her room. She turned off the light and went across the hall.

Looking through the blinds in her uncle's room, she saw the Dodge Durango sitting at the corner. She needed to move fast.

She went downstairs and put her puzzle book and photo into her backpack. She made sure that she had her wallet, cell phone, and car keys before going to the garage.

She got into her car, started the engine, and opened the garage door. She intended to leave the house as if nothing was wrong. She wanted her stalkers to believe that she was living her life as usual.

She backed out the driveway and drove onto the street. She drove to Fourth Street and then to Twenty-Third and pointed her car toward Amarillo. The Durango was right behind her at the traffic light.

They merged onto I-27, and Jade kept her eyes on her rearview mirror. It was dark, but she was sure he was still on her tail. She needed to lose this guy soon. She needed to make sure he didn't find her before she had a chance to open her uncle's bowling locker.

Jade drove to the mall, parked her car near an entrance, and went inside. She stood out of sight and watched the Durango drive through the parking lot, circle back, and park beside her car. The man with the royal flush tattoo got out and started toward the entrance.

She speed walked to the boutique to find Lisa and Paula talking at the checkout counter.

"What are you doing back here?" Paula asked.

"There's a creepy guy following me," Jade said. "He was behind me all the way into town, and he's coming into the mall. Will you help me lose him?"

"We should call the police," Lisa said.

"He hasn't done anything except follow me," said Jade. "I don't think the police can do anything about it at this point."

Jade turned and saw the man coming toward the store. "He's coming this way."

"Here, take these clothes into the dressing room," Paula said. "I'll block his view while you go into my office."

Jade took the clothes from Paula and went into the dressing room. She waited until Paula asked if the clothes fit before she squeezed through the door and went into Paula's office. She had time to decide what she was going to do next while she waited for Paula.

"He's sitting on that bench across from the store," Paula said when she entered the office. "You can't go out that way."

"I have an idea," Jade told her. "But I'll need to borrow a car."

"Oh honey, we can't help you with that," Paula said. "Lisa's car is in the shop, and my husband has my car. He's picking me up when we close. Why don't you slip out the back door and get back to your car?" Paula asked.

"He knows my car, and I'm afraid he'll catch me before I can get to it," Jade replied.

"We'll change your outfit," Paula said. "Change your style completely. He won't be expecting that."

"That's a good idea," Jade said. "Then I can slip out and go to my car."

Paula and Jade rummaged through the returns until they found clothes that would fit. Paula went to the dressing room and pretended to hand Jade more clothes to try on while Jade changed in the office.

Jade looked in the mirror when she'd finished. Tattoo man wouldn't recognize her in this get up. She wouldn't have recognized herself. She was wearing a grey pair of slacks with a forest green sweater. She wore a tan tweed jacket and her long hair was tucked under a tan knit cap. Her own clothes and her backpack were hidden inside a large shopping bag.

Paula returned to the office. "I've arranged for a little diversion. Mall security is going to distract him. Go out the back door into the hallway. Turn left, and you'll come out by Dillard's. Security should be keeping him busy long enough for you to circle back to your car."

Jade was about to thank her, but Paula pushed her out into the hallway and closed the door. She hurried down the hallway toward Dillard's, but she didn't circle back. She walked toward the Food Court instead and called for a cab.

She waited outside near the entrance and kept an eye out for the tattooed man. She left the mall when the cab drove up and got inside.

"Where are we going?" asked the driver.

"Fun 2 Bowl," she said, and they were on their way.

CHAPTER TWENTY-SIX

8:30 p.m.

When they arrived at the bowling alley, Jade paid the cab driver. She went inside with the key to her uncle's locker in the pocket of her jacket.

It was league night, and the bowling alley was packed with bowlers. Jade looked at the lockers, checking the numbers, looking for the one that corresponded with her key. She found it conveniently located near some restrooms.

She looked around to see if anyone was watching. The person at the counter was too busy to notice Jade.

She put the key into the lock and turned it. She opened the door and removed a bowling bag. She closed the locker and went to the ladies' room.

The restroom was empty. Jade went into a stall and slid the latch closed. She unzipped the bag and found an envelope with her name written on the front. She opened the envelope to find cash, a fake ID with her picture on it, and a letter. She opened the letter and saw her uncle's handwriting.

Jade, don't go through the bag at the bowling alley. Find a safe place where you won't be interrupted. Don't use your own name and don't use plastic. Use the cash to pay for anything you need. Use the ID only when necessary. Everything will be explained soon. Love, Uncle Erik.

She put the letter back into the bowling bag and zipped it closed. She took her backpack out of the shopping bag and hung it on the hook on the stall door. She stuffed the cash and the ID into one of the zippered pockets.

She changed into her own clothes and put the borrowed ones into the shopping bag. She took the backpack from the hook and slung it across her back. Picking up the shopping bag, she left the bathroom stall.

She opened the locker, put the shopping bag inside, and pocketed the key. She made her way through the crowd to the parking lot. She considered calling another cab but decided against it. She could see a lighted motel sign in the distance. It was close enough that she could walk, and no one that she knew would think to look for her there.

She took out her cell phone and called Hudson. She left him a message when it went to his voicemail. "Hi Hudson. I just wanted to let you know that I'm going to disappear for a while. Don't worry. I'm safe. I'll call you later."

Jade turned off her cell phone and put it in her pocket. She didn't want to talk to anyone at the moment. She squared her shoulders and set off toward the motel sign.

9:45 p.m.

The motel was further away than it appeared. She was cold and tired by the time she reached the front entrance.

The clerk at the desk greeted her with a smile. The name tag on the forty something woman's shirt said Lillian. Her hair was cut short and died jet black. She wore bright red lipstick with salon nails to match.

Jade walked to the counter and said, "I'd like a room for the night."

"We have lots of rooms available," said Lillian with a slow drawl.

"I just need a place to sleep," Jade replied. "And I need to pay cash."

Lillian leaned over the counter and looked at the bowling bag. She looked Jade over and said, "Are you running from someone, honey?"

Jade forced tears to her eyes and nodded. "It's my boyfriend. I can't let him find me."

"I understand, sweetie. It happens more often than you think," said Lillian.

"How much for a room?"

"Twenty dollars for the room. Another twenty buys my sealed lips and a warning phone call should anyone come looking for you."

Jade fumbled in her backpack and found two twenties. She handed them to Lillian and asked, "Do you need a name?"

"I'll make one up," said Lillian with a wink. "Makes it easier to keep my lips sealed, and you aren't going to give me your real name anyway."

She swiped a keycard through the machine and handed it to Jade. "It's on the second floor near the stairs. You'll be able to see the parking lot from the window."

"Thank you," said Jade. She took the key card and went in search of her room.

The room was nothing fancy. It could best be described as shabby chic, but it was clean, and the bed looked comfortable. She locked the door and put the security chain in place. She put the bowling bag and her backpack on the bed and moved a nearby desk chair under the doorknob just in case. She didn't know if it would keep anyone out, but it was worth a try.

She picked up the bowling bag and dumped the contents on the bed. A book, a cell phone with a charger, and a flashlight lay in front of her. She picked up the book and found another letter tucked inside.

She read the instructions twice.

Use the cell phone and text the first half of the family motto. The correct response is the second half. Call the number if you get the right reply. Throw the cell phone away if you don't.

She picked up the cell phone and tried to turn it on. The battery was dead. She plugged it in and waited until the phone had enough power to use. She tapped the contact button and found one number stored there. She tapped in the letters and made sure there were no mistakes. The text read "light on the outside." She pressed send.

She didn't have to wait long for the reply. She was relieved to read the words "light on the inside." She tapped the phone number and waited, wondering who would answer the call.

"Jade? Is that you? Are you safe?" asked a familiar voice.

"Mom! I'm fine for now. What's going on?"

"All I know is what I've been told," Mollie began. "There was a box waiting for me at the post office when I got back to Dallas. Erik must have mailed it a few days before he was killed. It had this cell phone and a letter with a set of instructions. The letter said that he was trying to keep us all safe. It said that he planned to tell us everything, but he'd set up some safe guards just in case."

"He hid messages and clues in the puzzle book he gave me," Jade told her mother. "I searched for days trying to find the last one."

"How did you find it?"

"It was in Teddy's harness." she said and began to cry. "Mom, they shot Teddy."

"Oh no! Is he gone?"

"No, we got him to the vet in time, and he'll be okay," Jade told her. "Uncle Erik's bowling locker key was hidden inside Teddy's harness. I might never have found it."

"I'm glad he'll be okay. Where is he now?"

"He's at the veterinary office. They wanted to keep him there for observation. And there's something else," Jade said. "Uncle Erik's friend Renee was killed at the museum."

"Oh my God! We need to get you away from there!"

"No, Mom! I have to finish this," Jade said feeling her anger surge. "These people have to be stopped. Uncle Erik left me the clues. No one else can do it."

"All right," Mollie said. "There was more information in the letter. He didn't want me to share it with you unless you were willing to keep going."

"I am. This has to stop!" Jade answered.

"Erik believed that your father was murdered. He was close to finding the evidence that would prove it. He's been investigating your father's death for years. He didn't share any of that information with us because he didn't want us to be in danger. He left the clues for you and sent me the package in case something happened to him. All of his notes, his records, and the evidence he's gathered over the years are locked away in a safe place. He wanted you to find it and take it to the police."

"Mom, I don't know that taking it to the police is a good idea."

"Why not?"

"Suzanne Walls and Hudson both think that the detective handling Uncle Erik's case has something against me. I was questioned about Renee's murder, too."

"Who is Hudson?"

"He's the police officer that took care of me when I found Uncle

Erik. He was there when Teddy was shot and helped me get him to the vet."

"Does he know where you are?" Mollie asked with worry in her voice.

"No, and I haven't told him about the clues or anything else. No one knows."

"Can you trust Hudson?"

"I think so, but I'm not taking the chance right now. I need to find Uncle Erik's evidence fast. Chances are that the police are already looking for me. Do you know where it's stored?"

"No, but I have another number for you. Use the same procedure you used to contact me."

Jade wrote the number on a notepad.

"I don't know who will answer," Mollie said, "but you should get more information from that person. Jade, be careful."

"I will. I love you, Mom."

"I love you, too!"

Jade texted "light on the outside" to the number that Mollie had given her. She waited until she got the response "light on the inside" before dialing.

Levi answered the phone. "Jade? Are you okay?"

"I'm fine. Tell me what's going on," Jade replied.

Levi received a package similar to the one that their mother had gotten. He gave Jade a series of numbers while she wrote them on a notepad. He told her that she was to use the book that she'd found to decipher a code.

"Did you find the code and the book?" Levi asked.

"I did," Jade assured him.

"I'd like to talk longer and find out more, but I'm on duty now. We're supposed to delete everything from these phones and dispose of them. You also need to keep Mom's birthday in mind. Be careful, Sis. I love you."

"I love you, too."

Jade deleted the text messages and the phone calls from the

phone and removed the battery. She put both in the bowling bag and would dispose of them later. She didn't want them to be found in the hotel trash.

She took her puzzle book from her backpack and pulled the photo from between the pages. She set the puzzles aside and picked up the book from the bowling bag.

She'd expected to find one of her uncle's favorite books or one of her own. Instead, it was her mother's favorite, *Pride and Prejudice*.

She opened the book and began working out the code on the photograph. There were numbers arranged in groups of three. She thought the first letter would be the page number, the second the line on the page, and the third the letter on the line.

It was tedious work, and it took some time to find all of the letters. Closing the book, she read her notes. There were no punctuations, and she had to read it several times before she realized it was a street address and a single letter.

She took her cell phone out of her backpack and turned it on. There were six missed calls and voicemails from Hudson. She ignored the notifications and tapped the internet icon. She typed in the address and discovered that it was the address of a storage facility. She looked up the directions. It was down the street from the motel.

She was safe at the motel, but she knew the best time to get inside the storage facility unseen was at night. She looked at the time. Eleven-thirty was still early for a Friday night, and she didn't want to be seen on the streets. Needing to rest before hiking to the storage facility, she set the alarm on her cell phone and did the best she could to get ready for bed.

She crawled under the covers wearing the workout clothes she wore under her jeans and sweatshirt. She was about to doze off when her cell phone rang.

It was Hudson. She let it go to voice mail again and got out of bed. She dug the new cell phone out of the bowling bag and reinstalled the battery. She set the alarm on that phone and turned hers off again.

She had a short time to rest, and she didn't want to be disturbed before it was necessary.

Saturday, January 5, 2018

3:30 a.m.

Jade was awake when the alarm sounded. She turned it off and stretched before padding to the bathroom. She felt better after the nap, but what she really wanted was to sleep for days. She knew that wasn't going to happen until things were resolved.

She got dressed and put everything she needed in her backpack. She decided to keep the extra cell phone a while longer. She turned it off and put it in her pocket.

Checking the room once more to make sure she wasn't leaving anything behind, her eyes fell on the notepad she'd been using. She decided to take it with her in case she needed it again. She put the backpack across her shoulders and left the room key on the night stand before she tiptoed out the door.

The storage facility was a little more than two miles from the motel. It would take forty-five minutes to an hour to get there walking a straight line. She was going to be staying in the shadows and avoiding busy streets. She had no idea how long it would take her.

Jade walked at a brisk pace keeping to the shadows as much as she could. She walked across vacant lots, through alleys, and parking lots until she reached the address.

She walked around the outside of the property, looking for the best place to begin her search. There were several buildings, each displaying a letter. She located the building indicated by the message she'd decoded. It was the building farthest from the office and near the northwest corner of the property.

She crept up to the fence, trying to see the unit numbers and any security cameras. She needed to get inside without being seen. She wondered what the chances were that the security cameras weren't working.

She walked along the fence line until she found unit four fifteen. It was her mother's birthdate. There was one security camera in that section. Watching it for a few minutes, she realized that it did a slow sweep of the area. She'd wait until it was focused on the opposite side of the property to make her move. Her more immediate problem was getting through the fence.

Jade went further down the fence line until she came to an indention in the landscape. She took off her backpack and searched inside for the flashlight. She turned on the light and discovered that it was a drainage ditch with enough room for her to crawl under the fence.

She turned off the flashlight and returned it to her backpack. She tossed the backpack under the fence before she lay on the ground and army crawled through the opening.

Returning the backpack to her shoulders, she backtracked to the storage unit. She waited until the camera was pointed in the opposite direction before moving out of the shadows. She swore when she saw a lock on the unit door.

She kept her eye on the security camera and tried the number series that Levi had given her. The lock didn't budge. She spun the dial and tried again. This time it worked. She opened the door enough that she could get through and closed it before the camera swept the area.

Jade stayed near the door while she removed her backpack and located the flashlight. She swept the beam around the room. A cabinet standing four feet high and three feet wide stood near the doorway. A piece of masking tape with the words "power supply" stretched across the top.

Jade opened the cabinet door and found a red switch. She moved it to the "on" position and gawked when light filled the room.

The space had all the comforts of home. A twin bed was in a back corner of the spacious unit. There were a desk, a chair, and a file cabinet.

All of the electrical appliances were battery powered. There were a small refrigerator, a hotplate, a space heater, and a fan.

The missing laptop and a hotspot for internet service waited on the desk. Above the desk was a bulletin board with photos and news articles pinned to it.

Everything she might need was there. All of his research and all of the evidence he'd gathered was cataloged. Half of the unit was used for workspace and living space.

Jade was still having trouble comprehending what she saw in the other half of the unit. She stared at the 1995 BMW 3 sedan. The paint was light blue, and it appeared to be in perfect condition except for a big dent in the grill and on the hood.

She shook her head, trying to focus. She didn't have time to stand around. She had work to do. The problem was that she didn't know where to start. She took out her cell phone and looked at the time. It was five a.m.

She went to the desk and stared at the laptop. A flash drive was in the USB port. She turned off the volume on her phone and set it aside. She put her backpack on the floor beside the file cabinet and sat in the desk chair.

She turned on the laptop and waited for it to boot up. A video file with her name on it was in the center of the screen. It was dated December thirteenth. She clicked it twice, and Uncle Erik's face filled the screen.

"Hi, Jade." Erik said. "I plan to tell you and your mother everything and show you all of this while we're together for Christmas. This is a precaution in case something happens to me before then.

I know that if you're watching this that the worst has happened.

I can't imagine what you're going through. I'm sorry for the pain, fear, and confusion that you must be feeling. Please, bear with me while I explain what this is about and why all of this stuff is here."

Jade listened while Erik explained why he had done the things he'd done and how he'd come to the conclusions that he'd made.

"Jacob had been killed in what we thought was a hit and run accident," Erik continued. "My time in the military was ending. I decided not to reenlist when Jacob died so that I could be close by for the three of you.

I'd been home for a month when I got a letter from Jacob. It was postmarked the day he died. It must have bounced around a dozen military posts before it finally got to me. He stumbled on to something that had him worried. I believed he'd been murdered after reading his letter. The letter is in a folder in the file cabinet along with everything I learned from the police investigation.

Everything you need to prove that your dad was murdered is in this room. I'm about to collect the last piece of the puzzle so that we can prove who killed him.

I'm sure you're wondering about the car. It's also evidence. It happens to be the car that killed your dad. It still has the license plates on it that it had back then. I tracked down the people who owned the car at the time. They reported it stolen the morning of the accident. I have my doubts.

Take care of yourself and remember that I love you. 'Light on the outside. Light on the inside.'"

The video ended and Jade sat for a moment, processing what she'd heard. She took a deep breath, stood, and went to the file cabinet. She took out the folder that contained her father's letter and began reading.

It was the first time she'd seen her father's handwriting. She had chills while reading his words. She understood why Uncle Erik believed he'd been murdered.

Jade spent hours reading through every piece of evidence. There were three people that Erik listed as suspects. One was scratched off and later added again.

No wonder he'd warned her not to trust anyone. These men were powerful and well connected. Together, they employed thousands of people in the area. Any one of them could be the actual killer.

The fact that she'd met and spoken several times with the three suspects concerned her. She wondered if the men following her worked for Jonathan Baxter, Wilson Lee, or Dino Stevens. She shuddered to think that any of them could have been responsible for the deaths of her father and uncle. She knew one of them wouldn't think twice about disposing of her.

The light on her cell phone attracted her attention. It was Hudson calling again. She didn't want to talk to him yet. She wasn't finished going through the evidence.

The clock on her phone showed that it was almost noon. She was tired and hungry, but she felt safe here. She knew that her uncle did, too.

She got up and found some nonperishable food in a crate under the bed. She took out some crackers and a can of soup with a pop top. She opened the can of soup and heated it on the hotplate then poured it into a disposable bowl. She took a bottle of water from the fridge and sat at the desk to eat.

While she ate, she stared at the photos and clippings on the bulletin board. There was still so much to go through. It would take her days. She'd have to leave the safety of the storage unit and go to work. And what about Renee's funeral?

Jade finished her meal and cleared away the trash. She glanced at the door of the unit and wondered if it locked from the inside. Uncle Erik must have locked it when he stayed here.

Inspecting the door, she noticed that a hinged bar stretched from one side of the door to the other. She listened at the door to make sure no one was near before she tested her theory. She pushed the hinged center of the bar down causing the ends to slide into a notch. The door wouldn't budge until the center of the bar was moved up, releasing the ends.

Jade left the door locked and went back to the desk. She picked up her phone and saw another missed call notification. She'd call Hudson, but first she needed to sleep. She turned off her cell phone and took the extra one from her backpack. She set the alarm for four o'clock. She turned off the lights and used the phone to find her way to the bed. She fell into a peaceful slumber in seconds.

CHAPTER TWENTY-SEVEN

SATURDAY, January 5, 2018

4:00 p.m.

It took a several minutes for the sound of the alarm to penetrate Jade's mind. She turned off the alarm when she realized it wasn't part of the dream she'd been having. She sat up and used the light on the phone to locate the light switch.

Something nagged at Jade. There was something she'd seen or read that she needed to revisit, but she didn't know what it was. She browsed through the notes and reports that she'd read, but she knew it wasn't there.

She walked around the room, looking at everything and seeing nothing. She was trying to focus on what was bothering her. She walked past the desk and glanced at the bulletin board. She took a few more steps and stopped.

She went back to the bulletin board. There near the center was a picture. She took it from the board for a closer look. It was a young man standing beside a BMW, smiling and waving at the camera.

She went to the front of the car and compared it to the one in the photograph. There was no doubt it was the same one. The license plates matched.

Jade shook her head. No, that wasn't what was bothering her. She looked at the photo closer. She stared at the young man's face. He appeared to be in his mid-twenties.

She gasped when she realized what this meant. The young man in the photo was waving with his left hand, and part of his left pinkie finger was missing.

She knew which of the three suspects was in this photo. All she needed now was proof that he'd killed her father and her uncle.

She sat down at the desk and turned on the computer. She searched all of the files to see if her uncle had anything saved that would prove who had killed her father. She turned on the hotspot so that she could search the internet history.

An email notification popped up when she accessed the internet. She clicked on the notification. It was from one of Uncle Erik's friends in law enforcement. The photo from the bulletin board was on the screen beside a more recent photo of the man. The email was confirmation that facial recognition had confirmed the photos were of the same man.

She opened a second email. It was a report saying that the two fingerprint samples that Uncle Erik sent were a match.

Jade knew these two emails confirmed her opinion of the man's identity, but she couldn't see how it proved anything other than he was somehow connected to the car that killed her father.

She browsed through the search history and past emails again. She found nothing else that was helpful. She closed the internet browser and turned off the hotspot.

She got up and walked around the room. She needed help if she was going to find the needle in this haystack.

She thought about calling Heather. She'd protected her and taken care of her in the Logan ordeal. Still, she didn't think that Heather was the right person for the job in this case.

Hudson was the person she needed. He had expertise that Jade needed and Heather lacked.

She picked up her cell phone and turned it on. She decided to listen to Hudson's voice mails before she called him. She found the phone charger that came with the other phone and plugged it in. She tapped the voice mail icon and listened.

The first three were the same. "Call me and let me know you're safe." The fourth and fifth calls were a bit more urgent, "I need to talk to you. Call me!" The last voice mail said, "There's been a development. It's urgent that you call me."

Jade looked at the time on her phone. It was almost six o'clock. It would be dark outside by now. She didn't want to meet Hudson here. She'd need to meet him somewhere nearby. She'd have to stay in the shadows while she walked to their meeting place.

She opened the text icon on her phone and tapped in Hudson's number. She texted the words "Can you talk?" The word "Later" was his reply.

She continued to search through the reports, papers, and files that Erik had accumulated during his research. The proof had to be here somewhere. She just had to find it.

She was startled when her phone buzzed. She looked at the caller ID before she answered.

"Hi, Hudson," she said.

"Are you in a safe place?"

"Yes, no one knows where I am."

"You need to stay put if you can."

"I can stay here for a while. What's happening?"

"Logan Rhodes was found dead last night."

"Oh my God!"

"He was shot with the same caliber weapon as your uncle. One shot to the chest."

"Do you think it was the same person?"

"We won't know for sure until the ballistics report comes back, but I wouldn't be surprised."

"Am I the primary suspect again?" she asked.

"It's possible, but that's the least of your worries right now," Hudson told her.

"Why is that?"

"Two men went to the Cantina last night and grabbed Heather when her shift ended. They wanted her to tell them where you're hiding."

"Is she okay?"

"She was scared but not hurt," he said. "You don't seem to be surprised."

"No, I'm not," Jade admitted. "That's why I decided to disappear. I don't want anyone else to get hurt. I don't want anyone else to die."

"Including me?"

"Including you," Jade told him, "but it's come to the point that I have to trust someone. Could you meet me somewhere so we can talk?"

"Any time, any place."

"There's a sandwich shop in a shopping center in Amarillo near Hillside and Western. I'll be there in an hour. I won't go in until you're inside, and I'm sure you haven't been followed."

"I'll be there," Hudson assured her. "What makes you think I'll be followed?"

"Those men knew where to find Heather. I'm sure they know where to find you."

"You have a point. Be careful."

"You, too."

The call ended, and she put her cell phone on silent. She opened her backpack and took out everything except her wallet and the flashlight. She needed to have her hands free and her pockets weren't big enough.

She listened at the door before raising the hinged bar. She listened again before pulling the hoodie over her head and opening the door. She closed it right away and put the lock back in place. She clicked it closed and walked toward the drainage ditch.

Jade got to the sandwich shop much too early, but she wanted to have plenty of time in case she had to hide. She found a dark place across the street where she could watch without being seen.

7:00 p.m.

Hudson parked in front of the restaurant and got out of the car. He looked around before going inside. He sat at a table facing the door.

Jade waited ten minutes before leaving her hiding place. She saw no one watching from a parked car. She stayed in the shadows until she reached the restaurant and went inside.

"Are you hungry?" asked Hudson.

"Yes, I'm starved."

"Let's order, and then we'll talk."

They went to the counter and ordered their sandwiches with chips and drinks. Jade scanned the parking lot before she sat back down.

They ate for a few minutes before Jade decided it was time to tell Hudson what she knew.

"Hudson, are you sure you want to get into the middle of this?" she asked.

"I think I'm already in the middle of whatever this is," he replied.

"This is going to be a long story with a surprise ending," she said.

"I love long stories and surprise endings," he said and smiled at her. "I know you're scared. I promise, I won't let you down."

"I don't know where to start," she said. "There's so much to tell you."

"I've always thought the best stories start at the beginning," he teased.

"Do you remember that I told you my dad died when I was little?"

"Yes, I remember that. You said your uncle stepped in and helped raise you."

"That's right," Jade said. "Well, it turns out that my dad was murdered."

She told Hudson the whole story. She told him how Erik had left messages and clues for her, and about the three men who had been following her, watching her every move. She told him how she had managed to lose the tattooed man and disappeared. She told him everything except where the evidence was hidden and who she believed was behind it all.

Hudson was speechless. He took a bite of his sandwich, sipped his drink, and finished off his chips before he said anything.

Jade watched him with apprehension. She wondered if she'd been wrong to trust him. She thought about bolting for the door.

"I'm sorry," Hudson said at last. "I'm trying to process everything you've just told me. I don't know how you've managed to keep it all together. This is the kind of stuff that drives cops to drink."

"I didn't have a choice," Jade replied. "Those men following me don't know about my part in this. They've followed and watched me all the same."

"That's true enough. Who did your uncle suspect was behind it all?"

"There are three men on his suspect list. They're all powerful, wealthy men who employ thousands of people. I'm sure most of them are legitimate employees. Some of them are not."

"The three stooges that have been watching you are a good example of that," Hudson replied.

"There could be more people watching. Those three, I saw on a regular basis."

"Your suspicions about Logan being in on the burglaries and

drugging Teddy has more merit now that I know the rest of the story."

"I don't understand why they killed him if he was working with them," Jade said.

"The question now is what are we going to do about it?" Hudson said.

"Does that mean you're going to help me?"

"I never figured it any other way," he said with a smile.

"In that case, I have to show you something," Jade said. "We'll need to hide your car."

"We could leave it in a parking lot somewhere and use your vehicle."

"I don't have access to my car at the moment. It's still at the mall as far as I know."

"How did you get here?"

"Alternate transportation."

10:00 p.m.

Hudson and Jade drove his car to his parents' house and parked it in their garage. They walked three blocks away, called a cab, and went back to the shopping center. Jade led Hudson to the storage facility and through the drainage ditch to the storage unit. She took the flashlight from her backpack and handed it to Hudson.

"Hold this so that I can dial the combination," she said.

He held the flashlight and waited until they were both inside before saying, "Have you been here the whole time?"

"No, I spent part of last night in a motel."

She turned on the light and locked the door. "What do you think?"

"This is incredible," he said and wandered around the room. "Is this the missing laptop?"

"Yes, he left a video for me on it. Some of the evidence is there, too."

"Have you gone through all of this?"

"Most of it," said Jade. "I knew I was in over my head after a while. Uncle Erik was an M.P. in the military. He understood all of this better than I do."

"Do you mind if I..." Hudson began.

"Please, help yourself. I'd like to know if you come to the same conclusion that I did. I'll stay out of your way."

She lay down on the bed and watched Hudson work for a long time before she fell asleep.

He worked for hours reading files, comparing notes, and looking at photographs. He wasn't satisfied with what he'd learned. He searched through drawers and boxes again until he found a VHS tape. There was no label on it. He searched the room for a player but found nothing.

Sunday, January 6, 2018

2:45 a.m.

"Jade," he said and shook her shoulder. "Wake up, Jade."

She opened her eyes and asked, "How long have I been asleep?"

"A long time," he said and held the tape so that she could see it. "Do you know what's on this?"

"No, where did you find it?"

"It was in a box that you hadn't opened yet. Did you happen to find a player or a TV in here?"

"No, but I may not have looked through everything."

"I've looked everywhere except under your bunk."

"Let's look then," Jade said and stood up.

They pulled everything from under the bed and searched all of the crates and boxes. They found an old video player and some cables under a case of SpaghettiOs.

"Do you know how to connect this to the laptop?" Jade asked.

"I'm not sure, but we'll try," Hudson replied and carried the video player to the desk.

It took some time, but they managed to get it to work. They put the tape in the player and watched a view of a parking lot.

"This looks like a copy of a surveillance tape," said Hudson.

"I think I know where that is," said Jade. "That may be where my dad worked."

They watched a few minutes longer until they saw a man walk across the parking lot and drop a letter in a mailbox near the entrance. The man disappeared inside.

"That may have been my dad," Jade said.

"Look," Hudson pointed to the screen with excitement. "Isn't that the car?"

"Hudson, I don't think I can watch this," Jade said, when she realized what was on the tape.

"You don't have too," Hudson replied. "I think this is the evidence that we need to put our guy away."

Jade turned away from the screen until Hudson asked her to look at something. He had stopped the tape and zoomed in to show the face of the man in the car.

"That's him. That's the same guy in the picture," Hudson said. "He ran over your dad. It was all caught on tape."

"Look at his hand," Jade said pointing at the screen.

The driver's side window was down and the man's left arm was resting on the door. Part of his pinkie finger was missing.

"I wonder why your uncle didn't copy this to a CD," Hudson said.

"He may not have had the chance. He said he was looking for the last piece of evidence."

"They must have grabbed your uncle after he called you. He didn't give them what they wanted. Either he told them that the evidence would be turned over, or they assumed he'd passed it on to you," Hudson told her.

"We can prove that he killed my dad. How are we going to prove he killed my uncle?"

"We may not be able to," Hudson said. "This is enough to put him away for the rest of his life."

"I know, but what about justice for my uncle and Renee and Logan?"

Hudson stood and walked around the room. He turned and looked at Jade.

"Are you sure its justice that you want or revenge?"

"Can't I have both?" she replied.

"It could be very dangerous."

"I've been in danger since Uncle Erik died," she said. "I don't want to live the rest of my life looking over my shoulder wondering when they'll decide to kill me. Renee didn't know any of this. I never told her, and I know my uncle didn't. They killed her anyway."

"That's a good point."

"They or he or whoever have to be stopped," Jade said. "They didn't hurt Heather last night, but who's to say they won't kill her, too. They might kill anyone who is remotely connected to me. I can't live with that."

"Okay, you've convinced me," Hudson said. "We'll have to make some plans, and we may have to recruit some help."

"Where do we start?"

"You'll have to resurface," Hudson began. "We'll need to find out where our man is going to be for the next few days, and we'll need to arrange for the two of you to cross paths."

"What day is it?" Jade asked.

Hudson looked at his watch. "It's four in the morning, so it's Sunday."

"Wow, it's easy to lose track of time in here," Jade began. "Any way, Renee's funeral is tomorrow at four. The board members attended Uncle Erik's funeral. I assume they'll attend hers, too."

"He's on the board?"

"All three of my uncle's suspects are on the board," Jade said and shook her head.

"What?"

"I just remembered something," she said. "I know why he was acting so weird that night."

"What are you talking about?"

"There was a big party at the museum one night. I went with my uncle and met the board members. I'd already met two of the suspects and was introduced to the third that night. Uncle Erik didn't like that I'd met them, but he tried to act like it was no big deal."

"He had every right to act weird, considering what he knew," said Hudson.

The pair began making their plan and discussed what they would need. Hudson suggested people who would be willing to help.

CHAPTER TWENTY-EIGHT

Sunday, January 7, 2018

5:00 a.m.

Jade and Hudson left the storage facility while it was still dark. They walked to the shopping center, and Hudson called an Uber. They went to his parents' house and got his car from the garage.

They drove to the mall where Jade's car was parked. They drove around looking for anyone who might be watching the car before they stopped. Hudson got out and inspected the car to see if it had been tampered with it. He nodded at Jade when he found nothing that concerned him.

Jade got into the car and turned the key. She drove out of the parking lot and drove back to Canyon while Hudson followed.

She turned onto her street and saw no cars parked where the occupants could watch the house. She'd been worried about what might happen when she returned. Seeing no one watching and waiting made her more nervous.

She opened the garage door and drove inside, leaving room for

Hudson's car. She turned off the engine and closed the garage door when he was inside. They got out of their cars and crept to the door.

Hudson unholstered his weapon and made a few hand signals, indicating that she should stay in the garage while he cleared the house. Jade nodded and unlocked the door. She stepped out of the way and waited for Hudson.

Jade stood still, listening for sounds of gunfire or a struggle. She was relieved when Hudson appeared in the doorway.

"It's all clear," he said. "It doesn't look like anyone has been here. I assume you made the mess in one of the upstairs bedrooms."

"I was in a hurry," she replied.

"You'll want to throw the clothes in the bathtub away," he teased.

"I forgot about those," Jade said. "I'll put them in a garbage bag later."

"Are there any guns in the house?"

"Not unless Uncle Erik had one hidden somewhere. I don't know where it would be."

"Do you know how to use a gun?"

"Yes, but I'm not a good shot," Jade admitted.

"Take this," Hudson said pulling a gun from a holster on his ankle. "It's ready to fire. Point it at the chest and pull the trigger."

Jade nodded and took the Glock from him.

"I need to leave while it's still dark," he told her. "I'll get things going and call you when everything is set."

"Watch your back," she said.

"I will," he said and touched her cheek with his fingertips. "Get some rest, and call me if anything happens. Keep that gun handy."

"I will," she said and waited until he was in his car before opening the garage door for him.

She closed the garage door as soon as he was clear. She went to the storage closet and found a step ladder and some duct tape. She set the ladder under the garage door opener and pulled the power plug. She tucked the emergency pull cord up over the mechanism and secured it with duct tape.

She moved the ladder to the side of the garage and put the tape away. She looked for anything that she could wedge into the track that would prevent the door from opening. She returned the ladder to the closet when she'd made sure no one could get in through the garage.

She went into the house and locked the door behind her. She took a garbage bag from the pantry and went upstairs to her room. She bagged up the bloody clothes and Teddy's harness and tied the bag in a knot. They were beyond saving and were beginning to smell.

She took the garbage bag downstairs and put it in the pantry. She made sure the house was secure before going back upstairs to shower.

Jade put the Glock and her phone on the bathroom counter and turned on the shower. She let the hot water ease the tension from her body and washed away the dirt and grime she'd accumulated while walking through vacant lots and crawling through the drainage ditch.

She toweled off and went in search of clean clothes. She dressed and put her dirty clothes in the laundry hamper before she retrieved her phone and Hudson's gun. She put them both on the nightstand and lay on the bed. She was asleep in minutes.

11:00 a.m.

Jade woke up with a start. She lay still and listened. The doorbell rang. She didn't move and struggled to hear over the thudding of her heart. No one was supposed to know she was home.

She thought she could hear a woman's voice, but she couldn't understand what was being said. She relaxed when she heard an engine start and the sound of a car driving away.

She rolled over and looked at the time. She'd been asleep for four hours. She stretched and relaxed in the comfort of her own bed until the silence was broken by the sound of her stomach growling.

She tucked her phone and Hudson's gun in the pocket on the front of her sweatshirt. She went to the kitchen and opened the refrigerator. There wasn't a lot to choose from.

I'll need to go shopping if I survive this, she thought and took some sandwich meat from the drawer. She took a Dr. Pepper from the shelf and closed the fridge. She found a partial loaf of bread in the cabinet and made a sandwich.

She sat at the bar and thought about Teddy while she ate. She wondered if anyone would be at the veterinarian's office. She wanted to find out how Teddy was doing. She hadn't checked on him since she went into hiding. She knew he must be wondering where she was and why she hadn't come to get him.

Wiping a tear from her eye, she fought the temptation to make the call. *I'll get the answering service anyway,* she told herself and wiped off the bar.

She didn't know what to do with herself. The house was supposed to be empty. She couldn't turn on the lights or make any noise that might give her away. There was nothing she could do other than wait for Hudson's call.

Jade wandered around the house looking for something to occupy her mind. She found a book on the bookshelf in the living room that she'd never read and took it upstairs. She made herself a comfortable place in the closet. She could use the light in there, and no one would see it from outside the house.

She put her phone and the Glock on a shelf and settled into her nest. Opening the book, she read until her cell phone buzzed.

2:30 p.m.

It was a text from Hudson that read, "I'll call you soon."

Jade stood and stretched before taking a bathroom break. She went downstairs for another Dr. Pepper. She was on her way back to the closet when she heard someone trying the knob on the front door. She froze on the stairs wishing she'd thought to carry the Glock with her.

The doorbell rang, and someone pounded on the door. They tried the knob again. She heard a man's voice and several curse words before she heard a car drive away.

She ran up the stairs and put the Glock back in the pocket of her sweatshirt. She texted Hudson and told him about the two visitors to the house. She was waiting for his reply when she heard someone pounding on the back door and trying the knob. She took the Glock from her pocket and kept it in her hand.

Her phone buzzed, and she read Hudson's reply. "They know car is gone."

She went across the hall to her uncle's room and peeked through the curtain. The tan muscular man was getting into the black Toyota and talking on his cell phone. She watched until he drove away.

3:10 p.m.

Jade sat in the closet with her cell phone in her right hand and the Glock in her left. She jumped when her cell phone buzzed.

"How are you doing?" Hudson asked.

"I'm a little rattled," she replied.

"I know. It's only a matter of time until they break into the house," Hudson said. "We're going to have to move you."

"Where?" asked Jade.

"A safe house has been arranged, but we'll have to wait until dark. Is anyone watching the house?"

"I haven't seen anyone," Jade told him. "One of them tried the back door after I texted you. I watched him get in his car and leave."

"My guess is that they're looking for you at every place you've ever been. They'd be stupid to try to break in before dark."

"What do you want me to do?"

"Pack a bag with anything you'll need for tonight and the funeral tomorrow," Hudson directed. "Be ready to go when it gets dark. Check to see if they're watching the house and call me."

"Okay," Jade said. "I'll talk to you later."

The call ended. She put the gun and her phone in her sweatshirt pocket. Going to the closet, she took out clothes to last her for two days. She packed them in a small suitcase and tucked a black dress on top for the funeral. She went to the bathroom and gathered her cosmetics.

Going over everything in her mind, she packed a few items that she'd forgotten before she zipped the bag closed and carried it to the bottom of the stairs. She sat down on the couch to wait.

5:45 p.m.

When it was dark outside, she went upstairs to her uncle's room and peeked through the curtains. There was no sign of her stalkers. Taking her cell phone out of her pocket, she tapped Hudson's number.

"There's no one watching that I can see," she told Hudson.

"Good, but we need to hurry," he replied. "Ronny and I are going to drive down your alley and stop at the end of your driveway. I'll text you when we're about to make the turn."

"What kind of car will you be in?" Jade asked.

"It's a Ford Explorer," Hudson said and gave her the license plate number. "You'll need to be ready to get in right away. Keep your cell phone and the gun handy."

"I will."

Ending the call, Jade went downstairs. She put her backpack on and picked up the suitcase. She paused the alarm and opened the back door. She hurried through and locked it behind her.

She hid in the shadows beside the storage shed. She turned the volume off on her cell phone and waited for Hudson's text.

Her phone buzzed, and the text read, "Let's go."

She went to the gate and waited until she saw the license plate illuminated by the street light. She opened the gate, slipped through, and closed it behind her before running to the Explorer. Hudson got out and opened the door for her. They sped down the alley as soon as both doors were closed.

Ronny drove while Hudson kept a lookout for anyone following them. There were sudden turns and unnecessary stops until both men were satisfied that they'd gotten away unnoticed.

Hudson turned in the front seat and smiled at Jade. "It looks like we've made a clean getaway."

"I hope so," Jade replied. "It's been a long day."

"It wasn't a good idea for you to go home, but I didn't like the idea of leaving you in that place."

"What happens now?"

"We're going to a safe house. There will be a team waiting for us so that we can work out the details of our plan. You'll be under guard the entire time, but Ronny and I will have to go to work and behave as though we're clueless about what's been going on."

"They know that you and Hudson are friendly," said Ronny. "They'll naturally assume that I'm part of it. We can't risk leading them to you."

"Do you trust the team members?" asked Jade, trying to hide the fear.

Ronny and Hudson looked at each other before answering. "Yes, but keep that Glock handy just in case," said Hudson.

The safe house was located north of Amarillo near the city limits. It was a modest house on a large lot. Ronny parked the Explorer in a barn that held three other vehicles. They escorted Jade inside and introduced her to the team.

The group worked out the details of their plan and explained the finer points to Jade. She would be in the most danger if anything went wrong. She was starting to get used to being in danger.

Monday, January 8, 2018

2:45 p.m.

Jade stood in the tiny bedroom where she'd spent the night and assessed her appearance in the mirror. She was dressed in the black dress and was ready to pay her respects at Renee's funeral.

A tap on the door told her that it was time to go.

Officer Cheryl Nordyke handed Jade a wallet. "The recorder is inside. Your cell phone will fit in here, too, so that you'll have one thing to carry. We want them to see that you're unarmed."

Jade nodded and followed the officer outside. Officer Jess Ann Vera stood beside a red Chrysler 300 with an Uber symbol on the windshield. She got into the backseat, and Officer Vera got into the driver's seat.

"It will take us forty-five minutes to get to the funeral home," said Officer Vera. "Try to relax and be yourself. There will be undercover officers there posing as friends of the deceased. You'll be as safe as you are with us."

Jade nodded and took a deep breath.

"Don't leave the funeral with anyone except me or Officer Bailey," she said and looked at Jade in her rearview mirror. "Remember that I'll be in a different car, so look for a lime green visor with Uber across the front."

They rode in silence for the remainder of the trip to Canyon. They arrived at the funeral chapel all too soon. Jade made a show of paying for the Uber and went inside.

The chapel was located on the grounds of the cemetery. Jade could see the tent set up for the graveside service a short distance away. She was relieved that she wouldn't have to get into a car with someone who might carry her to her own death.

She walked into the chapel with her head held high. She looked as though she'd been away for the weekend and returned relaxed and rested.

Nothing could have been farther from the truth. She felt exposed and vulnerable. Adrenaline coursed through her veins and made her feel ready to run at the first sign of danger.

She signed the register and took a seat behind the pews designated for the family. She sat quietly and held the wallet in her lap while she waited for the services to begin.

Tommy Carlile sat down beside her and said, "How are you doing, Jade?"

"I'm fine, Mr. Carlile. How are you?"

"Doing all right, considering the circumstances. You seem to be a little tense."

"I guess I am," she replied. "I can't help thinking about Uncle Erik's funeral. I'm trying to hold it together. I don't want to blubber like an idiot."

Tommy smiled at her and said, "It's okay if you cry. I may cry a little myself. Two friends gone in a matter of weeks. I still can't wrap my head around it."

They fell silent as Renee's family was escorted into the chapel, and the service began.

It was a closed casket service. A photo of Renee had been placed on top of the polished wood sarcophagus, and was surrounded by an assortment of colorful flowers.

When the service ended, people began to file past the family to offer their sympathy. Jade watched as all three of the men that Uncle Erik had suspected filed past. She avoided looking at any of them for more than a moment.

Jade stood and joined the line followed by Tommy. She shook hands with each of Renee's family members. She turned on the recorder and followed the crowd toward the tent on the cemetery grounds.

"Miss O'Neal, how are you this afternoon?" asked Jonathan Baxter.

"I'm fine, Mr. Baxter," she replied with a smile. "How are you?"

"I'm doing well, thank you. Do you mind if I walk with you?"

"I'm glad to have your company," she said

"This is such a sad business."

"Yes, it is," Jade agreed.

"Did you know Ms. Lanham well?"

"I knew her through Uncle Erik and the museum. She was kind and helpful to me when he died."

"Yes, I'm sure she was. She was a good person," Baxter said.

They arrived at the graveside and said nothing more. Everyone crowded under the tent and waited as the family took their seats. The brief service ended, and Jade stepped away from the crowd.

"Good afternoon, Miss O'Neal," said Dino Stevens. "I trust you're doing well."

"I am," she replied. "And you?"

"Quite well, thank you. If you'll excuse me, I have a meeting that I can't miss," he said. "Goodbye."

"Goodbye," Jade replied and walked back toward the chapel.

She stood on the walkway in front of the chapel and pretended to call for an Uber. Wilson Lee exited the chapel and waved at her.

"Hello, Mr. Lee."

"Don't you have a car?" Lee asked.

"It's having issues right now," she said.

"Ah, well, that happens to all us at some point," he said. "May I give you a ride?"

"Thank you, no. I have an Uber on the way."

"I'll be on my way then. It was good to see you."

"It was nice to see you, too."

Jade watched him walk to his car and drive away. She waited on the walkway for her ride. She was relieved to see a white Impala coming toward her. The driver wore a lime green visor. She could see the word Uber blazoned across the front.

She dashed to the car while the driver got out and opened the door for her. It was too late when she realized that it wasn't Officer Vera.

"Get in the car and don't make a scene," said Kathy Steen. "You'll regret it if you do."

Jade got in and looked for the under-cover police officers who were supposed to be protecting her. She thought about jumping out while Steen walked to the driver's side, but the handle had been removed. She was trapped.

She looked out the window trying to get someone's attention, but no one noticed. Steen got in the driver's seat and put the car into gear.

"I'll take that cell phone," she said and held out her hand. "I won't ask again."

Jade took the phone from her wallet and handed it to Steen. She prayed that someone would notice she was gone and that they'd find her in time.

CHAPTER TWENTY-NINE

MONDAY, January 8, 2018

4:00 p.m.

Hudson was waiting at the safe house for Jade's return when he received a text that said, "She's gone!" He tapped the call button and waited for Officer Randy Torres to answer.

"What do you mean she's gone?" Hudson asked, trying to contain his anger.

"We can't find her," said Torres. "She got into a car with a woman wearing the lime green visor, but it wasn't Vera."

"Are you sure?" Hudson asked, starting to panic.

"Yeah, we found Vera's body."

"Track her cell phone," Hudson demanded. "I turned the GPS on myself."

"We're trying, but the phone is either turned off or out of range."

"How long has she been gone?"

"Half an hour," Torres replied.

"She can't be out of range yet," said Hudson. "Jade wouldn't have turned it off herself. He's got her!"

"What do you want to do?" Torres asked.

"We need to regroup," said Hudson. "Let's call everyone in to the second safe house. I'll meet you there."

6:00 p.m.

Jade had been taken to an abandoned warehouse in Amarillo. She'd never been in this part of the city and wasn't sure where she was being held.

Steen had ordered her into the building at gun point. The tall man with the shaved head was waiting inside. He tied Jade to an uncomfortable straight back chair.

"You'd better go," King said to Steen. "You don't want to get caught with that car."

Kathy Steen nodded and walked outside. Jade heard the engine start, and the car drive away.

"It's good to see you again, Miss O'Neal," said King. "I feel like we're old friends."

"Who are you?" asked Jade.

"We haven't actually met, have we?" King taunted. "My name is Nelson King."

"Why have you been following me?" Jade asked.

"It was my job," he said. "I have to say that it was one of the most boring jobs I've ever had. You need a life."

Jade ignored the jibe and asked, "Why am I here?"

"Ace wants to talk to you. He should be here soon."

"Who is Ace?" she asked, trying to keep him talking.

"You don't know?"

Jade shook her head.

"Well, this may have all been for nothing," he said.

"Ace and King. Is there a Queen and a Jack?" she jeered.

"Yes, but you won't be meeting them."

336

"Why not?"

"There's no need," answered King.

"That explains the royal flush tattoo on the guy in the blue Durango."

"You're observant aren't you?" King said with irritation.

"Where are we?"

"This is one of Ace's old warehouses. We use it for...other things now."

"I can see that it's an abandoned warehouse," Jade said with disdain. "Where exactly are we?"

"Why do you want to know?"

"I'd like to know where I'm going to die," Jade said looking him in the eye.

"You've worked that out already, have you? You still have some time. Ace might let you live if you tell him what he wants to know."

"What does he want to know?"

"You'll find out soon enough."

Jade said nothing more.

"I'm going out for some fresh air and a smoke," King said. "Don't waste your breath screaming. There's no one around to hear you."

King went outside, and Jade tested the ropes binding her to the chair. She knew that she wasn't going to be able to escape. She remembered the recorder in her wallet. She hadn't turned it off.

The wallet lay on the floor beside her. Maybe the police would find the wallet and the recording when her body was found.

"I'm in a big building with a metal roof and walls. It reminds me of the metal that barns are built with. There are a lot of windows up high by the eaves. Most of them are broken. I know I'm in Amarillo. We drove through downtown to get here. I couldn't see a street sign, and I don't know what street I'm on."

She heard a loud rumbling noise. It sounded like it was within a few blocks of where she sat. She was trying to recall what the sound was when she heard a train whistle blow.

"I must be near railroad tracks," she said. "I know two names. Kathy Steen brought me here, and Nelson King is right outside."

She stopped talking when King opened the door. She didn't want him to find the recorder.

"Who were you talking to?" he asked with a sneer. "Your maker?"

"As a matter of fact, I was," she lied.

"It won't be long now," King said. "Ace is on his way."

7:00 p.m.

Ace entered the building, nodded at King, and walked toward Jade.

"Good evening, Miss O'Neal. I see you've met Mr. King."

"And you're Ace," she said.

"Have you and Mr. King been talking or did you already know that?" asked Ace.

"We've been talking. Why am I here?"

"That's a fair question. I'll pretend that you don't know the answer and tell you," Ace paused. "I believe that you have something I want."

"What would that be?" asked Jade.

"Information, Miss O'Neal. Just information."

"What kind of information?"

"I believe that your uncle left some information with you that pertains to my...past endeavors."

"He never said anything to me about you," Jade said.

"Hmmm," said Ace. "But he left something for you to read or give to the police, didn't he?"

"I don't know what you're talking about," she said, trying to buy time.

Ace rubbed the back of his neck with his left hand. Jade could see the nub where his pinkie finger used to be.

"Enough of this cat and mouse game," Ace said, his polite demeanor gone. "Where have you been?"

"I needed some alone time," Jade said.

"You haven't bothered to check on that monstrosity you call a dog. Why not?" Ace demanded.

The thought of Teddy being hurt, and Ace's words made her angry. She spoke without thinking.

"Because I didn't want to be found," Jade said. "I didn't know who shot him or why. I didn't want to be next!" she shouted.

"You didn't go into hiding when your uncle was killed," Ace pointed out.

"The police told me not to leave the area," she paused before continuing. "They work for you, don't they?"

"Some of them do, yes," Ace admitted. "There are still those like your friend Bailey who are too honest for their own good."

"Holloway and the men who searched the house work for you," she said, trying to confirm her suspicions.

"Yes, and there are others in police departments around the Texas Panhandle."

"Why did you kill my uncle?"

"He wouldn't tell me what I wanted to know," said Ace.

"And Renee Lanham?"

"I didn't touch Ms. Lanham," he said. "One of my people took care of her. She wouldn't talk."

"You have someone in the museum too, don't you? A guard or," Jade paused unsure how she knew, "Tommy Carlile."

"Very good," said Ace.

"What about Logan Rhodes?"

"Logan worked for us. He was supposed to bring you in, but he failed...twice."

"He shot Teddy!"

"Is there anything else you'd like to know?" Ace asked and put left hand in his jacket pocket.

"Renee didn't talk because she didn't know anything," Jade told him.

"But you do, don't you?" asked Ace.

Jade looked at him with defiance.

"That's the same look your uncle had on his face when I talked to him," Ace said and nodded at King.

King walked toward Jade and back handed her across the face.

Her head almost burst with pain. Her cheek throbbing, she tasted blood. She could feel blood dripping from her nose.

"Mr. King enjoys this part of his job the most," said Ace. "Tell me what I want to know unless you enjoy pain."

"Okay, I'll tell you what I know," she said. "May I have some water first?"

Ace nodded at King. King took a bottle of water from a bag by the door and poured some into her mouth. Jade swished it around and swallowed.

She looked at both men before she began. "My uncle left me messages. Most of them were warnings to be careful and not to trust anyone. The last few were clues. One clue led to another. I've been looking for the last one. I needed time alone to search, but I didn't find it."

"What was the last clue that you found?" asked Ace.

"The president holds the key," said Jade.

"The president holds the key," Ace repeated. "What president and what kind of key?"

"I don't know," answered Jade. "I searched the house. I looked around campus. I even looked in the museum. I didn't find anything."

"Where did you go while you were missing?"

"I went to the airport. I thought he might have hidden something there. It was the last place that I knew he'd gone," Jade said, amazed at the words that came out of her mouth.

"You found nothing there?"

Jade shook her head. Waves of pain rolled through her face.

"No one else has the information that you have?"

"No," answered Jade.

"Not even your mother and brother?" Ace asked with skepticism.

"No," she lied. "Uncle Erik was trying to protect us all. He didn't tell any of us what was happening."

"I think we've heard enough, don't you Mr. King?" said Ace, and he took his hand from his pocket, and pointed a gun at her chest.

"Is that the gun you used to kill my uncle?" Jade asked.

"Yes, it is," he said with a wicked grin. "And your friend Logan. Goodbye, Miss O'Neal."

"Goodbye, Dino Stevens."

Jade closed her eyes. She didn't want to see what was coming.

"Police! Drop the weapon!" someone shouted from the doorway.

Jade heard a shot and waited. *It didn't hurt,* she thought. *Am I still alive?* Stevens had turned and fired toward the voice.

All at once, gunfire seemed to come from every direction. King pulled a gun from behind his back and returned fire.

Jade tried to turn her chair over and get closer to the floor. She couldn't get enough leverage with her ankles tied to the legs of the chair. She heard a bullet whiz by and screamed.

Someone ran toward her and drug her out of the line of fire.

"Are you all right?" Hudson shouted and shielded her body with his own.

"What took you so long?" Jade shouted back.

"Well, you know. Did laundry, got a haircut."

Jade had never been so happy to see another person. She didn't know whether to laugh or cry. A round was fired over their heads, and she couldn't think about anything except staying alive.

The gun battle ended when Stevens and King ran out of ammunition. They obeyed orders to toss their weapons aside and to put their hands on their heads.

Hudson waited until the two men were handcuffed and in custody before he got up and untied Jade.

"How did you find me?" she asked and massaged her wrists.

"The recorder in the wallet," Hudson said and freed her ankles.

"The recorder?"

"Yeah, it works like a cell phone. Everything it picked up was sent to a machine on a wireless network. All we had to do was listen. The description you gave of the building and the GPS on Vera's second car led us right to you."

"Why didn't you tell me?" she asked.

"Ronny and I thought there might be a leak on our team. We didn't tell the others either."

"What happened to Officer Vera?"

"She was killed when her car was stolen," Hudson told her. "It turns out we had a leak after all. We picked him up once we figured it out."

Hudson helped Jade up and through the door. Ronny Hague met them with a blanket and put it around Jade's shoulders."

"Thank you," she said, realizing for the first time that she was cold.

"That was a great job getting them to talk like that. We have it all. Names of the victims and the motives, names of the people involved, and we know that we need to look at our own people."

"Why did you talk so much?" Hudson asked.

"I wanted to know the answers, and I thought it was a good way to buy time." She paused and said, "And I hoped you'd find the wallet with my body and arrest the right people."

Ambulances arrived, and the paramedics treated two officers who were wounded in the fire fight. Nelson King was unharmed, but Dino Stevens was taken to the emergency room with life threatening injuries.

The rope burns on Jade's wrists and ankles were treated and bandaged while officers collected evidence from the building. She was sitting in the ambulance, wrapped in a blanket, and drinking coffee when Hudson approached her with a plastic evidence bag.

He handed the bag to her and asked, "Do you recognize this?"

Jade looked at contents of the bag. It was a silver ink pen with a worn engraving. It read "We love you, Uncle Erik."

She nodded and said, "It was Uncle Erik's. He carried it all the time. I thought it had been lost."

Hudson took the bag from her and held her close while she cried. He knew that she'd realized this was where her uncle had died.

The suspects were arrested and brought to the Amarillo police station. Jade had been asked to stay and identify those who had a part in her own kidnapping.

She identified Kathy Steen and Nelson King. She identified the two men who had been following her although she didn't know their names.

Steen was charged with kidnapping and capital murder. Nelson King was charged with kidnapping, assault, and burglary. The tattooed man and the tan muscular man were also charged with burglary.

Dino Stevens was facing multiple murder charges, conspiracy to commit murder, and at least a dozen other charges. It would be a long time before he'd go to trial. His injuries from the gun battle with the police left him in critical condition.

Tuesday, January 9, 2018

12:00 a.m.

It was midnight by the time her things had been collected from the safe house, and Hudson drove her home.

"I'm taking the day off tomorrow," Hudson told her. "I thought we could go see if Teddy is ready to come home."

"I'd like that," Jade told him. "Would you like to come in for some coffee?"

"No, thanks. We both need some rest. The past few days have been kind of rough. I'll see you in the morning."

"What time do you want to go?" Jade asked.

"I'll pick you up at ten," he said.

"Okay. I'll see you tomorrow then."

"There's something that I've been wanting to do for a long time," Hudson said and looked into her eyes.

"What?" Jade asked, thinking it was something they'd do the next day.

Hudson didn't say a word. He took her in his arms and gave her a long, deep, passionate kiss.

Warmth spread through Jade's body, and her toes curled inside her shoes. Her body tingled. She melted closer to him and into the kiss.

Hudson broke away and smiled down at her while stroking her hair. "I should have done that sooner," he said.

"Yes, you should have," Jade said and smiled into his hazel eyes. "And I think you should do it again."

9:00 a.m.

Jade called the boutique and explained what had happened over the weekend. Paula told her to stay home for a few days.

Hudson picked her up at ten and they went to Dr. Burge's office. They found him talking with his receptionist.

"And put this in the file for collection," he was saying when they stopped at the front counter.

"Hi, Dr. Burge. How is Teddy?" asked Jade.

"He's doing just fine. Come with me, and you can see for yourself."

They followed Dr. Burge to the kennels, and Teddy sat up with his ears perked. He woofed and whined when he saw Jade.

Jade couldn't contain the tears. Dr. Burge opened the kennel door, and Teddy limped out to greet his favorite playmate. She wrapped her arms around the gigantic dog and cried while he licked the tears from her face.

"He's ready to go home when you're ready to take him," said the vet. "I heard you've had a busy few days."

"She has," Hudson replied, "but it's all over now."

"I'm glad to hear that. Jade, I have some paperwork for you to sign when you've finished in here. Then you can take Teddy home."

"Thank you, Dr. Burge."

"You might want to put this on him before we take him out of here," Hudson said and handed her the new harness they bought on their way over.

Jade put it on Teddy, being careful not to hurt him or make it too tight. She hooked the leash to the harness and led Teddy to the lobby. She handed the leash to Hudson while she signed the paperwork.

Teddy rode in the backseat of Hudson's car with his massive tail beating a cadence on the seat. Jade unhooked the leash and let him roam the backyard when they got home. He inspected every inch of the backyard and marked his territory before going into the house.

Jade put his leash on the hook and tossed him a cookie. He caught it and swallowed it whole. She filled his food bowl and his water dish. He ate a few bites and drank some water and then laid down on his blanket with a contented sigh.

"I think he's glad to be home," Hudson said.

"I think so, too. I'm glad he's back," Jade replied. "It was too quiet around here without him."

"Let's get your garage operational again, and then I'll replace that window pane."

"I'd make us some lunch, but I need to go shopping. What if I take you to lunch instead?" she asked.

"You're going to take me to lunch? I like the sound of that," Hudson said and kissed her.

"Mmmm, do you want dessert now or after lunch?" Jade asked.

Hudson grinned at her and asked, "Why can't we do both?"

"I like the way you think, Officer Bailey," Jade said and kissed him.

Teddy growled at them from his bed. They both looked at him.

"Teddy, is it okay if I kiss Jade?" Hudson asked with a smile.

Teddy woofed and laid his head on his paws.

"That sounds like a yes to me," said Jade and she kissed Hudson again.

6:00 p.m.

The story of the arrest of Dino Stevens made the local news. The news media didn't know the whole story.

Tommy Carlile admitted to killing Renee. She couldn't answer the questions he asked on Ace's behalf, and Ace ordered him to dispose of her.

He had sent the text to Renee from a burn phone. He waited outside Pioneer Town until he saw her go in. He followed her to the Goodnight Cabin and told her he'd gotten the same message.

He'd done a brief stint in the military and learned hand to hand combat. He grabbed Renee from behind and killed her. He put her body on the bed, covered her with the blanket, and walked away.

Tommy turned out to be the weak link in the organization. He told the police everything he knew in exchange for a plea deal and witness protection.

According to Jacob O'Neal's letter, he worked as a warehouse security guard. He took another man's shift when the man had a heart attack and was hospitalized.

Jacob noticed some strange things. He heard voices and odd sounds coming from the warehouse, security cameras were often on the fritz, and marks on the floor that hadn't been there earlier.

He started making notes whenever something odd happened. It wasn't long before he noticed a pattern. The odd things happened every other week during the Thursday night shift.

Jacob's partner, Kevin Leach, always went to investigate and reported that everything was fine. Jacob was beginning to feel uneasy and suspected that something wasn't right.

Leach was killed in a car accident on his way to work for one of the Thursday shifts, and Jacob worked the shift alone.

The security cameras were having issues again, and Jacob went to investigate. He saw three men that he didn't know loading crates onto a truck. They moved identical crates into the empty spaces. No one would have known the difference.

Jacob watched hidden from their view. The men behaved as if it was normal everyday work. He chose not to confront them because he had no weapon and no backup. He went back to the office and wrote the letter to Erik. He explained everything he'd seen.

He mailed the letter at the end of his shift the next morning and then went inside to talk to his boss. He was killed when he left the building.

Tommy's information filled in the gaps. He was one of the men moving the crates in and out of the warehouse.

The warehouse crew didn't learn about Leach's accident until they had returned to their base of operations. They knew that chances were good that Jacob had seen them at some point during the exchange.

Dino was closest to the warehouse at the time, and he took matters into his own hands. They never knew about the letter.

The contents of the replacement crates varied. Stolen goods, drugs, weapons, counterfeit money, and other items; it depended upon what the customer wanted.

Dino and his crew eventually took over the enterprise. They continued selling and moving contraband, but they began legitimate businesses, too.

Ace was Dino's nickname, and there was King. They decided to use the card theme to identify the various branches of the organization. Queen and Jack had not yet been identified. Queen oversaw the illegal activities, and Jack ran the legitimate businesses.

King was in charge of the dirty work. He liked it, and he was good at it.

Kathy Steen and Ed Kinnan were part of an extortion team. Their jobs were to gather information, photographs, documents, and anything else that could be used to blackmail their victims. Those victims were usually in positions to influence decisions or legislation.

Ace was the head of the entire operation. He funded organizations and supported judges, politicians, and other people in positions of power. Those people had no idea who he truly was until it was too late to escape.

The evidence that Erik had gathered remained locked away in the storage unit. Few people knew its exact location. The authorities didn't want to risk a member of the Stevens organization getting hold of it before Stevens went to trial.

EPILOGUE

2:00 p.m.

Jade was sitting with Heather and the other WTAMU students who were about to graduate. She was graduating summa cum laude.

The happiness she felt about graduating with highest honors paled in comparison to the fact that her mother and brother were here for the event.

She waved at her family in the audience. Hudson, her fiancé, sat with them.

Jade's job at the boutique was going well. She was to replace Paula as manager when Paula moved up to district supervisor.

Hudson proposed to Jade on Saint Patrick's Day. He tied a bright green ribbon around Teddy's neck and put a leprechaun's hat on his head. A sign that said "Will you marry Hudson?" hung around the giant dog's neck. Hudson was beside him on bended knee, holding an open ring box. They planned to marry in December. Heather was to be the maid of honor.

Levi had mustered out of the military and planned to use his GI bill to go to college at WTAMU. He was undecided on a major but leaned toward criminal justice.

Mollie was doing well in her new job in New York. She'd met a nice man, and they'd been dating for six weeks.

The family decided that Jade should have Erik's car. Jade and Hudson were to live in his house with the understanding that any future sale of the home would be a family decision. It was also decided that they would have custody of Teddy.

Teddy was fully recovered except for a slight limp. He still loved his walks, and getting into mischief.

Jade had been given the honor of addressing the student body. She went to the podium when her name was called. She spoke for ten minutes and ended with an Irish blessing.

> May the road rise to meet you. May the wind be ever
> at your back. May the sun shine warm upon your
> face and the rains fall soft upon your fields, and
> until we meet again may God hold you in the
> palm of His hand.

The End

ABOUT THE AUTHOR

Dianne Smithwick-Braden is an avid reader of fiction but mysteries are by far her favorite genre. It seemed only natural that her own novels would be mysteries.

The Wilbarger County Series is set near Dianne's home town of Vernon, Texas. She was raised on the family farm in the western part of Wilbarger County. She graduated from Vernon High School in 1979.

Dianne currently lives in Amarillo, Texas with her husband, Richard and their dog, Rowdy. Please, take a few moments to rate and/or review this book. Dianne would love to know what you think.

Subscribe to Dianne's monthly newsletter at www.diannesmithwick-braden.com.

TITLES BY DIANNE SMITHWICK-BRADEN

Coded for Murder

The Wilbarger County Series

Death on Paradise Creek (Book One)

Death under a Full Moon (Book Two)

Flames of Wilbarger County (Book Three)

Subscribe to Dianne's newsletter at:

www.diannesmithwick-braden.com

Follow Dianne at:

www.facebook.com/smithwickbraden

www.instagram.com/smithwickbraden

twitter.com/smithwickbraden

www.pinterest.com/smithwickbraden

www.goodreads.com

bookbub.com

Made in the USA
Lexington, KY
22 December 2019